Edward Everett Hale

Philip Nolan's Friends

A Story of the Change of Western Empire

Edward Everett Hale

Philip Nolan's Friends
A Story of the Change of Western Empire

ISBN/EAN: 9783337243562

Printed in Europe, USA, Canada, Australia, Japan

Cover: Foto ©Andreas Hilbeck / pixelio.de

More available books at **www.hansebooks.com**

"HE STOOD WATCHING THE RECEDING BOAT."

PHILIP NOLAN'S FRIENDS

A STORY

OF THE CHANGE OF

WESTERN EMPIRE.

BY

EDWARD E. HALE,

AUTHOR OF "A MAN WITHOUT A COUNTRY," "UPS AND DOWNS," "THE BRICK MOON," AND "SYBARIS."

NEW YORK:
SCRIBNER, ARMSTRONG, AND COMPANY.
1877.

Stereotyped and printed by
Rand, Avery, and Company,
117 Franklin Street,
Boston.

PREFACE.

THE silence of our historians on the subject of the annexation of Louisiana to the United States, or their indifference, is very curious. It is perhaps even necessary to explain to the general reader of to-day, that the "annexation of Louisiana" was the annexation of all that the United States holds west of the Mississippi, excepting the province of Alaska, and the regions secured by the Mexican war and consequent negotiation with Mexico. The standard histories, when they speak of the annexation, allude to the final debates in Congress; and the history of the negotiation, as given by Marbois, the French negotiator, is sometimes condensed. But little more is said. Yet it is the annexation of Louisiana which makes the United States of to-day to be one of the great powers. Without the immense region then known as Louisiana, no Pacific coast, no California, — no "empire from ocean to ocean."

I suppose it is safe to say that the Federalists had attacked the purchase so eagerly, that they were afraid their attack would be remembered. Of the distinguished Western men, the separate plans had been so diverse, sometimes so treasonable, that their representatives have not dwelt much on the story. On Mr. Jefferson's part, I think there was an uneasy feeling that the credit was none of his. The truth is, that the credit — so far as there is any to be given to one man — of this great transaction, which makes the United States what it is, is to be given to Napoleon Bonaparte. I mean that he originated the plan which was carried out, which no one else had proposed; and he is the only public character who had to do with it, who seems to have had, at the time, any clear sense of its importance, or of the results which would follow.

The belligerent operations of John Adams's administration are always spoken of by the historians as aimed at France. They were so spoken of at the time, in print. Twelve regiments of infantry and one of cavalry were authorized to serve "during the continuance of the existing differences with the French republic." A considerable part of these regiments was raised. The recruits — to fight against *France* — were assembled at our ports on the Ohio and Mississippi; that is, they were removed so far from any points where they could be used against France. The boats which were to take them down the river, to take Orleans, a *Spanish* post, were built and were in readiness. I have read the manuscript correspondence between Hamilton, the acting commander of the new army, and Wilkinson, the commander on the Ohio, with reference to this proposed attack on Orleans. Wilkinson himself made a visit to Hamilton, to adjust the details of the campaign. This mine was ready to be sprung upon poor Spain, when the republic of the United States should make war with "the French republic."

Two fortunate or unfortunate events, in which the War Office has been destroyed by fire, have put an end to many of the documents which once described the details of these preparations. In those days governments did not discount their victories, nor state their plans in advance in the journals. And so John Adams's expedition against the Spanish town of Orleans goes into history as a part of the "French War."

I felt that I owed something to the memory of Philip Nolan, whose name I once took unguardedly for the name of a hero of my own creation, who was supposed to live at another time. The part which the real Philip Nolan played in our history is far more important than that of many a man who has statues raised in his honor. So far as careful work among the memorials of his life would serve, I have tried to rescue him from the complete oblivion which hangs over him. He was murdered by the Spanish Government, who dishonored their own passport for his murder. Were such an event possible now, war within an hour would be the consequence. In the recent case of the "Virginius," the most angry of Cuban sympathizers did not pretend that there had been any such violation of the right of nations. But Spain was strong then, and America was weak, and Mr. Jefferson was "pacific."

America is now strong, and Spain is weak, — how strong, and how weak, the story of the "Virginius" showed. If we trace

events to their unconscious causes, we may say that no single day
has done so much to make America strong, and to make Spain
weak, as that day in 1801, when a Spanish officer, under his king's
commission, murdered Philip Nolan, bearing the same king's passport for his lawful adventure.

The documents which illustrate this history, in the archives of
San Antonio and of Austin, are very numerous. To the cordial
assistance of the officers of every name, who have helped me to find
and use them, I am greatly indebted. To Mr. Quintero, who gave
me the full use of his rich collections in the archives of Monterey,
which I have not visited, I have tried to express my obligations.
But, indeed, I have received so much kind help in the preparation
of this little book, from a thousand friends in the South and West,
that I cannot thank them all by name. My readers owe it to
them, if they gain any new light on our history, as they follow the
adventures of PHILIP NOLAN'S FRIENDS.

EDWARD E. HALE.

ROXBURY, MASS., Nov. 6, 1876.

CONTENTS.

ILLUSTRATIONS.

PHILIP NOLAN'S FRIENDS;

OR, SHOW YOUR PASSPORTS.

CHAPTER I.

A PARTING.

> "Oh! saw ye not fair Inez?
> She has gone into the West,
> To dazzle when the sun is down,
> And rob the world of rest."
>
> THOMAS HOOD.

"GOOD-BY!"

"Good-by, papa;" and the poor girl waved her handkerchief, and broke into tears, though she had held up perfectly till now.

"Tirez!" cried Sancho, the blackest of all possible black men; and he shook his fist at his crew of twenty willing rowers, almost as black as he. The men gave way heartily, and in good time; the boat shot out from the levee, and in a few minutes Inez could no longer see her father's handkerchief, nor he hers. Still he stood watching the receding boat, till it was quite lost among the crowd of flat-boats and other vessels in the river.

The parting, indeed, between father and daughter was such as did not often take place, even in those regions, in those times. Silas Perry, the father of this young girl, was a suc-

cessful merchant, who had been established near forty years
in the French and Spanish colony of Orleans, then a small
colonial trading-post, which gave little pledge of the great
city of New Orleans of to-day. He had gone there — a
young New Englander, who had his fortunes to make — in
the year 1763, when the King of France first gave Louisiana
to his well-beloved cousin, King of Spain. Silas Perry had
his fortunes to make — and he made them. He had been
loyal to the cause of his own country, so soon as he heard of
tea thrown over, of stamps burned in King Street, and of
effigies hanging on Liberty Tree. He had wrought gallantly
with his friend and fellow-countryman, Oliver Pollock, in for-
warding Spanish gunpowder from the king's stores, to Washington's army, by the unsuspected route of the Mississippi
and Ohio. He had wrought his way into the regards of suc-
cessive Spanish governors, and had earned the respect of the
more important of the French planters,

At this time the greater part of the handful of white people who made the ruling class in Orleans were French ; and
a brilliant "society" did the little colony maintain, But it
had happened to Silas Perry, whose business had often called
him to the Havana, that he had there wooed, won, and married
a Spanish lady ; and about the times of tea-parties, stamp-
acts, English troops recalled from the Mississippi, and other
such matters, Silas Perry had busied himself largely in estab-
lishing his new home in Orleans, and in bringing his bride
there. Here the Spanish lady was cordially made welcome
by the ladies of the little court, in which governor and commandant and the rest were of Spanish appointment, though
their subjects were of French blood. Here she lived quietly ;
and here, after ten years, she died, leaving to her husband
but two children. One of them had been sent to Paris for
his education, nine years before the time when the reader
sees his sister. For it is his sister, who was an infant when
her mother died, whom we now see, sixteen years after, waving her handkerchief to her father as the barge recedes from

the levee. Other children had died in infancy. This little Inez herself was but six months old when her mother died ; and she had passed through infancy and girlhood without a mother's care.

But her father had risen to the emergency in a New Englander's fashion. Not that he looked round to find a French lady to take the place of the Spanish donna. Not he. He did write home to Squam Bay, and stated to his sister Eunice the needs of the little child. He did not tell Eunice that if she came to be the child's second mother she would exchange calls with marchionesses, would dress in silks, and ride in carriages. He knew very well that none of these things would move her. He did tell her, that, if she did not watch over the little thing in her growth, nobody else would but himself. He knew what he relied upon in saying this ; and, on the return of Captain Tucker in the schooner " Dolores," sure enough, the aunt of the little orphaned baby had appeared, with a very droll assortment of trunks and other baggage, in the most approved style of Squam Bay. She was herself scarcely seventeen years old when she thus changed her home ; but she had the conscientious decision to which years of struggle had trained her before her time. She loved her brother, and she was determined to do her duty by his child. To that child she had ever since been faithful, with all a mother's care.

And so Miss Inez had grown up in a French town, under Spanish government, but with her every-day life directed under the simplest traditions of New England. With her little friends, and on any visit, she saw from day to day the habits, so utterly different from those of home, of a French colony not indisposed to exaggerate the customs of France. For language, she spoke English at home, after the fashion of the New Englanders ; but in the society of her playmates and friends she spoke French, after the not debased fashion of the Creole French of Louisiana. Through all her life, however, Louisiana had been under the Spanish rule. Silas

Perry himself spoke and read Spanish perfectly well, and he had taught Inez to use it with ease. The girl had, indeed, read no little of the masterpieces of Spanish literature, so far as, in a life not very often thwarted at home, she had found what pleased her among her father's books.

She was now parted from him for the first time, if we except short visits on one plantation or another on the coast. The occasion of the parting was an unrelenting storm of letters and messages from her mother's only sister, Donna Maria Dolores, the wife of a Spanish officer of high rank, named Barelo. For some years now this husband had been stationed at the frontier part of San Antonio, in the province which was beginning to take the name of Texas; and in this little settlement Donna Maria, lonely enough herself, was making such sunshine as she could for those around her. Forlorn as such a position seems, perhaps, to people with fixed homes, it was any thing but forlorn to Donna Maria. She had lived, she said, "the life of an Arab" till now; and now to know that her husband was really stationed here, though the station were a frontier garrison, was to know that for the first time since her girlhood she was to have the luxury of a home.

No sooner were her household gods established, than she began, by the very infrequent "opportunities" for writing which the frontier permitted, to hurl the storm of letters on Silas Perry's defenceless head. Fortunately for him, indeed, "opportunities" were few. This word, in the use we now make of it, is taken from the older vocabulary of New England, in whose language it implied a method of sending a letter outside of any mail. Just as in English novels you find people speaking of "franks" for letters, these older New Englanders spoke of "opportunities." Mail between Texas and Orleans there was not, never had been, and, with the blessing of God, never would be. "Had I the power," said the Gov. Salcedo, "I would not let a bird cross from Louisiana to Texas." But sometimes a stray priest going to confer with the bishop of Orleans, sometimes a government messenger from Mexico, sometimes a concealed horse-trader, and always camps of Indians, passed the frontier eastward, on one pretext or another; and, with proper license given, there was no reason left why they should not, after Louisiana became in name a Spanish province. No such stray traveller came to the city without finding Silas Perry; and inevitably he brought a double letter, — an affectionate note to Inez, begging her to write to her mother's sister, and an urgent and persuasive one to her father, begging him, by all that was sacred, not to let the child grow up without knowing her mother's only relations.

Silas Perry's heart was still tender. If he had lived to be a thousand, he would never have forgotten the happy days in the Havana, when he wooed and won his Spanish bride, nor the loyal help that her sister Dolores gave to the wooing and to the winning. But till now he had the advantage of possession; and the priests and soldiers and traders always carried back affectionate letters, explaining how much Inez loved her aunt, but how impossible it was for her to come. The concocting of these letters had become almost a family joke at home.

It may help the reader's chronology if we say that our story begins in the first year which bore the number of "eighteen hundred;" he may call it the last year of the eighteenth century, or the first of the nineteenth, as he likes to be accurate or inaccurate. At this time business required that Silas Perry should go to Paris, and leave his home for many months, perhaps for a year. Silas would gladly have taken his sister Eunice and his daughter with him; but travel was not what it is now, nor was Paris what it is now. And although he did not think his daughter's head would be cut off, still he doubted so far what he might find in Paris, that he shrank from taking her thither. As it happened, at this moment there came a particularly well-aimed shaft from Aunt Dolores's armory; and fortune added an "opportunity," not only for reply, but for permitting Inez and her aunt to make the journey into Texas under competent escort, if they chose to submit themselves to all the hardships of travel across prairies and through a wilderness. True, the enterprise was utterly unheard of : this did not make it less agreeable in Silas Perry's eyes. It was not such an enterprise as Donna Maria Dolores had proposed. She had arranged that the girl should be sent with proper companionship, on one of Silas's vessels, to Corpus Christi on the Gulf. She had promised to go down herself to meet her, with an escort of lancers whom their friend Gov. Herrera had promised her. But Silas Perry had not liked this plan. He said boldly, that, if the girl were to ride a hundred miles, she might ride three hundred. Mr. Nolan would take better care of her than any Gov. Herrera of them all. "Women always supposed you were sending schooners into mud-holes, where there was nothing to buy, and nothing to sell." And so the most improbable of all possible events took place. By way of preparation for going to Paris, Silas Perry sent his precious daughter, and his sister only less precious, on a long land-journey of adventure, to make a visit as long, at least, as his own was. It need not be said, if the reader apprehends what manner of man he was, that he had provided for her comfort, so far as forethought, lavish expenditure, and a wide acquaintance with the country, could provide for it. If he had not come to this sudden and improbable determination, this story would not have been written.

Inez, as has been said, fairly broke down as the rowers gave way. Her Aunt Eunice kept up the pretence of flying her handkerchief till they had wholly lost sight of the point of their embarkation. And then the first words of comfort which came to the sobbing girl were not from her aunt.

"Take one o' them Boston crackers ; they say they's dreadful good when you go on the water. Can't git none all along the coast ; they don't know how to keep 'em. So soon as ye father said you was to go, I told old Tucker to bring me some from home ; told him where to git 'em. Got 'em at Richardson's in School Street. Don't have 'em good nowhere else."

Inez, poor child, could as easily have eaten a horseshoe as the biscuit which was thus tendered her. But she took it with a pleasant smile ; and the words answered a better pur- pose than Dr. Flavel's homilies on contentment could have served.

The speaker was a short-set, rugged New Englander, of about sixty years of age, whose dress and appointments were in every respect curiously, not to say sedulously, different from those of the Creole French, or the Spanish seamen, or the Western flat-boatmen, all around him. Regardless of treaties, of nationalities, or of birthright privileges, Seth Ransom regarded all these people as "furriners," and so designated them, even in the animated and indignant conver- sations which he held with them. He was himself a Yankee of the purest blood, who had, however, no one of the restless or adventurous traits attributed to the Yankee of fiction or of the stage. He had, it is true, followed the sea in early life. But, having fallen in with Silas Perry in Havana, he had attached himself to his service with a certain feudal loyalty. The institution of feudalism, as the philosophical student has observed, made the vassal quite as much the master of his lord as the master was of his vassal, if not more. That this was the reason why Seth Ransom served Silas Perry, it would be wrong to say. But it is true that he served him in a masterful way, as a master serves. It is also true that he idolized Inez, as he had idolized her mother before her. Of each, he was the most faithful henchman and the most loyal admirer. Yet he would address Inez personally with the intimate terms in which he spoke to her when she was a baby in his arms, — when perhaps she had been left for an hour in his happy and perfect charge. If no one else were present, he would call her " Een," or " Inez," as if she had been his own granddaughter. In the presence of others, on the other hand, no don of the Governor's staff could have found fault with the precision of his etiquette.

The necessities of Mr. Perry's business often sent Seth Ransom back to New England, so that he could drink again from the waters of the pump in King Street, as he still called the State Street of to-day. It was as Hercules sometimes let Antæus put his foot to the ground. Ransom returned from each such visit with new contempt for every thing which he found upon other shores, excepting for the household of Silas Perry, and perhaps a modified toleration for that of Oliver Pollock. For Silas Perry himself, for Miss Eunice, and Miss Inez, his chivalrous devotion blazed out afresh on each return.

He was athletic, strong, and practical. Nobody had ever found any thing he could not do, excepting that he read and wrote with such difficulty, that in practice he never descended to these arts except in the most trying emergency. When, therefore, Silas Perry determined on his rash project of sending his daughter and sister under Mr. Nolan's escort to San Antonio, he determined, of course, to send Seth Ransom with them as their body-guard. The fact that he sent him, in truth, really relieved the enterprise from its rashness; for, though Seth Ransom had never crossed the prairies, any one who knew him, and the relation in which he stood to Miss Inez, knew that, if it were necessary, he would carry her from Natchez to the Alamo in his arms.

The boat was soon free from the little flotilla which then made all the commerce of the little port; and the steady stroke of the well-trained crew hurried her up stream with a speed that exacted the admiration of the lazy lookers-on of whatever nation.

Inez thanked her old cavalier for his attention, made him happy by asking him to find something for her in a bag which he had stowed away, and then kept him by her side.

"Do they row as well as this in Boston Harbor, Ransom?" she said. For some reason unknown, Ransom was never addressed by his baptismal name.

"Don't have to. Ain't many niggers there, no way. What

they is lives on Nigger Hill; that's all on one side. Yes: some niggers goes to sea, but them's all cooks. Don't have to row much there. Have sailboats; don't have no rivers."

The girl loved to hear his dialect, and was not averse to stir up his resentment against all men who had not been born under her father's roof, and all nations but those which ate codfish salted on Saturday.

"I don't see where they get their ducks, if they have no rivers," she said artfully, as if she were thinking aloud.

"Ducks! thousands on 'em. Big ducks too; not little critters like these. Go into Faneuil Hall Market any day, and have more ducks than you can ask for. Ducks is nothin'." And a grim smile stole over his face, as if he were pleased that Inez had selected ducks as the precise point on which her comparison should be made.

"Well, surely, Ransom, they have no sugar-cane," said she; and, by her eye, he saw that she was watching Sancho, the boatswain as he might be called, who, as he nodded to his men, solaced himself by chewing and sucking at a bit of fresh cane from a little heap at his side.

"Sugar-cane! Guess not. Don't want 'em. Won't touch 'em. Oceans of white sugar, all done up in sugar-loaves, jest when they want it. Them as makes sugar makes it in the woods, makes it out of trees; don't have to have them dirty niggers make it. Oceans of sugar-loaves all the time!" And again that severe smile stole over his face, and he looked up into the sky, almost as if he saw celestial beings carrying purple-papered sugar-loaves to Boston, and as if— next to ducks— the supply of sugar to that town was its marked characteristic.

Eunice Perry was glad to follow the lead which Ransom had given, sagaciously or unconsciously. Any thing was better for the voyage than a homesick brooding on what they had left behind.

"We must not make Inez discontented with Orleans and the coast, Ransom. Poor child! she has nothing but roses and orange-blossoms, figs and bananas ; we must not tell her too much about russet apples, or she will be discontented."

"I do like russet apples, aunty darling, quite as well as I like figs ; but I shall not be discontented while I have you on one side of me, and Ransom on the other, and dear old Sancho beating time in front." This, with a proud expression, as if she knew they were trying to lead her out from herself, and that she did not need to be cosseted. Old Sancho caught the glance, and started his rowers to new energy. To maintain a crack crew of oarsmen was one of the boasts of the "coast" at that time ; and, although Silas Perry was in no sort a large planter, yet he maintained the communication between his plantation above the city, and his home in the city, — which, for himself, he preferred at any season to any place of refuge, — by a crew as stalwart and as well trained as any planter of them all.

The boat on which the two ladies and their companions were embarked was not the elegant barge in which they usually made the little voyage from the plantation to their city home. It was a more business-like craft which Silas Perry had provided to carry his daughter as far as Natchitoches on the Red River, where she and her companions were to join the land expedition of Philip Nolan and his friends. The after-part of the boat was protected from sun or rain by an awning or light roof, generally made of sails, or sometimes of skins, but, in Inez's boat, of light woodwork ; it had among the *habitants* the name of *tendelet.* Under the tendelet a little deck, with the privileges of all quarter-decks, belonged to the master of the boat and his company. Here he ate his meals by day ; here, if he slept on board, he spread his mattress at night. It was high enough to give a good view of the river and the low shores, of any approaching boat, or any other object of interest in the somewhat limited catalogue of river experiences. In the preparations for the voyage of the ladies, curtains had been arranged, which would screen them from either side, from the sun, from wind, or even from a shower.

A long tarpauling, called the *piélat*, was stretched over the whole length of the boat, to protect the stores, the trunks, and other cargo, from the weather. The rowers sat at the sides, old Sancho watching them from the rear ; while a man in the bow, called the *bosman*,[1] who generally wielded a sort of a boat-hook, watched the course, and fended off any floating log, or watched for snag or sawyer.

The voyage this afternoon was not long. It was, as Inez said, only a "taste-piece." Eunice said it was as the caravans at the East go a mile out of town on the first night, so that they may the more easily send back for any thing that is forgotten.

"All nonsense !" said Ransom. "I told ye father might as well start afore sunrise, and be at the Cross to-night: would not hear a word on it, and so lost all day."

In truth, Inez was to spend her last night at the plantation, which had been her favorite summer home for years, to bid farewell to the servants there, and to gather up such of her special possessions as could be carried on the pack-horses, on this pilgrimage to her Spanish aunt. Her father would gladly have come with her, but for the possibility that his ship might sail for Bordeaux early the next morning.

[1] Was this word once "boatswain," perhaps?

CHAPTER II.

A MEETING.

"Pleased with a rattle, tickled with a straw."—ALEXANDER POPE.

BEFORE sunrise the next morning the final embarkation
was to take place.   The whole house was in an uproar.   The
steady determination of old Chloe, chief of the kitchen, that
Miss Inez should eat the very best breakfast she ever saw,
before she went off "to the wild Indians," dominated the
whole establishment.   In this determination Chloe was
steadily upheld by Ransom, who knew, by many conflicts
from which he had retreated worsted, that it was idle to try
to dictate to her, while at the same time he had views as
decided as ever on the inferiority of French cookery to that
of New England.   The preparation of this master breakfast had called upon Chloe and her allies long before light.
Cæsar and his allies, also preparing for a voyage which
would take them from home for many days, were as early
and as noisy.   The only wonder, indeed, was that the girl,
who was the centre of the idolatry of them all, or her aunt,
who was hardly less a favorite, could either of them sleep a
wink, in the neighborhood of such clamors, after midnight
passed.   When, they did meet at breakfast, they found the
table lighted with bougies, and preparations for such a repast
as if the governor and his staff, the commandant with his,
and half the merchants of Orleans, had been invited.   Be-

sides François and Laurent, who were in regular attendance on the table, Ransom was hovering round, somewhat as a chief butler might have done in another form of luxurious civilization.

"Eat a bit of breast, Miss Inez; and here's the second j'int; try that. Don't know nothin', — niggers, — but I see to this myself. Miss Eunice, them eggs is fresh: took 'em myself from four different nests. Niggers don't know nothin' about eggs. Made a fire in the barn chamber, and biled 'em right myself, jest as your father likes 'em, Miss Inez. Them others is as hard as rocks."

Inez was in the frolic of a new expedition now; and the traces of parting, if indeed they existed, could not be discerned. She balanced Ransom's attentions against the equal attention of the two boys, pretended to eat from more dishes and to drink from more cups than would have served Cleopatra for a month, amused herself in urging Aunt Eunice to do the same, and pretended to wrap in napkins, for the "smoking halt," the viands upon which her aunt would not try experiments. The meal, on the whole, was not unsatisfactory to Aunt Chloe's pride, to Ransom's prevision, or to the public opinion of the household. All who were left behind were, in private, unanimous on one point, — namely, that Miss Eunice and Miss Inez were both to be roasted alive within a week by the Caddo Indians; to be torn limb from limb, and eaten, even as they were now eating the spring chickens before them. But as this view was somewhat discouraging, and as Aunt Chloe, after having once solemnly impressed it upon Eunice, had been told by Silas Perry that she should be locked up for a day in the lock-house if she ever said another such word to anybody, it was less publicly expressed in the farewells of the morning, though not held any the less implicitly.

In truth, the bougies were a wholly unnecessary elegance or precaution; for the noisy party did not, in fact, get under way till the sun had well risen, and every sign of early

exhalation had passed from the river. Such had been Mr.
Perry's private orders to his sister; and, although the general custom of a start at sunrise was too well fixed to be
broken in upon in form, Eunice and Ransom had no lack of
methods of delaying the final embarkation, even at the risk
of a little longer pull before the "smoke."

The glory of the morning, as seen from the elevated quar-
ter-deck, was a new delight to Inez. She watched at first
for a handkerchief or some other token of farewell from one
or another veranda as they passed plantations which were
within the range of a ride or sail from her own home. Afterward, even as the settlement became rather more sparse,
there was still the matchless beauty of heavy clumps of
green, and of the long shadows of early morning. Even in
the autumn colors, nothing can tame the richness of the
foliage; and the contrast rendered by patches of ripening
sugar-cane or other harvests is only the more striking from
the loyal and determined verdure of trees which will not
change, but always speak, not of spring, but of perennial
summer.

The crew felt all the importance of the expedition. Often
as they had gone down the river with one or another cargo
to Orleans, few of them had ever voyaged for any considerable distance up the stream. This was *terra incognita* into
which they were coming. Not but they had heard many a
story, extravagant enough too, of the marvels of the river,
from one or another flat-boatman who had availed himself of
the hospitalities of the plantation for his last night before
arriving at the city. But these stories were not very con-
sistent with each other; and, while the negroes half believed
them, they half disbelieved at the same time. To go bodily
into the presence of these unknown marvels was an experience wholly unexpected by each of them. Even Cæsar the
old cook, Sancho, and Paul the bosman, were shaken from
their balance or propriety by an adventure so strange; and

the preparations they had made for the voyage, and the orders they had given to the men who were to leave home for a period so unusual, all showed that they regarded this event as by far the most important of their lives.

All the same the bosman gave out a familiar and sonorous song, and all the same the rowers joined heartily in the words. And when he cunningly inserted some new words, with an allusion to the adventures before them, and to the treasures of silver which all parties would bring back from the Caddo mines, a guffaw of satisfaction showed that all parties were well pleased. And the readiness with which they caught up such of the words as came into the refrain showed that they were in no sort dispirited, either by the fatigue or the danger of the undertaking before them.

The song was in the crudest French dialect used by the plantation slaves. The air was that of a little German marching song, which the quick-eared negroes had caught from German neighbors on the coast ; old veterans of Frederick's, very likely. In the more polished rendering into which Inez and her aunt reduced it, before their long voyage was over, still crude enough to give some idea of the simplicity of the original, it re-appeared in these words : —

> " Darkeys, make this dug-out hurry ; *Tirez.*
> Boys behind, begin to row ; *Tirez.*
> And don't let misses have to worry :
> Misses have to worry when the light of day is gone ; *Tirez.*
>
> Lazy dogs there behind, are your paddles all broke ?
> Lazy dogs there before, have you all lost the stroke ?
> Farewell ! Farewell ! Farewell — farewell,
> Farewell ! Dear girl ! Farewell — farewell.
>
> Up the Mississippi River ; *Tirez.*
> Caddoes have a silver-mine ; *Tirez.*
> My sweetheart takes to all I give her,
> All that I can give her when my misses is come home ; *Tirez.*

> "Lazy dogs there behind, are your paddles all broke?
> Lazy dogs there before, have you all lost the stroke?
> Farewell! Farewell! Farewell — farewell,
> Farewell! Dear girl! Farewell — farewell."[1]

It will not do, however, to describe the detail from day to day, even of adventures so new to Inez and all her companions as were these. For a day or two the arrangements which Mr. Perry had made were such, that they made harbor for each night with some outlying frontiersman's family. The only adventure which startled them took place one morning after they were a little wonted to their voyage in the wilderness.

By the laws of all river craft, the hands were entitled every day, at the end of two hours, to a rest, if only to take breath. Everybody lighted a pipe, and the rest was called the "smoking-halt." The boat was run up to the shore ; and the ladies would walk along a little way, ordering the boatmen to take them up when they should overtake them.

Inez had, one morning, already collected a brilliant bouquet, when, at a turning of the river, she came out on an

---

[1] Readers who find themselves on some placid lake, river, or bayou in an autumn day, should autumn ever come again, may like to intwine the words of the song in the meshes of the German air. Here it is.

unexpected encampment. A cloud of smoke rose from a smouldering fire, a dozen Indian children were chasing each other to and fro in the shrubbery, the mothers of some of them were at work by the fire, and the men of the party were lounging upon the grass. Four or five good-sized canoes drawn up upon the shore showed where the whole party had come from : each canoe bore at the head a stag's head fixed on a pronged stick, as a sort of banner, whether of triumph or of festivity.

Inez and Eunice had so often welcomed such parties at the plantation, that neither of them showed any alarm or anxiety when they came so suddenly out upon the little encampment. But Inez did have a chance to say, "Dear old Chloe! she is a true prophet so soon. There are the fires, and here are we. Dear auntie, pray take the first turn." Both of them, very likely, would have been glad enough to avoid the *rencontre;* but as they were in for it, and had no near base to retreat upon, they advanced as if cordially, and greeted the nearest woman with a smile and a few words of courtesy.

In a minute the half-naked children had gathered in three little groups, the smaller hiding behind the larger, and all staring at the ladies with a curiosity so fresh and undisguised, that it seemed certain they had never seen such people, or at the least such costumes, before. It was clear enough in a minute more that the Indian women did not understand a syllable of the words which their fairer sisters addressed to them. One or two of the men rose from the ground, and joined in the interview, but with little satisfaction as far as any interchange of ideas went. Both parties, however, showed a friendly spirit. The Indian women went so far as to offer broiled fish and fresh grapes to the ladies. These declined the hospitality; but Inez, taking from her neck a little scarlet scarf, beckoned to her the prettiest child in the group nearest to her, and tied it round the girl's neck. The little savage was pleased beyond words with the adornment, slipped from her grasp, and ran with absurd vanity from one group to another to show off her new acquisition.

"What would my dear Madame Faustine say, if she knew that her dearly beloved scarf was so soon adorning the neck of a dirty savage?"

"She would say, if she were not a goose," said Eunice, "that you will have the whole tribe on you for scarfs now; and, as you have not thirty, that you have parted with your pretty scarf for nothing."

Sure enough, every little brat of the half-naked company came around them, to try the natural languages of beggary. Inez laughed heartily enough, but shook her head, and tried if they would not understand "No, no, no!" if she only said it fast enough.

"We can do better than that," said Eunice. "We may as well make a treaty with them, as you have begun. We will wait here for the boat. I am horribly afraid of them; but, if we pretend not to be frightened, that will be next best to meeting nobody at all."

So she patted two dirty little brats upon the cheeks, took another by the hand, and led him to the shade of a China-tree which grew near the levee, and there sat down.

The children thought, perhaps, that they were to be roasted and eaten; for the tales of the Attakapas, or man-eaters of the coast, travelled west as well as east. But they showed all the aplomb of their race, and, if they were to be eaten, meant to be eaten without groaning. In a moment more, however, they had forgotten their tears.

Eunice had torn from the book she held in her hand the blank leaf at the end. She folded a strip of the paper six or eight times, and then with her pocket-scissors cut out the figure of a leaping Indian. The feathers in his head-dress were, as she said to Inez, quite expressive; and his posture was savage enough for the reddest. The children watched her with amazement, the group enlarging itself from moment to moment. So soon as the leaping savage was completed, Eunice unfolded the paper, and of course produced eight leaping savages, who held each other by the hands. These she brought round into a ring, and by a stitch fastened the outer hands together. She placed the ring of dancers, thus easily made, upon her book, and then made them slide up and down upon the cover.

The reticence of these babes of the woods was completely broken. They shouted and sang in their delight; and even their phlegmatic fathers and mothers were obliged to draw near.

Eunice followed up her advantage. This time her ready scissors cut out a deer, with his nose down; and, as the paper was unfolded, two deer were smelling at the same root in the ground. Rings of horses, groups of buffaloes, rabbits, antelopes, and other marvels, followed; and the whole company was spellbound, and, indeed, would have remained so as long as Eunice continued her magic creations, when Inez whispered to her, —

"I see the boat coming."

Eunice made no sign of the satisfaction she felt, but bade Inez walk quietly to the bend of the stream, and wave her handkerchief; and the girl did so.

Eunice quietly finished the group which engaged her, and then, singling out the youngest of the girls, with a pointed gesture gave one of the much-coveted marvels to each of them, flung away the scraps of cut paper from her lap, and sprang quickly to her feet.

The flying bits of paper were quite enough to arrest the attention of the warriors, and they scattered in eager pursuit of them.

A minute more, and the boat was at the rudiment of a levee which had already begun to form itself. The girls sprang on board again, not sorry to regain the protection of their party; and Eunice inwardly resolved to run no more such risks while she was commander of the expedition.

"Wouldn't have dared to do nothin'," said old Ransom, concealing by a square lie his own anxiety at the *rencontre.* "They's all cowards and liars, them redskins be; but if you go walkin' agin, Miss Eunice, better call me to go with you: they's all afraid of a white man."

"Ah, well, Ransom, they were very civil to us to-day; and I believe I have made forty friends at the cost of a little white paper."

None the less was Eunice mortified and annoyed that she should have had a fright — for a fright it was — so early in their enterprise. It had been arranged with care, that at night they should tarry at plantations, while plantations lasted; but from Point Coupée to Natchitoches, where they were to join Capt. Nolan's party, was fifty-five leagues, which, at the best the "patron" could do, would cost them six or seven days; and she did not hope for even a log-cabin on the way for all that distance. And now, even before that weakest spot in their line, she had walked into a camp of these red rascals, who would have made no scruple of stripping from them all that they carried or wore.

"All's well that ends well, auntie," said Inez, as she saw her aunt's anxiety.

But none the less did Eunice feel that anxiety. Ransom, she saw, felt it; and the good fellow was, not more careful, but ten times more eager to show that he was careful, at every encampment. The patron, who was wholly competent to the charge given him, with the utmost respect and deference vied with Ransom in his arrangements. From this moment forward the ladies were watched with a surveillance which would made Eunice angry, had she not seen that it was meant so kindly.

This caution and assiduity were not without their effect upon her. But, all the same, her relief was infinite, when on the night when they hauled up, rather later than usual, below the rapids of the Red River, she was surprised by hearing her own name in a friendly voice, and Capt. Nolan sprang on board.

He had met them two or three days earlier than he expected.

CHAPTER III.

PHILIP NOLAN.

" Bid them stand in the king's name."

To Philip Nolan and his companions is due that impression of American courage and resource, which for nearly half a century impressed the Spanish occupants of Texas, until, in the year 1848, they finally surrendered this beautiful region, however unwillingly, to the American arms and arts.

For ten years before the period of this story, scarcely any person had filled a place more distinguished among the American voyagers on the Mississippi, or the American settlers on its eastern banks, than had PHILIP NOLAN.

His reputation was founded first on his athletic ability, highly esteemed among an athletic race. He had had intimate relations with the Spanish governors of Louisiana; but no one doubted his loyalty to his native land. He understood the Indians thoroughly, as the reader will have occasion to see. He had a passion for the wilderness, and for the life of the forest and prairie ; but he was well educated, whether for commerce or for command ; and Spanish governors, Orleans merchants, and American generals and secretaries of state, alike were glad to advise with him, and profited by his rare information of the various affairs intrusted to their care, — information which he had gained by personal inspection and inquiry.

Once and again had Philip Nolan, fortified by official safeguards, crossed into Texas, hunted wild horses there, and brought them back into the neighborhood of New Orleans, or the American settlements of the Mississippi, to a good market. A perfect judge of horses, an enthusiastic lover of them, he was more pleased with such adventure than with what he thought the humdrum lines of trade. His early training, indeed, had been so far that of a soldier, that he was always hoping for a campaign. With every new breath of a quarrel between the United States and Spain, he hoped that his knowledge of the weak spots in the Spanish rule might prove of service to his own country. Indeed, if the whole truth could be told, it would probably appear, that, for the last year or two before the reader meets him, Nolan had been lying on his oars, or looking around him, waiting for the hoped-for war which, as he believed, would sweep the forces of the King of Spain out from this magnificent country, which they held to such little purpose. Disappointed in such hopes, he had now undertaken, for the third time, an expedition to collect horses in Texas for sale on the Mississippi.[1]

Silas Perry knew Nolan so well, and placed in him confidence so unlimited, that he had with little hesitation accepted the offer of his escort made first in jest, but renewed in utter earnest, as soon as the handsome young adventurer found that his old friend looked upon it seriously. Nolan had represented that he had a party large enough to secure the ladies from Indians or from stragglers. The ways were perfectly familiar to him, and to more than one of those with him. Their business itself would take them very near to San Antonio, if not quite there; and, without the slightest difficulty, he could and would see that the ladies were safely confided to Major Barelo's care.

---

[1] The writer of this tale, by an oversight which he regrets, and has long regretted, spoke of this venturous and brave young Kentuckian as *Stephen* Nolan in a story published in 1863. The author had created an imaginary and mythical brother of Nolan's, to whom he gave the name of *Philip* Nolan, and to whom he gave a place in the army of the United States. Ever since he discovered his mistake, he has determined to try to give to the true *Philip* Nolan such honors as he could pay to a name to which this young man gave true honor. With this wish he attempts the little narrative of his life, which forms a part of this story.

So soon as this proposal had been definitely stated, it met with the entire approval of Miss Inez. This needs scarcely be said. To a young lady of her age, three hundred miles of riding on horseback seems three hundred times as charming as one mile ; and even one, with a good horse and a good cavalier, is simply perfection. All the votes Miss Inez could give from the beginning were given in plumpers for the plan.

Nor had it met the objection which might have been expected from the more sedate and venerable Miss Eunice. It is true, this lady was more than twice Inez's age ; but even at thirty-five one is not a pillar of salt, nor wholly indisposed to adventure. Eunice's watchful eye also had observed many reasons, some physical and some more subtle, why it would be for the advantage of Inez to be long absent from Orleans. Perhaps she would have shed no tears had she been told that the girl should never see that town again. So long as she was a child, it had not been difficult to arrange that the society she kept should be only among children whose language, thought, and habit would not hurt her. But Inez was a woman now,— a very lovely, simple, pure, and conscientious woman, it was true ; but, for all that, Eunice was not more inclined to see the girl exposed to the follies and extravagances of the exaggerated French or Spanish life of the little colony, especially while her father was in Europe. And Eunice was afraid, at the same time, that the life, only too luxurious, which they led in the city and on the plantation, did not strengthen the girl, as she would fain have her strengthened, against the constitutional weakness which had brought her mother to an early grave. Eunice saw no reason why, at sixteen years of age, Inez should not lead a life as simple, as much exposed to the open climate, and as dependent on her own resources, as she herself, with the advantages and disadvantages of Squam Bay, had led when she was a girl just beginning to be a woman.

Eunice Perry and Philip Nolan were almost of the same age ; and those who knew them both, and who saw how intimate the handsome young Kentuckian was in the comfortable New England household of Silas Perry, whether in the town house or plantation house, were forever gossiping and wondering, were saying now that he was in love with Eunice, now that she was in love with him; now that they were to be married at Easter, and now that the match was broken off at Michaelmas.

From the time when he first appeared in Orleans, almost a boy, with the verdure of his native village still clinging to him, but none the less cheerful, manly, courageous, enterprising, and handsome, he had found a friend in Silas Perry; and the office of the New England merchant was one of the first places to which he would have gone for counsel. It was not long before the shrewd and hearty New Englander, who knew men, and knew what men to trust, began to take the youngster home with him. Those were in the days when Inez was in her cradle, and when Eunice was a stranger in Louisiana.

Silas Perry had been Philip Nolan's counsellor, employer, and friend. Philip Nolan had been Silas Perry's pupil, agent, messenger, and friend. Eunice Perry had been Philip Nolan's frequent companion, his more frequent confidante, and most frequently his friend; and, as such friendship had been tested, there were a thousand good offices which she had asked of him, and never asked in vain. An intimacy so sincere as this, the growth of years of confidence, made it natural to all parties that Eunice and Inez should undertake their journey under the escort of this soldier who was not quite a merchant, and this merchant who was not quite a soldier, — Philip Nolan.

"But you are all alone, Capt. Phil," said Inez, expressing in the very frankest way the pleasure which the meeting, hardly expected, with her old friend afforded her. "Where is our army?"

"Our army has gone in advance, to free the prairies of any marauding throngs who might press too close on the princess who deigns to visit them."

"Which means, being interpreted, I suppose, that the army is buying corn at Natchitoches," said Eunice.

"Yes, and no," said he, a little gravely, as she fancied. "We shall find them near Natchitoches if we do not find them this side. I must talk with my friend the patron, and see if I can persuade him to give up your luxurious boat for one that I have chartered above the rapids. I have not much faith that the 'Donna Maria,' or the 'Dolores,' or the 'Sea Gull,' — which name has she to-day, Miss Inez? — that this sumptuous frigate of ours can be got through the rapids so easily as we thought at your father's. But I have what is really a very tidy boat above; and, before you ladies are awake in the morning, we will see if you are to change your quarters."

"And must I leave thee, my Martha?" cried Inez in a voice of mock tragedy. "Capt. Nolan, she is the 'Martha,' named after the wife of the Father of his Country. In leaving the proud banner of Spain, under which I was born, to pass, though only for a few happy hours, under the stars and stripes, accompanied by this noble friend whom I see I need not present to you, — Miss Perry, Gen. Nolan; a lady of the very highest rank of the New England nobility, — accompanied, I say, by an American lady of such distinction, I ordered the steersman of my bark to keep always in the eastern side of the river, in that short but blessed interval before we entered this redder but more Spanish stream."

The young American of 1876 must remember that in 1800 both the east and west sides of the Mississippi were Spanish territory, up to the southern line of our present State of that name. Above that point, the eastern half of the river was "American," the western half was Spanish. For a few miles before the boat had come into the Red River, she had in fact been floating, as Inez thought, in American waters; and the girl had made more than one chance to land on American soil, though it was the mud of a canebrake, for the first time of her life. All parties had joined in her enthusiasm; and they had fixed a bivouac on this little stretch of her father's land. So soon as they entered the Red River, they were under Spanish jurisdiction once more.

Nolan entered into the spirit of the girl's banter; and they knew very well that it was not all fun.

"What a pity that your ladyship could not have come to Fort Adams, or to Natchez,[1] to begin with us!" he said.

Natchez, then a village of six hundred inhabitants, was the southernmost town in the United States. It was Nolan's own headquarters, and from there his expedition had started.

" Your grace should have seen the stars and stripes flying from the highest flagstaff in the West. I should have been honored by the presence of your highnesses at my humble quarters. Indeed, my friend the major-general commanding at Fort Adams would have saluted your royal highnesses' arrival by a salvo of sixteen guns; and, the moment your majesty entered the works of that fortress, every heart would have been yours, as every recruit presented arms. A great pity, Miss Inez, you had not come up to Natchez. But what does my friend Ransom think of all this voyaging ? "

Inez called him.

"Ransom! Capt. Nolan wants to know how you liked coming back into your own country."

" Evenin', captain."

This was Ransom's only reply to the cordial salutation of the young Kentuckian, who was, however, one of Ransom's very few favorites.

"Miss Inez says you spent Monday night in the United States."

"Patron says so too," replied the sententious Ransom. "Don't know nothin'. Much as ever can make them niggers pull the boat along. Wanted to walk myself: could walk faster than all on 'em can row, put together. Told the

[1] The reader must note that Natchez on the Mississippi, Natchitoches on the Red River, and Nacogdoches on the Angelina River, are three different towns. The names seem to have been derived from the same roots.

patron so. We slept in a canebrake ; wust canebrake we see
since we left home. Patron said it was Ameriky.[1] Patron
don't know nothin'. Ain't no canebrakes in Ameriky."

"There's something amazingly · like them for the first
thousand or two miles of Miss Inez's journey there," said
Nolan, laughing. " Any way, I'm glad the alligators did not
eat her up, and you too, Ransom."

"They'd like to. Didn't give 'em no chance," replied the
old man, with a beaming expression on his countenance.
"Loaded the old double-barrel with two charges of buck-
shot, sot up myself outside her tent. Darned critters knew
it 'zwell as I did ; didn't dare come nigh her all night long."

"You should have given them pepper, Ransom. Throw a
little red pepper on the water, and it makes the bull alligators
sneeze. That frightens all the others, and they go twenty
miles off before morning."

Inez was laughing herself to death by this time, but
checked herself in time to ask whether she might not fly the
stars and stripes on the "Lady Martha."

"What's the use of calling her the 'Lady Martha' only
for these four or five miles? And my dear silk flag: is it
not a beauty, Capt. Nolan? I made it with my own fair
hands. And if you knew how to sew, Capt. Nolan, you
would know how hard it is to sew stars into blue silk, — silk
stars too. I never should have done it but for Sister Félicie :
she helped me out of hours ; and I wish I did not think she
was doing penance now. But is it not a beauty? Look at
it !" and she flung her pretty flag open over her knees and
Eunice's. " All your stripes, you see, with the white on the
outside, as you taught me. And I did not faint nor shirk
for one star, though mortal strength did tire, and Sister
Félicie did have to help ; but there are all the sixteen there.
That one with the little blood-spot on it is Vermont : I
pricked my finger horridly for Vermont ; and that is your
dear Kentucky, captain ; and that is Tennessee."

1 The use of the words " America " for the United States, and " Americans "
for their people, was universal among the Spaniards, even at this early day.

Nolan bowed, and, this time with no mock feeling, kissed the star which the girl pointed out for his own State.

"May I not fly it to-morrow morning? Was it only made for that little sail through the canebrakes?"

Nolan's face clouded a little,— a little more than he meant it should.

"Just here, and just now," he said, "I think we had better not show it. Not that I suppose we should meet anybody who would care; but they are as stupid as owls, and as much frightened as rabbits. It was only that very same Monday, that we met a whole company of Greasers (that is what my men called them); and we had to show our passports."

Inez asked him what he showed; and with quite unnecessary precision,— precision which did not escape Eunice's quiet observation,— he told her that he had, for his whole party, Gov. Pedro de Nava's pass to Texas and to return; that he even had private letters from Gov. Casa Calvo to Cordero, the general in command at the Alamo. Eunice said that the marquis had been only too courteous in providing her also with a passport for their whole party; he would have sent an escort, had his friend Mr. Perry suggested. "Indeed, the whole army was at the service of the Donna Eunice, as he tried to say, and would have said, had my poor name been possible to Spanish lips. Why, Capt. Nolan, I have sealing-wax enough and parchment enough for a king's ransom, if your papers were not enough for us."

"My good right arm shall write my pass, in answer to my prayers," said Nolan a little grimly. "Is not there some such line as that in your father's Chapman, Miss Inez?" And he bade them good-night, as he went to seek his quarters in the wretched cabin by the very roar of the rapids, and intimated to the ladies that they had best spread their mattresses, and be ready for an early start in the morning.

In truth, Nolan was geographer enough to know that the ladies had perhaps shown their flag a little too early; but he would not abate a whit of the girl's enthusiasm for what, as

he said, and as she said, should have been her native land.
Even the novel-reader of to-day reads with an atlas of maps at
his side, and expects geographical accuracy even from the
Princess Scheherezade herself. The reader will understand
the precise position, by examining the little map below, which
is traced from an official report of that time.

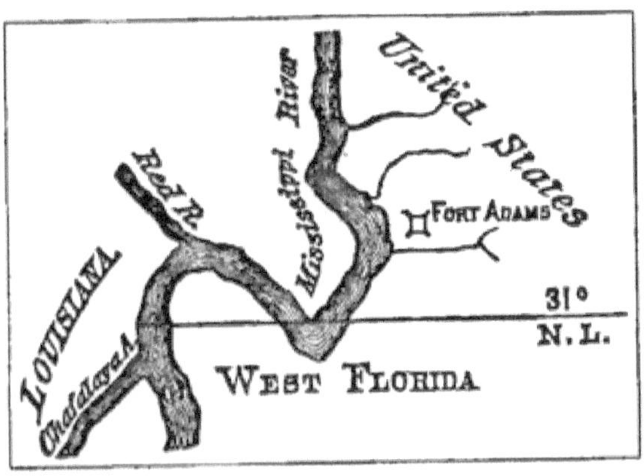

The western boundary of the United States was the middle
of the Mississippi River. The southern boundary was the
line of 31°. The girls knew, as everybody knew, where that
line crossed the river at different points. Was the little
projection opposite the Red River a part of the United
States, or of Florida? Inez and Eunice had thought they
were out of Spanish dominion there. Perhaps they were.
The reader can judge as well as the best diplomatist. Wars
have been made out of less material. The surveyors who
ran the boundary decided, not with the ladies, but with Nolan
and Ransom. Maps of that time vary ; and the river has
since abated all controversy, by cutting across the neck of
swampy land, and making the little peninsula into an
island.

And it was only for the wretched five miles of canebrake,
between the line of 31° and the mouth of the Red River,
that the eager Inez, by keeping her boat on the eastern

shore, had even fancied that she saw her own land, and was for once breathing what should have been her native air. As the boat hauled into the Red River, she had hidden her head in Eunice's lap, and had sobbed out, —

"This poor child is a girl without a country!"

CHAPTER IV.

"SHOW YOUR PASSPORTS!"

> " The pine-tree dreameth of the palm,
>   The palm-tree of the pine." — LORD HOUGHTON.

PHILIP NOLAN had his reasons for avoiding long tarry at the rapids ; and, when the new boat came with the party to the little port of Natchitoches, he had the same reasons for urging haste in the transfer of their equipment there.   These reasons he had unfolded to Eunice, and they were serious.

After all the plans had been made for this autumn journey, — plans which involved fatigue, perhaps, for the ladies, but certainly no danger, — the Spanish officials of Louisiana on the one side, and of Texas on the other, had been seized by one of their periodical quaking-fits, — fits of easy depression, which were more and more frequent with every year.   Nolan had come and gone once and again, with Spanish passports in full form, from the governor of Louisiana.   The present of a handsome mustang on his return would not be declined by that officer ; and, as the horse grew older, he would not, perhaps, be averse to the chances of another expedition. With just such free-conduct was Nolan equipped now ; and with his party of thirteen men he had started from Natchez on the Mississippi, to take up Miss Eunice and Miss Inez with their party at Natchitoches, the frontier station on the Red River.   Just before starting, however, the Spanish consul at Natchez had called the party before Judge Bruin, the United States judge there, as if they were filibusters.   But

Nolan's passport from Don Pedro de Nava, the commandant of the north-eastern provinces, was produced ; and the judge dismissed the complaint. This had been, however, only the beginning of trouble. Before Nolan joined the ladies, he had hardly passed the Mississippi swamp, — had, in fact, travelled only forty miles, — when he met a company of fifty Spanish soldiers, who had been sent out to stop him. Nolan's party numbered but twenty-one. The Spaniards pretended that they were hunting lost horses ; but, so soon as Nolan's party passed, they had turned westward also, and were evidently dogging them.

It was this unfriendly feeling on the part of those whom he was approaching as a friend, which had led Nolan to hasten his meeting with Eunice Perry and her niece, that he might, before it was too late, ask them whether they would abandon their enterprise, and return.

But Eunice boldly said " No." Her niece was, alas ! a Spanish woman born ; she was going to visit a Spanish officer on his invitation. If she had to show her passports every day, she could show them. If Capt. Nolan did not think they embarrassed the party, she was sure that she would go on : if he did, why, she must return, though unwillingly.

"Not I, indeed, Miss Eunice. You protect us where we meant to protect you. Only I do not care to cross these Dogberrys more often than I can help."

So it was determined that they should go on, — but go on without the little halt at Natchitoches, which had been intended.

Inez shared in all the excitement of a prompt departure, the moment the necessity was communicated to her. Before sunrise she was awake, and dressed in the prairie dress which had been devised for her. The four packs to which she had been bidden to confine herself — for two mules, selected and ready at L'Écore — had been packed ever since they left Orleans, let it be confessed, by old Ransom's agency, quite as much as by any tire-woman of her train. She was only too impatient while old Cæsar, the cook, elaborated the last river breakfast. She could not bear to have Eunice spend so much time in directions to the patron, and farewells to the boatmen, and messages to their wives. When it actually came to the spreading a plaster which Tony was to take back to his wife, for a sprain she had in her shoulder, Inez fairly walked off the boat in her certainty that she should be cross, even to Eunice, if she staid one minute longer.

Old Cæsar, at the last moment, blubbered and broke down. "Leave Miss Inez?" not he. What a pity that his voluble Guinea-French is not translatable into any dialect of the Anglo-American-Norman-Creole tongue! Leave her? not he. He had her in his arms when she was an hour old. He made her first doll out of a bulrush and some raw cotton. He taught her to suck sugar-cane ; and he picked pecan-meats for her before her mother knew that she could eat them. Should he leave her to be devoured alive by Caddo Indians? "*Jamais!* Imposible!"

"Come along with us, then," said Nolan ; and he indicated the mule which Cæsar was to ride.

And Cæsar came ; and his history is written in with that of Texas for the next ten years.

As the sun rose, the party gathered in front of the little shanty at which the most of the business of the landing was done. Ransom himself lifted Inez upon her saddle, adjusted the stirrups forty times, as if he had not himself cut the holes in the leathers, just as Inez bade him, a month before. Nolan watched for Eunice's comfort with the same care. Cæsar blubbered and bragged, and sent messages to the old woman, — messages which, if she ever received them, were the food on which she fed for the next decade of married life. Nolan was not displeased with the make-up of the little party. They were but eight in all ; but there was not a bad horse, a bad mule, a bad man, or a bad woman, in the train, he said. What pleased him most was the prompt obedience of the women, and the "shifty" readiness of the men. Old Ransom scolded a good deal, but was in the right place at the right time. And so, avoiding the village of Natchitoches by an easy detour, the party were in the wilderness an hour before the military commander of that fort knew that a boat had arrived from below, late the night before.

When the Spanish sentinel who had hailed her found that her passengers had all gone westward, he thought best not to report their existence to the governor; and so Philip Nolan's first manœuvre to escape frontier Dogberry No. 1 was perfectly successful.

In less than five minutes the whole party were in the pines, through which, over a sandy barren, they were to ride for two days. It was as if they had changed a world. To Eunice, why, the sniff of that pine fragrance was the renewal of the old life of her childhood. To Inez — not unused to forests, but all unused to pine-trees — the calm quiet of all around, the aromatic fragrance, the softness of the pine-leaves on which her horse's feet fell, all wrought a charm which overpowered the girl.

"Don't speak to me!"

And they left her alone.

"Does this seem more like home, Ransom?" said Nolan, letting his horse stand till the old man, who brought up the rear, might join him.

"Yes, sir! Pines is pines, though these be poor things. Pine-trees down East isn't crooked as these be; good for masts, good for yards; sawed one on 'em into three pieces when they wanted three masts for the 'Constitution.' But these has the right smell. These's good for kindlin's."

"You followed the sea once, Ransom?"

"Sarved under old Mugford first year of the war; was Manly's bo's'n when he went out in '77."

"Mugford?" asked Nolan. "I don't remember him."

"Pity you don't. Real old sea-dog; wasn't afraid of salt-petre. These fellers now, with their anchors, and gold braid on they coat-collars, don't know nothin'. Old Mugford never wore gold lace; didn't have none to wear. Wore a tarpaulin and a pea-jacket, when he could git it; ef he couldn't git it, wore nothin'."

"Where did you cruise?"

"All along shore. Went out arter Howe when the gineral druv him out of Boston. Kind o' hung round and picked up this vessel and that, that was runnin' into the bay, cos they didn't know the British was gone. Took one vessel with six guns, and no end of powder and shot. The old gineral he was glad enough of that, he was. No end of powder and shot: six guns she had. Took her runnin' into the bay. We was in the 'Franklin' then."

"Tell us all about it, Ransom."

"That's all they is to tell. I sighted our nine-pounder myself, — hulled her three times, and she struck. Old Mugford sent her into Boston, and stood off for more."

And the old man looked into the sky with that wistful look again, as if the very clouds would change into armed vessels, and renew the fight; and for a moment Nolan thought he would say no more. But he humored him.

"Next mornin'," said Ransom, after a minute, — "next mornin', when we was to anchor off the Gut, be hanged if they warn't thirteen boats from some of their frigates crawlin' up to us as soon as the light broke. We giv 'em blazes, cap'n. We sunk five on 'em without askin' leave. Then they thought they'd board us. Better luck 'nother time. Gosh! Poor devils caught hold of her gunnel; and we cut off their hands with broad-axes, we did."

"And Mugford?"

"Oh! you know Mugford reached arter one on 'em to cut at his head, and he got stuck just here with a boardin' pike, 'n he called Abel Turner. I stood with him in ma own arms. He called Abel Turner, and says he, 'I'm a dead man, Turner: don't give up the vessel. Beat 'em off, beat 'em off. You can cut the cable,' says he, 'and run her ashore.' Didn't say 'nother word: fell down dead."

Another pause. Nolan humored him still, and said nothing. And, after another wistful glance at the heavens, the old man went on, —

"Turner see the frigate was comin' down on him, and he run her ashore on Puddin' Point; and he sot fire to her, so that cruise was done. But none o' them fellers was ever piped to grog again, they wasn't; no, nor old Mugford, neyther."

A long pause, in which Nolan let the old fellow's reminiscences work as they might: he would not interrupt him.

But when he saw the spell had been fairly broken by some little detention, as they cared for the ladies in the crossing of a "sloo" or water-course, Nolan said to his old friend cautiously, —

"Did you see the general? Did you see Gen. Washington when he drove Howe out?"

Nolan spoke with that kind of veneration for Washington's name which was then, perhaps, at its very acme, — at the period when the whole country was under the impress of his recent death.

"Guess I did. Seen him great many times. I was standin' right by him when he cum into the old tavern at the head of King Street, jest where the pump is, by the Town House. Gage boarded there, and Howe and Clinton had they quarters there; and so the gineral come there when our army marched in.

"They was a little gal stood there starin' at him and all the rest; and he took her up, and he kissed her, he did.

"'Ne said to her, 'Sis,' says he, 'which do you like best, the redcoats or the Yankees?' 'N the child says, says she, she liked the redcoats the best, — gal-like, you know, — cos they looked so nice. 'N he laughed right out, 'ne says to her, 'Woll,' says he, 'they du have the best clothes, but it takes the ragged boys to du the fightin'.' Oh, I seen him lots o' times."

By this time Nolan thought he might venture to join Inez

again. She was now talking eagerly with her aunt, and seemed to have passed the depressed moment which the young soldier had respected, and had left to her own resolution.

The truth was, that a ride through a pine-forest in beginning a journey so adventurous, with no immediate possibility of a return to her father's care, had started the girl on the train of memories and other thoughts which stirred her most completely. For her mother she had a veneration, but it was simply for an ideal being. For her aunt she had an idolatrous enthusiasm, which her aunt wholly deserved. For the French and Spanish ladies and gentlemen around her, in their constant wars and jealousies with each other, she had even an undue contempt. Her father's central and profound interest in his own country and its prosperity came down to her in the form of a chivalrous passion for people she had never seen, and institutions and customs which she knew only in the theory or the idea. It would be hard, indeed, to tell whether her Aunt Eunice's more guarded narrative of her early life, or old Ransom's wild exaggerations of the glories of New England, had the most to do with a loyalty for the newly born nation which the girl found few ways to express, and indeed few ears to listen to.

Such a dreamer found herself now, for the first time, in the weird silence of a pine-forest, which she fancied must be precisely like the silent pine-groves of her father's home. Nor was any one cruel enough to undeceive her by pointing out the differences. She could hear the soughing of the wind, as if it had been throwing up the waves upon the beach. Her horse's feet fell noiseless on the brown carpet of leaves below her. And she was the centre, if not the commander, of a party all loyal to her, — strangers in a strange land, threatened perhaps, as it seemed, by the minions of this king she despised, though it was her bad luck to be born under his banner.

"Surely," she said to herself, "I am escaping from my

thraldom, if it be only for a few days. I am a woman now;
and in these forests, at least, I am an American."

In this mood Nolan found her.

"You have been talking with my dear old Ransom, Capt.
Nolan."

"Yes: he has been telling me of his battles. Did you
know how often the old fellow has been under fire ? "

"Know it ? Could I not tell you every shot he fired in the
'Franklin'? Don't I know every word of Mugford's, and
every cruise of Manly's ? I love to make him tell those old
stories. Capt. Nolan, why did we not live in such times ? "

"Perhaps we do."

"Do ? I wish I thought so ! " cried the girl. "The only
battles I see are the madame superior's battles with his excellency the governor, whether the Donna Louisa shall learn a
French verb or not. I am sick of their lies and their shilly-
shally : are not you ? "

"There is no harm in saying to you that for two years I
have been hoping to lead a hundred riflemen down this very
trail."

"Thank you, Capt. Nolan, for saying something which
sounds so sensible. Take my hand upon it, and count me
for number one when the time comes to enlist. Have you
been in battle, captain ? or are you a captain like " — and
she paused.

Nolan laughed.

"Like the governor's aids yonder, with their feathers and
their gold lace ? Woe's me, Miss Inez ! the powder I have
burned has been sometimes under fire from the Comanches,
sometimes when I did not choose to be scalped by another
redskin, but nothing that you would call war."

"But you have been in the army. You brought Capt.
Pope to our house, and Lieut. Pike."

"Oh, yes ! If being with army men will help you, count
me one. A good many of the older officers were in the war,
you know. Gen. Wilkinson was, and Col. Freeman was.

There is no end to their talk of war days. But I—I did nothing but train, as we called it, with the volunteers at Frankfort, when we thought the Indians would burn us out of house and home."

"Did you never—did you never—Capt. Nolan, don't think it a foolish question—did you never see Washington?"

"Oh, no!" he said, with a tone that showed her that he would not laugh at her eagerness. "But these men have: Wilkinson has; Freeman has. They will talk by the hour to you about what he said and did. I wish they had all loved him as well then as they say they did now. But really, Miss Inez, I do believe, that, in the trying times that are just now coming, young America is going to be true to old America. These twenty years have not been for nothing."

"Say it again," said the girl, with more feeling than can be described.

"Why, what goes there?" cried Nolan.

He dashed forward; but this time old Ransom rose before him, and was the person to receive the challenge of a Spanish trooper.

The man was in the leathern garments of the wilderness; but he had a sash round his waist, a cockade in his hat, and a short carbine swinging at his saddle, distinct enough evidences that he belonged to the Spanish army. In a moment more, the whole group of cavaliers approached him, so that the conversation, if such it may be called, which he began with Ransom, was continued by others of the party.

The Spanish horseman volubly bade them stop in the king's name, and show who they were. He had orders to arrest all travellers, and turn them back.

"What did you tell him, Ransom?" said Eunice, as soon as she came up.

"Told him to go and be hanged. Told him he hadn't got no orders to arrest us, cos the gov'ner had sent us. Told him he didn't know nothin' about it. Ye brother hed made it all right with the gov'ner, and had gone to see the king

about it. Wen I told him about the king, he seemed frightened, and said he would see."

The appearance of the Spanish sergeant was indeed a
surprise to all parties. Nolan had told Eunice that they
should meet no one before they came to the Sabine River,
and that he would keep himself out of the way when that
time came ; and now they had stumbled on just such another
party as he met the week before, sent out, as it would seem,
simply to look after him. Eunice, however, was quite ready
for the emergency.

She saluted the Spanish sergeant most courteously, apologized in a few well-chosen words of very good Castilian for
her servant's "impetuosity," and gave to the sergeant a little
travelling-bag which had swung at her saddle, telling him,
that, if he would open it, he would find the pass which the
Marquis of Casa Calvo had provided for them, and his
recommendation to any troops of Gen. Cordero.

"I cannot be grateful enough," she said, "to the good
Providence which has so soon given to us the valorous
protection of the chivalrous soldiers of the king of
Spain."

The sergeant bowed, a good deal surprised, did not say he
could not read, as he might have said with truth ; but, touching his hat with courtesy, turned to an officer approaching
him, whose dress had rather more of cloth and rather less
of leather than his own, and indicated that he would show
the passport to him.

Capt. Morales opened and scrutinized both papers, returned them silently to the leather satchel, and, with a low
bow, gave it back to Eunice.

"This is a sufficient pass for yourself, my lady, and for
the señorita who accompanies you, and for your party. How
many of these gentlemen and servants are of your party ?
My officer here will fill out the verbal catalogue, which the
secretary of the marquis has omitted."

"Let me present the Señorita Perry, my niece. Here is

my major-domo ; these three are servants with their duties in her household ; the old negro yonder is our cook."

The lieutenant entered on his tablet this answer, and Capt. Morales said, —

" And who is the hidalgo behind you, — the gentleman who says nothing ? "

CHAPTER V.

SAVE ME FROM MY FRIENDS.

" My heart's uneasiness is simply told, —
  I hate the Greeks, although they give me gold:
  This firm right hand shall foil my foemen's ends,
  If Heaven will kindly save me from my friends."

After DRYDEN.

"LET me present my friend," said Eunice at once, without the slightest confusion.

Nolan meanwhile was sitting listlessly on his horse, as if he did not understand one word of the colloquy.

"Mons. Philippe! Mons. Philippe!" cried Eunice, turning to him eagerly; and, as he rode up, she addressed him in French, saying, "Let me present you to Capt. Morales."

And then to this officer, —

"This is my friend, Mons. Philippe, a partner of my brother in his business, to whom in his absence in Paris he has left the charge of us ladies. He is kind enough to act as the intendant of our little party. May I ask you to address him in French?"

In this suggestion Capt. Morales, who was already a little suspicious when he found a woman conducting the principal conversation of this interview, found a certain excuse. The Spanish officers in the government of Louisiana all spoke French, as the people did who were under their command. They were, indeed, in large measure chosen from the Low Countries, that they might be at home in that language. But there was no reason for such selection in the appointment of officers who served in Mexico, like Morales; nor could Eunice, at the first glance, be supposed to know whether he spoke French or not.

In truth, he did speak that language very ill. And, after a stately "*Bon jour*," his first questions to Mons. Philippe halted and broke so badly, that with a courtly smile he excused himself, and said that if the lady would have the goodness to act as interpreter, he would avail himself of her mediation.

"Your name is not mentioned on this lady's passport, Mons. Philippe."

"I was not in Orleans when it was granted. It is, I believe, a general permit to the Donna Eunice Perry and her party."

"Have you, then, lately arrived from Paris?"

"The worshipful Don Silas has just now sailed for Paris. For myself, I only overtook the ladies, by the aid of horses often changed, at the rapids of the Red River. I count myself fortunate that I overtook them. His Excellency was himself pleased to direct me to use every means at his command in their service, and I have done so."

Nolan would not have said this were it not true. Strange to say, it was literally and perfectly true. For one of the absurdities of the divided command which gave Louisiana to one Spanish governor, and Texas to another, at this time, was the preposterous jealousy which maintained between these officers a sort of armed or guarded relation, as if one were a Frenchman because his province had a French name, and only the other were a true officer of the Catholic king, — an absurdity, but not an unusual absurdity. Just such an absurdity, not twenty years before, made the discord between Cornwallis and Clinton, which gave to Washington the victory of Yorktown, and gave to America her independence.

So was it, that, while the Marquis of Casa Calvo at New Orleans was Nolan's cordial friend, Elguesebal in Texas and De Nava at Chihuahua were watching and dogging him as an enemy.

"Will my lady ask the hidalgo what was the public news in Paris? Our two crowns, — or, rather, his Catholic Majesty's crown and the First Consul of France, — they are in good accord? What were the prospects of the treaty?"

"France and Spain were never better friends," replied Nolan, "if all is true that seems. The public journals announce the negotiations of a treaty. Of its articles more secret, even the Capt. Morales will pardon me if I do not speak. He will respect my confidence."

The truth was, that even at this early moment a suspicion was haunting men's minds, of what was true before the month was over, — that by the treaty of Ildefonso the Spanish king would cede the territory of Louisiana to Napoleon.

Capt. Morales had heard some rumor of this policy, even in Nacogdoches. The allusion to it made by Nolan confirmed him in his first suspicion, that this young Frenchman, who could speak no Spanish, was some unavowed agent of the First Consul, Napoleon.

If he were, it was doubtless his own business to treat him with all respect.

At the moment, therefore, that Nolan confessed he must speak with reserve, the Spaniard's doubts as to his character gave way entirely. He offered his hand frankly to the young Frenchman, and bade him and the lady rely on his protection.

"Your party is quite too small," he said. "I am only sorry that I cannot detail a fit escort for you. But I am charged with a special duty, — the arrest of an American freebooter who threatens us with an army of Kenny — Kenny — tuckians. The Americans have such hard names! They are indeed allies of the savages. But I will order four of my troopers to accompany you to Nacogdoches, and the commandant there can do more for you."

Nolan and Eunice joined in begging him not to weaken his force. They were quite sufficient for their own protection, they said. The servants were none of them cowards, and had had some experience with their weapons. But the captain was firm in his Castilian politeness ; and, as any undue firmness on their part in rejecting so courteous an offer must awaken his suspicions, they were obliged to comply with his wish, and accept the inopportune escort which he provided for them.

Inez, meanwhile, wild with curiosity and excitement, as the colloquy passed through its different stages of suspicion and of confidence, had not dared express her fear, her amusement, or her surprise, even by a glance. She saw it was safest for her to drop her veil, and to sit the impassive Castilian maiden, fresh from a nunnery, which Capt. Morales supposed her to be.

As for old Ransom, the major-domo of Eunice's establishment, he sat at a respectful distance, heeding every word of the conversation, in whatever language it passed, with a face as free from expression as the pine-knot on the tree next him. Once and again he lifted his eyes to the heavens with that wistful look of his, which was rather the glance of an astronomer than of a devotee. But the general aspect of the man was of an impatient observer of events, who had himself, Cassandra-like, stated in advance what must be and was to be, and was now grieved that he must await the slow processes of meaner intelligences.

At last his patience was relieved. Capt. Morales drew from his haversack a slip of paper, on which he wrote : —

" By order of the King :

Know all men, that the Lady Eunice and Lady Inez, with Mons. Philippe, the intendant of their household, with one Ransom and four other servants, have free

Pass and Escort

to the King's loyal city of   San Antonio
Bexar ; under direction of the military commandant, and after inspection by me.   MORALES,
Captain of Artillery.

Long live the King ! "

He then told off a corporal or sergeant with three troopers, and bade them, nothing loath, accompany the Orleans party to Nacogdoches. He gave his hand courteously to the Señora Eunice and Mons. Philippe, touched his hat as courteously to the Señorita Inez, and even threw his party into military order as the others passed, and gave them a military salute as his last farewell.

"Save me from my friends," said Nolan, as he joined the Donna Eunice after this formality was over, and each party was out of sight of each other. "Save me from my friends! This civility of your friend the captain is more inconvenient to us than the impudence of my captain on the prairie yonder."

"I see it is," said Eunice thoughtfully. "I am afraid I have done wrong. But really, Capt. Nolan, I was so eager to take you under our protection — I knew my brother would be so glad to serve you — I thought the governor had this very purpose in his mind — that I thought, even if the truth was for once good policy, I would tell him the truth still."

And she pretended to laugh, but she almost cried.

"Of course you could tell him nothing else," said he.

"Indeed I could not. Nobody could ask me actually to betray you by name to your enemies."

"I hope not," said the Kentuckian, laughing without reserve. "If indeed they are my enemies. I wish I could tell them at sight. If they would show their colors as they make us show ours, it would be well and good," he added. "If, when we see a buckskin rascal with the King of Spain's cockade, he would wear a feather besides, to say whether he is a Texan Spaniard or an Orleans Spaniard, that would do. But pray do not be anxious, Miss Eunice. My anxieties are almost over now. I can take good care of myself, and the King of Spain seems likely to take care of you. I am well disposed to believe old Ransom, that your father has gone to the king to tell him all about it."

Eunice said that she did not see how he could speak so. How could he bring his party up to them, if there were these four spies hanging on all the way?

"I can see," replied Nolan, laughing, "that dear Ransom would like nothing better than to blow out their brains, and throw them all into the next creek. But really that is a very ungracious treatment of men who only want to take care of fair ladies. We must not be jealous of their attentions."

Then he added more seriously, —

"I am afraid this meeting may cut off from me the pleasure of many such rides as this; and, believe me, I have looked forward eagerly to more of them than was reason. As soon as these fellows will spare me, I must ride across and meet my party, and warn them not to come too near your line of travel. But I can put another 'intendant' in my place, and, if need be, more than one; and I can leave you the satisfaction, if it is any, to know that I am not far away."

"If it is any! What would my brother think, if he did not suppose that five of you were behind Inez, and five before, five on the right hand, and five on the left? Still I suppose we are perhaps even safer now." This somewhat anxiously.

"Dear Miss Eunice, you are never so safe in this world as when you make no pretence of strength, while in truth you are well guarded. When I am weak, then I am strong." This he said with his voice dropping, and very reverently. "If this is true in the greatest things, if it is true in trials where the Devil is nearest, all the more is it true in the wilderness. A large party, with the fuss of its encampment, attracts every Bedouin savage and every cut-throat Greaser within a hundred miles. They come together like crows. But a handful of people like yours will most likely ride to San Antonio without seeing savage or Christian, except such as are at the fort and the ferries. Then, the moment these four gentlemen are tired of you, I shall be in communication, and my men in buckram will appear."

"Men in buckram! that is too bad," said Inez, who had joined their colloquy. "Where. may your men in buckram be just now?"

"They are a good deal nearer to us than your admirer,

Capt. Morales, supposes. But he is riding away from them as fast as he can ride, and they are riding away from him at a pace more moderate. You shall see, Miss Inez, when the camping-time comes, whether my men are in buckram, in broadcloth, or in satin."

Sure enough, when the sun was within an hour of setting, as that peerless October day went by, the little party, passing out from a tract rather more thickly wooded than usual, came out upon a lovely glade, where the solitude was broken. Two tents were pitched, and on one of them a little blue flag floated. Three or four men in leathern hunting-shirts were lying on the ground, but sprang to their feet the moment the new party appeared.

"My lady is at home," said Nolan, resuming the mock air of formal courtesy with which he and Inez so often amused themselves. "My backwoodsmen have come in advance, as Puss in Boots did, to arrange for my lady's comfort."

"Are these your men? You are too careful, captain, or too careless, I do not know which to say, — too careful for me, and too careless for your own safety."

"That for my safety," said the reckless young man, snapping his fingers. "If your ladyship sleeps well, we ask nothing more. To say true, my lady, I am the most timid of men : praise me for my prudence. Were I not caution personified, I should have commanded William yonder to fly the stars and stripes over your majesty's tent. But I had care for your majesty's comfort. I knew these Greasers would know those colors too well."

"And he has! and he has! Oh, you are good, Capt. Nolan! — See, aunty, the flag that flies over us!"

There is many a girl in Massachusetts who reads these words, who does not know that the flag of her own State displays on a blue field a shield bearing an Indian proper and a star argent — which means an Indian painted in his own manner as he is, and a star of silver. But in those days each State had had to subsist for itself, even to strike its own coin, and often to fight under its own flag ; and this New England girl, who had never seen New England, knew the cognizance of her own land as well as the Lotties and Fannies and Aggies — the Massachusetts girls of to-day — know the cognizance of England or of Austria.

"Welcome home, ladies," said the tall, handsome young soldier, who took Eunice's horse by the head, while Nolan lifted her from the saddle.

"This is the ladies' own tent, captain. We have set the table in the other." And the ladies passed in at the tent-door to find the hammocks swung for them, two camp-stools open, a little table cut with a hatchet from the bark of large pines, and covered with a white napkin, on which stood ready a candlestick and a tinder-box ; and another rough table like it, with a tin basin full of water ; and two large gourds, tightly corked, on the pine carpet at its side.

"We are in a palace," cried Inez. "How can we thank these gentlemen enough for their care ? "

"I must tell you who they are. — Why, William, where have the others gone ? — Miss Eunice, Miss Inez, this is my other self, William Harrod. William, you knew who these ladies were long before you saw them. Ladies, if I told you that William Harrod was Ephraim Harrod's brother, it would not help you. If I said he was the best marksman in the great valley, you would not care. When I say he is the best fellow that lives, you must believe me."

"Leave them to find that out, captain."

"The captain tells enough when he says you are his other self. In a country like this, one is glad to find two Philip Nolans."

Old Ransom and his party, meanwhile, were a little disgusted that the preparations they had made for the mistress's accommodation on her first night away from the river should be thus put in the shade by the unexpected encampment on which they had lighted. Before their journey was finished, they were glad enough to stumble on cattle-shed or abandoned camp which might save them from the routine of uncording and cording up their tents; but to be anticipated on the very first night of camp-life was an annoyance. When, however, Ransom found that these were Capt. Nolan's people, and that the preparation had been dictated by his forethought, his brow cleared, and the severe animadversions by which he had at first condemned every arrangement changed, more suddenly than the wind changes, into expressions of approval as absolute.

While the ladies were preparing for the supper, Ransom amused himself with the Spanish soldiers.

One of them had asked what the flag was which was displayed above the ladies' tent.

"Ignorant nigger!" said Ransom afterward, as he detailed the conversation to Miss Eunice. (The man was no more a negro than Ransom was; but it was his habit to apply this phrase to all persons of a Southern race.) "Ignorant nigger! I axed him ef he didn't know the private signal uv his own king. I told him the king uv Spain, when he went out to ride with the ladies uv the court, or when he sot at dinner in his own pallis, had that 'ere flag flyin' over his throne. I told him that he gin your brother a special permit to use it, wen he gin him the star of San Iago for wot he did in the war with the pirates."

"Ransom! how could you!" said Eunice, trying to look forbidding, while Inez was screaming with delight, and beckoning to her new friend, Mr. Harrod, to listen.

"Only way with 'em, marm. They all lies; and, ef you don't lie to 'em, they dunno wot you mean. Answer a fool accordin' to his folly, is the rule, mum. Heerd it wen I was a boy. Wen I'm in Turkey, I do as the turkeys do, marm: they ain't no other way."

Cæsar appeared, grinning, and said that supper was ready. One of Harrod's aids stood at the door of the second of his tents, saluted as his officer and Nolan led the ladies in; and Cæsar and Ransom followed, — Cæsar to wait upon the hungry travellers, and Ransom in his general capacity of major-domo, or critic-in-chief of all that was passing.

"We give you hunters' fare," said Nolan, who took the place and bearing of the host at the entertainment ; "but you have earned your appetites."

" It would be hard if two poor girls could not be satisfied with roasted turkey ; with venison, if that be venison ; with quails, if those be quails ; and with rabbits, if those be rabbits, — let alone the grapes and melons. You must have thought we had the appetite of the giant Blunderbore."

" I judged your appetite by my own," said Nolan, laughing. " As for Harrod, he is a lady's man : he has no appetite ; but perhaps he will pick a bone of the merry-thought of this intimation of a partridge ;" and he laid the bone on the plate of his laughing friend.

The truth was that the feast was a feast for kings. It was served with Cæsar's nicest finish, and with the more useful science and precision of the hunters. Ransom had made sure that a little travelling table-service, actually of silver, should be packed for the ladies ; and in this forest near the Sabine, under their canvas roof, they ate from a board as elegantly appointed as any in Orleans or in Mexico, partaking of fare more dainty than either city could command. So much for the hardships of the first day of the campaign.

CHAPTER VI.

GOOD-BY.

> "The rule of courtesy is thus expressed :
>   Welcome the coming, speed the parting guest."
>
> MENELAUS in the Odyssey.

"WHEN hunger now and thirst were fully satisfied," Nolan called Ransom to him, and asked the old man in an undertone where the Spanish soldiers were.

"They's off by they own fire. Made a fire for theyselves. The men asked 'em to supper, and gin 'em all the bacon and whiskey they'd take. Poor devils I don't often have none. Now they's made they own fire, and is gamblin' there."

By the word "gambling," Ransom distinguished every game of cards, however simple. In this case, however, it is probable that he spoke within the mark.

"Then we can talk aloud," said Nolan. "A tent has but one fault,— that you are never by yourself in it. You do not know what redskin or panther is listening to you."

Then he went on : —

"William, I have kept myself well out of these rascals' sight all the afternoon. I have not looked in their faces, and they have not looked in mine. For this I had my reasons. And I think, and I believe the ladies will think, that if you put on my cap and this hunting-shirt to-morrow, and permit me to borrow that more elegant equipment of yours, — if you will even take to yourself the name and elegant bearing of 'Mons. Philippe,' supposed *chargé d'affaires* of the Consul Bonaparte, and certainly partner of Mr. Silas Perry, — you may serve the ladies as well as at the Spanish guard-house yonder ; and I shall serve them better even than you, in returning for a day or two to our friends in buck-ram."

The ladies asked with some eagerness the reasons for such a change ; but in a moment they were satisfied that Nolan was in the right. Any stray officer at the fort might recognize him, well known as he was all along the frontier, and on both sides of it ; and, on the other hand, his own direction to his own party was, of course, the most valuable to all concerned. There was some laugh at the expense of the forest gear which was to be changed. The fringes to the hunting-shirts were of different dyes ; one hat bore a rabbit's tail, and one the feather of a cardinal : but, for the two men, they were within a pound of the same weight, and a hair-breadth of the same size, as Harrod said, and he said it proudly.

"My other self, I told you," said Nolan ; and then he assumed the mock protector, and charged the ladies that they must go to bed for an early start in the morning.

At sunrise, accordingly, the pretty little camp was on the alert. All the tents, except those of the ladies, were struck before they were themselves awake. Their toilet was not long, though it was elaborate ; and when Inez stepped out from her sleeping-apartment, and looked in to see the prog-ress breakfast had made, she was provoked with herself that she was the first person deceived by the new-made Dromio.

She slyly approached Mr. Harrod, who stood at the table with his back to her, tapped him smartly on the shoulder, and said, —

"Philopœna !   Capt. Nolan, my memory is better than you think "— to have the handsome "other self " turn round, and confuse her with his good-natured welcome.

"Philopœna ! indeed, Miss Perry, but it was not I who ate the almond with you."

"To think it," said the girl, "that a bird's feather and a strip of purple leather should change one man into another! Well, I thought I was a better scout. Do you know I enlisted among Capt. Nolan's rifles yesterday? If only my well-beloved sovereign would make war with you freemen, he would not find me among his guards."

The girl's whole figure was alive; and Harrod understood at once that she did not dislike the half-equivocal circumstances in which they stood, — of measuring strength and wit against the officers of the Spanish king.

Breakfast was as elegant and dainty as supper; but the impetuous and almost imperious Inez could not bear that they should sit so long. For herself, she could and would take but one cup of coffee. How people could sit so over their coffee, she could not see! "Another slice from the turkey?" No! Had she not eaten corn-cake and venison, and grapes and fricasseed rabbit, all because Ransom had cooked or gathered them himself for her? Would dear Aunt Eunice never be done?

Dear Aunt Eunice only laughed, and waited for her second cup to cool, and sipped it by teaspoonfuls, and folded her napkin as leisurely as if she had been on the plantation, and as if none of them had any thing to do but to look at their watches till the hour for lunch-time came.

"Miss Perry," said Harrod to her, "I believe you are a soldier's daughter?"

"Indeed I am," said Eunice heartily, and then, with a laugh, "and a rifleman's aunt, I understand, or a riflewoman's."

"Any way, you dear old plague, you have at last drunk the last drop even you can pretend you want, and I do believe you have given the last fold to that napkin. — Gentlemen, shall we not find it pleasanter in the air?"

And she dropped a mock courtesy to them, sprang out of the tent singing, —

"Hark, hark, tantivy: to horse, my brave boys, and away!"

And away they went.   The same delicious fragrance of the pines ; the exquisite freshness of morning ; the song of birds not used to travellers ; the glimpses now and then of beasts four-footed, who were scarcely afraid ! Every thing combined to inspirit the young people, and to make Inez rate at its very lowest the danger and the fatigue of the expedition.

Until they should come to the neighborhood of the Spanish post at San Augustine, the two united parties were to remain together.   To the escort provided by the eagerness or suspicion of Capt. Morales, the *rencontre* of the night before was only the ordinary incident of travel, in which two parties of friends had met each other, and encamped together. That they should make one body as they went on the next day, was simply a matter of course.   Nolan, therefore, had the pleasure of one day's more travel with his friends ; and, if the ladies had had any sense of insecurity, they would have had the relief of his presence and that of his backwoodsmen. But at this period they had no such anxiety except for him.

With laugh and talk and song of the four, therefore, varied by more serious colloquy as they fell into couples, two and two, the morning passed by ; and Inez and Eunice were both surprised when the experienced backwoodsmen ordered the halt for lunch.   They could not believe that they had taken half the journey for the day.   But the order was given ; the beasts were relieved of their packs ; a shaded and sheltered spot was chosen for the ladies' picnic ; and to Ransom was given this time all the responsibility and all the glory of their meal.

It was hardly begun, when, from the turn which screened the trail on the west, there appeared an Indian on horseback ; and, as Nolan sprang to his feet to welcome him, the rest of a considerable party of Indians, men and women and children, with all the paraphernalia of an encampment, appeared.

The leading man, whose equipment and manner showed, that, so far as any one ranked as chief of the little tribe, he assumed that honor, came readily forward ; and, after a min-

THE LANGUAGE OF PANTOMIME.

ute's survey, at Nolan's invitation he dismounted, and did due honor to a draught of raw West Indian rum which Nolan offered him in one of the silver cups which he took from the table. But, when Nolan addressed him in some gibberish which he said the Caddoes would understand, the chief intimated that he did not know what he meant. He did this by holding his hand before his face with the palm outward, and shaking it to and fro.

Nolan was a connoisseur in Indian dialects, and tried successively three or four different jargons ; but the chief made the sign of dissent to each, and intimated that he was a Lipan. Nolan had tried him in the dialects of the Adeyes, the Natchez, and the Caddoes, with which he himself was sufficiently familiar.

"Lipan !" he said aloud to his friends. "What devil has sent the Lipans so far out of their way ?"

With the other, he dropped the effort to speak in articulate language, and fell into a graceful and rapid pantomime, which the chief immediately understood, which Harrod followed with interest, and sometimes joined in, and in which two or three other lesser chiefs, still sitting on their horses, took their part as well.

Nothing could be more curious than this silent, rapid, and animated colloquy. Inez and Eunice looked from face to face, wholly unable to follow the play of the conversation, but certain that to all the interlocutors it was entirely intelligible. To all the tribes west of the river, indeed, there was this common language of pantomime, intelligible to all, though their dialects were of wholly distinct families of language. It still subsists among the southern Indians of the plains, and is perhaps intelligible to all the tribes on this side the Rocky Mountains.[1]

---

[1] The fullest account of this language of pantomime is probably from Philip Nolan's own pen. It is preserved in the Sixth Volume of the Transactions of the American Philosophical Society, and is the most considerable literary work known to me by this accomplished young man.

Hands, arms, and fingers were kept in rapid movement as the colloquy went on. The men bent forward and back, from right to left, now used the right arm, now the left, seemed to describe figures in the air, or tapped with one hand upon the other. An open hand seemed to mean one thing, a closed hand another. The forefinger was pointed to one eye, or to the forehead, or to the ear, now to the sun, now to the earth. All the fingers of one hand would be set in rapid motion, while the other hand indicated, as occasion might require, the earth, the sky, a lake or a river.

The whole group of whites and negroes on the one hand, and of "redskins" on the other, joined in a circle about the five principal conversers. Harrod's party had some slight understanding of the language, and occasionally gave some slight interpretation to their companions as to what was going on. All the Indians understood it in full, and, by grunts and sighs, expressed their concurrence in the sentiments of their leaders.

The interest reached its height, when Nolan took the right hand of the savage chief, passed it under his hunting-shirt and the flannel beneath it, so that it rested on the naked heart. Both smiled as if with pleasure ; and after an instant, by a reversal of the manœuvre, Nolan placed his hand on the heart of the Indian. Here was an indication, from each to the other, that each heart beat true.

After this ceremony, Nolan called one of the scouts from Harrod's party, and bade him bring a jug from their own stores. Then turning to Eunice he said, —

"Pray let all the redskin chiefs drink from your silver. I had a meaning in using this cup when I 'treated' Long-Tail here. And now none of them must feel that we hold ourselves above them. Perhaps they do not know that silver rates higher than horn in the white men's calendar, but perhaps they do."

Eunice had caught the idea already. She had placed five silver cups on a silver salver, and so soon as the liquor arrived gave them to the scout to fill.   The chiefs, if they were chiefs, grunted their satisfaction.   Nolan then, with a very royal air, passed down their whole line, and gave to each a bright red ribbon.   It was clear enough that most of them had never seen such finery.   The distribution of it was welcomed much as it would have been by children ; and after a general grunt, expressive of their satisfaction, the chief resumed his seat on horseback, and the party took up its line of march again.

"I asked them where they were going, and they lied; I asked them where they came from, and they lied," said Nolan a little anxiously, as he resumed his own place by the outspread blanket, which was serving for a tablecloth on the ground.

"They are hunting Panis," said Harrod ; "and they did not want to say so, because they supposed we were Spaniards. But I never knew Lipans so far down on this trail before."

"No," said Nolan : "I have never met Lipans but once or twice, — you know when."

"I thought you were going to show them what was in your heart."

Nolan laughed, and turned to the ladies.

"You would like to know what is in my heart, Miss Inez, would you not?   How gladly would I know what is in yours! To say truth, like most of us, I was not quite ready for the exposure ; and perhaps these rascals knew a little more than is best for them.   'A little knowledge is a dangerous thing.'"

"What are you talking about?" said Inez.   "I hate riddles, unless I can guess them."

Nolan produced from a secret fold in his pouch a little convex mirror, highly polished, with long cords attached to it.

"The memory of man does not tell how long ago it was that one of the French chiefs tied such a mirror as this on his heart.   Then, in a palaver with a redskin, monsieur said he would show him what was in his heart, stripped his breast, bade 'Screaming Eagle' look, and, lo! 'Screaming Eagle' himself was there. The 'One-Horned Buffalo' looked, and lo ! 'One-Horned Buffalo' was there."

"Lucky they knew themselves by sight," said Eunice.

"I have often thought of that. They would not have known their own eyes and nose and mouth. But they did know their feathers, their war-paint, and the rest ; and from that moment he enjoyed immense renown with them.

"Nor do I count it a lie," said Nolan, after a pause. "What is all language but signs, just such as we have all been using ? Here was a sign carefully wrought out, like the 'totem,' or star of the 'Golden Fleece,' which, according to Ransom, the king will give to your father, Miss Inez."

"I am sure I have them all in my heart. I am very fond of them, and I wish them well so long as they are not scalping me ; and, when I am far enough from trading-houses, I do not scruple to use the glass on my heart, as the best symbol by which I can say so."

As they resumed the saddle, Inez begged her friends to tell her more of this beautiful language of signs.

"It is twenty times as graceful as the pantomime of the ballet troupe," said she.

"They all understand it," said Nolan, "at least as far as I have ever gone. Harrod will tell you how it served us once on the Neches."

"It is quickly learned," said Harrod, not entering on the anecdote. "Indeed, it is simple, as these people are. See here," said he eagerly : "this is *Water*."

And he dropped his rein, brought both his hands into the shape of a bowl, and lifted them to his mouth, without, however, touching it.

"Now, this is *Rain*," he added ; and he repeated the same sign, lifting his hands a little higher, and then suddenly turned his fingers outward, and shook them rapidly to represent the falling of water.

"*Snow* is the same thing," he said, " only I must end with white. This is white ;" and with the fingers of his right hand he rubbed on that part of the palm of the left which unites the thumb with the fingers.

"Why is that white?" said Inez, repeating the movement.

"Look in old Cæsar's hand, and you will see," said Harrod.

"Oh, yes! I see; how bright it all is! But, Mr. Harrod, how do you say *go*, and *come?* where do the verbs come in?"

"This is *go*," said he; and he stretched his right hand out slowly, with the back upward. "Here is *come;*" and he moved his right finger from right to left, with a staccato movement, in which the ladies instantly recognized the steps of a man walking.

Harrod was perhaps hardly such a proficient in this pantomime as was Nolan, to whom he often turned when Inez asked for some phrase more abstract than was the common habit of the "bread-and-butter" talk of the frontier. But the two gentlemen together were more than competent to interpret to her whatever she asked for; and, when at last she began a game of whispering to Nolan what he should repeat to Harrod, the precision and fulness of the interpretation were as surprising as amusing.

"But you have not told us," said Eunice in the midst of this, "what you said to the Learned Buffalo, if that was his name, and what he said to you, in all your genuflexions and posturings."

"Oh! I told you what they said, or that it was mostly lies. They said they had lost some horses, and had come all this way to look for them. That is what an Indian always tells you when he is on some enterprise he wants to conceal. He said it was fourteen days since he had seen any of his white brethren. That was a lie. He stopped at Augustine last night, and stole that cow-bell that was on the black mule. He said his people had been fighting with the Comanches, and took thirty-two scalps. That was a lie. I heard all about it from a Caddo chief last week. The Comanches whipped them, and they were glad to get away with the scalps they wore."

"The language of pantomime seems made to conceal thought," said Inez.

"Oh ! he tells some truth. He says the Spaniards have a new company of artillery at San Antonio. He says your aunt was out riding on the first day of October : you can ask her if that was true, when you see her. He says she had with her a calash with two wheels, in which sat a black woman who held a baby with a blue ribbon. I ought to have told you this first of all ; but this *galimatias* of his about the Comanches put it out of my head."

Inex turned to him almost sadly.

"Capt. Nolan, how can you tell me this nonsense ? Fun is well enough, but you were so serious that you really cheated me. I do not like it. I do not think you are fair." And in an instant more the girl would be shedding tears.

"Indeed, indeed, Miss Inez ! " cried the good fellow, " I know when to fool, and when not. I have told you nothing but what the man said to me. Blackburn ! " and he beckoned to one of the mounted men who had accompanied Harrod, " you saw this redskin, you know his signs. Miss Perry thinks I must have mistaken his news from San Antonio."

The man was a rough fellow in his dress, but his manner was courteous, with the courtesy of the frontier. " He said, miss, that they left San Antonio when the moon had passed its third quarter three days. He said that, the day before he came away, a new company came up from below, with big guns, — guns on carts, he called them, miss. He said that same afternoon, the officer in command rode out horseback, mum, and a lady with him ; and that a cart with a kiver over it went behind, with a black hoss, miss. He said there was a nigger-woman in the kivered cart, an' she had a white baby, 'n the baby had a blue ribbon round her head. I believe that was all."

The man fell back, as he saw he was no longer wanted ; and Inez gave her hand very prettily and frankly to Nolan, and said, —

"I beg your pardon, captain : I was very unjust to you. But this seemed impossible."

Harrod was greatly pleased with this passage, in its quiet testimony to his leader's accomplishment, though it was an accomplishment so far out of the common course. Nolan had not referred to him because he had heard the interpretation which Inez had challenged. The talk went on enthusiastically about the pantomime language ; and the young men vied with each other in training the ladies to its manipulations, so far as these were possible to people pinioned in their saddles.

"You can say any thing in it," cried Inez.

"I don't see that," said Eunice. "You can say any thing a savage wants to say."

"You cannot say the Declaration of Independence," said Harrod.

"Nor the Elegy in a Country Churchyard," said Nolan.

And so the day wore pleasantly by, till, as they came to the ferry where they were to cross the Sabine, Nolan confessed he had kept in company to the last moment possible, and bade them, "for a few days at most," he said, farewell.

He left, as an escort, Harrod and the three scouts who had joined with him. Harrod was willing to appear as Mons. Philippe, and the others were to meet the Spanish challenge as best they could. It might be, Nolan said, that he should have joined again before they had to pass inspection once more.

CHAPTER VII.

THE SAN ANTONIO ROAD.

> " I called to the maid :
>   I whispered and said,
>   ' My pretty girl, tell to me,
>   The man on the sly
>   Who kissed you good-by, —
>   Is he Frenchman, or Portugee ? ' "
>
> *Tom Tatnall's Courtship.*

AND so Philip Nolan bade his friends good-by for a day or two as they all supposed, but, as it proved, for a longer parting.

The escort of a squad of Spanish cavalry, unexpected and unsatisfactory as it was, removed the immediate or actual necessity for the presence of his troop with the little party of Eunice's retainers. None the less did he assure her that he should rejoin the party with his larger force, though he did think it advisable to keep these out of the sight of the officers at the Spanish outposts. The outposts once passed, he and his would journey in one part of the province as easily as in another.

To a reader in our time, it is difficult indeed to understand why all this machinery of passport should be maintained, or why Nolan should have had any anxiety about his welcome. Such a reader must learn, and must remember, therefore, that, under the old colonial system of Spain, the crown held its colonies in the state of separation which we speak of sometimes as Japanese or Paraguayan, though it be now abandoned in both Japan and Paraguay. On the theory that it was well to maintain colonies for the benefit of what was called the metropolis, that is, the European state, the people of the Spanish colonies were sternly forbidden to manufacture any article which could be supplied from home. With the same view, all trade between them and other nations than the metropolis was absolutely forbidden; and, to prevent trade, all communication was forbidden excepting at certain specified ports of entry, and with certain formal passes. At the time with which we have to do, the people of Mexico, and therefore the few scattered inhabitants of this region which we now call Texas, a part of Mexico, were not permitted to cultivate flax, hemp, saffron, the olive, the vine, nor the mulberry; and any communication between them and the French colony of Louisiana, to the east of them, had been strictly forbidden. What the line between Mexico and Louisiana was, no man could certainly say; but it was certain Natchitoches in Louisiana had been a French outpost, while Nacogdoches in Texas, and San Antonio, were Mexican outposts. The territory between the Rio Grande and the Red River had always been claimed, with more or less tenacity, by both crowns.

That there should be animosity between Mexico and Louisiana while one was French and one was Spanish, was natural enough, even if the crowns of France and Spain were united in a family alliance. It is not so easy to see why this animosity did not vanish when Louisiana became a Spanish province, as it was in this year 1800, in which we are tracing along our party of travellers. And it is certainly true that a guarded trade was springing up between Orleans and Natchitoches on the one hand, and the Mexican province on the other; but it is as sure that this trade was watched with the utmost suspicion.

For it involved the danger, as the Mexican authorities saw, of a violation of their fundamental principle of isolation. They doubtless feared that the silver from their northern mines might be a tempting bait to the wild Anglo-Americans of the Mississippi, of whose prowess they heard tales which would quite confirm the boast that their adventurers were half horse and half alligator. Trade with the civilized Frenchmen, who had a few weak posts on the Mississippi, might be tolerable, now that their colonists were under the flag of Spain ; but who and what were these sons of Anak, on the other side of the Mississippi River, who carried a starry flag of their own ?

It must be remembered also, that, from the moment that the independence of the United States was secure, the new settlers of the West had determined that they would have a free navigation to the sea, Spain or no Spain. They had made many different plans for this, none of them very secret. There were those who hoped that Louisiana might become French again, and were willing to annex Kentucky to Louisiana as a French province. There were agents down from the Canadian Government, intimating that King George could get command of a route through to the sea, and would not the people of Kentucky and Tennessee like to join him ? There were simple people who did not care what stood in the way, but were ready to march in their might, and sweep out of the valley anybody who hindered the Kentucky tobacco from finding its way to the markets of Europe. None of these plans regarded the King of Spain, or his hold of the mouth of the Mississippi River, with any reverence or favor.

Philip Nolan, however, had made his earlier expeditions into Texas with the full assent and approval of the Spanish governors of Louisiana. When he came back, as has been said, he gave the governor some handsome horses from the wild drove which he had collected ; he received the governor's thanks, and had no difficulty in getting leave to go again. And if Philip Nolan's name had been Sancho Panza or Iago del Toboso, and if his birthplace had been in Andalusia or Leon, he might perhaps have gone back and forth, with horses or without them, for fifty years ; and this little history would then certainly never have been written.

But his name was not Sancho Panza ; it was Philip Nolan :
and his companions were not Mexican cattle-drivers, nor
even young hidalgos hanging about town in Orleans. There
were a few young Kentuckians like Harrod and himself ;
there were Americans from a dozen different States ; and
there were but six Spaniards in his whole party.

He seems to have regarded it as a matter of indifference
where this party made its rendezvous. As he had the permission of the Spanish governor to trade, it certainly should
have made no difference. But, in fact, his men made their
rendezvous and were recruited at Natchez, within the United
States territory,—a town of which the Spaniards had but
lately given up the possession to the American authorities,
and that only after much angry talk, and in very bad blood.
That a party of twenty-one young adventurers, under the
lead of an American as popular and distinguished as Philip
Nolan, should cross west into Mexico from Natchez,—this
was, it may be supposed, what excited the jealousy of the
military officers in command in Northern Mexico. The local
jealousy between them and the officials of their own king in
Orleans came in also to help the prejudice with which the
young American was regarded.

Nolan rode away with one of the men in buckskin who
had joined with Harrod, throwing a kiss to Inez with that
mixture of mock gallantry and real feeling which might have
been traced in all their intercourse with each other. "*Au
revoir,*" cried she to him ; and he answered, "*Au revoir,*"
and was gone.

"We shall miss him sadly," said Eunice, after a moment's
silence ; "and I cannot bear to have him speak with anxiety
of his expedition. He has staked too much in it to be disappointed."

The travellers followed on their whole route what was even
then known as the Old San Antonio Road,—a road which
followed the trail made by the first adventurers as early as
1715. It was not and is not, by any means, as straight as

the track of a bee or a carrier-pigeon; and it was after they had had the experience of four nights under canvas that they approached the Spanish post of Nacogdoches.

The conversation had again fallen on the probable danger or safety of Nolan's party.

William Harrod said what was quite true,— that Nolan would never be anxious for a moment about his own risks; but he was too loyal to these young men who had enlisted with him, to lead them into danger of which he had not given warning.

"For himself he has no fear," said Inez.

"Nor ever had," was Harrod's reply. "Why, Miss Inez, I was with him once when a party of Apaches ought to have frightened us out of our wits, if we had had any. I dare not tell you how many there were, but the boys said there were five hundred; and, if they had said five thousand, I would not have contradicted them; and we poor white-skins, we were but fourteen all told. And there was Master Nolan as cool as a winter morning. He was here, he was there. I can see him now, asking one of our faint-hearted fellows for a plug of tobacco, just that he might say something pleasant to the poor frightened dog, and cheer him up. He was in his element till it was all over."

"And how was it over?" said Inez. "Did you have to fight them?"

"Yes, and no. We did not get off without firing a good many shots before that day was over; and if, whenever we come to dance with each other, Miss Inez, you ever find that my bridle arm here is the least bit stiff, why, it is because of a flint-headed arrow one of those rascals put through it that day. But Master Phil outgeneralled them in the end."

"How?"

"Oh! it was a simple enough piece of border strategy. He brought us down to a shallow place in the river, not commanded, you know, by any bluffs or high land; and here, with great difficulty, we crossed, and got our wild horses across, and all our packs, and went into camp, with pickets out, and so on. And then at midnight he waked every man of us from sleep, took us all back under a sky as dark as Egypt, marched us full five miles back on the trail where they had been hunting us ; and, while my red brethren were watching and waiting to cut our throats at daybreak, — having crossed the river to lie in wait for us as soon as we started, — why, we were 'over the hills and far away.'

"I don't think the captain likes the Apaches," he said grimly, as he finished his little story.

"But he can be very kind with the Indians. How pleasant it was to see him talking with those — Lipans, did you call them ? "

"Oh, yes ! and they know him and they fear him, and so far as it is in savage nature they love him. Far and wide you will hear them tell these stories of the Captain of the Long-knives — that is what they call him ; for they have seen him twenty times oftener than they have seen any other officer, Spanish, French, or American. Twenty times ? They have seen him a hundred times as often."

"For he has done good service to the Spanish crown," said Eunice, joining again in the conversation. "Though these Spanish gentlemen choose to be suspicious, the captain has been their loyal friend. The Baron Carondelet trusted him implicitly, and Gov. Gayoso either feared him or loved him. This is certain, — that the captain has done for them all that he ever said he would do, and much more."

"You say 'Spanish and American,'" said Inez, laughing. "And, now that he is the confidential agent of Gen. Bonaparte, you must say ' French ' as well."

"You remind me," said William Harrod, "to ask what I am to say if our Spanish friends at the fort yonder should wish to *parlez-vous* a little. The captain would give them as good as they sent, or better. But poor I — when I have said 'Bon jour ! ' 'Comment vous portez-vous ? ' and ' Je n'entends pas,' — I have come to the end of my vocabulary. What in the world shall I do ? "

"You must have a toothache," said Inez, laughing as usual.

"Oh, no!" said Eunice. "The confidential agent is a diplomatist; and this for a diplomatist is a very large stock in trade. Let me try.

"I will be Capt. Alfonso Almonte, Acting Major Commandant of His Most Catholic Majesty's Presidio and Fort of Our Lady of the Bleeding Heart on the Green River of the West. One of my pickets brings in, in honorable captivity, the Señora Eunice Perry of Orleans, with the Señorita Inez Perry of the same city, and a mixed company of black, white, and gray, including three men in buckskin, and M. Philippe, the confidential officer of First Consul Bonaparte, major-general commanding.

"Well, all the others prove to be just what they should be, — amiable, charming travellers, and only too loyal in their enthusiasm for His Most Catholic Majesty King Charles the Fourth. After I have sent them all to feast from silver and gold; then I turn to you, M. Philippe, and I say, —

"'When did you leave Paris, monsieur?'"

Harrod entered into the joke, and replied bravely, —

"I say, 'Bon jour!'"

"Do you? Well, then, I say, 'Good-day. I hope I see you very well; and may heaven preserve your life for many years!'

"What do you say now?"

"If you would say that in nice homespun English," said Harrod, "I would say, 'The same to you. Long life and many years to you. Suppose we have something to drink.'"

"No; you must not say that to a major commandant: it is not etiquette. Besides, he does not speak in English: he speaks in French. What do you say?"

"I think the best thing I could say would be, 'Je n'entends pas.' See. I would put up my hand, so, as if I did not quite catch his Excellency's meaning; and then, very cautiously, and a little as if I would deprecate his anger, I would say, 'Je n'entends pas.'"

"But this is mere cowardice. You only postpone the irrevocable moment. I should speak a great deal louder. I should scream and say, ' Bon jour! Dieu te benisse ! Quel heureux hasard vous a conduit dans ce pays?' I should say this with the last scream of my lungs. And you?"

"Why, I think I would then say, ' Comment vous portez-vous, monsieur?' Perhaps it would be better to say that at the beginning."

"Well, we shall soon find out," said Eunice; "for here is the picket, and there is the challenge."

Sure enough: as they approached the adobe buildings of the fort, a trooper rode out, sufficiently well equipped to show that he was in the royal service, and asked, " Who goes there ? "

Ransom was ready for him, and had learned this time that civility was the best policy. The corporal of the Spanish escort rode forward, and exchanged a word or two with the sentry of the garrison, who threw up his lance in salute, and they all filed by. A Mexican woman at work making cakes looked up, and smiled a pretty welcome. She was "grinding in a mill." That means that she had two stones, one somewhat concave, and the other, so to speak, a gigantic pestle, which filled or fitted into the cavity. Into the cavity she dipped in corn, which had been already hulled by the use of lye; and with the stone she ground it into an impalpable paste. Had the ladies staid long enough to watch this new form of household duties, they would have seen her form with her hands and bake the *tortilla*, with which they were destined to be better acquainted. As it was, they paused but a moment, as the *cortége* filed by. But they had seen enough to know that they were indeed in a foreign country, and that now they were to begin to see the customs and hear the language of the subjects of their unknown king.

Orleans, after all, was a pure French city; and till now none of this party, excepting Harrod, had any real experience of Mexican life. Nacogdoches was not even a town, though the rudiments of a civil settlement were beginning to appeal around the garrison. The party were halted until their different passes could be examined ; but the news of the arrival of such a *cortége* had, of course, run like wild-fire through the post. In a very few minutes Don Sebastian Rodriguez, the commandant, had come forward in person, bareheaded, to tender his respects to the ladies, and to beg them to leave the saddle. He introduced Col. Tréviño, the officer of the day, who said his wife begged them to honor her by accepting her poor hospitality, and trusted that they would feel at home in her quarters.

The uniform of the " officer of the day " was quite different from the uniform of any Spanish officers whom Inez had ever seen before ; for Nacogdoches, like the rest of Mexico, was under the rule of the Council for the Indies, while Orleans was governed directly by the Crown. This gentleman had such a coat and waistcoat as the ladies had seen in pictures of a generation before. He had on boots which resembled a little an Indian's leggings gartered up, so soft and pliable was the leather. His coat and vest were blue and red, so that the costume did not lack for brilliancy ; but the whole aspect, to the man, was of efficiency. His costume certainly met the old definition of a gentleman's dress, for there was no question but he could " mount and ride for his life."

He sent a negro back to call his wife, and stepped forward eagerly to lift Inez from her saddle, while Don Sebastian rendered the same service to Eunice.

The lady sent for came forward shyly, but with great courtesy, to meet the ladies, and was evidently immensely relieved when Eunice with cordiality addressed her in Spanish. For the word had been through the station, that a party of Americans had arrived ; and there was some terror, mixed with much curiosity, as one and another of the natives met the strangers. When Eunice spoke to the Donna Maria Tréviño in Spanish rather better than her own, the shadow of this terror passed from her face, and, indeed, Col. Tréviño's face took on a different expression.

In far less time than people who call in carriages and keep lists of visitors can conceive, the three women were perfectly at home with one another. In less than five minutes appeared a little collation, consisting of chocolate and wine and fruit, and, as the Senora Tréviño with some pride pointed out, a cup of tea. Neither Eunice nor Inez implied, by look or tone, that this luxury was not an extreme rarity to them. To have said that tea had been served by Ransom morning and night at every resting-place, and at every bivouac, since they left Orleans, would have done no good, and certainly would not have been kind.

Meanwhile, in the outer room, which served the purpose of an office for Col. Tréviño, this functionary and Harrod were passing through an examination none the less severe that it was couched with all the forms of courtesy. But with the colonel, as with his lady, the Castilian language worked a spell to which even the wax and red tape of the Governor Casa Calvo were not equal. Nor was any curiosity expressed because Mons. Philippe did not speak in French. And when, after this interview, the colonel and Harrod joined the ladies, as they did, Ransom having respectfully withdrawn under the pretext of seeing personally to the horses of the party, Inez was greatly amused to see the diplomatic agent, Mons. Philippe, and the colonel commanding, Don Francesco Tréviño, talking Spanish together with the ease and regard of old companions in arms.

Harrod said afterward that a common danger made even rabbits and wolves to be friends. "And my friend the colonel was so much afraid of this redoubtable filibuster 'Nolano,' with his hundreds of giant 'Kentuckians,' that when he found a meek and humble Frenchman like me, with never a smack of English on my tongue, he was eager to kiss and be friends."

The conversation, indeed, had not been very unlike that which they had but just now rehearsed in jest. Ransom, with perfect civility this time, had explained that these were

Spanish ladies with their servants, travelling to San Antonio, on a visit to their relations. The name of Barelo, his brother officer, was enough to command the respect of Col. Treviño, who was only too voluble in expressing the hope that his pickets and sentries had been civil.

"In truth," he said, "we have been cautious, perhaps too cautious. But no, a servant of the king is never too cautious; a soldier is never too cautious. But we have received now one, two, three alarms, that the Americans are to attack us. We do not know if there is peace, we do not know if there is war; but we do not love republics, we soldiers of the king. And if my men had taken you for the party of Nolano, — well, well — it is well — that there were ladies was itself your protection. The filibusters do not bring with them ladies."[1]

Harrod was troubled to find that Nolan's reputation on the frontier was so bad, and felt at once that his chief had not rated at the full the perils of his position, when he ascribed them merely to a difference between Orleans Spaniards and Spaniards of Texas. Of course the young man let no sign escape him which should show that he was interested in Nolan or his filibusters. He was only hoping that Blackburn and the other men outside might be as prudent. In a moment more the colonel said, with some embarrassment, —

"I beg your pardon that I addressed you in the Castilian. I see from Capt. Morales's pass that you are a French gentleman. We forget that our friends in Orleans yonder do not all use our language."

Harrod laughed good-naturedly, and, speaking in the Castilian as before, said, —

"It is indeed a pleasure to me to speak in the Spanish when I am permitted. As the language is more convenient to the ladies, let us retain it, if you please."

---

1 This word "filibusters," originally the English word "freebooters," and as such familiarly used on the coast of Mexico and the Spanish main, had degenerated on Spanish tongues into the word "filibustier." It was familiarly used for an invader who came for plunder, whether he crossed the frontier by land or by sea. It has passed back into our language without regaining its original spelling and pronunciation.

The colonel had been about to say that he would call a lieutenant upon his staff, who spoke the French more freely than he did; but the readiness of the French gentleman saved him from this necessity; and, with relief only next to that which he had shown when he found he was not talking to the dreaded Nolan, he entered into free conversation in his own tongue. In this language Harrod had for many years been quite at home.

The colonel finished his examination of the elaborate pass furnished by Casa Calvo, intimated that he would prepare a more formal document than that given in the saddle by Capt. Morales, and then, having made himself sure that the little collation was prepared, proposed that they should join the ladies.

The ladies felt, as Harrod had done, that a single word even of English might prejudice the cordiality of their reception. Even old Ransom had made this out, by that divine instinct or tact which was an essential part of his make-up; and when he came for orders, so called, from the ladies, even if he whispered to them and they to him, it was always in the Spanish language. Indeed, Inez said afterward, that, when he chose to swear at the muleteers, it was in oaths of the purest Castilian.

As he left the room for the first time, Harrod called him back, and whispered to him also. This was to bid him tell Blackburn, and the others of his immediate command, that, as they loved Capt. Nolan, they were not to speak in English, either to Harrod or to one another, while they were in Nacogdoches. They were to remember that they were all French hunters, and, if they did not speak French, they must speak Choctaw, — an alternative which all three accepted.

"Let me present to you, my dear wife, Mons. Philippe, the gentleman who accompanies these ladies, — a French gentleman, my dear."

Harrod bowed with all the elegance of Paris and Kentucky united.

"I have been explaining, ladies, to your friends, the causes of these preparations of war, — the oversight of passports, and the challenge of travellers, so unusual, and so foreign to hospitality in the time of peace ; if, indeed, this be peace. May God bless us!   Only he knows, and the blessed Virgin."

"Is it, then, a time of war ?" asked Eunice, — "and with whom ?"

"The good God knows, señora : if only I were equally fortunate !   Whether our gracious master, the good King Charles IV., is not at this moment in war with this great Gen. Bonaparte," — and he bowed, with a droll and sad effort at civility, toward "Mons. Philippe," as if that gentleman were himself the young Corsican adventurer, " — or whether these wild republicans of the American States have not made war upon us, the good God — may he bless us all ! — and the holy Mother know ; but I do not."

"Surely I can relieve your anxiety, colonel," said Eunice, in her most confiding manner.   "We are not yet a fortnight from Orleans, and we had then news only nine weeks from Europe.   So far from war, the First Consul was cementing peace with our august king.   I shall have pleasure in showing you a French gazette which makes us certain of that happy intelligence.   Then, from our neighbors of the American States there were no news but such as were most peaceful."

"But your ladyship does not understand," said Col. Tréviño, hoping that she might not see how much he was relieved by the intelligence, — "your ladyship does not, can not, understand the anxieties of a command like ours.   It is not the published war, it is not the campaigns which can be told in gazettes, and proclaimed by heralds, which we soldiers dread." Again with an approving glance at Mons. Philippe, as if he were Bonaparte in person.   "It is the secret plots, the war in disguise.   This Nolano will not send word in advance that he is coming."

Inez started, in spite of herself, as she heard the name ;

and then she could have punished herself by whatever torture for her lack of self-control. She need not have been distressed. The Col. Tréviño did not suspect a girl of seventeen of caring any more for what he said, than the cat who was purring in the Donna Tréviño's arms.

"This Nolano will not send word in advance that he is coming. He will swoop down on us with his giants, as a troop of buffalo swoops down upon a drinking-pond in yonder prairie. And he must return, — yes, may the Holy Lady grant it! God be blessed ! — he must return as a flock of antelopes return when they have caught a glimpse of the hunters."

The colonel was well pleased with this bit of rhetoric. Eunice, meanwhile, had not changed glance nor color.

"Who is this Nolano of whom you speak? Is he an officer of Gen. Bonaparte ? "

"Grace of God ! No, madame ! He is one of these Americans of the north, who propose to march from their cold, wintry recesses to capture the city of Mexico ; to take the silver-mines of our king, and divide them for their spoil. Our advices, madam, are not so distinct as I could wish ; but we know enough to be sure that this man has recruited an army in the east, and, if the way opens, will attack us."

"Impossible," said Eunice bravely, " that he should have recruited an army, and the Marquis of Casa Calvo know nothing of it ! Impossible that the marquis should permit me and this lady to travel in a country so soon to be the scene of war ! "

" A thousand pardons, señora," persisted the other. " We speak under the rose here. Let it be confessed that the Marquis of Casa Calvo is not so young as he was forty years ago, nor so sharp-sighted. Our sovereign places him, perhaps, at Orleans ; let us say — yes, may the Holy Mother preserve us ! — because that is not the place of action and · of arms. For us, — why, we have seen Philippo Nolano, and that within two years."

Poor Inez ! She did not dare to glance at Harrod ; but she longed to strike an attitude rivalling the colonel's, and to say, —

"And we have seen Philippo Nolano, and that within two days."

But the position, though it had its ludicrous side, was of course sufficiently critical to keep them all seriously watchful of word and glance alike.

"Indeed !" said Eunice seriously, "how was this? and what manner of man is he? What do you say his name is ?"

"His name is Nolano, my lady ; his baptismal name, if these heretics have any baptism, is Philippo : may the Saint Philippo pardon me, and preserve us ! Do we know him ? Why, he made his home in this very presidio of Nacogdoches, and that not two years ago. My lady, he has sat in that chair, he has drunk from this cup. To think that such treason should lurk in these walls, and study out in advance our defences ! "

At this point, the little lady of the group took courage.

"My dear husband," said the Señora Tréviño, "let us admit that we were very glad to see him. — Indeed, ladies, he is a most agreeable person, though he be an American of the north, and a filibuster. He was here for some time ; and he knew the language of the 'Americans so well, that in all business he served my husband and the other officers here as an interpreter. There were some Americans arrested for illicit trade, — silver, you know," and she dropped her voice, — "two men with a hard name ; but I learned it, so often did I hear it. There was a process about these men : Eastridge was their name. Oh ! it lasted for months ; and often was your namesake Don Philippo in the chair you sat in, Mons. Philippo ; he was discussing their business with my husband " —

"And playing chess with my wife," said the colonel, interrupting her. "Ah, he was a very cunning soldier, was your

Don! There is no secret of our defences but is known to him; and now he comes with an army."

"Surely," said Eunice as bravely as before, "you do not speak of the Capt. Nolan who was so near a friend of the Baron Carondelet? Why, he was presented to me by the Baron himself at a ball."

Col. Tréviño confessed that Nolan brought him letters at one time from the Baron.

"And my brother has dined with him at Gen. Gayoso's palace. Oh! it is impossible that this person can lead an American army."

"Ladies," said the colonel, clasping his hands, "a soldier must believe nothing, and he must believe every thing also. May all the saints preserve us!"

And Eunice felt that she had pressed the defence of her friend as far as was safe, or to his advantage.

CHAPTER VIII.

THE DRESSED DAY.

> "A visit should be of three days length.
> 1. The Rest Day.   2. The Dressed Day.
> 3. The Pressed Day." — MISS FERRIER.

THE respect due to a reception so courteous as that with
which the Colonels Tréviño and Rodriguez welcomed the
party, compelled a stay in Nacogdoches over one full day.
In truth, Philip Nolan had advised a stay so long, and had
told the ladies that he had a thousand ways of informing
himself at what moment they should leave the fort to proceed westward. The morning of the day after the arrival of
the ladies was spent in a prolonged breakfast, in which the
señora did her best to show her guests that the resources of
a military post were not contemptible. And indeed she
succeeded. When she had made it certain that they were
not too much fatigued by their five days' ride from the river,
she took order to assemble at supper all the officers of the
command and their wives ; and the preparations for this little
fête filled the colonel's quarters with noisy bustle, quite
unusual, through the morning.

In the midst of this domestic turmoil, — not so different,
after all, from what Eunice and Inez had seen on the plantation, when Silas Perry had brought up an unexpected company of guests, — a new turmoil broke out in the square, and
called most of the occupants of the house out upon the
arcade which fronted it. The Lady Tréviño was not too

dignified to join the groups of curious inquirers; and she did not return at once to her guests.

Ransom did come in, under the pretence of asking if they needed any thing, but really because there was news to tell. He satisfied himself that in this dark inner room there were no eavesdroppers, and that those heavy stone walls had no ears; and then he indulged himself, though in a low tone, in the forbidden luxury of the vernacular.

"Pray what is it, Ransom?" asked Inez, speaking always in Spanish.

"All nonsense," said the old man, —"all nonsense: told 'em so myself, but they would not hear to me. Spanishers and niggers all on 'em, nothin' but Greasers: don't know nothin', told 'em so — all nonsense."

Then after a pause: —

"White gal 'z old as you be, Een:" this was his short-hand way of saying "Miss Inez," when he was off guard.

"White gal dressed jest like them Injen women ye see down on the levy. They catched her up here among the Injens, and brought her away. She can't speak nothin' but Injen, and they don't know what she says. They brought her down from up there among the Injens where they catched her. She's dressed jest like them Injen women ye see on the levy; but she's a white gal — old as you be, Een."

Inez knew by long experience that when one of Ransom's speeches had thus balanced itself by repetition backward to the beginning, — as a musical air returns to the keynote, — she might put in a question without disturbing him.

"Who found her, Ransom? Who brought her in?"

"Squad o' them soldiers; call 'em soldiers, ain't soldiers, none on 'em: ain't one on 'em can stand the Choctaw Injens two minutes. Was ten on 'em goin' along, and had a priest with 'em, — 'n they met a lot o' Injens half-starved, they said. Men was clean lost, — hadn't got no arrows, and couldn't git no game. Didn't b'long here: got down here'n got lost; didn't know nothin'. Injens had this white gal, —

white as you be, Een, — 'n the priest said he wouldn't gin
'em nothin' ef they wouldn't let him have the white gal.
They didn't want to, but he made 'em, he did; said they
should not have nothin' ef they wouldn't let him have the
white gal. White as you be she is, Miss Eunice."

Inez was all excited by this time, and begged her aunt to
join the party in the arcade, — which they did.

True enough, just under the gallery, was this tall wild girl,
of singularly clear brunette complexion, but of features
utterly distinct from those of an Indian squaw. Eunice and
Inez, indeed, both felt that the girl was not of Spanish, but
of Anglo-Saxon or Scotch-Irish blood, though, in the unpop-.
ularity of their own lineage in Nacogdoches, neither of them
thought it best to say so. Three or four of the Mexican
women of the post were around the girl, some of them
examining her savage ornaments, some of them plying her
with tortillas and fruit, and even milk, under the impression
that she must be hungry. The girl herself looked round,
not without curiosity, and in a dozen pretty ways showed
that she was not of the same phlegmatic habit as her recent
possessors.

In a few moments the Señora Tréviño returned, having
given some orders for the poor girl's comfort, the results of
which immediately appeared.

But when she called the girl to her most kindly, and when
she came under the arcade as she was beckoned, the ladies
could make no progress in communicating with her. She
seemed to have no knowledge of Spanish, nor yet of French.
If she had been taken prisoner from either a Spanish or
French settlement, it was when she was so young that she
had forgotten their language.

Inez tried her with "madre" and "padre;" the Señora
Trévino pointed reverently to a crucifix, and a Madonna with
folded hands. But the girl showed no other curiosity than
for the other articles of taste or luxury — if such simple
adornments can be called such.

"Still, Eunice," cried Inez, "I am sure she understood 'mamma.' Say 'ma' to her alone."

Meanwhile Mme. Tréviño called one and another woman and servant who had some smattering of Indian dialects; but the girl would smile good-naturedly, and could make nothing of what they said. But this suggested to Eunice that she might beckon to Blackburn the hunter, who was lounging in the group in front; and in a whisper she bade him address the girl in the Choctaw dialect.

This language was wholly distinct from any of the dialects of the west of the Mississippi — as these, indeed, changed completely, even between tribes whose hunting-grounds were almost the same.

Blackburn did as he was bidden, but without the least success; but in a moment he fell back on the gift of silence, and began in the wonderful pantomime, which the ladies had already seen so successful between Nolan and the Lipan chief.

The girl smiled most intelligently, nodded assent, and in the most vivid, rapid, and active gesture, entered on a long narration, if it may be called so, of her life with the Indians. Blackburn sometimes had to bid her be more slow, and repeat herself. But it was clear enough that they were both on what he would have called the right trail, and he was coming at a full history of her adventures.

But a new difficulty arose when Blackburn was to interpret what he had learned. He made a clumsy effort in a few words of bread-and-butter Spanish, such as all Western men picked up in the groceries and taverns at Natchez. But this language was very incompetent for what he had to tell. Still the good fellow knew that he must not speak English in the presence of these Greasers; and he bravely struggled on in a Spanish which was as unintelligible as his Choctaw.

In the midst of this confusion Ransom came to the front, and addressed him boldly: —

"Est-ce-que vous ne parlez Français bien, mon camarade?

Then speak hog English, but I'll tell 'em it's Dutch. Say *parlez-vous* at the beginning, and *oui monsieur* at the end."

Then he turned to the Señora Treviño, and bowed with a smile, and told her that the man was a poor ignorant dog from Flanders, who had been in the woods as a hunter ever since he came abroad as a boy; that he spoke very little French, and that very badly; but that he, Ransom, had seen him so much that he could understand him.

. Then he turned to Blackburn: —

" N'oubliez pas, mon ami, — don't forget a word I tell you. Pepper it well, and don't git us hanged for nothin'. Ensuite — tout ensemble — oui, monsieur."

"Oui, monsieur, vraiment," said Blackburn bravely. "The gal don't remember when she did not live with the redskins. sacrement! parbleu! mon Dieu! But she does not remember her own mother, who died ten years ago. Parlez-vous Français, Saint Denis! Since then she has lived as they all live. Comment, monsieur. She says she wants to go to the East, that her mother bade her go there. Morbleu! sacrement! oui, monsieur. She says the redskins wasn't kind to her, and wasn't hard on her, but didn't give her enough to eat, and made her walk when her feet was sore. Mère de Dieu, sacrement! Saint Denis — bon jour!"

It was clear enough that poor Blackburn's French had been mostly picked up among the voyagers on the river, and, alas! from their profane, rather than their ethical or æsthetic moments. It may be doubted whether to the Señora Treviño the poor smattering would not have betrayed rather than helped the poor fellow, but that her sympathies were so wholly engrossed by the condition of the captive that she cared little by what means her story was interpreted.

In a moment more, Ransom had explained it in voluble Spanish.

"Ask him for her name, Ransom; ask if she knew her mother's name; ask him how old she is," cried Inez eagerly.

"She says the Indians call her the White Hawk, but that

her mother called her Mary, and bade her never forget," said the old man, really wiping his eyes. "She says she is sixteen summers old."

Inez seized the girl's hand, and said "Marie," of which she made nothing; but when the girl said squarely "Mary," "Mary," and then said "Ma" — "Ma" — "Ma," the poor captive's face flushed for the first time; and she seized both Inez's hands, repeated all these syllables after her, and broke into a flood of tears.

"Ma-ry," said Eunice slowly to the Señora Tréviño: "it is the way they pronounce Marie in the eastern provinces."

In a moment more appeared the portly and cheerful Father Andrés, who had by good fortune accompanied the foraging party which had brought in this waif from the forest. To his presence with the soldiers, indeed, it is probable that she owed her redemption.

Ransom's story was substantially correct. This was a little band of Apaches, who had by an accident been cut off from the principal company of their tribe, and by a series of misfortunes had lost their horses and most of their weapons. They were loath to throw themselves on Spanish hospitality, and well they might be. Still, when the troopers had struck their trail and overtaken them, the savages were in great destitution and well-nigh starving. They were out of their own region, were trying to return to it on foot, and were living as they might on such rabbits as they could snare, and such wild fruits as they could find. Father Andrés, with a broader humanity, had agreed to give a broken-down mule and a quarter of venison as a ransom for the girl; and both parties had been well satisfied with the exchange.

For the girl herself, — she was tall, graceful in movement, eminently handsome, with features of perfect regularity, eyes large and black, and with her head fairly burdened with the luxuriant masses of hair, which were gathered up with some savage ornament, but insisted upon curling in a most un-Indian-like way. There was a singular unconsciousness in her demeanor, like that of an animal. Inez said she never knew that you were looking at her. Once and again, in this little first interview, she started to her feet, and stood erect and animated, with an eagerness which the Spanish women around her, or their Indian servants, never showed, and could not understand. Perhaps she never seemed so attractive as in these animated pantomimes in which she answered their questions, or explained the detail of her past history.

Soon after the arrival of Father Andrés, Harrod returned from riding with the officers. He explained to Donna Isabella that he had acquired some knowledge of the Indian pantomime in his hunting expeditions. By striking out one superfluous interpreter from the chain, he gave simplicity and animation to the stranger's narrative.

She remembered perfectly well many things that her mother had told her, though she showed only the slightest knowledge of her mother's language. But, on this point, Harrod and the ladies from Orleans were determined to try her more fully when they were alone. The village, whatever it was, of her birthplace, had been fortified against savages; but a powerful tribe had attacked it, and, after long fighting, the whites had surrendered. But what was surrender to such a horde? So soon as they had laid down their weapons, the Indians had slaughtered every man, and every boy large enough to carry arms. Next they had killed for convenience' sake every child not big enough to travel with them in their rapid retreat. The women they had kept, and if any woman chose to keep her baby the whim was indulged. Such a baby was this " Ma-ry,"—the White Hawk just now rescued. Her mother had clung to her in every trial. Long, long before the White Hawk could remember any thing, she and her mother had been sold to some other tribe, which took them far from other captives of their own race. With this tribe — who were Apaches, of Western Texas — she had lived ever since she could remember. She had always heard of whites. She had always known she was one of them. But she had never seen a white man till yesterday.

"And, now you are with us, you will stay with us," said Donna Isabella eagerly.

The girl did not so much as notice her appeal; for she happened to be looking on one of the thousand marvels around her, so that she did not catch the eagerness of the Spanish lady's eye, and she understood not a syllable of her language. Harrod touched her gently, and repeated the appeal to her in a pantomime which the others could partly follow.

Then the White Hawk smiled, — oh! so prettily, — and replied in a pantomime which they could not follow; but she placed her hand in Donna Isabella's, in Eunice's, and in Inez's, in rapid succession, just pausing long enough before each to give the assurance of loyalty.

"She says that she promised her mother every night, before she slept, that she would go to her own people, — the whites. Whenever she can go to the rising sun to find them, she must go. But she says she is sure you three will be true to her, and that she will be true to you. She says she must find her mother's brothers and sisters, and she says you must be her guides."

Inez's eyes were brimming with tears.

"Can we find them, Mons. Philippe? How can we find them? Where was this massacre, and when?"

The Spanish officers shrugged their shoulders at this, and said that, alas! there was only too much of such cruelty all along the frontier. The story, Harrod said, was like that of the massacre at Fort Loudon, but that was too long ago. The truth was, that for seventy years, from the time when the Indians of Natchez sacrificed the French garrison there, down to that moment, such carnage had been everywhere. Harrod told the ladies afterward that in only seven years, about the time of which the White Hawk spoke, fifteen hundred of the people of Kentucky had been killed or taken prisoners, and as many more on the Ohio River above Kentucky. Which village of a hundred, therefore, was White

Hawk's village, of which mother of a thousand was hers, it would be hard to tell.

But Eunice thought that in that eye and face she saw the distinct sign of that Scotch-Irish race which carries with it, wherever it emigrates, such matchless beauty of color, whether for women or for men. But of this to their Spanish friends she said nothing.

So unusual a ripple in the stagnant life of the garrison threw back the memory of the arrival of the ladies from Orleans quite in the distance. Still, when the evening came, and the Donna Isabella's guests gathered, it proved that the several ladies of the little "society" had not been unmindful of the duties they owed to fashion. Most of them were attired in the latest styles of Mexico and Madrid which were known to them. Others relied boldly on the advices they had received from their correspondents, and wore what they supposed the latest fashion of Europe outside of Spain. All came, eager with curiosity to see what were the latest dates from Orleans and from Paris. With some difficulty, and in the face of many protests from Ransom, Eunice and Inez were able to indulge them. It was necessary to open some packs which had been put up for San Antonio, and San Antonio only.

Ransom said this was impossible. Eunice said it must be done. Ransom said he would not do it. Eunice said that then she should have to do it herself. Ransom then knew that he had played his last card, went and opened the packs in question, brought them to the ladies, and declared that it was the easiest thing in life to do so, and that, in fact, they ought to be opened, because they needed the air. For such was Ransom's way when he was met face to face.

We ought to tell our fair readers how these two ladies were dressed on that October evening. Not so different in the effect at a distance from the costumes of to-day ; but the waists of their frocks were very close under their arms, as if they were the babes of 1876 at the baptismal font. For the rest, the skirts were scant, as Inez's diary tells me, and the trimming was their glory.

Would you like to see Mme. Fantine's account of the dress which Inez wore that evening? It is, " Coiffure à l'hirondelle. Robe à soie bleue à demi traine ; la jupe garnie des paillettes." Now, paillettes were little round steel spangles.

There! Is not that the loyal and frank way for the novelist of the nineteenth century when he has his heroine's costume to describe?

But Mme. Fantine could not have described the White Hawk's dress, — "Ma-ry's ;" and, after all, she was the belle of the evening. The Donna Isabella and Inez, principally Inez, had devoted themselves to her toilet through the afternoon. To dress her as a Christian woman had been Donna Isabella's first idea ; but, to say truth, Donna Isabella's idea of Christianity was not unlike that of the missionaries in Africa, whose first great triumph was the persuading the natives to bury their dead in coffins. If the Donna Isabella could have seen the White Hawk in a mantilla and long silk wrapper, she would have been as well satisfied as Father Andrés if he could place baptismal waters on her forehead. To such costume White Hawk herself objected. Could she have spoken Hebrew, she would have said, with Jesse's son, "I have not proved them." And here our pretty Inez proved her loyal friend. How charming it was to see these lovely girls together! No: White Hawk had come to them in savage costume, and so it was best that she should come to the party. Only these feathers must be crisp and new ; and the presidio was quite competent to furnish crisp, new crane's feathers. This doeskin tunic, — yes, it did have a bad smell, even Inez had to confess that ; but the quartermaster produced a lovely new doeskin, at the sight of which those black eyes of White Hawk's flashed fire ; and what with Inez's needle, and Eunice's, and the Mexican maid of Donna Isabella, and White Hawk's own nimble fingers, every pretty fringe, every feather, with every bead and every shell, from the old wilderness-worn dress, were transferred in an hour to the new robe. As for hair, as Inez said, there was not a major's wife, nor a captain's, at the party, but envied White Hawk her magnificent coiffure.

For slippers — *alias* moccasins — they were fain to go to the storehouse of the presidio again, and select one of the smallest pair they found there made ready for women's wear. They gave these to White Hawk, who laughed merrily. Before the "party" began, they were embroidered with the brightest colors, discovered only White Hawk knew where or how.

Thus apparelled, White Hawk certainly drew all eyes. Inez confessed that she paled her ineffectual fires. Her ivory fan, fresh from Paris, did not win the homage, she said, which White Hawk won by her crane's feathers.

"And what could you expect," said the enthusiastic girl, "when she has those wonderful cheeks, those blazing eyes, and that heavenly smile? Eunice, if you do not take her to Antonio with us, why, Eunice, I shall die!"

The garrison, at its best, furnished twelve ladies — confessed as ladies — when there was any such occasion for festivity as this evening. Of gentlemen, as at all military posts, there was no lack. The frontier garrison towns of Mexico presented at that time a series of curious contrasts. Gentlemen of the best training of Europe, who had perhaps brought with them ladies of the highest culture, — as Gov. Herrara had at this very time,— were stationed for years, in the discharge of the poor details of frontier duty, in the midst of the simplest and most ignorant people in Christendom. In the same garrison would be young Mexican gentlemen in training for the same service, not deficient in the external marks of a gentleman, but without any other culture than training in the details of tactics. Between the wives was a broader contrast, perhaps, than between the husbands. Very few Mexican ladies of the Spanish blood, "Creoles," if we may take the expression of the day, were educated for any conversation with intelligent men, or expected to bear a share in it. But such a lady as Mme. Herrara, with whom the persevering reader of these pages will meet, or the Señora Maria Caberairi, or the Señora Marguerite Valois, accustomed to the usages of Europe, lived as rational beings; that is, they received visits, and discharged the duties of an elegant hospitality. Such a protest against the Oriental seclusion, which perhaps the Moors introduced into Spanish life, whether in Old Spain or in New Spain, met with no favor from the handsome, indolent, and passive ladies who made up the majority of garrison society. And the line was marked with perfect distinctness, on this occasion, between four on the one side and eight on the other, of the ladies who attended at Donna Isabella's ball.

This contrast added greatly to the lively Inez's enjoyment of the evening. She had no lack of good partners, only too eager to take her out to the minuet. The lively girl showed that she, at least, had no objection to talking to young officers, and that she had enough to say to them.

"Do not disgrace your duenna," said Eunice laughing, as Inez left her on one of these campaigns of conquest. And Inez said, —

"Dearest duenna, if I could only use a fan as well as you do!"

Harrod said to Eunice that he should find his occupation gone, now that there was a little army of Dons and hidalgos only too eager to take charge of the ladies of his convoy. Indeed, in brilliancy of costume, the gentlemen of the party quite held their own in comparison with even the French and Spanish toilets of the ladies. The dragoons wore a short blue coat, with red cape and cuffs, with small-clothes of blue velvet always open at the knee. Every gentleman brought with him a tall dress hat, such as the modern reader associates with banditti on the stage. It was etiquette to bring this even into the ballroom, because the ribbon of gay colors with which it was bound was supposed to be a lady's gift and a mark of gallantry. Many of the men were tall and handsome, and you would have said that dancing and cards were the only business of their lives.

Although Inez had spent her whole life in what was called a Spanish colony, in a town which thought much of itself, while Nacogdoches was but a garrison post, she had never seen, till now, any of the peculiar forms of Spanish society. Orleans held its head very high in the social way, but it was as a French city. The governors and their courts could make no head against the proud Gallicism of the people they found there ; and French travellers said with pride that Spaniards were " *Francised*," but Frenchmen were not " *Españoled* " in Orleans.

The minuet was at that moment the property of the world. The fandango and the bolero were dances Inez had never seen before ; nor would she have shed tears if she had been told she should never see them again. The White Hawk, who joined even merrily in the gayeties of the evening, seemed hurt and annoyed at the intimacies of the fandango, and showed that she was glad when it was over. None of the strangers, indeed, could take part in it ; and they observed that a part of the ladies among their hosts would not take part in it. Naturally enough, the talk turned on national dances, in a circle of such varied nationalities. The White Hawk frankly and simply performed an Apache *pas de seul* for the surprise and amusement of her hosts, so soon as she found they would take pleasure from it. And then, after a little conference with Donna Maria and her husband, and a word with Col. Rodriguez the commander of the garrison, one of the band-men was sent out to bring in a party of dancers from the vulgar crowd without, who would show a pure Mexican dance to the visitors.

This was the dance of the Matachines, which dates back even to the court of Montezuma. A boy, gayly dressed, rushed in with his bride: these were Montezuma and Malinche. The girl's rattle took the place of the castanets of the fandango. In an instant more the other dancers, armed also with rattles, followed in two parallel rows, soon breaking into four; and a large man with a hideous mask, — the devil of the scene, — whip in hand, ruled the pageant. Nobody but Montezuma and Malinche escaped his blows.

At times the emperor and his bride sat in chairs which were placed for their thrones, and received from the other dancers the most humble protestations.

Friar Andrés said that the whole was typical of astronomical truths. Perhaps it was. I remember Margaret Fuller once told me, who write these words, what the quadrille called "pantalon" typified. If I only remembered! That is the figure where the gentleman leaves his partner for a while in captivity on the other side.

Meanwhile all the men were not occupied in minuets, in fandangos, in boleros, or in fanning ladies. Parties of officers, not inconsiderable, sat at cards in the card-rooms; and, if one could judge from their cries now and then, the play was exciting and high.

In such amusements the "dressed day" came to a close, and it stole an hour even from the day of departure.

CHAPTER IX.

TALKING AND WALKING.

"Such noise as I can make to be heard farthest I'll venture." — MILTON.

IT was decided in solemn assembly, the next morning, that the White Hawk should join the party of travellers for San Antonio. Donna Isabella had seen too much of garrison life to wish to keep the girl longer than was necessary at a post like Nacogdoches. Indeed, if she ever were to seek her birthplace, it must be from such a point as San Antonio, and not from a garrison town. Eunice and Inez gladly took the care of her; and Col. Tréviño formally prepared a new passport which should describe her and her condition also.

"I have added your name, Mons. Philippe," said the hospitable colonel. "I see you joined the party after the marquis's pass was filled. Ah me! the marquis is growing a little drowsy, after all!" and he laughed with that conceit with which a rival bureau always detects errors in the administration of the establishment "over the way."

And so, after every conceivable delay, innumerable *adios*, and commendations to the Virgin, the little party started again. To the last, Blackburn, Richards, Adams, and King were taken for granted as part of the party. They asked no questions; and the colonel, with all his formalities, never asked them where they joined or where they were to leave.

With no prospect of other detention before arriving at San Antonio, they all pushed out into what was very nearly desert country.

The afternoon was well advanced, when they made the halt — which with an earlier start would have been made earlier — for a rest from the saddle, and to give the beasts a chance for food. The ladies sat on their shawls a little away from the caravan proper ; and Harrod, with some help from Ransom, improvised a screen from the wind by stretching his own blanket above some stakes driven into the ground.

The first care had been to send notes and messages to Capt. Nolan, who was supposed to be not far away. These were intrusted to Blackburn, and to old Cæsar, whom Blackburn had persuaded to join him for a few days. After their departure, the encampment took on an air of tranquil repose.

"We are as happy as Arabs," said Inez.

"As happy as Ma-ry here would be in your father's salon on the plantation," said Harrod. "Ask her if she sees any thing piquant or strange in lunching *al fresco* here."

"Ask her," said Eunice, "what she makes of Ransom's Boston crackers, and whether she would rather have a rabbit *à la mesquit.*"

"Ah, well!" said Harrod, "the rarity of the thing is all very well ; but, when Miss Inez here has lunched twenty days more *al fresco*, she will be glad to find herself in her aunt's inner chamber " —

"As Ma-ry will, after twenty days of the salon life, to find herself on a mustang horse, riding after antelopes," said Inez, this time sadly.

"Miss Inez, I do not believe a word of it."

"A word of what?"

"Of what you are afraid of, — that this girl has become a child of the forest, and is going to love mustangs and antelopes and mesquit-bushes and grilled rabbits, more than she will love books and guitars and the church and a Christian home. Blood is a good deal thicker than water, Miss Inez ; and blood will tell."

"Seventeen years go a good way, Mr. Harrod ; and she must be as old as I am," said Inez, as if she herself were the person of most experience in this world.

"But seventeen centuries go farther," said he; "and I may
say eighteen, lacking two months, I believe. Oh, Miss Inez!
trust a man who has seen white skins, and black skins, and
red skins, and olive skins, and skins so dirty that they had
no color. Trust me who speak to you. If the sins of the
fathers go to the children for the third and fourth generation,"— there was no banter in his tone now; but all this
was in serious earnest, — "shall not the virtues of the mothers, and their loves, and even their fancies and their tastes?
Shall not their faith and hope, shall not their prayer, have a
hold deeper than a little calico or flannel? Does not your
commandment say, 'through all generations for those who
love Him?' and do you not suppose that means something?"

It was the first time Harrod had spoken with quite this
earnestness of feeling. To Eunice it was not unexpected,
however. She had seen, from his first salute at the encampment, that he was every inch a man. To Inez there was all
the satisfaction which comes to every girl of yesterday when
some person of insight sees that she is a woman to-day. The
change from boy to man takes years, and is marked by a
thousand slow graduations. The change from girl to woman
is well-nigh immediate. But the woman just born cannot
scream out, "The world is all changed to me. Why will
you talk to me as if I were playing with my doll?" All the
same is she grateful to him or her who finds out this change;
and so Inez was grateful to William Harrod now.

"You see," said Harrod, "I was born close to the frontier;
and since I can remember I have been on it and of it. Dear
old Daniel Boone — have you ever 'hearn tell' of him, Miss
Perry?— dear old Daniel Boone, many is the time that he
has spent the weeks of a winter storm and clearing at my
father's; and many is the tramp that I have taken with him
and with his sons. I fired his rifle before I was ten years
old. Yes; and I have seen this thing always. Why! when
I was a little boy I have seen our dear Elder Brainerd take
these savage boys, and be good to them, and helpful, and let

them cheat him and lie to him; and since then I have seen them go off like hawks when they smelt carrion. And I have seen — well, I have seen Daniel Boone, who had slept under the sky as they sleep, had starved as they starve, had frozen as they freeze; and he would come to my dear mother's table as perfect and finished a gentleman as there is in Orleans or Paris. Dear Miss Perry, there is such a thing as race, and blood does tell."

"And I hope it tells in something better than choice of places to lunch in," said Inez.

"Yes, indeed," said the young fellow, who was on one of his hobbies now. "You shall see that your pretty Ma-ry will be a lady of the land, if you can once see her in her land. As for these *Greasers*, I do not know that I rate them as of much more help to her than so many Caddoes or Apaches. Oh, dear! how I hate them!" and he laughed heartily.

"Pray do not say so to Inez," said her aunt. "You do not guess yet how hard I find it to make her loyal to her sovereign."

"Most estimable of duennas," cried Inez, "pray do not say that again for a week. Let me mildly represent to your grace, that your unsuspected loyalty to the most gracious of masters, and to the loveliest of queens, has led you to make this protest daily, since her Majesty's sacred birthday — blessed be her gracious life and her sweet memory! — recalled to your loveliness's recollection you duty to your honored sovereign. There, you darling old tease, can I not do it as well as you can? And do not the adjectives and compliments roll out rather more graciously in the language of Squam Bay than even in the glorious Castilian itself? Oh, dear! I wish I could set Ransom to translate one of the Bishop's prelections on royalty into genuine Yankee."

"Do it yourself," said Harrod, who was rapidly gaining all Nolan's enthusiasm for the old man.

And Inez attempted a rapid imitation.

"There," said she, "it is the day of our Lady of the Sacred Torch ; and, by a miraculous coincidence, it happens also to be the day of the Santissima Luisa, the patron saint of my beloved, most honored, and never-to-be-forgotten queen and sovereign lady. · And, as the bishop rides to the cathedral, by a great misfortune the wheels of the carriage of the most right reverend and best-beloved father come off in the *fosse* or ditch just in front of the palace of the governor of my most gracious sovereign Charles the Fourth, and the holy father is thrown forward into the mud."

" Inez, you shall not run on so."

" Dear duenna, hold your peace : I shall and I will.   And all shall be said decently and in order.

" Word is carried of the misfortune to the cathedral, where Ransom is waiting in the sacristy, with a note from Miss Eunice Perry, heretic though she be, and fated to be burned when her time comes, inviting the most reverend and beloved father to dinner.   Ransom observes the dangers to the elect, should the prolocution in honor of my gracious and never-to-be-forgotten queen be omitted.   By a happy instinct he slips off his white jacket, and with grace and ease slips on the tunic, which seems to him most to resemble the Calvinistic gown of his childhood ; and then, preceded by acolytes, and followed by thurifers, he mounts to the pulpit, just as the faithful are turning away disappointed, and says, —

" ' It's all nonsense, 'n I told the biship so, last time I see him.   I says, says I, them hubs to the wheel of your coach ain't fit for nothin', they ain't ; and ef you will ride in it you'll break down some day, an' good enough for you.   ' N now he has broke down, jest as I told him he would, 'n he can't preach the queen's sermon.   I tell you the queen ain't much, but she's a sight better than you deserve, any on you.   Ye ain't fit to have a queen, none on ye ; ye don't know nothin', 'n ye don't know what a real good queen is.   Ye'd git more'n ye've got any rights to, ef ye had old George the Third, the beggar ; 'n he's the wust king that ever wos, or ever will be.

The queen's birthday is to-day, so they sez ; but they's all liars, and don't know nothin', as how should they, secin' they's all Catholics and niggers together, and ain't learned nothin' ?   I tell the biship they ain't no good preachin' to such a crew as you be ; but, becos he can't come himself, I've come to tell ye all ye may go home.' "

" Inez, you shall not run on so," said Eunice, really provoked that the girl, who had so much deep feeling in her, should sweep into such arrant nonsense.

" Dearest Aunt Eunice, you are afraid that I shall lose my reputation in the eyes of dear White Hawk and of Mr. Harrod.   Would you perhaps be so kind as to preach the queen's sermon yourself ? "

"That is a way she has, Mr. Harrod ; and I recommend it to you, if you are ever so fortunate as to have the education of a young lady of seventeen intrusted to you."

" This dear Aunt Eunice of mine, who is the loveliest and kindest duenna that ever was in this world, if I do say so, she will rebuke me for my sins, because I do not sin to please her ; and then she will set the example of the way the thing ought to be done.

" For instance : suppose I am tempted by the spirit of evil to imitate the Donna Dulcinea del Tobago, I call her, because her husband, the chief justice, smokes all day long ; suppose I am tempted to imitate her, — I sit down at my piano-forte, and I just begin, —

'Oh, happy souls ! by death at length set free,'

when my dear aunt says, 'You shall not do so, Inez: it is very wrong.'   And then I begin again, and she says, 'Inez, it is very improper.'   And then, if I begin a third time, she says, 'Inez, if you will do any thing so absurd, pray do it correctly.   Let me sit there.   I will show you how she sings it ;' and then she makes the Donna Dulcinea ten times as absurd as I could, because she has heard her ten times as often. — You are the dearest old aunt that ever was, and I am the worst tease that ever was born."

And she flung herself on the neck of her aunt, and kissed her again and again.

Meanwhile the White Hawk sat amused beyond expression, and mystified quite as much by what was to her only a pantomime, in which she could not make out one term in ten.

As Inez ceased her eulogy, she looked around upon the girl, and caught the roguish twinkle of her eye, and could not but turn to her, and kiss her as eagerly as she had kissed her aunt, though from a sentiment wholly different.

For both these ladies watched the White Hawk with the feeling with which you would watch an infant, mingled with that with which you regard a woman. "What does she think? How does this all seem? What would she say if she could speak to us?"

The range of her pantomime, and the spirit and truth of Harrod's interpretation of it, were enough to express things, and to make them feel, just up to a certain point, that here was a woman closely tied to them, sympathizing with them, as they, indeed, with her. But where things stopped, and ideas began, — just where they wanted language most, — language stopped for them, and White Hawk seemed like a child of whose resources even they knew nothing. It was a comfort to Inez to overwhelm her with this storm of kisses, and a comfort to the other also.

"She must learn to speak to us. And, while we are on the trail here, she shall learn her own language. We will not make her talk about your 'loftiness,' and your 'serenity,' Miss Eunice."

"Dear, dear Ma-ry," said the girl, turning to her again, and speaking very slowly, as if that would help, "do say something to me. Talk baby-talk, dear Ma-ry."

And then she tried her with "ma-ma;" and, as before, it was very certain that "Ma-ry" knew what these syllables meant. And with a wild eagerness she would listen to what Inez said to her, and then would try to form words like Inez's words. Perhaps she had some lingering memory of what her mother had taught her; but the words would not come.

"Then, if I cannot teach you, you shall teach me, dear Ma-ry." And so the two girls began, with Harrod's aid, to work out the chief central signs of the language of panto-mime; and, when Inez found her chance, she would make "Ma-ry" repeat in English this word or that, which the girl caught quickly. The readiness of her organs for this speech was enough to show that she had had some training in it when she was yet very young.

In this double schooling the girls passed the afternoon, for many miles after they were all in the saddle again. Indeed, it became occupation and amusement for all the leaders of the party for day after day in their not very event-ful journey. Their fortune did not differ from that of most travellers in such an expedition. The spirit and freshness of an open-air life lifted them well over the discomforts of a beginning; and when the bivouac, the trail, and the forest began to be an old story, the experience gained in a thou-sand details made compensation for the lack of novelty and consequent excitement. For some days from Nacogdoches, the trail led them through woods, only occasionally broken by little prairies. A little Spanish post at the Trinity River, and once or twice the humble beginnings of some settler on the trail, vary the yellow pages of poor little Inez's diary. But the party were beginning to grow reckless, in comparison with their caution at the outset, — reckless merely because they had been so favored in the weather and in the monoto-nous safety of their march, — when they were recalled, only too suddenly, to the sense of the danger which always hangs over such travellers in the wilderness.

Harrod had sent on his men in advance, as had come to be the custom, with directions to select the position for the camp, and have the ladies' tents ready before the caravan proper arrived. Adams and Richards found that a bayou known as the Little Brassos was so swollen that the passage would be perhaps circuitous and certainly difficult, and, with fit discretion, fixed their camp on high land above the water's edge, although by this location the party made a march shorter by an hour than was usual. Nobody complained, however, of the early release from the saddle, the two young people least of all. A few minutes were enough for them to refit themselves; and there was then half an hour left before the late dinner or early supper — now called by one name, and now by another — which always closed the day.

Harrod's directions were absolute, and Ransom's as well, that there should be no straggling, not the least, from the camp; and the girls were least inclined of any to disregard them. Certainly poor little Inez had no thought of disobedience, when she pointed out to Harrod a little knoll, hardly five rods from where they stood, and said to him that it must command a better view of the bayou than they had at the camp itself, and she would try once again if she could make any manner of sketch there, which would serve as a suggestion of the journey to her father. For both Eunice and Inez had cultivated some little talent they had in this way; and besides the fiddle-faddle in work on ivory, which was a not unusual accomplishment for French ladies in their time, each of them had tried to train herself — and Eunice had with some success trained Inez — in drawing, in the open air, from nature. In the close forest of the first few days from Nacogdoches, Inez had found few opportunities for her little sketch-book; and Harrod encouraged her in her proposal now, and promised to join her so soon as the horses were all unpacked and fitly tethered for the night.

Inez sat there for a minute, made the notes in her diary (which in yellow ink on yellow paper still appear on that page), and then left the book open while she ran down to the edge of the bayou to fill the water-bottle of her paint-box.

She was surprised and interested to see the variety of the footmarks of the different beasts who had come to the same spot before her for drink. A large log of a fallen tree lay over the water ; and the fearless girl, who was not without practice in such gymnastics in her plantation life, ran out upon it to fill her little flask with water as clear as she could find.

Here her view up and down the little lake — for lake it seemed — widened on each side. The sky was clouded so that Inez lost the lights of the afternoon sun, but still it was a scene of wonderful beauty. The dark shadows, crimson and scarlet, of the autumn foliage, the tall, clear-cut oak, whose lines were so sharp against the sky, were all perfectly reflected in the water, with a distinctness so vivid that she had only to bend her head, and look under her arm, to make the real heavens seem the deception, and the reflection the reality. From the distance her attention was gradually called to her own shore: a great water-snake poked his head above the water, and really seemed to look at her for a moment, then with an angry flash broke the smooth surface for a moment, and plunged out of sight. Great bunches of water-grapes hung near her ; bright leaves of persimmon, red oak and red bay, swamp oak and tupelo, were all around her, and tempted her to make a little bouquet for the supper-table. Her quarters in the branches of the fallen tree were not extensive. But the girl was active, and was diligently culling her various colors, when her eye caught sight in the water of a treasure she had coveted since she met the Caddo Indians, — the great seed-vessels, namely, of the gigantic water-lily of those regions, the *Nelumbo lutea*, or sacred "bean of India."

Were they beyond reach ? If they were, Ransom would come down for her in a minute in the morning, before they started. But, if she had not this provoking hat and shawl on, could she not clamber down to the water's edge among the small branches, and with a stick break them off so they could be floated in? It was worth the trial. And so the girl hung up the offending hat with the shawl, broke off the strongest bough she could manage, and descended to the water's edge again for her foraging.

It took longer than she meant, for the rattles were very provoking. Rattles, be it said, these great seed-vessels are, in the Indian economies; and it was for rattles in dancing that Miss Inez thought them so well worth collecting. But, with much pulling and hauling, three of them consented to loosen themselves from their anchorage, and, to Inez's delight, began to float slowly across to the other side of her little cove. Now she had only to run around there, and secure her prizes. But as she turned to recover her hat and shawl, and to work shoreward with her not-forgotten bouquet, looking out through the bushes upon the little opening in the shrubbery which had been her path, the girl saw what she knew in an instant must be the gigantic Texas panther, quietly walking down to the water, with two little cubs at its side. Inez was frightened: of that there is no doubt. And to herself she owned she was frightened. She would have been frightened had she met the beast on the travelled trail; but here the panther had her at disadvantage. She had, however, the presence of mind to utter no sound. If the panther had not made her out hidden in the shrubbery, she would not call his attention. Would he be good enough to lap his water, and go his way, perhaps?

So she waited, her heart in her mouth, not daring to wink, as she looked through the little opening in the tupelo beside her. These, then, were the footmarks which she had been wondering about, and had thought might be the prints of bears. Bears, indeed! Much did she know of bears! Would the creature never be done? What did she know about panthers? Did panthers drink enough for nine days, like camels? At last the panther had drunk enough — and the little panthers. But then another process began. They all had to make their ablutions. If Inez had not been

INEZ HAS AN ADVENTURE.

wretched she could have laughed to see the giant beast lapping her paws, just as her dear old Florinda did at home, and purring its approval over the little wretches, as they did the same. But now she had rather cry than laugh. Should she have to stay here all night? Had she better stay all night, or risk every thing by a cry that they could hear at camp? Would they hear her at the camp if she did cry?

There is no reason to suppose that the poor girl was left twenty minutes in her enforced silence, stiff with the posture in which she stood, and cold with fear and with the night mist which, even before the sun went down, began to creep up from the bayou ; but it seemed to her twenty hours, and well it might. Still it did not last forever. The cubs at last finished washing the last claw of the last leg ; and the old lady panther, or old gentleman, whichever the sex may have been, seemed satisfied that here was no place for spending the night. Perhaps some rustle in the shrubbery gave sign of game. Any way, without noise, the great beast turned on its tracks, paused a moment, and then made one great bound inland, followed by the little ones. Inez had some faith left in her in the power of the human voice ; and she did her best to stimulate their flight by one piercing scream, which she changed into a war-whoop, according to the best directions which White Hawk had given her, — a feminine war-whoop, a war-whoop of the soprano or treble variety, but still a war-whoop. As such it was received apparently by the panthers, who made no tarry, but were seen no more.

Inez hastened to avail herself of her victory. Hat and shawl were recovered. Firmly and quickly she extricated herself from the labyrinth of boughs of the fallen cottonwood tree, and almost ran, in her nervous triumph, along its trunk to the shore. Up the beaten pathway she ran, marking now the fresh impression of the beasts' tracks before her. Once and again she cried aloud, hoping that she might be heard in the camp. She had left, and remembered she had left, her note-book and her sketch-book on the knoll. But they might go. For herself, the sight of the tents was all in all; and she turned from the path she followed as she came down, all the more willingly because she saw the panthers had followed it also, to run along the broader way, better marked, which kept upon the level to the beaten trail of travel.

"Broader way, and better marked." Oh, Inez, Inez! broad is the way that leads to destruction; and how many simple wood-farers, nay, how many skilled in wood-craft, have remembered this text when it was too late to profit by it! Three minutes were enough to show the girl that this better-marked track did not lead to the travelled trail. It turned off just as it should not do, and it clung to the bayou. This would never do. They would miss her at the tents, and be frightened. Panther or no panther, she would go up over the knoll. So she turned back on her steps, and began to run now, because she knew how nervous her aunt would be. And again the girl shouted cheerily, called on the highest key, and sounded her newly learned war-whoop.

But, as she ran, the path confused her. Could she have passed that flaming sassafras without so much as noticing it? Any way, she should recognize the great mass of bays where she had last noticed the panthers' tracks. She had seen them as she ran down, and as she came up. She hurried on; but she certainly had returned much farther than she went, when she came out on a strange log flung up in some freshet, which she knew she had not seen before. And there was no clump of bays. Was this being lost? Was she lost?

Why, Inez had to confess to herself, that she was lost just a little bit, but nothing to be afraid of.; but still lost enough to talk about afterwards, she certainly was.

Yet, as she said to herself again and again, she could not be a quarter of a mile, nor half a quarter of a mile, from camp. As soon as they missed her, — and by this time they had missed her, — they would be out to look for her. How provoking that she, of all the party, should make so much bother to the rest! They would watch her now like so many cats all the rest of the way. What a fool she was ever to leave the knoll!

So Inez stopped again, shouted again, and listened, and listened, to hear nothing but a swamp-owl.

If the sky had been clear, she would have had no cause for anxiety. In that case they would have light enough to find her in. She would have had the sunset glow to steer by; and she would have had no difficulty in finding them. But, with this horrid gray over every thing, she dared not turn round, without fearing that she might lose the direction in which the theory of the moment told her she ought to be faring. And these openings which she had called trails — which were probably broken by wild horses and wild oxen as they came down to the bayou to drink — would not go in one direction for ten paces. They bent right and left, this way and that; so that, without some sure token of sun or star, it was impossible, as Inez felt, to know which way she was walking.

And at last, as this perplexity increased, she was conscious that the sun must have set, and that the twilight, never long, was now fairly upon her. All the time there was this fearful silence, only broken by her own voice, and that hateful owl. Was she wise to keep on in her theories of this way or that way? She had never yet come back, either upon the fallen cottonwood tree, or upon the bunch of bays which was her landmark; and it was doubtless her wisest determination to stay where she was. The chances that the larger party would find her were much greater than that she alone would find them; but by this time she was sure that, if she kept on in any direction, there was an even chance that she was going farther and farther wrong.

But it was too cold for her to sit down, wrap herself never so closely in her shawl. The poor girl tried this. She must keep in motion. Back and forth she walked, fixing her march by signs which she could not mistake, even in the gathering darkness. How fast that darkness gathered! The wind seemed to rise, too, as the night came on ; and a fine rain, that seemed as cold as snow to her, came to give the last drop to her wretchedness. If she were tempted for a moment to abandon her sentry beat, and try this wild experiment or that to the right or left, some odious fallen trunk, wet with moss and decay, lay just where she pressed in to the shrubbery, as if placed there to reveal to her her absolute powerlessness. She was dead with cold, and even in all her wretchedness knew that she was hungry. How stupid to be hungry when she had so much else to trouble her! But at least she would make a system of her march. She would walk fifty times this way, to the stump, and fifty times that way ; then she would stop, and cry out, and sound her war-whoop ; then she would take up her sentry march again. And so she did. This way, at least, time would not pass without her knowing whether it were near midnight or no.

"Hark! God be praised, there is a gun! and there is another! and there is another! They have come on the right track, and I am safe!" So she shouted again, and sounded her war-whoop again, and listened, — and then again, and listened again. One more gun! but then no more! Poor Inez! Certainly they were all on one side of her. If only it were not so piteously dark! If she could only work half the distance in that direction which her fifty sentry beats made put together! But when she struggled that way through the tangle, and over one wet log and another, it was only to find her poor wet feet sinking down into mud and water! She did not dare keep on. All that was left for her was to find her tramping ground again ; and this she did.

"Good God, take care of me! My poor dear father, — what would he say if he knew his child was dying close to her friends? Dear mamma, keep watch over your little girl!"

CHAPTER X.

LIFE ON THE BRASSOS.

> "As yet a colt he stalks with lofty pace,
>   And balances his limbs with flexile grace ;
>   First leads the way, the threatening torrent braves,
>   And dares the unknown arch that spans the waves.
>   Light on his airy crest his slender head,
>   His belly short, his loins luxuriant spread ;
>   Muscle on muscle knots his brawny breast ;
>   No fear alarms him, nor vain shouts molest.
>   But, at the clash of arms, his ear afar
>   Drinks the deep sound, and vibrates to the war ;
>   Flames from each nostril roll in gathered stream ;
>   His quivering limbs with restless motion gleam ;
>   O'er his right shoulder, floating full and fair,
>   Sweeps his thick mane, and spreads its pomp of hair ;
>   Swift works his double spine, and earth around
>   Rings to his solid hoof that wears the ground."
>   SOTHEBY.

BUT it is time that this history should return from tracing the varying fortunes of one of the companies of Philip Nolan's friends, to look at the fortunes of that other company whom he had himself enlisted, and to whom he had returned when he left Eunice and Inez, in care of Harrod for the moment, near the ferry of the Sabine River.

Had we diaries as full of these movements as we have of those of Eunice and Inez, which have proved of less account in history, this chapter might take fuller proportions than those which have brought those ladies to the waters of the Brassos River. It proved that the expedition of young men led by Nolan, from Natchez and Texas, was destined to meet the Spanish army in array of battle. Here was the first of those trials of strength between the descendants of Cortez and his men on the one hand, and the descendants of New Englanders and Virginians on the other, which were to end in the independence of Texas forty years after. But of this expedition we have now scarcely a record, — none excepting one memoir from its youngest member, as drawn up by him after the expiration of a quarter of a century. Of the false and crafty pursuit by the Spanish forces, the archives of Texas and Mexico are full. The Spanish Armada did not cause more alarm in England than poor Phil Nolan's horse-hunting expedition among the very officers who had given him his right to enter their territory.

As has been already said, the party gathered at Natchez, which was Nolan's home, so far as a man of affairs like him, a man of so many languages and so many lands, can be said to have had one. Natchez, a settlement of some six hundred persons, was now an American town, having passed under the flag of the United States a year or two before. It had been founded by the French, however; and the Spanish Government gave up the administration only after severe pressure, and indeed with riotous disturbances of the inhabitants. For it was becoming the headquarters of the Western race of men; and, when they suspected that the Spanish Government was slow in its execution of the treaty which provided for the surrender of Natchez to our own sway, their indignation knew no bounds. In such a community as this it is not difficult to fancy the feeling excited by the examination of Nolan — of which we have already spoken — when Vidal, the Spanish consul, complained that he was about to invade the territory of Mexico.

Nolan had, in fact, enrolled a company of more than twenty men on this expedition — the third which he had undertaken in his trading for wild horses. It was admitted on all hands, that this trade was prohibited under the general restrictions which grew out of the hateful policy of that hateful wretch, Philip the Second — Bloody Mary's husband, let it be reverently remembered in passing. But in this case Don Pedro de Nava, the commandant-general of the north-eastern provinces of New Spain, had given Nolan a formal permission to carry it on. The horses were indeed needed in the Spanish garrisons in Louisiana. On his several returns to Orleans, Nolan had sent presents of handsome horses to the governor, as token of his success. And when these facts appeared on the hearing before Judge Bruen, the American judge, he said that this could not be regarded as a hostile expedition against a friendly power; it was a trading expedition permitted in form by the authorities of that power. The United States, he said, was not bound to intervene, nor would it intervene in any way.

Accordingly the gay young party started, full of life and hope. I am afraid no man of them would have turned back had Judge Bruen addressed them paternally, and told them that they were violating the neutrality of the United States by an attack upon the territory of its friends. I am afraid none of them loved the King of Spain. But I am bound to say, that, so far as three-quarters of a century has unlocked the secrets of the past, there is no evidence that Philip Nolan spoke untruly that day, or that he had any foolish notion of invasion or conquest. The reader will see that his conduct, and that of his men, show no signs of any such notion; and neither the archives of Mexico nor of America have divulged any word to imply it.[1]

---

[1] The writer begs to acknowledge the courtesy with which Mr. Fish and Mr. Jefferson, the accomplished keeper of rolls, as well as Gen. Belknap at the War Office, have made every research in the national archives which would throw any light on the darker places of this history. The following letter to Philip Nolan, a copy of which has been preserved in the State Department, is so curious, that even the reader of a novel may pause to look at it: —

THOMAS JEFFERSON TO PHILIP NOLAN.

PHILADELPHIA, June 21, 1798.

SIR, — It is some time siuce 1 have understood that there are large herds of horses in a wild state in the country west of the Mississippi, and have been desirous of obtaining

The young fellows crossed the Mississippi at Walnut Hills,[1] above Natchez, and rode westerly. Their route would thus lie between the posts of Natchitoches and Washita — both of them old French posts, now held by Spanish garrisons. The Spanish consul at Natchez had sent word to the commandant at Washita that this band was coming; and he sent out a party of dragoons to meet them. This was the party of which the reader has heard already. They were more than twice as numerous as Nolan's men, but they hesitated to attack him, as well they might. For, whether he had or had not any right to bring horses out from New Spain, he was not yet in New Spain : he was still in Louisiana. More than this, as has been said, he carried with him the permission of the Spanish governor to cross the frontier for the purposes of his trade.

The Spanish captain therefore pretended that he had only come out to hunt for some horses he had lost. But, as Nolan observed, so soon as he advanced with his friends, the Spanish soldiers turned and dogged him; nor did he lose

details of their history in that State.   Mr. Brown, Senator from Kentucky, informs me it would be in your power to give interesting information on this subject, and encourages me to ask it.   The circumstances of the Old World have, beyond the records of history, been such as admitted not that animal to exist in a state of nature.   The condition of America is rapidly advancing to the same.   The present, then, is probably the only moment in the age of the world, and the herds above mentioned the only subjects, of which we can avail ourselves to obtain what has never yet been recorded, and never can be again, in all probability.   I will add that your information is the sole reliance, as far as I can at present see, for obtaining this desideratum.   You will render to natural history a very acceptable service, therefore, if you will enable our Philosophical Society to add so interesting a chapter to the history of this animal.   I need not specify to you the particular facts asked for, as your knowledge of the animal in his domesticated, as well as his wild state, will naturally have led your attention to those particulars in the manners, habits, and laws of his existence, which are peculiar to his wild state.   I wish you not to be anxious about the form of your information : the exactness of the substance alone is material ; and if, after giving in a first letter all the facts you at present possess, you could be so good on subsequent occasions as to furnish such others in addition as you may acquire from time to time, your communications will always be thankfully received.   If addressed to me at Monticello, and put into any post-office of Kentucky or Tennessee, they will reach me speedily and safely, and will be considered as obligations on, sir,

Your most obedient, humble servant,

Mr. Nolan.   Th : Jefferson.

1 Now Vicksburg.

sight of them till he passed the garrison to which they belonged. He declined to go into Washita, and for the same reason declined to bring his party into Natchitoches, as we have seen. They crossed the Washita River, rode merrily on and on till they came to the Red River, their party being diminished only by the absence of Harrod, Richards, Adams, and King. When Blackburn had joined, Cæsar had joined also; for Cæsar had an enthusiasm for Capt. Nolan, and thought to see wild life, to collect silver, and to return soon to Miss Inez. Under the captain's lead, so soon as he had determined to give Natchitoches the go-by, they kept on the east side from the Red River, till they came to the village of the Caddoes. Among these good-natured and friendly people, they staid long enough to build a raft, and ferry their horses over; and now the real enterprise for which they had started was begun.

The Caddoes were not yet used to visits from whites, though they had learned to take their furs to Natchitoches every year to sell. The Americans found them in this "month of turkeys," as they called October, or the "moon" which filled the greater part of October, enjoying the holiday of an Indian's life. Their lodges were made by a framework of poles placed in a circle in the ground, with the tops united in an oval form. This framework was tightly bound together, and the whole nicely thatched. Within, every person had a "bunk" of his own, raised from the ground, and covered with buffalo-skins, — not an uncomfortable house. Many of these youngsters who visited them here had been born in log cabins which had not so much room upon the floor; for these lodges covered a circle which was twenty-five feet in diameter. More than once, as the party went forward, were the members of it glad to accept the hospitality which such lodges offered, and more than once glad to build such for their own quarters.

And, from this moment, the work and the play of the little party began. Nolan was encouraged so soon as he learned that his presence and escort for the party of ladies were no longer needed. One day he was negotiating with Twowokanies, — friendly people enough when they saw the strength of the long-knives ; he bought from them some fine horses, and so the business of the expedition prospered. Six days more brought them to Trinity River, and across it. All these young men were used to open prairie life, with its freedom and adventure ; but only the six Spaniards of the party, Nolan himself, and one or two of the Americans, had ever taken wild horses in fair chase with the lasso. The use of it was still to be taught and learned, as the warm days of October and November passed. While Eunice and Inez were wending westward from Nacogdoches, many was the frolic, and many the upset, the empty saddle, and the hair-breadth escape, by which the greenhorns of this other party were broken into their new business. But it was a jolly and a hearty life ; and no man regretted the adventure while buffalo-meat and fine weather lasted.

As they crossed the divide between the Trinity and the Brassos, moving on a parallel line with the smaller party, the supply of buffalo-meat gave out ; and they had to try the experiment of horse-flesh. Bnt there were few of them whose fathers and grandfathers had not tried that before them, though few of them guessed that it was to be made fashionable in Parisian *cafés*. As long ago as the days of Philip of Mount Hope, the savage who entertained Capt. Church offered him his choice of " cow-beef " or " horse-beef." With the Brassos River came good fare again, — elk, antelope, turkeys, buffaloes, and wild horses by thousands.

So the captain directed that here the camp should be established ; and here " Nolan's River " still flows, to maintain the memory of this camp, and of the gallant pioneer who built it for a generation which has, alas ! well-nigh forgotten him. Wild horses are but an uncertain, shall one say a skittish, property ? It is said of all riches, that " they take to themselves wings, and fly." Of that form of wealth which

Nolan and his friends were collecting, the essential and special worth is that they do not have to take to themselves legs, but are all ready at any moment to flee. Without this quality, indeed, it would cease to be wealth. In this case, moreover, the neighborhood of Twowokanies, Comanches, Apaches, Lipans, and redskins without a name, made the uncertainty of wealth still more uncertain. Whatever else was doubtful, this was sure, that, if these rascals could run off the horses as fast as they were corralled, they would do so. And thus to hunt all day, and to keep watch all night, was the duty of the little party as the long nights of winter came on.

The first necessity, therefore, at " Nolan's River," was to build a corral, or pen, of logs, to be enlarged from time to time, as the success of hunting warranted.[1] When the task was over, the hunting went forward with more animation; and, as the new year turned, the young fellows rejoiced in a drove of three hundred fine horses, which, as they promised themselves, they should take to a good market in Louisiana and in the Mississippi territory, as soon as the spring should open. Camp-life had its usual adventures ; but the great occasion of the winter was the arrival of a party of two hundred Comanches, men, women, and children, on their way to the Red River. Several tribes of different names met at this place. A great chief named Nicoroco had summoned them together there. The young whites smoked the pipe of peace with them all, gave them presents as they could, and thought they had opened amicable relations with them. And so they returned to their corral and their hunting.

Blackburn had joined, with Cæsar. But to the surprise of all, — that of the captain most of all, — Harrod and his squad did not appear.

Of all the winter's sojourn there, this reader need now be

---

[1] The spot is not known. Some of my correspondents in Texas place it as far south as Waco County, but the name " Nolan's River " makes this doubtful.

delayed only by the following letter, which opens the plans and hopes, the annoyances and failures, of Capt. Nolan : —

PHILIP NOLAN TO EUNICE PERRY:
NOLAN'S RIVER, IN THE WILDERNESS,
4th day of the month of chestnuts.
Last year of the old century.

MY DEAR MISS PERRY, — If you think me dead, this letter undeceives you. If you think me faithless, let me try to undeceive you. If, which is impossible, you think I have forgotten you or Miss Inez, no words that I can write will undeceive you.

Blackburn joined us safely at the crossing of Trinity River, and brought us news from you not three days old. I have to thank you for your letter, and Miss Inez for her little postscript, for which I will repay her yet. You were right in thinking that the news which Will sent of the cordiality of the two colonels, and of their determination to provide escort for you, combined with your own great courtesy in relieving me from my promise to your brother, were the causes which changed my plans as formed when we parted. Nothing but the statement of your own judgment and wish would have debarred me from the pleasure of seeing you and your niece soon.

It is very true, as you suspected, that my presence with my men gives vigor and unity to their work, which it must have if it is to succeed. They are a good set, on the whole ; but boys are boys, and rangers are rangers, and Spaniards are Spaniards. I am sometimes tempted to leave them to cut each others' throats when they stumble into one of their quarrels ; and then, another day, when all has worked well, and they are dancing or singing, or telling camp stories round their fire, I wonder that I have ever thought them any thing but a band of brothers.

My only anxiety arises from the detention of Will Harrod and his men, who have not joined me ; but I suppose you know, better than I, the cause of their delay.

The great enterprise goes forward happily. I shall hope to send Mr. Jefferson a valuable letter. If only I can send him a horse across the Alleghanies ! I have for your brother's own saddle the handsomest black charger he ever set his eyes upon, the stud of the First Consul himself, or of your Gracious Majesty Charles the Fourth, not excepted. If only the beast escapes "One Eye," and the distemper and yellow-water, — which may Castor and Pollux grant ! Are not they the protectors of horses ? An exciting life is ours. In the saddle for the whole of daylight, we do not lose our anxiety when the night comes on : at least

"THEY TOOK MASTER ONE EYE AND TIED HIM TO A TREE FOR
THE NIGHT."

we chiefs do not. My boys are snoring around this pine-knot fire, while I am writing, as if they knew no care. But it is always so.

"Uneasy lies the head that wears a crown."

But my fair enemy Miss Inez will never be satisfied, if in the wilderness here I end by quoting Shakspeare. Tell her it is for her sake that I end my letter with an adventure, which she may introduce into her first romance. You must know, and she must know, that I and half a dozen of my boys have been on a visit to Nicoroco, the great chief of chieftains in these regions. The great Wallace himself was not so bare-legged as Nicoroco is, nor did his sway extend nearly so far. Yes, and we smoked calumets of peace enough to make Miss Inez sick ten times over, and Miss Perry also, unless your new waif — Hawk-Eye, is her name ? — have taught you, faster than I believe, the peaceful habits of the wilderness. Heavens ! if your royal master's handsome chief commander, the "Prince of Peace," as I am told he is called, could but have presided, he would never have feared the *salvajos Americaños* any more ! Ah, well ! We returned from these pacifications to our corral, our buffalo-meat, and our horses, and alas ! a few pacified Comanches returned with us.

What faith can you put in man ? Early one morning our dear friends departed ; and when we shook ourselves a few hours after, for our break-fast, we found, that, by some accident not to be explained, they had taken with them all of our eleven saddle-horses, and that for the future we were to pursue the mustangs on foot, and on foot were to drive them through the deserts to Natchez and Orleans ! This was the interpretation given in effect to all our pacifications !

What to do ? *Quien sabe?* Certainly I did not know. But I did know I was neither going to ride a wild mustang home, nor appear on foot in the presence of my townsfolk the other side of the Father of Waters. So I called for volunteers, and your dear old Cæsar stepped forth first. Three white men joined, ashamed to be outdone by a darkey. On foot we started. On foot we followed their trail for nine days. Day by day they were more careless. Day by day we were more cheer-ful. The ninth day we walked gently into their camp, unsuspected and unexpected. There was my old chéstnut, whom you rode that Tuesday ; there were three other of our beasts ; and there that evening came in, as innocent as a lamb, my old friend *One Eye*, of whom I have told you before, with some excellent friends of his, mounted on the other seven of our brutes. This time I took Master One Eye, and tied him to a tree for the night, to give him a chance to ponder the principles of the Great Cal-umet. The next morning we helped ourselves to all the bear-meat we could carry, and turned our faces to Nolan's River. We were not nine days coming home.

There, Miss Inez! had ever Amadis such an adventure, or Robert Bruce, or the Count Odoardo de Rascallo, or your handsome hero Gen. Junot?

It is near midnight, unless Orion tells lies ; and the fire burns low.

My homage is in all these lines. *Adios.*

Your ladyship's most faithful vassal,

To come or to stay away,

PHILIP NOLAN.

CHAPTER XI.

RUMORS OF WARS.

"With chosen men of Leon, from the city Bernard goes,
 To protect the soil of Spain from the spear of foreign foes, —
 From the city which is planted in the midst between the seas,
 To preserve the name and glory of old Pelayo's victories."

LOCKHART.

CAPT. PHILIP NOLAN was, when he wrote, in far greater danger than he supposed.

As I write this morning, if any gentleman now by the side of "Nolan's River" were curious to know if King Alfonso spent an agreeable night last night, he could sènd to some station not far away, and his curiosity would be relieved before dinner. At least, I suppose so. I know that I was favored some hours ago with the intelligence, which I did not want, that King Alfonso was about to leave Madrid this morning, and ride to his army. In truth, as it happens, I know better what he is going to do to-day than I know where my next neighbor at the foot of the hill is going.

But, when Philip Nolan wrote these merry words to Eunice Perry, he knew little enough of what was doing at Madrid ; and he knew still less, as it happened, of what was in the wind at a capital much nearer to him. This was the famous and noble city of Chihuahua, — a city some three hundred miles west of Nolan's corral. To this distant point I shall not have to ask the reader to go again ; but, before the several pieces on our little board advance another step, I must ask him to look for a moment now behind all intermediate pawns, and see what is the attitude of him who represents the king, protected here by his distant and forgotten bishops, knights, and castles.

Chihuahua was, in the year 1800, a city quite as imposing in aspect as it is to-day. To those simple people who had to come and go thither for one or another measure of justice, injustice, protection, or vengeance, it seemed the most magnificent city in the world, — wholly surpassing the grandeurs of all other frontier or garrison towns. Around the public square were built a splendid cathedral, the royal treasury, and a building which served as the hotel-de-ville of the administration of the city. The cathedral was one of the most splendid in New Spain. It had been erected at enormous cost, and was regarded with astonishment and pride by all the people, who had seen no statues or pictures to compare with those displayed in its adornments. Several noble "missiones," a military academy, the establishments of the Dominicans, Franciscans, and those which the Jesuits had formerly built, added to the European aspect of the city.

Our business with Chihuahua is that, in this city, Don Pedro de Nava, the general-commandant of the north-eastern provinces at this time, held his court. Under the administration then existing in New Spain, this was an unlimited military authority. In the more southern provinces of what is now the Republic of Mexico, a system of a sort of courts of appeal known as "audiences" had been created as some check upon the viceroy and the intendants. But in the northern provinces no such system was known, and the military law corresponded precisely to the definition given in Boston in Gen. Gage's time : —

"1st, The commander does as he chooses.

"2d, Military law is the law that permits him to do so."

This Gov.-Gen. de Nava had, as the reader has been told, issued to Nolan a formal permission to come from Louisiana for horses, to take such as were needed for the remount of the Spanish army, and for these purposes to bring with him two thousand dollars' worth of goods for trade with the Indians. I have seen De Nava's own account of this order in the curious archives at San Antonio. Alas! I am afraid poor Phil Nolan had no two thousand dollars' worth of goods, and that that part of the permit served him little. After De Nava issued it, — on some report to Madrid on the subject, or on some new terror there, — much stricter orders came to him, which he was obliged to repeat to all the local governors. He became painfully aware that his permit to Nolan exceeded by far his present power. He does not seem to have thought of notifying him that it was recalled. He did write to San Antonio and to Nacogodoches, to say that nobody else must come for the same purpose, but that his permit to Nolan was still an excuse for his coming. He said, that, as Nolan might have with him the two thousand dollars' worth of goods permitted, the commanders at San Antonio might take them off his hands for the royal service. At the same time he intimated that it was so long since his permit was given, that Nolan ought not to come. But these papers all show a weak man, conscious that his superiors will be displeased by what he has already done, and hoping against hope that something may turn up so that no harm may come of it.

Gov. Salcedo, of whom the reader will hear again, was the evil spirit of the Spanish administration of these regions, as the worthless " Prince of Peace " was its evil spirit at home.

Gen. Salcedo was the governor who had expressed the wish, cited in an earlier chapter, that he could even prevent the birds from crossing from Louisiana into Texas. He was a faithful disciple of the extremest views of King Philip. While the local governor of Coahuila, and the commandant at San Antonio, both of them intelligent men, saw without uneasiness an occasional traveller from Natchitoches, or Philip Nolan proposing to go to Orleans, — Salcedo raved when he heard of such obliquity or carelessness. If they had told him that the primate of Mont El Rey, the beloved Bishop Don Dio Primero, had extended his episcopal visitation as far as Natchitoches, he would have been beside himself with indignation. "What devils should take the bishop so far?" And, when they told him that the bishop went to fight the Devil, he expressed the wish that his holiness would leave as many devils as he could to harry those damnable French and the more damnable Americaños beyond them. Ah me! if Don Salcedo had been permitted to live to see the day, forty years later, when Sam Houston's men charged on poor Santa Anna's lines at San Jacinto, screaming, "Remember the Alamo!" he would have said that none of his black portents were too black, and none of his prophecies of evil gloomy enough. He would have said that he was the Cassandra who could not avert the future of Texas and Coahuila.

De Nava had seen no danger in permitting poor Philip Nolan to drive a few horses, more or less, across the frontier of Texas into the king's colony of Louisiana. If the horses had gone there at their own will, as doubtless thousands of horses did yearly, *quien sabe?* and what harm? If Philip Nolan chose to come to San Antonio, and spend there a little Orleans money in his outfit for such an expedition; if he hired for good dollars a handful of Spanish hunters to go with him, — what harm? said Don Pedro de Nava. And so he gave Philip Nolan the passport and permission aforesaid.

But the authorities in the city of Mexico, and those in the city of Madrid, did not know Philip Nolan, and did not understand such reasoning. The only Philip they chose to remember in the business was that Most Gracious and Very Catholic Philip, Lord of both Indies, who was good at burning heretics. It was certain that he would have had no horse-hunting in his domains but by loyal, God-fearing subjects of his own. And if De Nava and those lax and good-natured men, the governors of the eastern provinces of Coahuila and Texas, had assented to such heretical horse-hunting, it was time for them to know who was master in these deserts; and the orders should proceed "from these headquarters." And if that broken-down old fool Casa Calvo, away in that bastard province of Louisiana, which was neither one thing nor another, — neither colony nor foreign state, — if he chose to go to sleep while people invade us, why, we must be all the more watchful!

By some wretched accident, as we must suppose, some account of Nolan's plans, enormously exaggerated, seems to have come even to the city of Mexico. The traditions are that Mordecai Richards, — the same Richards whom we have already introduced to our readers, — after he had engaged in Nolan's service, sent traitorous information to some Spanish authority, of the plan of the expedition and of its probable route. Be this as it may, Spanish governors of the suspicious race were far too much excited then to receive such news with satisfaction. Old John Adams's messages about the mouth of the Mississippi [1] had not been very pacific. Everybody knew, what everybody has long since forgotten, that he had half his army on that stream, and fleets of flatboats at every post, which were waiting only for the time when he should say "Go," and his army would pounce upon Orleans. Nobody could say at what moment European combinations might make this step feasible, without the least danger that the "Prince of Peace," the commander-in-chief of the armies of King Charles, should strike any return blow. "Hunting horses, forsooth!" said Don Nemisio de Salcedo: "are we fools to have such stories told to us? It is an army of these giants of Kentuckianos; they must be driven back before it is too late." And poor Governor De Nava, unwillingly enough had to "take the back track," and act as if he thought so too.

His military force was not large. In times of absolute peace, seeing no foreign army was within five hundred miles of Chihuahua, the garrison of that city was usually not more than two or three hundred men. But in this terrible exigency, with the Kentuckianos mustering in force on his distant

---

[1] Not Harrod's John Adams, but President John.

border, De Nava withheld every unnecessary band that would otherwise have gone after Apaches or Comanches, refused all leaves of absence and furloughs, made his most of the loyalty of the military academy, and against poor Phil Nolan, fearing nothing in his corral, was able to equip an army of a hundred and fifty men.

Military men, whose judgment is second to none, assure us that there was never better material for an army than the Mexican soldier of that day. This force of dragoons were all of them men who had seen service against the mounted Indians. Each man had a little bag of parched corn meal and sugar, the common equipage of the hunters of those regions. Travellers of to-day, solicited in palace-cars to buy sugared parched-corn, do not know, perhaps, that this is the food of pioneers in front of Apaches. Besides this, a paternal government provided good wheat biscuit and shaved dry meat, which they ate with enormous quantities of red pepper. With such outfit the troop would ride cheerily all day, taking no meal excepting at the encampment at night; and, if any man were hungry in the day, he bit a piece of biscuit, or drank some water with his corn-meal and sugar stirred into it.

After orders and additional orders which need not be named, the little army assembled in the square in front of the cathedral. It was to march against the heretics : that was all they knew. A priest came out with holy water, to bless the colors. Every man had been confessed ; and every man, as he shook himself into his saddle, understood that, whatever befell, he had a very considerable abatement made from the unpleasantness of purgatory, because he was on this holy errand. As they were on special service, not against Indians but whites, the lances which they carried on the prairies were taken away. But every man had a carbine slung in front of his saddle, a heavy horse-pistol on each side, and below the carbine the shield, which was still in use, even in this century, to ward off arrows. It was made of triple sole-leather. It was round, and two feet in diameter. The officers carried oval shields bending on both sides, and in elegant blazonry displayed the arms of the king or of Spain, with other devices. So that it would have been easy to imagine that Fernando del Soto had risen from his grave, and that this was a party of the cavaliers of chivalry who were starting against poor Nolan and his fifteen horse-hunters in buckskin.

The governor, with the officers of his staff, in full uniform, had assisted at the sacred ceremonials in the church. The men marched out and mounted. The governor, standing on the steps of the cathedral, gave his hand to the commander of the party.

"May God preserve you many years!" he said.

"May God preserve your Excellency!"

"Death to the savage heretics!" said the governor.

"Death to the invaders!" said Col. Muzquiz, now in the saddle. Then turning to his men, he waved his hand, and cried, "Long live the king!"

"Long live the king!" they answered cheerily.

"Forward, march!" A hand kissed to a lady — and the troop was gone!

CHAPTER XII.

"LOVE WAITS AND WEEPS."

" The stranger viewed the shore around :
   'Twas all so close with copsewood bound,
   Nor track nor pathway might declare
   That human foot frequented there."

Lady of the Lake.

THE little camp which Harrod had formed on the Little Brassos was not much more than a hundred miles below the corral in which, some weeks later, Nolan wrote his merry letter to the ladies. Now that farms and villages spot the country between, — nay, when it is even vexed by railroad lines and telegraphs, — now that this poor little story is perhaps to be scanned even upon the spot by those familiar with every locality, — it is impossible to bear in mind that then the region between was all untrodden even by savages, and that, had Harrod and the ladies loitered at their camp till Nolan arrived at his, they would still be as widely parted as if they were living on two continents to-day.

The disappearance of poor little Inez was not noticed in the camp till she had been away nearly an hour, — indeed, just as the sun was going down. Harrod had told her that he would join her on the knoll, and had hurried his necessary inspection, that he might have the pleasure of sitting by her, talking with her, and watching her at her work. But, when he turned to walk up to her, he saw that she was no longer there ; and, seeing also that the curtain in front of her tent was closed, he supposed, without another thought, that she had returned from the hillside, and was again in her tent with Eunice. A little impatiently he walked to and fro, watching the curtain door from time to time, in the hope that she would appear. But, as the reader knows, she did not appear. Yet it was not till her aunt came forth fresh from a late siesta, in answer to Ransom's call to dinner, that Harrod learned, to his dismay, that Inez was not with her. If he felt an instant's anxiety, he concealed it. He only said, —

"How provoking! I have been waiting for her because she said she would make a sketch from the knoll here ; and now she must be at work somewhere all alone."

"She is a careless child," said Eunice, "to have gone away from us into this evening air without her shawl. But no: she has taken that. Still she ought to be here."

But Harrod needed no quickening, and had already run up the hill to call her.

Of course he did not find her. He did find the note-book and the sketch-book, and the open box of colors. Anxious now indeed, but very unwilling to make Eunice anxious, he ran down to the water's edge, calling as loudly as he dared, if he were not to be heard at the camp, but hearing no answer. He came down to the very point where the cotton-wood tree had fallen ; and he was too good a woodsman not to notice at once the fresh trail of the panther and the cubs. He found as well tupelo leaves and bay leaves, which he felt sure Inez had broken from their stems. Had the girl been frightened by the beast, and lost herself above or below in the swamp ?

Or had she, — horrid thought, which he would not acknowledge to himself ! — had she ignorantly taken refuge on the fallen cottonwood tree, — the worst possible refuge she could have chosen ? had she crept out upon it, and fallen into the deep water of the bayou ?

He would not permit himself to entertain a thought so horrible. But he knew that a wretched half-hour — nay, nearly an hour—had sped since he spoke with her; and what worlds of misery can be crowded into an hour! He ran out upon the tree, and found at once the traces of the girl's lair there. He found the places where she had broken the branches. He guessed, and guessed rightly, where she had crouched. He found the very twig from which she had twisted the bright tupelo. And he looked back through the little vista to the shore, and could see how she saw the beasts standing by the water. He imagined the whole position; and he had only the wretched comfort, that, if she had fallen, it must be that some rag of her clothing, or some bit of broken branch below, would have told the tale. No such token was there; that is, it was not certain that she had fallen, and given one scream of agony unheard before the whole was over.

He must go back to camp, however unwillingly. He studied the trail with such agony, even, as he had not felt before. He followed down the side track which Inez had followed for a dozen yards, but then was sure that he was wasting precious daylight. He fairly ran back to camp,— only careful to disturb by his footfall no trace which was now upon weed or leaf; and when he came near enough he had to walk as if not too eager.

"Has she come home?" said he, with well-acted calmness.

"You have not found her? Dear, dear child, where is she?" And in an instant Eunice's eagerness and Harrod's was communicated to the whole camp. He showed the only traces he had found. He told of the open color-box and drawing-book; and Eunice instantly supplied the clew which Harrod had not held before.

"She went down to fill her water-bottle. Did you find that there,—a little cup of porcelain?"

No, Harrod had not seen that: he knew he should have seen it. And at this moment Ransom brought in all these sad waifs, and the white cup was not among them. Harrod begged the poor lady not to be distressed: the fire of a rifle would call the girl in. But Eunice of course went with him ; and then even her eye detected instantly what he had refrained from describing to her,—the heavy footprints of the panther.

"What is that ? " she cried ; and Harrod had to tell her.

In an instant she leaped to his conclusion, that the child had taken refuge somewhere from the fear of this beast ; and in an instant more, knowing what she should have done herself, knowing how steady of head and how firm of foot Inez was, she said,—

"She ran out on that cottonwood tree, Mr. Harrod. Look there, — and there, — and there, — she broke the bark away with her feet ! My child ! my child ! has she fallen into the stream ? "

Now it was Harrod's turn to explain that this was impossible. He confessed to the discovery of the tupelo leaves. Inez had been on the log. But she had not fallen, he said, lying stoutly. There was no such wreck of broken branches as her fall would have made. And, before he was half done, the suggestion had been enough. Two of the men were in the water. It was deep, alas ! it was over their heads. But the men had no fear. They went under again and again ; they followed the stream down its sluggish current. So far as their determined guess was worth any thing, Inez's body was not there.

In the meanwhile every man of them had his theory. The water terror held to Eunice, though she said nothing of it. The men believed generally that those infernal Apaches had been on their trail ever since they left the fort ; that they wanted perhaps to regain White Hawk, or perhaps thought they would take another prisoner in her place. This was the first chance that had been open to them, and they had pounced here. This was the theory which they freely communicated to each other and to Ransom. To Eunice in person, when she spoke to one or another, in the hurried preparations for a search, they kept up a steady and senseless lie, such as it is the custom of ignorant men to utter to women whom they would encourage. The girl had missed the turn by the bay-trees ; or she had gone up the stream looking for posies. It would not be fifteen minutes before they had her " back to camp " again. Such were the honeyed words with which they hoped to re-assure the agonized woman, even while they charged their rifles, or fastened tighter their moccasons, as if for war. Of course she was not deceived for an instant. For herself, while they would let her stay by the water-side, she was pressing through one and another quagmire to the edge of the cove in different places. But at last, as his several little parties of quest arranged themselves, Harrod compelled her to return. As she turned up from the stream, one of the negroes came up to her, wet from the water. He gave her the little porcelain cup, which had lodged on a tangle of sedge just below the cottonwood tree. Strange that no one should have noticed it before !

Every instant thus far, as the reader knows, had been wasted time. Perhaps it was no one's fault, — nay, certainly it was no one's fault, — for every one had " done the best his circumstance allowed." For all that, it had been all wasted time. Had Harrod fired a rifle the moment he first missed Inez, with half an hour of daylight still, and with the certainty that she would have heard the shot, and could have seen her way toward him, all would have been well. But Harrod had, and should have had, the terror lest he should alarm Eunice unduly ; and, in trying to save her, he really lost his object. At the stream, again, minutes of daylight passed quicker than any one could believe, in this scanning of the trail, and plunging into the water. The shouts — even the united shouts of the party — did not tell on the night air as the sharp crack of a rifle would have done. Worst of all, in losing daylight, they were losing every thing ; and this, when it was too late, Harrod felt only too well.

Considering what he knew, and the impressions he was under, his dispositions, which were prompt, were well planned and soldierly. It is but fair to say this, though they were in fact wholly wrong. Yielding to the belief, for which he had only too good reason, that the Apaches were on the trail, and had made a push to secure their captive again, Harrod bade the best soldiers of his little party join him for a hasty dash back on the great trail, in the hope that traces of them might be found, and that they could be overtaken even now, before it was wholly dark. One thing was certain, — that, if they had pounced on their victim, they had turned promptly. They had not been seen nor suspected at the camp itself, by their trail.

Silently, and without Eunice's knowledge, he bade Richards work southward, and Harry, the negro boy who had brought in the water-bottle, work northward, along the edges of the bayou. If there were — any thing — there, they must find it, so long as light lasted. And they were to be in no haste to return. "Do not let me see you before midnight. The moon will be up by and by. Stay while you can see the hand before your face."

He should have given rifles to both of them. Richards, in fact, took his; but the negro Harry, as was supposed in the fond theory of those times, had never carried a gun, and he went with no weapon of sound but his jolly "haw-haw-haw" and his vigorous call. Once more here was a mistake. Harry's rifle-shot, had he had any rifle to fire, would have brought Inez in even then.

Meanwhile Ransom led Eunice back to the camp-fire; and, when his arrangements by the bayou were made, Harrod hastily followed. His first question was for the White Hawk; but where she was, no one knew. Two of the men thought she had been with Miss Perry; but this, Eunice denied. Ransom was sure that she came to him, and pointed to the sky, while he was carrying in the dinner. But Harrod doubted this, and the old man's story was confused. Were the girls together? Had the same enemy pounced on both? Harrod tried to think so, and to make Eunice think so. But

Eunice did not think so. She thought only of the broken bit of tupelo, and of this little white cup which she still clutched in her hand. From the first moment Eunice had known what would have happened to her, had that beast driven her out over the water. And from the first moment one thought, one question, had overwhelmed her, "What shall I say to him, to tell him that I let his darling go, for one instant, from my eye?"

Then Harrod told Ransom that he must stay with Miss Eunice while they were gone.

Ransom said bluntly, that he would be hanged if he would: Miss Inez was not far away, and he would find her before the whole crew on 'em saw any thing on her.

But Harrod called him away from the throng.

"Ransom, listen to me," he said. "If Miss Perry is left alone here, she will go crazy. If you leave her, there is no one who can say one word to her all the time we are gone. I hope and believe that we will have Miss Inez back before an hour; but all that hour she has got to sit by the fire here. You do not mean to have me stay with her; and I am sure you do not want me to leave her with one of those 'niggers.'"

Harrod for once humored the old man, by adopting the last word from his vocabulary.

"You're right, Mr. Harrod; I'd better stay. 'N' I'll bet ten dollars, now, Miss Inez'll be the first one to come in to the fire, while you's lookin' after her. 'Tain't the fust time I've known her off after dark alone."

"God grant it!" said Harrod; and so the old man staid.

But Harrod had not revealed, either to Eunice or to Ransom, the ground for anxiety which had the most to do with his determinations and dispositions. In the hasty examination of the trail which he made when he first searched for the girl, and afterwards when he, with Richards and King — better woodsmen than he — examined the path which they supposed the girl had taken, and the well-marked spot at the shore of the bayou, where the beasts came to water, they had found no print of Inez's foot; but they had found perfectly defined marks, which no effort had been made to conceal, of an Indian's footprint. · Harrod tried to think it was White Hawk's, and pointed to Richards the smallness of the moccason, and a certain peculiarity of tread which he said was hers. Richards, on the other hand, believed that it was the mark of an Indian boy whom he described; that he had been close behind Inez, and had been trying, only too successfully, to obliterate every footstep. With more light, of course, there might have been more chance to follow these indications; but, where the regular trail of the brutes coming to water had broken the bushes, they led up less successfully; and the indications all agreed, that, if the Apaches were to be· found at all, it was by the prompt push which they were now essaying.

They all sprang to saddle; and even Harrod tried to give cheerfulness which he did not feel, by crying, —

"They have more than an hour's start of us, and they will ride like the wind. I will send back when I strike the trail; but you must not expect us before midnight." And so they were gone.

Poor Eunice Perry sat alone by the camp-fire. Not two hours ago she had congratulated herself, and had let Inez, dear child, congratulate her, because, at the Brassos River, more than half, and by far the worst half, of their bold enterprise was over, — over, and well over. And now, one wretched hour, in which she had been more careless than she could believe, and all was night and horror. Could she be the same living being that she was this afternoon? She looked in the embers, and saw them fade away, almost careless to renew the fire. What was there to renew it for?

Ransom, with the true chivalry of genuine feeling, left her wholly to herself for all this first agony of brooding. When he appeared, it was to put dry wood on the coals.

"She'll be cold when she comes in. Night's cold. She

didn't know she'd be gone so long." This was in a soliloquy, addressed only to the embers.

Then he turned bravely to Eunice, and, bringing up another camp-stool close to where she sat, he placed upon it the little silver salver, which he usually kept hid away in his own pack, where he reserved it for what he regarded as the state occasions of the journey.

" Drink some claret, Miss Eunice ; good for you ; keep off the night air. Some o' your brother's own private bin, what he keeps for himself and ye mother, if she'd ever come to see him. I told him to give me the key when he went away ; told him you might need some o' the wine ; and he gin it to me. Brought a few bottles along with me. Knew they wouldn't be no good wine nowhere ef you should git chilled. Told him to give me the key ; his own bin. Better drink some, Miss Eunice."

He had warmed water, had mixed his sangaree as carefully as if they had all been at the plantation, had remembered every fancy of Eunice's in concocting it, grating nutmeg upon it from her own silver grater, which lay in his stores, much as her brother's silver waiter did. And this was brought to her in her silver cup, as she sat there in the darkness in the wilderness, with her life darker than the night. Eunice was wretched ; but, in her wretchedness, she appreciated the faithful creature's care ; and, to please him, she made an effort to drink something, and sat with the goblet in her hand.

"It is very good, Ransom : it is just what I want ; and you are very kind to think of it."

Ransom leaned over to change the way in which the sticks lay across the fire. Then he began again, —

" Jest like her mother, she is. Don't ye remember night her mother scared us all jest so ? Got lost jest as Miss Inez has, and ye brother was half crazy. No, ye don't remember : ye never see her. Ye brother was half crazy, he was. Her mother got lost jest as Miss Inez has ; scared all on us jest so. She's jest like her mother, Miss Inez is. I said so to Mr. Harrod only yesterday."

Eunice was too dead to try to answer him; and, without answer, the old man went on in a moment, —

"We wos out on the plantation. It wos in the fall, jest as it is now. It wos the fust year after ye brother bought this place; didn't have no such good place on the river before: had the old place hired of Walker.

"After he bought this place, cos she liked it, — two years afore this one was born, — it wos in the fall, jest as it is now" —

"I'd sent all the niggers to bed, I had, 'n wos jest lookin' 'round 'fore I locked up, w'en ye brother come up behind me, white as a sheet, he was. 'Ransom,' says he, 'where's ye missus?'"

"Scared me awfully, he did, Miss Eunice. I didn't know more'n the dead where she wos; 'n I said, says I, 'Isn't she in her own room?' — 'Ransom,' says he, 'she isn't in any room in the house; 'n none on 'em seen her,' says he, 'since she had a cup o' tea sent to her in the settin'-room,' says he; ''n it wasn't dark then,' says he.

"'N none on 'em knew where she wos or where she'd gone. Well, Miss Eunice, they all loved her, them darkeys did, jest as these niggers, all on 'em, loves this one; and, w'en I went round to ask 'em where she wos, they run this way an' that way, and none on 'em found her. 'N in an hour she come in all right: got lost down on the levee, — went wrong way 'n got lost; had been down to see how old Chloe's baby was, 'n got lost comin' home. Wosn't scared herself one bit, — never was scared, — wosn't scared at nothin'. Miss Inez just like her mother."

Now there was a long pause; but Eunice did not want to discourage him, though she knew he would not encourage her.

"Tell me more about her mother, Ransom."

"Woll, Miss Eunice, ye know how handsome she wos.

That 'ere picter hangs in the salon ain't half handsome enough for her.   Painted in Paris it wos, fust time they went over : ain't half handsome enough for her.   Miss Inez is more like her, she is.

" She wos real good to 'em all, she wos, ma'am.   She wos quiet like, not like the French ladies ; 'n when they come and see her, they knowed she wos more of a lady than they wos, 'n they didn't care to see her much, 'n she didn't care to see them much.   But she wos good to 'em all.   Wos good to the niggers : all the niggers liked her.

" Took on a good deal, and wos all broke down, when she come from the Havannah to this place.   Kissed this one, Dolores here, that we's goin' to see, — kissed her twenty times ; 'n Dolores says to me, says she, — that's this one,— she says, says she, in her funny Spanish way, ' Ransom, take care of her ev'ry day and ev'ry night ; 'n, Ransom, when you bring her back to me,' says she, ' I'll give you a gold doubloon,' says she.   'N she laughed, 'n I laughed, 'n we made this one laugh, — Miss Inez's mother.   She did not like to come away, 'n took on a good deal."

Another pause, in which Ransom wistfully contemplated the sky.

" Took her to ride myself, I did, ev'ry time, after this one was born, — I did.   Coachman didn't know nothin'.   Poor crittur, ye brother got rid on him afterward.   No : he died. I drove the kerridge myself, I did, after this one was born. She was dreadful pleased with her baby, cos it wos a gal, 'n she wanted a gal, 'n she took it to ride ev'ry day ; 'n she says to me, ' Ransom,' says she, ' we must make this a Yankee baby, like her father,' says she.   She says, says she, ' Ransom, next spring,' says she, ' we will carry the baby to Boston,' says she, ' 'n show 'em what nice babies we have down here in Orleans,' says she.   'N she says to me, says she one day, when she had had a bad turn o' coughin', ' Ransom,' says she, ' you'll take as nice care of her as ye do of me,' says she ; ' won't you, Ransom ? ' says she.

"And you said you would, Ransom, I'm sure," said Eunice kindly, seeing that the old man would say no more.

"Guess I did, ma'am. She needn't said nothin'. Never thought o' doin' nothin' else. Knew none on 'em didn't know nothin' 'cept ye brother till you come down, ma'am. It was a hard year, ma'am, before you come down. Didn't none on 'em know nothin' 'cept ye brother."

Eunice was heard to say afterward that the implied compliment in these words was the greatest praise she had ever received from human lips ; but at the time she was too wretched to be amused.

There was not now a long time to wait, however, before they could hear the rattle of hoofs upon the road they had been following all day.

It was Harrod's first messenger, the least competent negro in his train. He had sent him back to relieve Eunice as far as might be with this line, hurriedly written on a scrap of brown paper : —

"We have found the rascals' trail — very warm. I write this by their own fire.   H."

The man said that they came upon the fire still blazing, about three miles from camp. King and Adams and Capt. Harrod dismounted, studied the trail by the light of burning brands, and were satisfied that the camp had been made by Indians, who had followed our travellers along on the trail, and now had turned suddenly. King had said it was not a large party ; and Capt. Harrod had only taken a moment to write what he had sent to Miss Eunice, before they were all in the saddle again and in pursuit.

So far, so good. And now must begin another desperate pull at that wait-wait-wait, in which one's heart's blood drops out most surely, if most slowly.

Old Ransom tended his fire more sedulously than ever, and made it larger and larger.

"She'll be all chilled when she comes in," said he again,

by way of explanation. But this was not his only reason. He bade Louis go down to the water's edge, and bring up to him wet bark, and bits of floating wood. He sent the man again and again on this errand ; and, as fast as his fire would well bear it, he thrust the wet sticks into the embers and under the logs. The column of steam, mingling with the smoke, rose high into the murky sky ; and the light from the blaze below gave to it ghastly forms, as it curled on one side or the other in occasional puffs of wind.

Tired and heart-sick, Eunice lay back on her couch, with her tent-door opened, and watched the wayward column. Even in her agony some sickly remembrance of Eastern genii came over her ; and she knew that the wretched wish passed her, that she might wake up to find that this was all a phantasm, a fairy tale, or a dream.

So another hour crawled by. Then came a sound of crackling twigs ; and poor Eunice sprang to her feet again, only to meet the face of the negro Harry, returning from his tour of duty. He had worked up the stream, as he had been directed ; he had tried every access to the water. He said he had screamed and called, and whooped, but heard nothing but owls. The man was as fearless of the night or of loneliness as any plantation slave used to the open sky. But he had thought, and rightly enough, that his duty for the night was at an end when he had made a tramp longer than was possible to so frail a creature as Inez ; and came back only to report failure. He was dragging with him a long bough for the fire ; and it was the grating of this upon the ground which gave warning of his approach.

Nothing for it, Eunice, but to lie down again, and watch that weird white column, and the black forms of the three men hovering about it. Not a footfall, not even the sighing of the trees : the night is so still ! It would be less weird and terrible if any thing would cry aloud. But all nature seems to be waiting too.

A halloo from Richards—who comes stalking in, cross, wet, unsuccessful, and uncommunicative.

"No—see nothin'. Knew I shouldn't see nothin'. All darned nonsense of the cappen's sending me thar. Told him so w'en I started, that she hadn't gone that way, and I knew it as well as he did. Fired my rifle? Yes, fired every charge I had. Didn't have but five, and fired 'em all. She didn't hear 'em; no, cos she wasn't there to hear 'em. Hain't you got a chaw of tobacco, Ransom? or give a fellow somethin' to drink. If you was as wet as I be, you'd think you wanted sunthin!"

Wait on, Eunice, wait on. Go back to your lair, and lie upon your couch. Do not listen to Richards's grumbling: try to keep down these horrible imaginings of struggles in water, of struggles with Indians, of faintness and death of cold. "Sufficient for the day is the evil thereof."

Yes: poor Eunice thinks all that out. "But is not this moment the very moment when my darling is dying, and I lying powerless here? Why did I not go with them?"

"Too-oo — too-oo " —

"Is that an owl?"

"Hanged if it's an owl. Hark!"

"Whoo — whoo — whoo — whoo," repeated rapidly twenty times; and then again, "Whoo — whoo — whoo — whoo," twenty times more, as rapidly.

Ransom seized his gun, fired it in the air, and ran toward the sound. Eunice followed him, gazing out into the night.

"Whoo — whoo — whoo — whoo," more slowly; and then Ransom's, "Hurrah! All right, ma'am. She's here," through the darkness.

And then, in one glad minute more, he had brought Inez in his arms; and her arms were around her aunt's neck, as if nothing on earth should ever part them more.

The White Hawk had brought her in.

And now the White Hawk dragged her to the fire, pulled off the moccasons that were on her feet, and began chafing her feet, ankles, and legs, while Ransom was trying to make her drink, and Eunice kneeling, oh ! so happy in her anxiety, at the poor girl's side.

CHAPTER XIII.

NIGHT AND DAY.

"The camp affords the hospitable rite,
   And pleased they sleep (the blessing of the night);
   But when Aurora, daughter of the dawn,
   With rosy lustre purpled o'er the lawn,
   Again they mount, the journey to renew." — *Odyssey.*

WITH the first instant of relief, old Ransom bade Harry saddle the bay mare, which Ransom had never before been known to trust to any human being but himself. With an eager intensity which we need not try to set down in words, he bade him push the mare to her best, till he had overtaken the captain, and told him the lost was found.

Meanwhile poor little Inez was only able to speak in little loving ejaculations to her aunt, to soothe her, and to cry with her, to be cried with, and to be soothed.

"Dear auntie, dear auntie, where did you think I was?" and, —

"My darling, my darling, how could I lose sight of you?"

And the White Hawk — happy, strong, cheerful, and loving — was the one "effective" of the three.

But Ransom had not chosen wrongly in his prevision for her return. "Knew ye'd be cold w'en ye come in, Miss Inez; knew ye warn't drowned, and warn't gone far." He had a buffalo-skin hanging warming, ready for her to lie upon. He brought a camp-stool for her head to rest upon, as she looked into the embers. And when Eunice was satisfied at last that no hair of her darling's head was hurt; when she saw her fairly sipping and enjoying Ransom's jorum of claret; when at last he brought in triumph soup which he had in waiting somewhere, and the girl owned she was hungry, — why, then Eunice as she lay at her side, and fed her and fondled her, was perhaps the happiest creature, at that moment, in the world.

And when words came at last, and rational questions and answers, Inez could tell but little which the reader does not already know; nor could they then learn much more from White Hawk, with language so limited as was theirs.

"Panther? yes, horrid brute! I have seemed to see him all night since. When it was darkest, I wondered if I did not see the yellow of those dreadful eyes.

"Apaches? No, I saw no Indians, nor thought of them; only my darling 'Ma-ry' here;" and she turned to fondle the proud girl, who knew that she was to be fondled. "O Ma-ry, my sweetheart, how I wish you knew what I am saying! Why, Eunice, when I thought it was my last prayer, when I asked the good God to comfort you and dear papa," — here her voice choked, — "I could not help praying for dear 'Ma-ry.' I could not help thinking of her poor mother, and the agony in which she carried this child along. And then, why, Eunice, it was not long after, that all of a sudden I was lying in her arms, and she was cooing to me and rubbing me; and I thought for a moment I was in bed at home, and it was you; and then I remembered again. And, dear auntie, what a blessing it was to know I was not alone!"

In truth, the brave girl had held resolute to her purpose. She would save her voice till, at the end of every fifty sentry turns, she would stop and give her war-whoop and other alarm-cry. Then she would keep herself awake by walking, walking, walking, though she were almost dead, till she had made fifty turns more; and then she would stop and scream again. How often she had done this, she did not know: Eunice could guess better than she. Nor did she know how it ended. She must have stumbled and fallen. She knew she walked at last very clumsily and heavily: all else she knew was, as she said, that she came to herself lying on the ground, while White Hawk was rubbing her hands, and then her feet, and that White Hawk would say little tender things to her, — would say, " Ma-ry," and would stop in her rubbing to kiss her ; then, that White Hawk pulled off those horrid wet stockings and moccasons which she had been tramping in, and took from her own bosom a pair dry and strong, — " oh, how good it felt, auntie ! " — and then, that White Hawk made her rest on her shoulder, and walk with her a little, till she thought she was tired, and then sat down with her, and would rub her, and talk to her again.

" How in the world did she know the way ? "

" Heaven knows ! She would stop and listen : she would put her ear to the ground, and listen. At last she made me sit at the foot of a tree, while she climbed like a squirrel, auntie, to the very top ; and then she came down, and she pointed, and after she pointed she worked always this way. She made this sign, auntie ; and this must be the sign for ' fire.' "

The girl brought her hands near her breast, half shut, till they touched each other, and then moved them quickly outward. Both of them turned to White Hawk, who was listening carefully ; and they pointed to the embers, as Inez renewed the sign. White Hawk nodded and smiled, but repeated it, extending her fingers, and separating her hands, as if in parody of the waving of flame. This part of the gesture poor Inez had not seen in the darkness.

From the moment White Hawk had seen Ransom's white and rosy column of smoke, it had been a mere question of time. By every loving art, she had made the way easy for her charge. She would have lifted her, had Inez permitted. " But, auntie, I could have walked miles. I was strong as a lion then."

Lion or lamb, after she was roasted as a jubilee ox might have been, she said, her two nurses dragged her to her tent and to bed.

"It is too bad, auntie!   I ought to thank dear Capt. Harrod, and all of them.   Such a goose as to turn night into day, and send them riding over the world!"

All the same they undressed her, and put her to bed; and such is youth in its omnipotence, whether to act, to suffer, or to sleep, that in five minutes the dear child was unconscious of cold, of darkness, or of terror.

And Eunice did her best to resist the reaction which crept over her, oh, so sweetly! after her hours of terror.   But she would start again and again, as she lay upon her couch.   One instant she said to herself, —

"Oh, yes, I am quite awake! I never was more wakeful. But what has happened to them?   Will they never be here?" And the next instant she would be bowing to the First Consul, as Mr. Perry presented her as his sister, and renewed his old acquaintance with Mme. Josephine, once Beauharnais. Then she would start up from her couch, and walk out to the fire, and Ransom would advise her to go back to her tent.   At last, however, just when he, good fellow! would have had it (for his preparation of creature comforts for the scouting party was made on a larger scale, if on a coarser, than those for Miss Inez), the welcome tramp of rapid hoofs was heard; and in five minutes more Harrod swung himself from the saddle by the watch-fire, and was eagerly asking her for news.

For himself, he had but little to tell.   Since all was well at home, it would wait till breakfast.

"What have you got for us now, Ransom? a little whiskey? Yes, that's enough; that's enough.   The others are just behind."

Then, turning to Eunice, —

"Yes, Miss Perry.   All is well that ends well.   I have said that to myself and aloud for this hour's gallop. — Ransom! Ransom! don't let those fools take her to water. Make Louis rub her dry. — Yes, Miss Perry, we found the rascals' fire.   God forgive me for calling them rascals! They are saints in white, for all I know.   But really, — this whiskey does go to the right place!—but really, when you have been trying to ride down a crew of pirates for a couple of hours, it is hard to turn round and believe they were honest men.

"Yes, we found their fire; and, if I ever thanked God, it was then, Miss Perry. Though why, if they were after the girls, why they should have built a fire just there by that little wet prairie, I could not tell myself. Still there was the fire. Up till that moment, Miss Eunice,—up till that moment,—I believed she was stark and dead under the water of the bayou. I may as well tell you so now," and he choked as he said it; and she pressed his hand, as if she would say she had been as sure of this as he.

"Yes, I thought that the painter there, or the Indians, or both together, had driven her out on that infernal cotton-wood log—I beg your pardon, Miss Eunice: I am sure the log has done me no harm; but I thought we were never to see her dear face again." And he stopped, and wiped the tears from his eyes with the back of his hand.

"So I thanked God when I saw their fire, because that confirmed what all the rest of them said. And we got off our horses, and we could see the trail was warm: they went off in a hurry. Why they did not put their fire out, I did not know, more than why they lighted it.

"If we could have made a stern chase, as Ransom would say, we would have overhauled them soon; but this I did not dare. King knew from what he saw this morning how to take us round the edge of that wet prairie,—by a trail they had followed by mistake then; and he said we could head them as they travelled, at the sloo where we lunched, if you remember. For we could see that they had one lame mule at least. They seemed to have but few beasts any way; and of course none of them was a match for Bet there, or for that Crow, the bay that King rides. So I took him with me, told the others to keep the main trail slowly; and sure enough, in an hour, more or less, King had me just where you and Miss Inez lay under that red-oak to-day.

"And there we waited and waited; not long, not long. We could hear them grunting and paddling along, and beating the mule, till I stepped out, and struck an old fellow over the shoulder, and cocked my pistol. They do not know much, but they knew what that meant. They all stopped meek as mice, for they thought I was an army.

"But, good heavens! there were but four of them; three old men and a squaw, and these four miserable brutes. It was no war-party, that was clear. I could have talked to them if it were daylight; but now it was as much as ever I could see them, or they me. King understood none of their gibberish, nor I. I hoped perhaps Adams might; meanwhile I tied the old fellow hand and foot: he did not resist, none of them resisted. In a minute the others came up; and then we struck a light, and, after some trouble, made a fire.

"Then, when we could see, I began to talk to them in gestures; and now I can afford to laugh at it: then I was too anxious and too mad.

"I went at the old man. You should have seen me. He said he could not answer because his hands were tied, which was reasonable. So I untied him, but told him I would blow his brains out if he tried to run away. At least, I think he knew I would.

"I asked him where the girls were.

"He said we had them with us.

"I told him he lied.

"He said I did.

"I asked him again where they were, and threatened him with the pistol.

"He said he knew nothing of the girl with the long feather, since she sat there with her back to the oak-tree, and mended the lacing of her shoe.

"Only think, Miss Eunice, how the dogs watch us!

"As for White Hawk, he said he sold her to Father Andrés for the lame mule he had been riding, and that he supposed Father Andrés sold her to me; that he had not seen her since I mounted you ladies, and White Hawk went on in advance. He said they staid and picked up what dinner the men had left, and ate it, as they had every day.

"I asked him why he left his fire. He said they were frightened. They knew we were in the saddle, and they were afraid, because they had stolen the blacksmith's hammer and the ham-bones: so they mounted and fled.

"Well, you know, I thought this was an Indian's lie, — a lie all full of truth. I told him so. I took him, and tied him to a tree, and I tied the other man and the big boy. The woman I did not tie: Miss Eunice, applaud me for that. I believe you have a tender heart to the redskins; and I determined to wait till morning. But in half an hour I heard the rattle of the mare's heels, and up came Harry to say that all was well."

"And all's well that ends well."

"Yes, Ransom: no matter what it is. I did not know I should ever feel hungry again.

"But, dear Miss Perry, how thoughtless I am! For the love of Heaven, pray go into your tent, and go to sleep. How can we be grateful enough that she is safe?"

Then he called her back.

"Stop one moment, Miss Perry: we are very near each other now. What may happen before morning, none of us know. I must say to you, therefore, now, what but for this I suppose I should not have dared to say to you, — that she is dearer to me than my life. If we had not found her, oh, Miss Perry, I should have died! I would have tried to do my duty by you, indeed; but my heart would have been broken.

"Yes. I knew how eager you were, and how wretched. Pray understand that my wretchedness and my loss would have been the same as yours. Good-night! God bless her and you!"

A revelation so abrupt startled Eunice, if it did not wholly surprise her. But she was too completely exhausted by her excitements of every kind even to try to think, or to try to answer. She did not so much as speak, as he turned away, and only bade him good-by by her kindly look and smile.

It was late when they met at breakfast. Harrod would gladly have permitted a day's halt after the fatigues of the night, but not here. They must make a part of the day's march ; and already all of the train which could be prepared was ready for a start. Inez appeared even later than the others ; but she was ready dressed for travelling. The White Hawk welcomed her as fondly and proudly as if she were her mother, and had gained some right of property in her. Eunice was so fond and so happy, and Harrod said frankly that he did not dare to tell her how happy the good news made him when it came to him.

"Woe's me," said poor Inez, hardly able to keep from crying. "Woe's me, that, because I was a fool, brave men have had tô ride, and fair women to watch ! You need none of you be afraid that I shall ever stray two inches from home again."

But, as she ate, Harrod drew from her, bit by bit, her own account of her wanderings.

"And to think," said he, "that this girl here knows how to follow a trail better than I do, and finds one that I have lost ! I believe the flowers rise under your tread, Miss Inez ; for on the soft ground yonder by the lick we could not find your foot-tread. Could it have been hers that frightened me so ? "

Then he told her how they were sure they caught the traces of an Indian boy, and thought he had been stepping with his feet turned outward in her footprints.

"And pray what did you think I wore, captain ? I had taken off my shoes, and I was walking in the moccasons the Senora Trévino gave me at Nacogdoches."

"And I did not know your footfall when I saw it. I will never call myself a woodsman again ! "

CHAPTER XIV.

A PACKET OF LETTERS.

" I warrant he hath a thousand of these letters."
Merry Wives of Windsor.

BUT it is time that the reader should welcome the party of travellers, no longer enthusiastic about camp-life, to the hospitalities — wholly unlike any thing Inez had ever seen before — of San Antonio de Bexar.

The welcome of her dear aunt, of Major Barelo, — who held the rank of *alfarer*, which in these pages will be translated " major," — indeed, one may say, of all the gentlemen and ladies of the garrison, had been most cordial. The energy of the march made it a matter of nine days' wonder; and the young Spanish gentlemen thanked all gods and goddesses for the courage which had brought, by an adventure so bold, such charming additions to the circle of their society. Donna Maria Dolores was not disappointed in her niece; nor was she nearly so much terrified by this wild American sister-in-law as she had expected; and Inez found her aunt, ah! ten times more lovely than she had dared to suppose.

But the impressions of both ladies will be best given by the transcript of three of their letters, — which have escaped the paper-mills of three-quarters of a century, — written about a week after their arrival. True, these letters were written with a painful uncertainty lest they were to be inspected by some Spanish official. They were severely guarded, therefore, in any thing which might convict Nolan or Harrod, or their humbler adherents. For the rest, they describe the position of the ladies sufficiently.

INEZ PERRY TO HER FATHER.

IN MY OWN ROOM, SAN ANTONIO DE BEXAR,
Nov. 26, 1800.

DEAR, DEAR PAPA, — Can you believe it ? We are really here. See, I write you in my own room, which dear Aunt Dolores has arranged for me just as kindly as can be. I would not for the world tell her how funny it all is to me ; for she has done every thing to make it French or American, or to please what are supposed to be my whims. But, if you saw it, you would laugh so, papa ! and so would Roland, if he is any thing like you.

I shall write Roland a letter, and it will go in the same cover with this. But he must not cry, as you used to say to me, if I write to you first of all.

I have kept my journal very faithfully, as I said I would ; and some day you shall see it. But not now, dear papa ; for the general — Herrara, you know— is very kind to let this go at all, and it must be the smallest letter that I know how to make, and Roland's too.

I think you were wholly right about the journey, dear papa ; and if we had it to do over again you would think that this was the way to do it, if you knew all that we have seen and all that we have enjoyed, and even if you knew all the inconveniences. It has been just as you said, that I have learned ever so many things which I should never have learned in any other way, and seen ever so much that I should never have seen in any other way. Dear papa, if you will keep it secret, and not tell Roland, — for I am dreadfully afraid of Roland, you know, — I will tell you that I do not think that I am near so much of a goose as I was when I left home. I hope you would say that your little girl is rather more of a woman. And I am as well, papa, as I can be. Eunice says I have gained flesh. We cannot find out, though we were all weighed yesterday in the great scales in the warehouse. But they weigh with *fanegas* and all sorts of things ; and nobody seems to know what they mean in good honest livres. I know I am stouter, because of the dresses, you know. There, pray do not read that to Roland.

Aunt Eunice is writing, and she will tell you all the business, — the important business of the journey. She will explain why we changed the plans, and how it all happened. I know you will be very sorry that we had not Capt. P. all the way. I am sure I was. He was just as nice as ever, and as good as gold to me. If Roland is to be a soldier, I hope he will be just such a soldier. But then, I hope Roland is not to be a soldier. I hope he is to come home to me some day. Aunt Eunice will tell you whom we had to escort us instead of Capt. P. When you come home you will know how to thank him for his care of us. I only wish I knew when we are to see him or the captain again. Papa, if you or Roland had been with us, I do not think there was one thing you could have thought of which he did not think of and do, so bravely and so pleasantly and so tenderly. I knew he had sisters, and he said he had. I can always tell. I only hope they know that it is not every girl has such brothers. I have ; but there are not many girls that do. Why, papa, the night I was lost, he — there ! I did not mean to tell you one word of my being lost, but it slipped out from the pen. That night he was in the saddle half the night, hunting for me. Perhaps you say that was of course. And he tied up some Indians that he thought knew about me. Perhaps that was of course too. But what was not of course was this : that from that moment to this moment, he never said I was a fool, as I was. He never said if I had done this or that, it would have been better. He was perfectly lovely and gentlemanly about it all, always : papa, he was just like you. I wish I knew when we should see him again. He left yesterday, with only three men, to join the captain. I wish we could see him soon. When we are all at home again, in dear, dear Orleans, I shall coax you to let me ask his sister to spend the winter with us. There are two of them : one is named Marion, — really after the Swamp-Fox, papa, — and the other is named Jane. Jane is the oldest. Is not Marion a pretty name ?

But, papa, though there is only this scrap left, I want to tell you earnestly how much I want to take Ma-ry with us when you come home ; how much I love her, and how necessary it is that she shall not stay here. Aunt Eunice says she will explain it all, and who Ma-ry is, and why I write her name so. She will tell you why it is so necessary as I say. But, dear papa, only I can tell you how much, how very much, I want her. You see, I have a sister now, and I do not want to lose her. And, papa, this is not the coaxing of a little girl : this is the real earnest wish of your own Inez, now she has seen things as a woman sees them. Do not laugh at that, dear papa ; but think of it carefully when you have read dear auntie's letter, and think how you can manage to let me have Ma-ry till she finds her own home. Oh, dear ! what will happen to me when she finds it ?

Oh papa ! why is not this sheet bigger ? It was the biggest they had. Ever so much love to Roland, and all to you.

From your own little   INEZ.

Silas Perry read this letter aloud to his soldier-son, as they sat together in their comfortable lodgings in Passy. And then Roland said, " Now let me try and see how much the little witch explains to me of these mysteries. It is just as she says: she is afraid of me without wanting to be, and we shall find the words are longer, though I am afraid the letter will be shorter. We will fix all that up when I have been a week on the plantation."

INEZ PERRY TO ROLAND PERRY.

SAN ANTONIO DE BEXAR, Nov. 27, 1800.

MY DEAR BROTHER, — You have not the slightest idea what sort of a place a Spanish city is, though you have been the subject of our gracious and Catholic king ten years longer than I have. There are many beautiful situations here, and some of the public edifices are as fine any we have in Orleans ; but it is the strangest place I ever saw.

" That is curious," said Roland, stopping to keep his cigar alive, " as she never saw any other place but Orleans. You see that I have the dignified letter, as I said. I shall be jealous of you if it keeps on so."

Then he continued his reading : —

We have had a beautiful journey through a very interesting country. I am sure you would have enjoyed it ; and as we spent three days at Nacogdoches, which is a garrison town, perhaps it would have been instructive in your profession. But perhaps a French military student does not think much of Spanish officers. All I can say is, we saw some very nice, gentlemanly men there, who danced very well ; and we saw those horrid dances, the Fandango and Bolero.

All the escorts say that we had a very fortunate journey across the wood-country and the prairies. I am told here that I have borne the fatigue very well. There was not a great deal of fatigue, though sometimes I was very tired. One night there was a Norther, — so Mons. Philippe called it.

" Does she mean Nolan, by ' Mons. Philippe ? ' " said Roland, stopping himself again. " I thought she said Nolan was not with them. There's a blot here, where she wrote something else at first. Can the man have two names ? "

So Mons. Philippe calls it, but the people here call it *Caribinera.* What it is is a terrible tempest from the north, which tears every thing to pieces, and is terribly cold. We were so cold that we needed all our wraps to make us comfortable, and Ransom had to build up the fire again.

I am sure I shall enjoy my visit here. My aunt and Major Barelo are as kind as possible; and all the ladies in the garrison have been very thoughtful and attentive. But how glad I shall be to come home again, and meet you and papa!

Dear Roland, do not go into the army.

"What is this? Something more scratched out?" But he held it to the light.

There is fighting enough to be done here.

"That is what Miss Een thinks, is it?"

"But she did not dare trust that to the post-office in Mexico. That is a prudent girl."

"Is that all?" said his father.

"Yes, all but this:" —

Dear Roland, I do want to see you, and I love you always.
Truly yours,

INEZ.

"I call that a nice letter, sir; and, on the whole, I will not change with you. Of course she has changed a hundred times as much as I have, and I cannot make out that she is any thing but a baby. Dear Aunt Eunice will fill all blanks."

EUNICE PERRY TO SILAS PERRY.

SAN ANTONIO DE BEXAR, Nov. 26, 1800.

MY DEAR BROTHER, — We are safe here, and have a most cordial welcome. Having no chance to write by Orleans, I send this, through Gen. Herrara's kindness, by the City of Mexico, whence there is a despatch-bag to some port in Europe.

"Roland, she thinks the letters were to be examined on their way, and I believe this has been."

"I am certain mine has been, sir. Here is the mark which shows what was copied from mine in some Mexican office, — this that poor little Een tried to scratch out, about fighting."

"Much good may it do them!" said his father, and continued reading his sister's letter aloud : —

Inez has borne her journey famously. Indeed, when we were well started, and were once used to the saddle, it was tedious, but nothing more. She lost herself one night, and frightened me horribly ; but no harm came of it. As for Indians, we saw but few. From the first post the Spanish officers furnished us escorts of troops on their return to this garrison. Perhaps that frightened away the Indians, as it certainly did *los Americaños.*

"'As it certainly did *los Americaños.*' Roland, Phil Nolan found that his room was better than his company. He would never have left them if it were not better for them that he should leave. Eunice knew these letters were to be opened, and she has written for more eyes than mine."

When you see Mons. Philippe, you must express what I have tried to tell, — how much we value his constant and kind attention.

"Who the dickens is Mons. Philippe ? That I shall learn when the 'Hamilton' comes in."

We have brought with us a charming girl, who makes a dear companion for Inez, being, I suppose, about her age. She is an American girl, whom a Spanish priest found among the Apaches, and bought of them. From the first moment the two girls fancied each other, though at first neither could understand the other's language. But now Mary has learned a great deal of English and a little Spanish, and dear little Inez is quite glib in Apache ! The girl's name is Mary ; she calls it Ma-ry, as if it were two words ; it is the only word she remembers which her mother taught her.

Inez wants to take her home ; and, unless I hear from you that you object, I shall agree to this, unless some other arrangement is made for sending her East. Donna Dolores agrees : the garrison is not a very good place for her.

To tell you the truth, the regular lessons which Inez gives her, and the reading which the dear girl undertakes in books you bade her read, keeps them out of mischief for two or three hours every day. The ladies here do so little, and have so little to do in this dull Moor-like life, that this seems strange to them. But I encourage them both in it. They ride a good deal under dear old Ransom's escort ; and sometimes he drives them out in one of these solemn old carriages which I believe were inherited direct from Cortez.

This is an interesting place, such as I suppose you have often seen, but as different from a French city, or from our French city, — do not let Roland laugh at me, — as that is from Squam Bay. Oh, do not think that we will be homesick here. Donna Dolores is all that you described her to be, and as happy in her new plaything as she hoped to be, and deserved to be. She persuades herself that she sees Inez's mother's face in hers, and is sometimes startled by a tone of her voice. She delights the dear child, as you may suppose. There are several ladies here who are accomplished and agreeable. I do not know but you have heard the major speak of the families of Garcia, of Gonzales, and Tréviño. Col. Tréviño is now at Nacogdoches : he was very civil to us.

We have found two governors here, — fortunately for us, for I believe neither of them strictly belongs here. Gen. Herrara is, as you know, a remarkable man : we are great friends. His wife is an-English lady whom he married at Cadiz, and it is a great pleasure to me to see so much of her. He was in Philadelphia when Gen. Washington was president, and spoke to me at once of him. Of course we have been firm friends ever since that. He is governor, not of this province, but of New Leon, our next neighbor, and is very much beloved there. I hardly know why he resides so much here. Gov. Cordero, whose real seat of government is Monte Clovez, is here a great deal, — for military reasons, I suppose. He is a bachelor : the more is the pity. He is Spanish by birth, and every inch a soldier. Gov. Elquezebal you will remember.

Young Walker is here from the military school. You remember his mother. He came at once to see me.

But my paper is at an end, and I must let my pen run no longer. Give much love to my dear Roland. This letter is his as much as yours.

Always your own loving sister,

EUNICE PERRY.

"Gov. Cordero is there for military reasons, Roland, and Gen. Herrara is there also. What military reasons but that President John Adams has stirred up the magnificoes a little? But if I have sent our doves into a hawk's nest, Roland, I do not know how we are to get them out again."

"It is one comfort," he added, after a pause, "that there will be a good strip of land and water between Gen. Herrara and Gen. Wilkinson."

And the father and son resumed their cigars, and sat in silence.

What Silas Perry meant by "a good thick strip," will appear from his own letter to Eunice, which shall be printed in the next chapter. He had written it as soon as possible after his arrival in Paris. It had crossed her letter on the ocean. Written under cover to his own house in Orleans, and sent by his own vessel, it spoke without hesitation on the topics, all-important, of which he wrote.

CHAPTER XV.

COURTS AND CAMPS.

Well loved that splendid monarch aye
    The banquet and the song,
The merry dance, traced fast and light,
The maskers quaint, the pageant bright,
    The revel loud and long.
Here to the harp did minstrels sing;
There others touched a softer string;
While some, in close recess apart,
Courted the ladies of their heart,
    Nor courted them in vain.—*Marmion.*

OUR little history draws again upon these yellow files of ancient letters.

SILAS PERRY TO EUNICE PERRY.

PASSY, near PARIS, Nov. 16, 1800.

MY DEAR SISTER,—We have had a wonderful run. Look at the date, and wonder, when you know that I have been here a week. I have good news for you in every way. First, that our dear boy is well,—strong, manly, gentlemanly,—and not unwilling to come home. He thought I should not know him in his cadet uniform, as he stood waiting for me in the court-yard where the *post-chaise* brought me. But, Lord! I should have known him in a million. Yet he is stronger, stouter, has the *air militaire* wonderfully; and they do not wear their hair as our officers do. This is my first great news. The second you would read in the gazettes, if you were not sure to read this first. It is, that France and America are firm friends again: no more captures at sea, no more mock war. This First Consul knows what he is about. He told his brother Joseph what to do, and he did it. On the 30th of September the treaty was signed: the right of search is all settled, and commerce is to be free on both sides. Had I known this on the 30th of September, I might not have come. For all that, I am glad I am here.

Third bit of news; and this is "secret of secrets," as our dear mother would have said. You may tell Inez; but swear her to secrecy. I have only told Turner and Pollock. We are no longer Spanish subjects! We are French citizens, — citizens and citizenesses of the indivisible French Republic. Perhaps I do not translate *citoyennes* right; but that is what you and Inez are. Is not that news?

I only knew this last night. There are not ten men in Paris who know it. But, by a secret article in a treaty made in Spain last month, this imbecile King of Spain has given all Louisiana back to France. There! does not that make your hair stand on end?

Of course, dear Eunice, if there should be any breath of war between the two countries, your visit must end at once. Heaven knows when you will hear from me; but act promptly. Do not be caught among those Mexicans when the Dons are fighting the Monsieurs. But I think there will be no war before we are well home. When war comes I am glad we are on the side that always wins.

Roland will tell you in his letter, in what scene of vanity I picked up my information. If I can I shall add more; but I must now sign myself,

Your affectionate brother,

SILAS PERRY.

ROLAND PERRY TO INEZ PERRY.

PASSY, near PARIS, Nov. 16, 1800.

DEAR LITTLE SISTER, — Father has left me his letter to read and seal, and has bidden me give you all the particulars of his triumphs at court. I tell him that nobody has made such an impression as he, since Ben Franklin. It has all been very droll; and, when I see you, I can make you understand it better than I can write it. To be brief, papa is what they call here "*un grand succès.*"

He says, and you say, that I have not written enough about how I spend my time. I can see that he is surprised at knowing the chances I have for good society. But it has all come about simply enough. When I came here, M. Beauharnais, as you know, welcomed me as cordially as a man could; and, when there was an off-day at school, they made me at home there. Just as soon as Eugène entered at the Polytechnic — well, I knew the ways a little better than he did. As dear old Ransom used to say, "I had the hang of the schoolhouse." Any way, he took to me, and I was always glad to help the boy. You see, they called him an American, because of his father and mother : so, as the senior American in *l'École*, I had to thrash one or two fellows who were hard upon him. Now that he is one of the young heroes of Egypt, I have reason to be proud of my *protégé*. I only wish I had gone with them. Well, if I have not told you of every call I have made there, — I mean at his mother's, — it is because it has been quite a matter of course in my life. When Eugène and the general were both away, there were many reasons why I should be glad to be of service to her; and she has never forgotten them.

Well, when papa came, I told him that his first visit must be to Mme. Buonaparte at Malmaison; and he must thank her, if he meant to thank any one, for my happy life here. You know how papa would act. He said he was not going to pay court to First Consuls, and put on court dresses. Some fool had told him great lies about the state at Malmaison. I told him, if I did not know how to take my own father to see a friend of mine, I did not know any thing. He was very funny. He asked if he need not be powdered. I told him, No. I told him to put on his best coat, and go as he would go to a wedding at Squam Bay.

Inez, he was very handsome. He was perfectly dressed, — you know he would be, — and his hair, which is the least bit more gray than I remember it, was very *distingué* in the midst of all those heads of white powder. We drove out to Malmaison, and I can tell you we had a lovely time. I was as proud as I could be. There is not much fuss there, ever, about getting in; and with me, — well, they all know me, you know, — and the old ones have, since I was a boy. By good luck, Madame was alone (you know we say *Madame* now, without having our heads cut off). She was alone, and I presented papa. She was so pleased! Inez, I cannot tell you how pleased she was. You see, she does not often see people of sense, who have any knowledge of the islands, or of her father and mother, or her husband's friends. Then it was clear enough, in two minutes, that papa must have been of real service to Major Beauharnais and to her, which he had never told me of. He lent her money, perhaps, when she was poor, — or something. My dear Inez, she treated papa with a sort of welcome I have never seen her give to any human being.

Well, right in the midst of this, who should come in but the Gen. Buonaparte himself, the First Consul, boots muddy, and face all alive! He had ridden out from the Thuilleries. He looked a little amazed, — I thought a little mad. But Mme. Josephine has tact enough. "*Mon ami*," she said to him, "here is an American, my oldest and best friend. I present to you Mons. Perry, — the best friend of the Vicomte, and but for whom I should never have been here. Mons. Perry, you had the right to be the godfather of Eugène."

Dear papa bowed, and gave the First Consul his hand, and said he hoped he was well. Was not that magnificent? Oh, Inez, it was ravishing to see him! The consul was a little amazed, I think; but he is a man of immense penetration and immense sense. So is papa. The general asked him at once about Martinique and all the islands, and Toussaint and St. Domingo, and every thing. Well, in two minutes, you know, papa told him more than all their old reports and despatches would tell him in a month, — more, indeed, than they knew.

Well, the general was delighted. He took papa over to a sofa, and there they sat and sat; and, Inez, there they sat and sat; and they talked *for two hours.* What do you think of that? People kept coming in; and there was poor I talking to Madame, and to half the finest women in France; and everybody was looking into the corner, and wondering who "*l'Americain magnifique*" was, whom the consul had got hold of. Madame sent them some coffee. But nobody dared to interrupt; and at last Gen. Buonaparte rose and laughed, and said, "Madame will never forgive me for my boots;" but he made papa promise to come again last night. Now, last night, you know, was one of the regular court receptions, — one of the Malmaison ones, I mean. You know the state receptions are at the Thuilleries. Of this I must take another sheet to tell you.

When Inez read this letter, she said to her aunt, —

"Do you know what Malmaison is? It is not a very nice name."

"It must be their country-house: read on, and perhaps you will see."

I have shown papa what I have written. He laughs at my account of him, and says it is all trash. But it is all gospel true, and shall stand. He also says that you will not know what Malmaison is. Malmaison is an elegant place, about ten miles from Paris, which Mme. Buonaparte bought, — oh! two years or more ago. She carries with her her old island tastes, and is very fond of flowers; and at this house with the bad name she has made exquisite gardens. She really does a good deal of gardening herself, — that is, such gardening as you women do. I have gone round with her for an hour together, carrying strings and a watering-pot, helping Mlle. Hortense, — who, you know, is just your age, — to help her mother.

Well, so much for Malmaison.

Papa had really had what he calls a "very good time" talking with the First Consul. He says he is the most sensible man he has seen since he bade Mr. Pollock good-by. I am afraid I did not take much pains to tell him that the grand reception of last night was to be a very different thing from that informal visit; for, if I had told him, he never would have gone. But when he was once there, why, he could not turn back, you know.

And it was very brilliant. Indeed, since the battle of Marengo, nothing can be too brilliant for everybody's expectations; and, although Malmaison is nothing to the Thuilleries, yet a *fête* there is very charming. When

papa saw lackeys standing on the steps, and found that our carriage
had to wait its turn, and that our names were to be called from sentry
to sentry, he would gladly have turned and fled. But, like a devoted son,
I explained to him that this would be cowardly. I reminded him that he
had promised Gen. Buonaparte to come, and that his word was as good
as his bond. Before he knew it, a chamberlain had us in hand; and we
passed along the brilliant line to be presented in our turn.

Inez, dear, I confess to you that I had an elegant little queue, and a
soupçon of powder upon my hair. So had most of the gentlemen around
me. But. Gen. Buonaparte hates powder, they say, when it is not gunpowder; and he and dear papa had no flake of it on the locks, which
they wore as nature made them. They were the handsomest men in that
room, — I, who write, not excepted. Now, my dear sister, never tell me
that I am vain again.

Well, when our turn came, Mme. Buonaparte gave papa her hand,
which is very unusual, and fairly detained him every time he offered to
move on. This left me, who came next, to talk to Mlle. Hortense, who
was *charmante.* She never looked so well. I did not care how long the
general and madame held papa. I asked Hortense about the last game
of Prison Bars, which is all the rage at Malmaison. I engaged her for
the third dance. I promised her some Cherokee roses, and I must write
to Turner about them. She asked why papa did not bring you, and I
said you were to enter a Spanish convent. She guessed by my eye that
this was nonsense, and then we had a deal of fun about it. The chamberlain was fuming and swearing inwardly; but the general and Mme.
Buonaparte would not let papa go on. Papa was splendid! You would
have thought he had been at court all his life. At last he tore himself
away. I bowed to Madame, who smiled. I bowed to the First Consul,
and he said, "*Ah, monsieur, Eugène est au désespoir de vous voir.*" I
smiled and bowed again. And so papa and I were free.

But there were ever so many people looking on, and I was so proud to
present to him this and that of my friends! I brought Lagrange to him,
who taught us our mathematics when I was in the Polytechnic. Lagrange
brought up La Place, who is another of our great men. I presented him
to Mme. Berthollet, and to Mme. Campan, who is a favorite here, and to
Mme. Morier; and they all asked him such funny questions! You know
they all think that we live close by Niagara, and breakfasted every day
with Gen. Washington, and that all of us who were old enough fought in
the battle of Bunker Hill, while of course we were all playmates with
Mme. Buonaparte.

At last the dancing came. The rooms are not very large, but large
enough; and the music, — O Inez dear! it was *ravissante.* The First
Consul took out a hideous creature: I forget her name; but she was

a returned *émigrée*, of a great royalist family, who had buried her prejudices, or pretended to. Gen. Junot took out Madame: that was a couple worth seeing. I danced with Mlle. Poitevin, a lovely girl; but I must tell of her another time. O Inez! the First Consul dances — well — horridly! He hates to dance. He called for that stupid old "Monaco," as he always does, because he cannot make so many mistakes in it. Well, he only danced this first time; and I had charming dances with Mlle. Julie Ramey, and then with the lovely Hortense. Was not I the envied of the evening then!

It was then that, looking round to see how papa fared, Mlle. Hortense caught my eye, and said so roguishly, "*Ah, Monsieur, que vous épouvante!* we will take care of your papa. See, the consul himself has charge of him." True enough, the consul had found him, and led him across to a quiet place by the conservatory door; and, Inez, they talked the whole evening again.

And it was in this talk, — when papa had been explaining to him what a sin and shame it was that so fine a country as Louisiana should have been given over to that beast of a Charles Fourth, and that miserable Godoy: only I suppose he put it rather better, — that the consul smiled, tapped his snuff-box, gave papa snuff, and said, "Mons. Perry, you Americans can keep secrets. You may count yourselves republicans from today." Papa did not know what he meant, and said so plumply.

Then he told papa that he had received an express from Madrid that very morning. Inez, an article is signed by which Louisiana is given back to France. Think of that! The Orleans girls may dance French dances and sing French songs as much as they please; and old Casa Calvo may go hang himself.

Only, Inez, you must not tell any one: it is a secret article, and the First Consul said that no public announcement of any sort was to be made.

Now, after that, who says it is not profitable to go to court? I am sure papa will never say so again. But the paper is all out, and the oil is all out in my new argand. Salute dear Aunt Eunice with my heart's love; and believe me, *ma chère sœur*,

Votre frère tres devoué,

ROLAND PERRY.

CHAPTER XVI.

NEWS? WHAT NEWS?

"News! great news! in the 'London Gazette!'
But what the news is, I will not tell you yet;
For, if by misfortune my news I should tell,
Why, never a 'London Gazette' should I sell."

Cries of London.

THESE letters from Paris did not, of course, reach Eunice
and Inez till the short winter — if winter it may be called —
of Texas was over ; and February found them enjoying the
wonders and luxuries of that early spring.

The surprising news with which both letters ended gave
them enough food for talk when they were alone ; and the
White Hawk, almost their constant companion, saw that
some subject of unusual seriousness had come in, — a subject
too, which, with her scanty notions of European politics, she
could hardly be expected to understand. In her pretty
broken English she would challenge them to tell her what
they read, and what they said.

"Te-reaty — what is te-reaty, my sister?　F-erance — what
is F-erance, my auntie ?"

But to make the girl understand how the signing of a piece
of parchment, by an imbecile liar in a Spanish palace, should
affect the status, the happiness, or the social life of the two
people dearest to her in the world, was simply impossible.

The ladies were both glad to receive such news.　Everybody in Orleans would be glad, excepting the little coterie of
the governor's court.　Everybody in America would be glad.

Better that Louisiana should be in the hands of a strong power than a weak one.   But still their secret gave the ladies anxiety.   If, — as Silas Perry had suggested, — if the dice-box should throw war between Spain and France, here they were in San Antonio at the beginning only of a visit which was meant to last a year.   And, worse, if the dice-box should throw war between France and England, everybody knew that an English squadron would pounce on Orleans, and their country would be changed again.

"I told Capt. Nolan one day," said Inez, in mock grief, which concealed much real feeling, "that I was a girl without a country.   I seem to be likely to be a girl of three countries, if not of four."

Three months of garrison life, with such contrivances as the ladies around them had devised to while away time, had given to all three of the new-comers a set of habits quite different from those of the home at Orleans.   The presence of Cordero and of Herrara there, both remarkable men, seemed almost of course.   Eunice Perry was right in saying that neither of them belonged there.   But they both liked the residence, and, still more, they liked each other.   This was fortunate for our friends ; for it proved that in Mme. Herrara, who was herself an English lady by birth, they found a charming friend.   The ladies named in Miss Perry's letter to her brother were all women of brilliancy or of culture, such as would have been prizes in any society.   The little *tertulias* of the winter became, therefore, parties of much more spirit than any Eunice had known, even in the larger and more brilliant social circle of Orleans ; and in the long hours of the morning, when the gentlemen were pretending to drill recruits, or to lay out lines for imaginary buildings, or otherwise to develop the town which the governors wanted to make here, the ladies made pleasant and regular occasions for meeting, when a new poem by Valdez, or an old play by Lope de Vega, entertained them all together.

In all these gatherings the Donna Maria Dolores, whom

our fair Inez had gone so far West to see, was, if not leader, the admired, even the beloved, centre of each little party. Eunice Perry came to prize her more highly, as she wondered at her more profoundly, with every new and quiet interview between them. Her figure was graceful; her face animated rather than beautiful; her eyes quick and expressive. There was something contagious in her welcome; and so sympathetic was she, in whatever society, that her presence in any *tertulia* was enough to put the whole company at ease, — certainly to lift it quite above the conventional type of formal Spanish intercourse. There were in the garrison-circle some officers' wives who would have been very unfortunate but for Maria Dolores. Either for beauty, or wealth, or something less explicable, they had been married by men of higher rank than their own ; and now they found themselves among ladies who were ladies, and officers most of whom were really gentlemen, while their own training had been wholly neglected, and they were absolutely in the crass ignorance of a Mexican peasant's daughter, or of the inmate of a Moorish harem. They could dress, they could look pretty, and that was absolutely all. There were not quite enough of them, this winter, to make a faction of their own, and send the others to Coventry. Indeed, the superior rank, as it happened, of Mme. Herrara, of the Señora Valois, and of Donna Maria Dolores, to say nothing of others who have been named, made this impossible. So was it that Donna Maria had her opportunity, and used it, to make them at ease, and to see that they were not excluded from the little contrivances by which the winter was led along. She always had a word even for the dullest of them. A bit of embroidery, or some goose-grease for a child's throat, or a message to Monteclovez, something or other, gave importance, for the moment, even to a stupid wax-doll, who had perhaps but just found out she was a fool, and had not found out what she should do about it.

It was in a little gathering, rather larger than was usual,

in which they were turning over two or three plays of Lope de Vega, and wondering whether they could spur the gentlemen up to act one with them, that Eunice and Inez both received a sudden shock of surprise, which made them listen with all their ears, and look away from each other with terrible determination.

"Who shall take Alfonso?" said the eager Madame Zuloaga.

"Oh, let Mr. Lonsdale take Alfonso! He is just mysterious enough! And then he has so little to say."

"But what he does say would kill us with laughing: his English-Spanish is so funny! Do the English really think they know our language better than we do?"

"I am sure I should never advise him. But anybody can take Alfonso. Ask Capt. Garcia to take it, — Luisa, do you ask him: he will do any thing you ask."

The fair Luisa said nothing, but blushed and giggled.

One of the wax-doll people spoke up bluntly, and, in a language not absolutely Castilian, said, —

"Capt. Garcia will be gone. His troop is ordered out against Nolano."

"Gone!" cried two or three of the younger ladies. And only Eunice cared whether the troop went against Apaches or Comanches, or to relieve a garrison in New Mexico, so it was to go: it was the loss of partners for which they grieved, not any particular danger to friends or to enemies.

Eunice, however, picked up the dropped subject.

"Did you say they went against Nolan?"

"Why, yes, or rather no. They go to take the place at Chihuahua, you know, of the two troops who go, you know, against the Americaños. Who go? or are they now gone, Donna Carlotta? Was it not you who told me?"

No, it was not Donna Carlotta who had told her; and soon it proved that nobody should have told her, and that she should not have told what she had heard. De Nava had intentionally sent his troopers from distant Chihuahua, because the Americaños would not watch that city; and he had not meant to give any sign of activity eastward in San Antonio, which they would watch. The truth was, he was jealous and suspicious both of Cordero and of Herrara, though they were his countrymen.

But by some oversight a letter had been read in presence of the wax-doll, which she should never have heard ; and thus the secret of secrets, which Herrara and Cordero and Barelo had preserved most jealously, was blurted out in the midst of four-and-twenty officers' wives.

So soon as the ladies parted, Eunice made it her business to find the husband of her sister, and spoke to him very frankly. She told him that she knew Nolan, and knew him well ; that he even accompanied them for a day or two on their expedition. She told him on what cordial terms he was with all the Spanish governors of Orleans. She ridiculed the idea of his making war with a little company of " grooms and stablers " (for into Spanish words of such force was she obliged to translate the horse-hunters of his party) ; and she explained to Major Barelo, that, though the people of the West were eager to open the Mississippi, the very last thing they wanted was to incense the military commanders of Mexico.

Major Barelo was an accomplished officer of European experience, and a man of rare good sense. He heard Eunice with sympathy all through, and then he said to her, —

" I can trust you as I can trust my wife. You are right in saying that this folly is the most preposterous extravagance that has crossed any ruler's brain since the days of Don Quixote.

" You are right in saying that Don Pedro de Nava gave to this very Nolan a pass, not to say an invitation, to carry on this very trade. Why, we know him here : he has been here again and again.

" But it seems that you do not know that De Nava has been told to change his policy. New kings, new measures.

He is a Pharaoh who does not know your Joseph, my dear sister.

"He does not dare give his commands to us. We have too much sense. We have too much civilization. We have too much of the new century. Herrara or Cordero would laugh his plan to scorn. Far from incensing the Kentuckianos, they would let the captain slip through their fingers, and wisely. We have had a plenty of despatches from Nacogdoches about him ; but we light our cigars with them, my dear sister."

"Yes, yes," said Eunice eagerly ; "but what does De Nava do? Is he sending out an army?" Then she saw she was too vehement: she collected herself, and said, "You see, my dear brother, I know the American people. I know that, if injustice is done, there is danger of war."

"And so do I," said Barelo sadly. "And when war comes, now or fifty years hence, who has the best chances on these prairies, — your Kentucky giants, or my master four thousand miles away in the Escorial?"

"Do you know when the army started?" said Eunice, giving him time to pause.

"Army! there is no army, — a wretched hundred or two of lancers. Oh! they left, I think they left Chihuahua just before Christmas. We heard of them at El Paso last week. That was when we got this order for two troops of the queen's regiment to go back to the commandant to take their places." And then he added, "I am as much annoyed as you can be, — more. But a soldier is a soldier."

"A soldier is a soldier," said Eunice almost fiercely, to Inez afterward, when she told her of this conversation, "and a woman, alas, is a woman. How can we put poor Nolan on his guard, — tell him that these brigands are on his track? If only we had known it sooner!"

How, indeed! For William Harrod had left them so soon as San Antonio was in sight. He had called off with him Richards and King and Adams, and had said lightly, in his really tender parting from Inez and Eunice, that he should be with Nolan in five days' time. He counted without his host, alas! but of this Eunice and Inez knew nothing till long after.

"Do you believe Ransom could slip through?" said Eunice thoughtfully.

"He could and he could not," said Inez. "In the first place, he would not go. The Inquisition could not make him go. He is here to take care of you and me: if you and I want to go, he will take us; and we shall arrive safely, and Nolan, dear fellow, will be saved. But, if we think we cannot tell Aunt Dolores that we want to go up to the Upper Brassos, why, as you know, Ransom will not budge." And the girl smiled sadly enough through her tears.

"Me will go," said White Hawk, who was looking from one to the other as they spoke, judging by their faces, rather than their words, what they were saying.

"Where will me go?" said Inez, hugging her and kissing her. The wonder and depth of White Hawk's love for her was always a new joy and new surprise to Inez, who, perhaps, had not been fortunate in the friends whom her schoolgirl experiences had made for her among her own sex.

"Me go on horse-trail; me go up through mesquit country — find prairie country; come up through wood three day, four day, five day — White Wolf River; me swim White Wolf River; more woods — more woods five day, six, seven day — no matter how much day; me find Harrod, find King, find Richards, find Blackburn, find Nolan — find other plenty white men, good white men, your white men — hunt horses, plenty horses — plenty white men."

"You witch!" cried Inez; "and how do you know that?"

White Hawk laughed with the quiet Indian laugh, which Inez said was like Ransom's choicest expression of satisfaction.

"Know it with my ears — know it with my eyes. See it. Hear it. Think it. Know it all — know it all."

" And you would go back to those horrid woods and those fearful Indians, whom you hate so and dread so, for the love of your poor Inez ! " Inez was beside herself now, and could not speak for crying.

Of course White Hawk's proposal could not be heard to for an instant. But all the same : it had its fruit, as courage will.

That afternoon there was some grand parade of the little garrison, so that the cavaliers whom Eunice and Inez relied upon most often were detained at their posts. But Eunice proposed, that, rather than lose their regular exercise, they should ride with the attendance of Ransom, and rely on meeting the major and the other gentlemen as they returned. The day was lovely ; and they took a longer ride than was usual past the Alamo, and up the river-side.

Six or seven miles distant from the Presidio, as they came out on a lovely opening, which they had made their object, they found, to their surprise, a little camp of Indians, who had established themselves there as if for a day or two. There was nothing unusual in the sight ; and the riding party would hardly have stopped, but that the little red children came screaming after them, with tones quite different from the ordinary beggar-whine, which is much the same with Bedouins, with lazzaroni, and with Indians. White Hawk, of course, first caught their meaning. " Friends, friends," she said, laughing, — " old friends," as she put her hand upon Inez's hand, to arrest her in the fast gallop in which she was hurrying along.

Inez thought White Hawk meant they were friends of hers, and for a moment drew bridle. Eunice and Ransom stopped also.

" No, no ! Friends, — your friends, Inez, — your friends." And, as Inez turned, indeed, she saw waved in triumph a scarf which was no common piece of Indian finery ; and which, in a minute more, she saw was the scarf she had given to a child on the levee of the Mississippi, in the very first week of their voyaging.

"Have the wretches come all the way here?" she said, surprised; and she stopped, almost unconsciously now, to see what they would say.

To her amusement, and to Eunice's as well, with great rapidity and much running to and fro from lodge to lodge, there were produced, from wrappings as many as if they had been diamonds or rubies, all the little cuttings of paper, — horses, buffaloes, dancing boys and girls, — with which Eunice had led along the half-hour while they were waiting for the boatmen, on that day of their first adventure.

She smiled graciously, not sorry that she had a good horse under her this time, and acknowledged the clamorous homage which one after another paid to her. Then, remembering her new advantage, she asked the White Hawk to interpret for her; and the girl had no difficulty in doing so.

Eunice bade her tell them that she could make them no buffaloes now, — not even an antelope; but, if they would come down to the Presidio the next morning, they should all have some sugar.

They said they were afraid to come to the Presidio: one of their people had been flogged there.

A grim smile appeared on Ransom's face, which implied, to those who knew him, a wish that the same treatment had gone farther.

"Tell them, then, that I will send them some sugar, and send them some antelopes, if they will come to-morrow morning to the Alamo;" and the White Hawk told them, and they all rode on.

"Do you not see," said Eunice quickly, "if the White Hawk can go up the Brassos, these people can go up there? If she knows the way, she can tell them. There must be some way in which they can take a token or a letter."

She turned her horse, so soon as they had well passed the camp, beckoned Ransom from the rear to join her, and bade the girls fall in behind.

Taking up the road homeward, but no longer galloping, or even trotting, she said to the old man,—

" Ransom, Capt. Nolan is in great danger."

" Een told me so," replied he, too much occupied with anxious thought to care much for etiquette.

"There are a hundred or two Spanish troopers hunting him, if they have not found him ; and, what is worse, they mean to fight him, Ransom."

" The cap'n 'll give 'em hell, ma'am."

" The captain will fight them if they find him ; but, Ransom, they must not find him. Ransom, I don't want the people down below to know any thing about this ; but to-morrow morning, some of these Indians must start with a letter to the captain ; and they must make haste, Ransom. Will you bring it out here before daylight ? "

" Yes'm. But it ain't no use. Can't send no letter. Poor set, — liars, all on um. Show the letter to the priest before they go. Priest got hold uv every darn one on um. Tell um all he'll roast um all, ef they go nigh white man. Liars all on um, — can't send no letter. Tain't no use."

" Do you think the priest knows these people ? "

" Know it, jest as well as nothin'. Hearn um tell at market to-day. Old Father José cum ; and the young one, black-haired rascal, he cum too ; cum and gin um a picter-book, and cum back with five beaver and three antelope skin, and two buffaloes. Gin um a picter-book. Hearn all about it at market. All liars ! Injuns is liars ; priests is liars too."

Eunice thought of tokens which messengers had carried, who knew not what they bore. She longed to tell Ransom some story of Cyrus or of Pyrrhus ; but she contented herself with saying, —

" I must send word." And she called Inez to her, and the White Hawk.

" Ma-ry, can I send these people to the captain ? Can you tell them how to go ? "

" Tell — yes — now," and the girl checked her horse, as if to return with the message.

"No, not now, Ma-ry. Can I write? Will these people take the letter?"

"Give sugar, — much sugar, — take letter. Take it, throw it in river, throw it in fire. All laugh. Eat sugar, throw letter away. All lie. All steal.

"Give sugar, little sugar, — give letter, — letter say Nolan send other letter. Other letter come, you give sugar, — oh, give heap sugar! heap sugar — see?"

"Yes, yes, — I see," said Eunice. "When they come back with other letter from Capt. Nolan, I will pay them with sugar."

"See — yes — yes — see? Heap sugar all come."

Then she opened and shut her hands quickly.

"Five, five, five days, heap sugar. Five, five, five, five days, little heap sugar. Five, five, five, five, five, five, days, gourd of sugar. More days, no sugar, no sugar, bad Indian. Nolan dead. No sugar at all."

"Ma-ry, these people know the priest. Father José they know. Father Jeronimo they know. Priests do not love Nolan. Will they show the priest my letter?"

The girl took the question in an instant, — took it, it would seem, before it was asked. Her face changed.

"Show old White Head letter, — White Head tear letter, burn letter."

But in an instant she added, —

"White Hawk send skin. Old White Head no read skin." And she flung up her head like a princess, proud of her superior accomplishment. Eunice took her idea at once, praised her, and encouraged it. The girl meant, that, if she traced on the back of an antelope-skin one of the hiero-glyphic pictures of the Indian tribes, Nolan would under-stand the warning she gave; while the average Franciscan, with all his accomplishments, would let it pass without com-prehending its meaning.

In such discussions, on an easy gallop, they returned homeward. As they approached the garrison, they met Mr.

Lonsdale, the stranger whom the gossiping party of ladies had pronounced so mysterious. Eunice, to say the truth, was much of their mind. Who Mr. Lonsdale was, what he was, and why he was there, no one knew. And, while she disliked the gossiping habit of most of the people around her, she did not like to be in daily intercourse with a man who might be a spy from the headquarters at the City of Mexico, might be an agent of the King of England, might be any thing the Mexican ladies said he was.

For all this, he and the ladies were on terms externally friendly. He stopped as they approached, and asked permission to join their party, which Eunice, of course, granted cordially. He turned, and rode with her. The two girls dropped behind.

After a moment's hesitation, he said, —

" I should be sorry to be the bearer of bad news, Miss Perry. Perhaps you are indifferent to my news. But I came out hoping to meet you."

And he stopped as if hesitating anew.

Eunice said, with a shade of dignity, that she was much obliged to him.

" I thought — I supposed — I did not know," said the Englishman, with more even than the usual difficulty of his countrymen in opening a conversation, "you may not have heard that a military force is in the upper valleys, looking for the American horse-hunters."

What did this man mean ? Was he a quiet emissary from the provincial capital, whose business it was to gain information about poor Nolan ? Was he trying to get a crumb from Miss Perry ? She was quite on her guard. She felt quite sure of her ground, too, — that she could foil him, by as simple an artifice as — the truth.

" Oh, yes, Mr. Lonsdale ! I have heard this. I heard it from Mme. Malgares, and in more detail from one of the officers."

" Then perhaps you know more than I do."

"Very probably," said Eunice, not without the slightest shade of triumph.

The mysterious Mr. Lonsdale was thrown off his guard. Eunice had no wish to relieve him; and they rode on in silence. With some gulping, and possibly a little flush, he said, "I had thought you might be anxious about Mr. Nolan, or about the Kentucky gentlemen. I understood Miss Inez to speak as if some of them were your escort here."

How much did he know, and how little? Eunice's first thought was to say, "The Kentucky gentlemen will take care of themselves." But this tone of defiance might complicate things. Once more she tried the truth.

"Oh, yes! Mr. Harrod and two or three more of that party came to Antonio with us." She longed to say, "Why did not your king pounce on them then?" but again she was prudent.

Mr. Lonsdale tried to break her guard once more. "The Spanish force is quite a large one," said he.

Eunice longed to say, "I know that too." But her conversation with Major Barelo had been confidential. She said, "Indeed!" and the Englishman was disarmed. He made no further attempt. They came without another word to the colonel's quarters; he helped the proud Miss Perry to dismount, and the ladies sought their own apartments.

Before bedtime the White Hawk brought her letter to Eunice. She came into the double room which Eunice and her niece occupied; and she bore on her back a parcel of skins, exactly as a squaw might bring them into the warehouse for trade. She flung them down on the floor with just the air of a tired Indian, glad his tramp was at an end. Then, with a very perfect imitation of the traders' jargon, she said, —

"Buy skin? ugh? good skin? ugh? Five skin, six skin, good skin. Buy? ugh? Whiskey, sugar, powder, — one whiskey, two sugar, four powder, — six skin. Ugh?"

And she held up one hand, and the forefinger of the other.

Eunice and Inez laughed ; and Inez said, —

"Yes, yes! good skin — buy skin — one skin, five skin. Heap sugar, heap whiskey, heap powder!"

So the mock bargain was completed. The girls knelt, and untied the cords ; and the White Hawk affected to praise her skins, — the color, the smoothness, the age, and so on. And when she had played out her joke, and not till then, she turned them all over, and showed the grotesque figures which she had drawn on the back of one of them. Even to Eunice's eye, although she had the clew, they showed nothing. Perhaps she began at the top when she should have begun at the bottom : perhaps she began at the bottom when she should have begun at the middle. Ma-ry enjoyed her puzzled expression, but made no sign till Eunice said, —

"I can make nothing of it. You must show me."

Then the White Hawk laughed and explained. From point to point of the skin her finger dashed — who should say by what law? But here was a group made up of an eagle and ten hands, ten feet, and ten other hands. This meant a hundred eagles and fifty more, — and eagles were "enemies." In a distant corner was a round shield, in another a lance with scalps attached, in another the feather of a helmet. This showed that she supposed the enemies were lancers ; that they wore the Spanish helmet, and carried the Spanish shields. Another character had three Roman crosses : these were the crosses of the cathedral at Chihua-hua. Nolan had seen them, and the White Hawk had heard of them. Far and wide had their fame gone among those simple people ; for that cathedral was as the St. Peter's of the whole of Northern Mexico. And so the record went on. The White Hawk assured her friends that so soon as Nolan or Harrod saw the skin they would know what, as the ladies could very well understand, very few white men would know: that a hundred and fifty Spanish lancers had left Chihuahua in search of him. Then she showed where the representa-tion of six bears' paws showed that on the sixth day of the moon of the bears the expedition started ; and then where a chestnut-burr, by the side of men fording a river, showed that they crossed the Rio Grande after the month of chestnuts had come in.

All this Eunice heard and approved with wonder. She praised the girl to her heart's content.

"Where did you find your colors, my darling?"

And Ma-ry confessed, that, failing walnut-husks and oak-galls, she had contented herself with Inez's inkstand.

"But this red around the scalps, this red crest of the turkey's head, these red smooches on the lances?"

The White Hawk paused a moment, turned off the question as if it were an idle one ; but, when she was pressed, she stripped up the sleeve of her dress, and showed the fresh wound upon her arm, where she had, without hesitation, used her own blood for vermilion.

Then Inez kissed her again and again. But the girl would not pretend that she thought this either pain or sacrifice.

Eunice thanked her, but told her she must always trust them more. And then they all corded up the pack together ; and, under the White Hawk's hands, it assumed again the aspect of the most unintelligent bale of furs that ever passed from an Indian's hands to a trader's. It was agreed, that at daybreak Ransom and Ma-ry should carry the parcel to the Indian camp, and Ma-ry should try the force of her rhetoric, backed with promises of heaps of sugar, to send a party with the message.

"It is all very fine," said Inez ; "and, if that skin ever reaches him, I suppose that he or Capt. Harrod will disentangle its riddles. But I have more faith in ten words of honest English than in all this *galimatias.*"

"So have I, dear child, if the honest English ever comes to him. See what I have done. I have begged from Dolores this pretty prayer-book. There is no treason there. I have loosened the parchment cover here, and have written on the inside of it your ten words, and more. See, I said, —

"' The governor sent a hundred and fifty lancers after you at Christmas. They were at El Paso last week, and mean fight.'

"You see I printed this in old text, and matched the color of the old Latin, as well as its character. These people shall take that to Capt. Nolan with this note."

And she read the note she had written : —

"' MY DEAR COUSIN, — May the Holy Mother keep you in her remembrance ! My prayer for you, day and night, is that you may be saved. Forget the vanities and sins of those shameless heretics, and enter into the arms of our mother, the Church. Study well, in each day's prayers, the holy book I send you. On our knees we daily beg that you may see the errors of your wandering, and return.'

"That will make him search the book through and through ; and if he does not rip off this parchment cover, and find what I have written on the inside, he is not the man I take him to be.

"And now, girls, go to bed, both of you : Ma-ry will need to be moving bright and early, if she is to take this to the redskins before the fort is stirring."

CHAPTER XVII.

MINES AND COUNTER-MINES.

"Seek not thou to find
The sacred counsels of almighty mind:
Involved in darkness lies the great decree,
Nor can the depths of fate be pierced by thee ;
What fits thy knowledge, thou the first shalt know."
HOMER.

WITH the gray of the morning the White Hawk left the house, and found her way out of the little settlement. The girl's history was perfectly known to every one at the post, and any waywardness in her habits attracted no surprise ; indeed, it attracted no attention. On his part, Ransom had saddled his own horse, had fastened behind the saddle the pack of furs, and a package, only not quite so large, of the much-prized sugar.

"All nonsense," he had said to Eunice. "Gin um two quarts whiskey, and they'll go to hell for you. Sugar's poor sugar : your brother would not look at it, it's so bad ; but it's too good for them redskins. Gin um whiskey."

But Eunice was resolute ; and the old man knew that he must throw the sugar away, because she so bade him. He satisfied himself, therefore, with taking from the storehouse on her order just twice as much as she had bidden him. He was well clear of any observation from the Presidio when he saw Ma-ry in advance of him, moving so quickly that he had to abandon the walk of his horse, and come to a trot, that he might overtake her.

"Mornin', Miss Mary: better jump up here: The old bay's often carried Miss Inez."

And in a moment he had lifted the girl, who was an expert in horsemanship in all its guises, so that she sat behind him on the pack of furs, steadying herself by placing one hand upon his shoulder. Having entirely satisfied himself, after the first few days of his observation of the White Hawk, that she was, in very truth, neither a "nigger" nor an "Ingin," he had taken her into the sacred chamber of his high favor, and did not regard her as humbug or liar, which is more than can be said of his regard for most men and women.

"Want ye to tell them redskins to keep away from them priests and friars, Miss Mary. Priests and friars ain't no good nowhere. These here is wuss than most on um be. Tell the redskins to keep clear on um."

The White Hawk thought she understood him, and said so.

"Tell um to make haste, lazy critters, if they can. Wanted to go myself to tell Mr. Nolan. Can't go, cos must stay with the young ladies. But I could get there and back 'fore them lazy redskins will go half way. Tell um to be here in a week, and we'll give um five pounds of good sugar, every man on um."

Ma-ry understood enough to know that this proposal was absurd. She told Ransom, in language which he did not understand, that if the messengers reached Nolan in less than eight or ten days it would be by marvellous good luck. As she did not use his words, spoke of suns and nights, and of hands whenever she would say "five," the old man did not at all follow her ; but he was relieved by thinking that she understood him, and said so.

"That's so: let um travel all day and all night too. I'd get there myself by day arter to-morrow ; but them redskins don't know nothin'."

The truth was, that he was as ignorant as a mole of Nolan's position and of the way thither. But he had always relied, and not in vain, on his own quick good sense, his iron

THE INTERVIEW WITH CROOKED FEATHER.

strength, and his intense determination to achieve any task he had in hand more promptly than those around him. He did not, therefore, even know that he was bragging. He meant merely to say that the Indians were as nearly worthless as human beings could be; that their ability was less than his in the proportion of one-fifth to one; and, by the extravagance of his language, to wash his hands, even in the White Hawk's eyes, of any participation in the responsibility of this undertaking.

They were soon in sight of the smoke of the lodges; and in a moment more were surrounded by the beggar children of a beggar tribe, eager for paper gods, for whiskey, for sugar, for ribbons, for tobacco, or for any thing else that might be passing.

Ma-ry sought out and found the man who could best be called the chief of the party. Ransom had dismounted; but she sat upon the saddle still, and took an air which was wholly imperial in her dealings with the Crooked Feather. Ransom said afterward to Inez, "The gal's a queen in her own country, she is." Ma-ry did not ask: she directed.

The man was amazed that she spoke to him in his own language. No white man or woman of the Presidio had ever accosted him so till now. He had seen her only the day before with a party from the fort; and he knew very well that they represented the dignitaries of the fort. He did not know who she was, nor did the girl make any endeavor to explain.

Simply she bade him, in the most peremptory way, take the skins and the little parcel which she gave him to the hunting-party whom he would find on the Tockanhono, and to be sure he was there before the moon changed. When he had done this he was to come back, also as soon as might be; and when he returned, if he brought any token from the long-knife chief whom he found there, he was to have sugar in heaps which almost defy the powers of our numeration. All the party were to have heaps of it. In guerdon, or token, Ransom was now permitted to open the little pack of sugar which he had brought with him, which then lay in tempting profusion in its open wrapper while Ma-ry spoke. She was a little annoyed to see that her order — for it was hers originally — had been so largely exceeded.

As for the size of the party, the Crooked Feather might go alone, or he might take all the lodges, as he chose : only he must not tarry. For all who went, and all who returned, there would be sugar if they were here before the third quarter of the new moon. If as late as the next moon, there would be no sugar ; and the White Hawk's expression of disgust at a result so wretched was tragical. The so-called stoics to whom she spoke affected feelings of dismay equal to hers.

Crooked Feather ventured to suggest that a little whiskey made travel quicker.

The imperial lady rebuked him sternly for the proposal, and he shrunk back ashamed.

In a rapid council he then decided that only five horses with their riders should go, and this under his own lead. As for the sugar which Ransom had brought and laid before them, it was nothing : even a rabbit would not see that any sugar lay there. In token of which, as they talked, the Crooked Feather and his companions scooped it up in their hands, and ate it all ; it would not have vanished sooner had it been some light soup provided for their refreshment. But he understood that his supposed " White Father " who had provided this had sent it only as a little token of good-will, — clearly could not, indeed, send more, besides the furs and the princess, on the back of Ransom's saddle. A chief of the rank and following of Crooked Feather was substantially, he said, the equal of his Great Father personally unknown to him. But he wore and showed a crucifix, which his Great Father had sent to him ; and as the Great Father had set his heart on sending these skins to the long-knife chieftain, who was an intimate friend of Crooked Feather's, according to that worthy's own account, why, Crooked Feather would personally undertake their safe conduct.

Even while this harangue went on, the squaws detailed for that duty were packing the beasts who were to go on the expedition, hastily folding the skins of the lodge which was to go.

Ma-ry was a little surprised to find that she was mistaken for an emissary of King Charles the Fourth, or of the Pope of Rome. In truth, she could not herself have named these dignitaries, nor had she the least idea of their pretensions. It was idle to try to explain that her Great Father was a very different person from the Great Father who had started the crucifix. She simply applauded the purpose of the Crooked Feather to do what she had told him to do ; and she did not hesitate to give precise instructions to the women who were packing the horses, in the same queenly manner with which she had spoken before.

In less than an hour the party was on its way, having long before consumed to the last crumb all the sugar. Ransom and Ma-ry returned home. They parted at the spot where they had met. Ma-ry entered the Presidio on one side, and Ransom on the other, and it was clear that the absence of neither of them had challenged any remark in the laziness of a Spanish town. Ma-ry told her story with glee to the ladies. Inez fondled and Eunice praised her, only trying to warn her of the essential difference between such a great father as Silas Perry and such another as Pope Pius ; of which, however, to repeat again MacDonald's remark to the Japanese governors, "She could make nothing."

The same evening the Crooked Feather, who had been true to his promise of speed, had advanced as far as Gaudaloupe River. He found there a camp-fire, a little tent, and three horses tethered. It proved that the party there consisted of three fathers of the Franciscan order, who had left the Alamo for an outpost mission.

The fathers were patronizing and courteous. They asked

the purpose of Crooked Feather, and he told them. They then produced some grape brandy, such as the missions were permitted to make for their own use, in contravention of the royal policy which weighed upon persons not ghostly. Crooked Feather took his portion large, and allotted lesser quotas to his companions.

With the second draught he went into more minute particulars as to his enterprise, and those who sent him. But the fathers seemed to take no interest in his narrative.

As soon as the liquor had done its perfect work, and all the Indians slept in a drunken sleep, Father Jeronimo cut open the bale of furs, and shook them to see what might be hidden. When nothing came out, he examined the skins, and at once found Ma-ry's runes. Of these " he could make nothing." But he said, with a smile, to the worthy Brother Diego who assisted him, that it was a pity to lead others into temptation ; and he took out that skin from the parcel to place it under his own blanket.

As the Crooked Feather slept heavily, there was no difficulty in relieving him also of the smaller parcel which Ma-ry had given to him. Father Diego crossed himself, and so did the other, on opening it. They found the familiar aspect of a little book of devotion. None the less did the older priest cut open the stitches which held on the parchment over-cover. When he noticed, among the words which covered the inside, some which he knew were neither Spanish nor Latin, he folded the parchment carefully, and put it in his bosom. He enclosed in it, as he did so, Eunice's friendly note, of which he could read no word. He then tied up the book in its wrapper precisely as it had been folded before.

With his "tokens " thus improved upon, and with the worst headache he had ever known in his life, the Crooked Feather started the next morning, at a later hour than he had intended, on his mission.

At an earlier hour the three Fathers had started on theirs.

CHAPTER XVIII.

WILL HARROD'S FORTUNES.

"The fragrant birch above him hung
  Its tassels in the sky;
And many a vernal blossom sprung
  And nodded careless by.

But there was weeping far away;
  And gentle eyes, for him,
With watching many an anxious day,
  Were sorrowful and dim."

BRYANT.

IT is time to go back to the fortunes of poor Will Harrod, who had fared, as the winter passed, much less satisfactorily than any of the rest of our little party.

With no other adventure which we have thought need detain the eager or the sluggish reader, Harrod had held on his pleasant journey with the ladies till they were fairly within sight of the crosses of the church, as they approached San Antonio. Then he bade them farewell, with more regret than the poor fellow dared express in words, — not with more than Eunice expected, or than Inez knew.

He said, very frankly, that his duty to his commander was to join him as soon as might be, with three companions, who were so much force taken from the strength of the hunting-party. He said, that, if he took these men with him into the Presidio, there was the possibility that they might all be detained, whatever the courtesy of Major Barelo, and in face of the permission which De Nava had given to Nolan. And therefore, he said, though each day that he was with them was indescribably delightful to him, — nay, happier than any days had ever been before, — he should tear himself away now, hoping that it might not be very long before at Antonio, or perhaps at Orleans, they might all meet again.

And the loyal fellow would permit himself to say no more. Not though he had given every drop of his heart's blood to Inez, — though he was willing enough that she should guess that he had given it to her, — yet he would not in words say so to her, nor ask the question to which the answer seemed to him to be life or death. The young reader of to-day must judge whether this loyalty or chivalry of his was Quixotic. Poor Harrod had time enough to consider it afterward, and to ask himself, in every varying tone of feeling and temper, whether he were right or wrong. At every night's encampment on this journey he had gone backward and forward on the " ifs " and " buts " of the same inquiry. He had determined, wisely or not wisely, that he would not in words ask Inez if she would take that heart which was all her own. First, because he had no home to offer her. He was an adventurer, and only an adventurer ; and just now the special adventure in which he was enlisted promised very little to any engaged in it. Second, he had known Inez only because she had been intrusted to his care ; and she was intrusted to his care, not by her father, but by Philip Nolan, whom he almost adored, who was the person to whose care her father had intrusted her. Perhaps her father would not have intrusted her to him. Who knew ? Very certainly Mr. Perry would not have intrusted her to him, Master William Harrod thought, had he supposed, that, before a month was over, he was going to play the Moor to this lovely Desdemona, and steal her from her father's home.

So William Harrod spoke no word of love to Inez. To Eunice Perry he had committed himself through and through. To Inez he said nothing — in words. If every watchful attention meant any thing in the girl's eyes ; if the most delicate remembrance of her least wish, if provision for every whim, if care of her first in every moment of inconvenience or trial, — if these meant any thing, why, all that they meant he meant ; but he said nothing.

It is not fair to say or to guess whether Inez understood all this, how far she understood it, or, which is a question more subtle, whether she ever asked herself if she understood it. Inez laid down to herself this rule, — not an inconvenient one, — that she would treat him exactly as she treated Philip Nolan. Philip Nolan did not want to marry her, she did not want to marry him : yet they were the best of friends. She could joke with him, she could talk rhodomontade with him, she could be serious with him. They had prayed together, kneeling before the same altar ; they had danced together at the same ball ; they had talked together by the hour, riding under these solemn moss-grown trees. She would be as much at ease with Philip Nolan's friend as she was with Philip Nolan. That ease he had no right to mistake, nor had any one a right to criticise.

There was but one thing which gave the girl cause to ponder on her relations to this young man : it would be hardly right to say that it gave her uneasiness. But here was her aunt Eunice, who had never before had any secret from her, and from whom she had never had any secret. There was not a theme so lofty, there was not a folly so petty, but that she and Aunt Eunice had talked it over, up and down, back and forth, right and left. Why did Aunt Eunice never say one word to her about William Harrod ? She never guarded her, never snubbed her, never praised him, never blamed him. If Harrod and Inez rode together all through an afternoon, talking of books, of poets, of religion, or of partners, of ribbons, or of flowers, or of clouds, or of sunset, when they came in at night, Aunt Eunice had no word of caution, none of curiosity. This was not in the least natural ; but it was a reserve which Inez did not quite venture to break in upon.

Be it observed at the same moment, that Inez was not one of the people who have been spoken of, who believed that there was a tenderness between Phil Nolan and her aunt. Inez knew the absurdity of that theory. On the other hand, Inez had never forgotten twenty words of confidence which Philip Nolan gave her two years before the time of which we speak, when she was beginning to feel that dolls were not all in all, when she was growing tall, and was very proud of such confidence. Philip Nolan had shown Inez a picture then, — a very lovely picture of a lady with a very charming face ; and this picture was not a picture of her Aunt Eunice. Inez believed in men, and as she knew Phil Nolan's secret, she had never been misled by the theory that there was any tender understanding between him and her aunt.

Was there, then, any mysterious understanding between William Harrod and her aunt? No! Inez did not believe that either. True, it would happen that there would be rides as long when he and her aunt were together, and when Ma-ry and Inez were together, as there were when he and she talked of any thing in heaven above, and earth beneath, and the waters under the earth. And when Aunt Eunice and Capt. Harrod had been thus talking together all the afternoon, or all the morning, when they came into camp, while the men were tethering the horses, and the women, in the relief of moccasons, were lying alone before the fire, even then never did Aunt Eunice say one word beyond the merest outside-talk of ford or mud, or sun or rain, which made any allusion to William Harrod.

There was one person, however, who made not the slightest question as to the relation between these parties. The White Hawk knew, without being told, that Harrod loved Inez as his very life. When the two girls were alone, she never hesitated to tell Inez so ; and she never hesitated to add that it would be strange indeed, seeing what manner of girl her own Inez was, if he did not love her as his very life. Nay, there were times when, with such language as the girls had, this waif from the forest would venture the question to which she never got any answer, — whether Inez did not have the least little bit of thought of him, though his back were turned and he far away.

The reader now knows more than William Harrod knew of the state of his own affairs, on the afternoon when he made his last good-bys to the two ladies, and, with King and Richards and Adams, turned back to join the captain on the expedition from which they had been now for more than a fortnight parted. Of these men, Harrod had learned early to distrust Richards. He seemed to him to be himself distrustful, morose, and sulky without cause; and Harrod did not believe him to be a true man. Of the others he had formed no judgment, for better or worse, except that they were like the average of Western adventurers, glad to spend a winter on ground which they had never seen before. He had been a little surprised that all of them had assented, without question or murmur, to so long a separation from the main party of hunters.

He was more surprised, that, now this separation was so near an end, none of the men showed any interest in the prospect of reunion. They rode on, for the four days' forced march which brought them back to that famous camp where Inez had lost herself, — a party ill at ease. Whenever Harrod tried to lead the conversation to the business of the winter, it flagged. The men dropped that subject as if it were a hot coal. For himself, poor Harrod gladly turned back in his own thoughts to every word that had been spoken, to every look that had been looked, as he and she rode over this road before. If the men did not want to talk about mustangs and corrals, he certainly did not. And so, as they brought down five days of ordinary travel so as to compass them in little more than three, it was but a silent journey.

Of such silence, the mystery appeared, when they had discussed the jerked venison of their noonday meal at camp at the same point as that where Eunice watched and wept.

To go to Nolan's rendezvous from this point, they would have to follow up the valley of the Brassos River, known to the Indians as the Tockanhono. The trail would not be as easy as the old San Antonio road which they had been following, nor could they expect to make as rapid progress upon it. But, at the outside, Nolan was not two hundred miles above them, perhaps not one hundred miles. With the horses they had under them, this distance would be soon achieved.

As the men washed down the venison with the last drop of the day's ration of whiskey, Harrod gave his commands for the evening, in that interrogative or suggestive form in which a wise officer commands free and independent hunters.

"Had we not better hold on here till daybreak ?" he said. "That will give the horses a better chance at this feed. We will start as soon as we can see our hands in the morning ; and by night we shall have made as much as if we had started now."

None of the men said a word — a little to Harrod's surprise, though he was used to their sulkiness.

"Well," said he, "if you want to play cards, you must play by yourselves this evening. I shall take a nap now, and then I have my journal to write up ; and Mr. Nolan wants me to take the latitude here as soon as the stars are up. So good luck to you all."

Upon this, King — who was perhaps the most easy speaker of the party — screwed himself up, or was put up by the others, to say, —

"Cap'n, I may as well tell you that we's going home. There won't be no horses cotched up yonder this year. Them blasted Greasers is too many for Cap'n Nolan or for you ; and we sha'n't get into that trap. We uns is going home ; 'n, if you's wise, you goes too."

Harrod stared at first, without speaking. This was the mystery of all this sulky silence, was it ? And this Mordecai Richards was at the bottom of it ! Harrod was too angry to speak for a moment. Before he did speak, he had mastered

that first wish to give the man a black eye, or to choke him
for a few minutes, as fit recompense for such treachery. He
did master it, and succeeded in pretending this was a half-
joke, and in trying persuasion.

They battled it for half an hour. Harrod coaxed, he
shamed, he threatened ; and, at the end, he saw the traitors
saddle and pack their horses, and they rode off without a
word of good-by, leaving Harrod alone, as he had left Eunice
Perry on that spot, only that Harrod had no loyal Ransom.

"There is no use crying for spilled milk," he said, as if it
were a comfort to him to speak one clean and strong word
after paddling in the ditch of those men's lies and cowardice.
"Half an hour of a good siesta lost in coaxing cowards and
convicting liars!"

And on this the good fellow threw himself on the ground
again, drew a buffalo-robe over his feet and knees, adjusted
his head to his mind on a perch which he took from his
saddle, and in ten seconds was asleep ; so resolute was his
own self-command, and so meekly did wayward thought,
even when most rampant, obey him when he gave the order.
He slept his appointed hour. He woke, and indulged himself in pleasant memories. He went down to the bayou.
The moccason-tracks of Inez's little foot were not yet all
erased. He crept out upon the log of cottonwood; he
peeped through the opening in the underbrush. He came
back to the false trail which she had followed. He worked
along in the effort to reproduce her wanderings. As night
closed in, he tried to fancy that he was where the girl was ;
and he paced up and down fifty times, as he indulged himself
in the memory of her courage. Then he came up to his
post, took the altitude of the North Star, and of Algol and
Deneb, as the captain had bidden him. By the light of his
camp-fire he made an entry in his journal longer than usual.
Let it be not written here whether there were there, or were
not, a few halting verses, between the altitude of Mizar and
that of Deneb.

Before ten o'clock the fire was burning low, and the fearless commander was dreaming of Inez and of home.

But it is not every night that passes so smoothly for him; and it is not every evening that he can write verses or enter altitudes so serenely.

The next day, with no guide, — and, indeed, needing none but the indications of an Indian trail, — the brave fellow worked his way prosperously toward his chief; and at night, after he had taken his altitudes, and written up his journal, he lay by his camp-fire again, with the well-pleased hope that two or three more such days might bring him to the captain. At the outside, five would be enough, unless all plans were changed. On such thoughts he slept.

He woke to find his hands tightly held, — to hear the grunts and commands of two stout Comanches who held him, — to struggle to his feet between them, with daylight enough to see that he was in the power of a dozen of them. His packs were already open, and were surrounded by the hungry and thirsty cormorants. One was draining his whiskey-flask. Two or three were trying experiments with his sextant. The chief of the party had already appropriated his rifle; and as Harrod turned to look for the precious pack, on which his head had rested, he saw that that also was in the hands of the savages, and that one of them was already fighting with another on the questions which should be possessor of a cigar-case, and which should be satisfied with the diary.

This misfortune of the young Kentuckian will explain to the reader what was a mystery to Philip Nolan when he wrote the letter which we have read, — why Harrod and the rest had not rejoined him within a fortnight, more or less, after he had received their letters by Blackburn.

CHAPTER XIX.

THE WARNING.

> " Before the clerk must bend
>   Full many a warrior grim,
> And to the corner wend,
>   Although it please not him."
>
> HEINRICH KNAUST.

PHILIP NOLAN'S letter to Eunice had not reached her on that morning in March when Ma-ry had sent away the joint letter to him, of whose fate the reader has been apprised. He had no prizes to offer to the Carankawa squaw to whom he intrusted it ; and her occasions of travel were so varied, and her encampments were so long, that it was many months before Eunice Perry received it.

She was one of the *Indios reducidos*, — that is, the Indians who could make the sign of the cross, — and not one of the *Indios bravos*, who were redskins without that accomplishment. But her "reduction" had not yet brought her to that more difficult stage of religion in which people tell the truth, or do what they promise to do.

Meanwhile the winter wore away, — not unpleasantly to the young leader and his party. He had characterized them fitly enough in that letter. They could fight over their cards as hotly as they would have fought for a king's crown ; and the next day, in the wild adventures of the chase, the man who had, the last night, sworn deadly vengeance because a two of clubs was not an ace, would risk his life freely to save

the man whom he had then threatened. The moon of cold
meat, as the Indians call the tenth month from March, crept
by; and through the month the young hunters had no lack of
hot supplies every night. The moon of chestnuts followed ;
and they were not reduced to roasted chestnuts. The moon
of walnuts followed ; and they had walnuts enough, but they
had much more. They hunted well, they slept well, they
woke with the sun. They hardly tired of this life of adventure ; but they were all in readiness, so soon as the spring
flood should a little subside, to take up their line of march
with their frisky wealth to Natchitoches and Orleans.

All fears of the Spanish outposts had long since died away.
The only question which ever amazed the camp was the question which the last chapter solved for the reader, — what had
become of Harrod and of his companions? There was not a
man of them who really liked Richards ; but they knew nothing to make them distrust King and Adams ; and of course
every man knew that William Harrod was another Philip
Nolan.

Things were in this pass, when, as they returned from the
day's hunting to the corral one afternoon, they found sitting
by the cooks, the home-guard, and the camp-fire, the five
Indians of whom Crooked Feather was the spokesman,
whom the reader saw last when they left the Guadaloupe
River five days before, with such benediction as the Franciscan fathers had given them.

Crooked Feather rose at once, laid aside his pipe, and presented to Nolan a little silver-mounted hunting-whip, with an
address which Nolan scarcely understood. The man spoke
rapidly, and with much excitement.

Nolan controlled him a little, by praising him and the
whip, and giving his hand freely to every member of the red
party, and then persuaded Crooked Feather to begin again.
He asked him to speak slowly, explaining that, while his heart
was right to the Twowokanies, his ears were somewhat deaf
when he heard their language.

Crooked Feather began again, and this time with gesture enough to make clear his words. Nolan immediately called Blackburn ; and by an easy movement he led the Indian away from the other men, who were already hobnobbing with the redskins of lesser rank or lesser volubility.

"Blackburn, see and hear what he says. He gives me this riding-switch from old Ransom. Ransom is no fool, as you know, Blackburn ; and this means simply that he thinks we should be going, and going quickly. The man left Antonio only on Tuesday ; he saw the ladies Monday ; and early Tuesday morning Ransom came with that girl they call the White Hawk, bade him bring me this whip, and promised him no end of plunder if he returned in twelve days. Now, they had some reason for sending the redskins."

"They have sent something besides the whip," said Blackburn ; and he turned to the impassive Crooked Feather, and with equal impassivity said to him, "Give me what else the young squaw sent to you."

Then for the first time, and as if he had forgotten it, or as if it were a trifle among braves, the Crooked Feather crossed to his packs, loosened and brought to the others the parcel of skins, dusty and defaced by the journey.

" Crooked Feather brought these skins also. There are six skins, which the white squaw, whom the white-head father took from the Apaches, sends to the chief of the long-knives."

"You lie !" said Blackburn, as impassive as before, and with as little sign of displeasure. "There are but five skins. The Crooked Feather has stolen one."

"There are six skins," said the savage, holding up one hand, and one finger of the other ; and he explained that he had himself opened the parcel, counted the skins, and folded them again. He showed his own memorandum,— an open hand in red, and a red finger, — on the other side of the outer skin.

Even the impassive face of an Indian gave way to a surprise which could hardly be feigned when he also counted the skins, and there were but five.

"Perhaps he is lying, Blackburn; but I think not. Do not let the other boys hear you, but go and talk with the other redskins, and find out what you can. I will play with him here. You see, Ransom never sent that bale of skins all the way here with nothing in it. Bring me our long pipe first."

Blackburn brought the pipe, lighted. Nolan spread one of the skins, and invited Crooked Feather to sit on it. He sat on another himself. He threw one on his knees. He threw another on the Feather's knees. He drew a few whiffs of smoke, and gave the pipe to the other. They renewed this ceremony three or four times. Then Nolan opened his private flask of whiskey, and drank from it. He offered it to the other, who did the same, not with the same moderation which his host had shown. After these ceremonies, the white man said gravely, without even looking the other in the face, —

"The white squaw and the gray-haired chief gave to my brother another token. I am ready to receive that from the Crooked Feather."

The Crooked Feather, who had till this moment conceived the hope that he might retain the little prayer-book for a medicine and benediction for himself and his line forever, gave way at the moment, took it from his pouch, and gave it to Nolan.

"The chief of the long-knives says well. The old chief and the white squaw gave me this medicine for the chief of the long-knives."

Nolan cut, only too eagerly, the thongs which bound the missal-book, and opened it. He wholly concealed his surprise when he saw what it was. Rapidly he turned every page to make sure that no note was concealed within them. He placed it in his own pouch, drew three more whiffs from the pipe, and waited till the Crooked Feather did the same. He pretended to drink from the flask again; and the Feather did so, without pretence or disguise.

Nolan then said, —

"The white squaw and the white chief gave my brother another medicine. They gave him a white medicine, like the bark of a canoe-birch folded."

He looked, as he spoke, at a distant tree, as though there were no Crooked Feather in the world.

Crooked Feather, looking also across at the camp-fire, as though there were no Nolan in the world, said, —

"The chief of the long-knives lies. I have given to him all the tokens and all the medicines which the white squaw gave me, or the white-haired white chief. Let the chief of the long-knives give his token to the Crooked Feather. The Crooked Feather will give it to the white squaw before seven suns have set. The white squaw will give the Crooked Feather more sugar than a bear can eat in a day."

This dream of heaven was put in words without a gesture or a smile.

"It is well," said Nolan quietly. "Let us come to the camp-fire. The Crooked Feather has ridden far to-day. My young men have turkey-meat and deer-meat waiting for him."

They parted at the fire, and in a moment more Nolan was in consultation with Blackburn.

Blackburn told him what he had drawn from the others without difficulty. They had confirmed all that the Crooked Feather had said. They had added what he would have added had he been asked the history of their march. In the first place, they knew nothing of Harrod or of the other lost men. They had not long been camping by Antonio, nor had they any knowledge of the existence of such a party as his. In the second place, they had carefully described Miss Eunice, Miss Inez, the White Hawk, and Ransom, with precision of details such as none but Indians would be capable of. There could be no doubt, in the mind of either Nolan or Blackburn, that on the very last Tuesday they had left their camp by the river, and had started with the parcel of furs, the packet, and the riding-whip. That the parcel contained

six skins when they started, Blackburn was sure. The men
all said so. They had opened it, and counted them. Nor
did they even now know that its tale was not full. Blackburn was sure, that, if Crooked Feather had tampered with it,
they had not. Nolan was equally sure that the chief had
not. He had, indeed, no motive to do so. His only object
must be to discharge his mission thoroughly, if he discharged
it at all. Had he wanted to steal a wretched antelope-skin,
why, he would have stolen the whole pack.

Blackburn thought he gave more light when he told his
chief the story of the encampment by the Guadaloupe River ;
and here Nolan was at one with him. If a Franciscan
father plied them all with brandy, he had his reasons. If
he plied them with brandy, they all slept soundly, and kept
no watch that night. If he were curious about their enterprise, he would inform himself of it.

"Blackburn, on the other skin there was a picture-writing
which told us just what we want to know."

"That's what I say too," said Blackburn promptly.

"Blackburn, in this parcel, with this little prayer-book,
was a note which told us just what we want to know."

"That's what I say."

"And that fellow with a long brown nightgown, tied up
with a halter round his waist, has got it."

So saying, Nolan for the last time turned over the book
of hours, and Blackburn turned to leave his pensive chief.

"Halloo ! Blackburn, come back ! "

And Nolan led him to a secluded shelter, where they
were out of ear-shot or eye-shot.

"See here, and here, and here, and here ; " and he pointed
one by one to the four ornamented pages of the prayer-book.

"Miss Perry was as much afraid of these nightgown men
as I am. She has sent her message in writing they do not
learn at Rome."

Sure enough : in miniature work quite as elegant as many
a priest has wrought in, Eunice had substituted for the

original illustrations of the book a series on vellum which much better answered her present purpose. The pictures were all Bible pictures; and the figures were drawn in the quaint style of the original. But every scene was a scene of parting, and illustrated the beginning of a retreat.

Here was Abraham going up out of Egypt, very rich in cattle. Strange to say, the cattle were all horses, and in Abraham's turban was a long cardinal feather. "Do you remember, Blackburn, the feather I wore the day I bade the ladies good-by?"

Then here was Lot and his troop turning their backs on the plain. Once more the preponderance of horses was remarkable; and once more a brilliant red feather waved in Lot's helmet.

Blackburn began to be interested. The next picture was of Gideon crossing the Jordan in his retreat. There were spoils of the Midianites, and especially horses; and in Gideon's head waved still the red feather.

By and by Ezra appeared, leading the Israelites over the Euphrates. Horses again outnumbered all the cattle, and Ezra again wore a red feather; but the chief next to Ezra, just of his height and figure, wore a crest of fur.

"See there, Blackburn! She thinks Harrod is here! That is his squirrel-tail."

They turned on, but there were no more pictures. Both men looked back upon these four; and it was then that Nolan's eye caught the figures in black-letter at the bottom of the first, —

Exod. xii. 31, 32; Deut. ii. 9.

"Halloo, Blackburn! what is this?" cried he. "There is nothing about Abraham in Deuteronomy, nor in Exodus either."

In a moment Blackburn had brought to his chief, from a little box at the head of his sleeping-bunk, the Bible which accompanied him in his journeys. A moment more had found the warning texts, —

"Rise up, and get you forth from among my people, both ye and the children of Israel ; and go, serve the Lord as ye have said.

" Also take your flocks and your herds, as ye have said, and be gone ; and bless me also."

" And the Lord said unto me, Distress not the Moabites, neither contend with them in battle ; for I will not give thee of their land for a possession."

Nolan read aloud to Blackburn ; and then, as he looked for more messages, he said, —

" It is all of a piece with old Ransom's token.   They think the country is too hot for us, and they mean to put us on our guard.   See, Blackburn, what comes next."

Under Lot and his party were the letters, —

Josh. ix. 1, 2.

" Lucky the Franciscan blackleg did not know Lot was not cousin of Joshua," growled Nolan.

He turned up the text to read, —

" And it came to pass when all the kings which were on this side Jordan, in the hills, and in the valleys, . . . heard thereof ;
"That they gathered themselves together, to fight with Joshua and with Israel, with one accord."

Under the next pictures were the letters, —

Judg. xi. 17.

And the interpretation proved to be, —

" Then Israel sent messengers unto the king of Edom, saying, Let me, I pray thee, pass through thy land ; but the king of Edom would not hearken thereto."

" This is plain talk, Blackburn," said the chief after a moment's pause.

" Yes, captain ; and do you see ? " —

The man took the book carefully from his chief, and showed him, far in the distance of each picture of the four, a three-domed cathedral with three crosses.

"Them's the crosses of Chihuahua; I've heard on 'em hundreds of times. Has not thee, captain?"

"Heard of them! I have seen them. You are right, Blackburn. It is from Chihuahua that our enemy is coming, and from Chihuahua that we must look for him. Now what is this?"

And he turned once more to the picture of Ezra with his cardinal. The warning texts were, —

𝔈𝔷𝔯𝔞 𝔳𝔦𝔦𝔦. 10; 𝔈𝔵𝔬𝔡. 𝔦𝔟. 8.

"And of the sons of Shelomith; the son of Josiphiah, and with him an hundred and threescore males."

"I do not care what his name is, Blackburn; but, if he has a hundred and sixty Spanish lancers of the male sort after him, they are too many for us. What is her other text?"

"And it shall come to pass, if they will not believe thee, neither hearken to the voice of the first sign, that they will believe the voice of the latter sign."

"I should think so," said Nolan sadly or dully, as Blackburn might choose to think. "I should think so, unless they wanted to be marched, every man of them, into the mines at New Mexico.

"Blackburn, an hour after sunrise to-morrow we will be gone."

"I say so too," replied the subordinate, by no means ill pleased.

"Get the redskins well off to-night. We will say nothing to the boys till they are well gone."

Accordingly a grand farewell feast was improvised for Crooked Feather. The very scanty stores of whiskey which were left in the hunters' provisions were largely drawn upon. A pipe of peace was smoked; and Crooked Feather and his men were started on their return with haste which might have have seemed suspicious, had they been more sober.

Perhaps it seemed suspicious as it was.

Crooked Feather bore with him the "medicine-paper" which he coveted, the display of which to White Hawk, to the white-haired chief, or to the white lady, to either or to all, would produce the much-coveted and well-earned sugar.

CHAPTER XX.

A TERTULIA.

" Come to our *fête*, and bring with thee
 Thy newest, best embroidery;
 Bring thy best lace, and bring thy rings:
 Bring, child, in short, thy prettiest things."
         After MOORE.

CROOKED FEATHER was not false to his promise; and on this occasion he met neither medicine-man nor ghostly father to hinder him on his way. On the thirteenth day from that on which he started, he came in sight of the crosses of Antonio. He found his own party encamped not far distant from the place where he had left them. No sign of surprise or affection greeted the return of the party. They swung themselves sullenly from their horses, and gave them to the care of the women. Crooked Feather satisfied himself that neither of the three whites who were authorized to receive his token had come out to meet him. He was too taciturn and too proud to confess his disappointment, — for disappointment he really felt. He solaced himself by devouring a bit of the mesquit, — a rabbit which he tore limb from limb with his fingers. He then bade his wife bring out another horse; and, without his companions this time, he rode into the Presidio with his token.

He gave a wide berth to every man who wore a black coat or cassock. His memories of the headache which followed his last debauch were too fresh, and the shame he felt at being outwitted by the scalped fathers was too great, for him to trust himself to such guides again.

Lounging in part of Major Barelo's quarters, he found old Ransom.

"Back agen, be ye?" said the old man with undisguised surprise. "Come into the yard with me. Yarg! Go ask the Señora Perry if she will have the kindness to come down."

The savage swung himself from his beast; and Ransom bade an attendant idler secure him, while he led Crooked Feather into the more private courtyard. In a minute Eunice appeared. The two girls were not with her.

No interpreter was needed, however. The savage was too eager to be well done with his disagreeable expedition. In a moment he produced the tobacco-pouch which Nolan had given him. In a moment more Ransom had found the secret of its fastening, and had opened it. In a moment more Eunice had torn open the letter, and had read it.

PHILIP NOLAN TO EUNICE PERRY.

MARCH 21.

Thank you a thousand times for your warning. Fortunately you are in time. A rascally priest stole your letter, and whatever was on an antelope-skin. But I have the prayer-book, and I have Ransom's whip. Thank the old fellow for us. We are off before daylight; and I send this red-skin off now, that he may not see our trail. Good-by, and God bless you all!

P. N.

"God be praised, indeed!" said Eunice, as she read the letter a second time, this time reading aloud to Ransom, but in her lowest tones, that not even the walls might hear. "God be praised! This is good news indeed. See the man has his sugar, Ransom;" and then she turned, gave her hand to the savage, smiled, and thanked him. With a moment more she was in her own room, and had summoned the two girls to share her delight and triumph.

The letter was read to Inez, and it was translated to the White Hawk. Then Inez took it, and read it herself, and turned it most carefully over. It was only after a pause that she said, " Are you sure there was no other letter, that there was nothing more ?" And then Eunice wondered too, and sent to recall Ransom. There might have been something else in the tobacco-pouch.

No ! there was nothing more in the tobacco-pouch. Inez even clipped out the lining of it with her scissors. There was nothing more there ; there had been nothing more there.

None the less was Inez resolved that she would ride out with the White Hawk the next morning, and have an interview with the Crooked Feather. The Crooked Feather could, at the least, tell whom he had ·found at the encampment.

And then the three ladies began their preparations for the *tertulia* of the evening, with more animation and joyfulness than they had felt for many, many days.

" What in the world shall I say to your horrible Mr. Lonsdale, aunt, if he should take it into his grave old island head to ask me what makes me so happy ? "

" What, indeed ? " said Eunice. " We must not tell him any lies. You must change the subject bravely. You must ask him what are the favorite dances in London."

" Eunice, I will ask him if his old Queen Charlotte dances the bolero. I will. I should like to show him that I know him perfectly well, and through and through."

" I wish I did," said Eunice, stopping in her toilet, and looking at Inez almost anxiously.

" Wish you did? Then I will tell you in one minute. He is a hateful old spy of a hateful old king. And what he is here for, I do not see. What was the use of our beating the redcoats and Hessians all out of our country, if, after it is all over, we are to have these spies coming back to look round and see if they have not forgotten something ? "

" Don't talk too loud, pussy," said her aunt, taking up the comb again. " What would Gen. Herrara say if he heard

you call this your country, and if you told him you thought
he ought to turn all travelling Englishmen out of it ? "

" Travelling fiddlesticks ! " cried the impetuous girl.   " Do
you tell me that an English gentleman, like dear Sir Charles
Grandison, who was a gentleman, has nothing better to do
than to cross the ocean and come all the way up to this
corner of the world to pay his respects to the Señora Valois,
and to dance a minuet with me ? "

" He might be worse employed, I think," said Aunt Eunice,
catching and kissing the impetuous girl, whose cheeks glowed
as her eyes blazed with her excitement ; " and I believe dear
Sir Charles's grandson would say so too, if he were here.
Come, come, come ! Mary is wondering what you are storm-
ing about, and all your pantomime will never explain to her.
Come, come, come !   How nice it is to be able to go to a
party without setting foot out of doors ! "

It was indeed true, that, by one of the corridor or cloister
arrangements which gave a certain Moorish aspect to the
little military station, there was a passage, quite " practicable," through which, without putting foot to the earth, the
three ladies passed to the saloons of Madame .de Valois,
where the brilliant party of the evening was gathering.   The
home of this lady was in the city of Chihuahua ; but, fortunately for our ladies, in this eventful winter she was making
a long visit at San Antonio.   She had chosen this evening
to give a brilliant party, by way of returning the civilities
which she had received from the ladies of the Presidio.

All three of the American ladies were welcomed with
cordial and even enthusiastic courtesy.   The White Hawk
was quite used, by this time, to the pretty French dresses in
which Inez was so fond of arraying her.   She could speak
but little English, less French, and still less Spanish ; and
she could dance but little English, less French, and less
Spanish.   But the minuet, as has been intimated, was the
common property of the world ; and Inez had spent time
enough in compelling Ma-ry to master its intricacies, to be

rewarded by no small measure of success. She said, herself, that Ma-ry's mistakes were as pretty as other people's victories. For the rest, in all civilizations, the language of the ballroom requires but a limited vocabulary, so there be only fans and eyes to supply the place of words.

Inez had not been wrong in suspecting that she should come to a trial of wits with Mr. Lonsdale. "See what he will get out of me," she whispered disdainfully to her aunt, as Mr. Lonsdale was seen bearing down to cut her out from the protection of Miss Perry's batteries.

"And what is your news from home, Miss Inez?"

This was his first question after they had taken their places for the dance.

"Oh, we feel that we bring home with us! It would be quite home were only papa here, and my brother."

Thus did Inez reply.

"Indeed, you are more fortunate than the rest of us. We cannot carry our household gods with us so easily."

Inez bit her lip that she need not say, "Why do you come at all if you do not like to be here?" But she said nothing.

Mr. Lonsdale had to begin again, — a thing which was then, as it is now, difficult to men of his nation engaged in conversation.

"I meant to ask what is your news from the United States. Is Mr. Jefferson the President? or does President Adams continue for another term of office?"

Inez was indignant with the man, because he had not in any way thrown himself open to her repartee. The question was perfectly proper, perfectly harmless; and it was one, alas! which she could not answer.

"I did not know what to say to him," she said afterward to her aunt. "So I told him the truth."

What she did say was this : —

"I do not know, and I wish I did, Mr. Lonsdale."

"And which candidate do you vote for, Miss Perry?"

"The hateful creature!" This was Inez's inward ejaculation. "He means to draw out of me the material for his next despatch to the tyrant. Sooner shall he draw out my tongue, or my heart itself from my bosom."

Fortunately, however, it would have been difficult for Inez to tell which her predilections were. She answered, still with the craft of honesty, —

"Oh, papa thinks President Adams is too hard on our French friends. For me, I am a Massachusetts girl, and I cannot bear to have a Massachusetts president defeated ; and then, Mr. Lonsdale, Col. Freeman says that Col. Burr is a very handsome man, and a very gallant soldier. He fought at Monmouth, Mr. Lonsdale : did you see him there, perhaps?"

And here the impudent girl looked up maliciously, well satisfied that she had in one word implied that Lonsdale was at least forty years old, and that he had turned his back in battle.

He was well pleased, on his part, and amused with the *rencontre.*

"I did not see him at Monmouth," he said, with more animation than she had ever seen him show before. "I do not remember: I had not begun my diary then. I think I must have been knocking ring-taws against an old brick wall we had in the garden. But I have seen Col. Burr. I have seen him take Miss Schuyler down the dance, and he did dance very elegantly, Miss Perry."

"Pray where was that?" said Inez ; and then she was enraged with herself, that she should have betrayed any interest in the spy's conversation.

"Oh! it was at a very brilliant party in New York. Col. Burr seemed to me to be a favorite among ladies, and I see you think so too. But I think that even in America they have no votes."

"I was even with him, auntie. I said that in New Jersey they had votes, and that Col. Burr came from New Jersey."

"You little goose!" said Eunice, when Inez made this confession. "What in the world had that to do with it?"

"Well, auntie, it had nothing to do with it; but it was very important to prove that Mr. Lonsdale was always in the wrong."

And in such a spirit Miss Inez's conversation with poor Lonsdale went forward, till this particular dance was done.

The pretty and lively girl was demanded by other partners; and she had, indeed, wasted quite as much of her wit, not to say of her impertinence, as she chose, upon the man whom she called a "British spy," and who, let it be confessed, added to other mortal sins that of being at least three and thirty years of age, and that of dancing as badly as the First Consul himself. Inez did not pretend to disguise her satisfaction, as he led her back to her duenna, and she was permitted to give her hand to some ensign of two and twenty.

Lonsdale turned, amused more than discomfited, to Eunice.

"Miss Perry will not forgive me for the sin of sins."

"And what is that?" said Eunice, laughing.

"Oh, you know very well! The sin of sins is, that I am born the subject of King George, and that at her behest I do not renounce all allegiance to him, whenever I pray to be delivered from all the snares of the Devil."

Eunice laughed again.

"I hope you pardon something to the spirit of a girl who is born under a sceptre much more heavy than that of the 'best of kings.'"

Lonsdale might take "best of kings" as he chose. It was the cant phrase by which King George was called by poets-laureate and others of their kidney, till a time long after this.

"Oh! I can pardon any thing to seventeen, when seventeen is as frank, not to say as piquant, as it is yonder. Miss Inez does not let her admirers complain of her insincerity."

"No! She has faults enough, I suppose; though I love her too well to judge her harshly enough, I know. But, among those faults, no one would count a want of frankness."

"Still," said Lonsdale, hesitating now, and approaching his subject with an Englishman's rather clumsy determina tion to say the thing he hates to say, and to be done with it, "still it seems to me a little queer that Miss Inez can forgive all enemies save those of her own blood. After all, it is English blood ; her language is the English language, and her faith is the English faith. Why should she speak to an Englishman with a bitterness with which no French girl speaks, and no Spanish girl? We have fought the French, and we have fought the Spaniards, harder and longer than we ever fought your people ; and I may say," said he, laughing now, "we have punished them worse."

."Oh! Mr. Lonsdale," said Eunice, who would gladly have parried a subject so delicate, "do not be so sensitive. Pardon something to 'sweet seventeen,' and something to the exaggeration of a girl who has never set foot in her own country."

"What do you mean?"

"I mean that this poor child is an exaggerated American. She was born under the flag of Spain. She has heard of the excellences of Washington and Adams and Franklin. She has never seen the littlenesses of their countrymen. She has heard of the trials of her father's friends. She has never seen the pettiness of daily politics. She wants to show her patriotism somewhere, and she shows it by her raillery of an Englishman. I trust, indeed, that she has not been rude, Mr. Lonsdale."

"Indeed, indeed, your pupil does you all credit and honor, Miss Perry. Miss Inez could not be rude, be assured. But it is not of her only that I am speaking. Remember, — nay, you do not know, — but I have met your fair countrywomen in their homes, in Boston, in New York, in Philadelphia. I have met them, I have danced with them, as with Miss Inez on this outpost. Always it is the same. Always courtesy, — hospitality if you please, — but always defiance. France, Spain, poor Portugal even, — nay, a stray Dutchman, — they welcome cordially. But an Englishman, — because he speaks their language, is it? — because he prays to God, and not to God's mother, is it?"—and this Lonsdale said reverently,—"an Englishman must be taught, between two movements of the minuet, that George III. is the worst of tyrants, and that a red coat is the disguise of a monster. Why is this, Miss Perry? As I say, no French girl speaks so to an English traveller: no Spanish girl speaks so. Yet our arms have triumphed over France and Spain; and—hear me confess it—they have been humbled, as they never were humbled elsewhere, by our own children. Is that any reason why our children should hate us?"

It was a pretty sight to see Eunice Perry look now timid, and now brave. It was a pretty sight to see her look him full in the face, and then look down upon the ground without speaking. She tried to speak, and she stopped. She hesitated once and again. Then, after a flush, the blood wholly left her cheek. But she looked him square in the eye, and said,—

"You are frank with me, Mr. Lonsdale: let me be frank with you. Surely I can be frank,—it is best that I should be. For it is not of you that I speak: it is of your country, or of your king. Will you remember, then, that you introduced this subject, and not I?"

Lonsdale was startled by her seriousness, though he had been serious. But he said,—

"Certainly, certainly: pray say what is on your heart. Whatever you say, I deserve. You parried my questions as long as you could."

"Surely I did. The conversation is none of my seeking," said Eunice, really proudly.

Then she paused, and looked again upon the ground; but, when she had collected herself, she looked him fairly in the face, as before.

"Mr. Lonsdale, when you fight France, you fight her navies; when you fought Spain, you fought her armies. No French girl has seen an English soldier on French soil since Cressy and Agincourt. But, when you fought us, you fought

us in our homes.   Nay, where we had no armies, your cruisers
and squadrons could easily land soldiers on our shores, and
did.   Where we had no forts, it was easiest to burn our
villages.   From Falmouth (you do not know where Falmouth
is), to Savannah (you do not know where that is), there are
not fifty miles of our coast where an English cruiser or an
English fleet has not landed English troops.   There is not a
region of my country fifty miles wide, but has seen an inroad
of marauding English seamen or soldiers.   Your journals
laughed at your admirals for campaigns which ended in stealing sheep.   But, Mr. Lonsdale, because my father's sheep
were stolen by Admiral Graves's fleet, I, who talk with you,
have walked barefoot with these feet for twelve months at a
time in my girlhood.   Nay, Mr. Lonsdale, I have seen my
mother's ears bleeding, because an English marine dragged
her ear-rings from her ears.   What French girl lives who
can tell you such a story? — what Spanish girl?   There is
not a county in America, but a thousand girls, whom you
meet as you meet Inez, could tell you such ; would tell you
such, but that our nations are now, thank God ! at peace,
and you have come among them as a stranger who is a friend.
They do not tell the story.   It is only I who tell the story.
But they remember the thing.   Pardon me, Mr. Lonsdale.   I
did not want to say this ; and yet perhaps it is better that it
is said."

"Better!" said the Englishman ; "a thousand times better.
It is the truth.   And really — I would not, — really, you
know, — I would not, I could not, have pressed, had I thought
for a moment that I should give you pain."

" I am quite sure of that," said Eunice simply ; and, with
an effort, she changed the subject.   But, after a beginning
like this, the Englishman could not, even if he would, bring
round her talk to the subject of Philip Nolan and his hunters.

CHAPTER XXI.

THE MAN I HATE.

"But Wisdom, peevish and cross-grained,
Must be opposed to be sustained."

MATT. PRIOR.

BUT Inez had no chance for further colloquy with her aunt that evening. And, when they came home from the little ball, perhaps Inez was tired, perhaps her aunt was tired. Inez was conscious that she was cross; and she felt sure that Aunt Eunice was reserved and not communicative.

The next morning she attacked her to find out what she had learned from the mysterious Englishman; the spy, as she persevered in calling him.

"Is he Blount, dear aunt? I have felt so sure that he was Blount under a false name. I suppose he has a new name for every country he goes into, and every time he changes his coat. I only wish I had called him 'Mr. Blount,' to see the color come for once on those sallow cheeks. I mean to teach Mary to call him 'Blount.'"

"Nonsense, child! you have not the least idea of what you are talking about. Mr. Blount is dead, in the first place: he died last spring. In the second place, and in the third place, he was not an Englishman at all: he was a Tennessee senator." She dropped her voice, even in their own room, and said, "Capt. Phil told me his father knew him."

Miss Inez was a little put down by this firstly, secondly, and thirdly. But she came to the charge again. "Well, I was only a girl, and I did not understand politics. I thought that Blount was a sort of English spy, and I know this man is."

Eunice took the magisterial or duennaish manner; and the White Hawk looked from the one to the other, wondering why Inez was so much excited, and why Eunice seemed so grave.

"Dear Inez," said her aunt, "the Senate of the United States thought, or said they thought, that Mr. Blount was mixed up in a plot which King George's people had for getting back the whole of our region — I mean of the American shore of the Mississippi — to the English. And they punished him for it. And he died. And that is the end of Mr. Blount."

"What a provoking old aunt you are! Of course I do not care whether his name is Blount, or what it is, so long as I am sure that it never was Lonsdale till he landed in Mexico. I am sure I used to hear no end of talk about Mr. Blount; and — and — I have it — it was Capt. Chisholm, aunt. There!" And the girl jumped up, and performed an Apache war-dance with the White Hawk, in token that she had now rightly detected the name of her enemy.

"You look as if you could scalp him, Inez. Take care, or White Hawk will."

"Scalp him! scalping is too good for him, dear aunt. I could scalp him beautifully. Let me show you." And she flew at poor Aunt Eunice on the moment, seized from her luxuriant hair a pretty gold stiletto on which it was wound, gathered the rich curls up in her own left hand, and then, waving the stiletto above her head, with a perfect war-cry, affected to plunge it into the offending *chevelure.* The White Hawk laughed in a most un-Indian way; and poor Eunice fought valiantly to liberate herself.

When peace was restored, by a ransom on both sides of a few kisses, Inez flung herself on the floor, and said, —

"Respectable lady, will you tell me now what was your

conversation with Capt. Chisholm, now disguised in this presidio under the fictitious name of Lonsdale, called an *alias* to procurators and counsel learned in the law; otherwise known as 'The Man I Hate'?" And she waved the stiletto again wildly above her head.

"My dear pussy, Mr. Lonsdale is no more a soldier than you are; and I do not believe he ever heard of Capt. Chisholm. When he goes to Orleans they will talk to him about those things perhaps; but in England they were as much secrets as they are here."

"About what things, dear aunt?" said Inez, as serious now as she had been outrageous.

"About that foolish plan of the governor of Canada to pick up the stitches they dropped when they lost the Mississippi River. It was all a bold intrigue of the people in Canada, who probably had some instructions from London, or perhaps only asked for some. But there were not ten men in England who ever heard of the plan. The governor of Canada sent this Capt. Chisholm through to us, to see what could be done. And some foolish people fell into the plot: that is all."

"And Mr. Lonsdale the spy, otherwise known as 'The Man I Hate,'" — these words were accompanied as before by the brandishing of the stiletto, — "has been sent again on just the same errand. Only this time he begins at Vera Cruz and Mexico. He travels north by Monterey and Monteclovez. He pretends to be interested in volcanoes and botany and in butterflies. He makes weak little water-color pictures, almost as bad as mine, of the ruins of Tlascala and Cholula. All this is a mask, a vain and useless mask, to disguise him from my eyes and those of my countrymen. But see how vain is falsehood before truth! The moment he looks me in the face, the mean disguise falls off, and the spy appears. Another André, another Arnold, stands before me, in the presence of 'THE MAN I HATE.'"

"How did you find him out?" asked Eunice, laughing.

" First, Mme. Malgares said that he was a hidalgo of the highest rank at King George's court, that he was a duke of the blue blood, and that Lonsdale was only the name by which he travels incognito."

" But it is not a week since you told me that Mme. Malgares was a fool. I do not believe English princes of the blood travel incognito in the heart of Mexico."

" Mme. Malgares may be a fool," said little Inez wisely ; " but none the less may an acute and adroit man, who has even deceived Miss Eunice Perry, have dropped his guard when he spoke to her."

Inez was, however, a little annoyed by her aunt's retort, and she tried her second reason.

" Second, his talk of butterflies and of flowers is not the talk of a virtuoso, nor even of an artist. It is assumed." Here she waved the dagger again. " He talks with interest when he drops his voice, when he inquires about President Adams, or Mr. Jefferson, about Capt. Nolan, or " —

" Heigh-ho ! " and her animation was at an end ; and, poor girl, she really looked sad and pale.

" About whom ? " said Eunice thoughtlessly.

But Inez was not to be caught.

" I wish I knew who was president. What a shame it should take so long for news to come, when we came so quickly ! Why, I dare say Roland knows, and papa ; and we know nothing."

But Eunice Perry was not deceived by Inez's change of subject. She was as much surprised as Inez was, that they had no message nor token from William Harrod ; and she was quite as anxious about Philip Nolan, too, as her niece could be.

Meanwhile, at the moment when the ladies were discussing Mr. Lonsdale so coolly, he was trying to take old Ransom's measure. With or without an object of pressing his inquiries, he had walked out to the stables to have the personal assurance which every good traveller needs, that the horses which had brought him all the way from Mexico, and were to carry him farther on his journey, were well cared for. At the stables he found, and was well pleased to find, old Ransom.

"Good-morning, Ransom," he said, half shyly and half proudly. He spoke, unconsciously, with the "air of condescension observable in some foreigners," and with an uncertainty which was not unnatural as to whether Ransom were or were not a servant.

The truth was, that Ransom was entitled to all the privileges of a servant, and took all the privileges of a master. He noticed Mr. Lonsdale's hesitation instantly, and from that moment was master of the situation.

"Mornin', sir," was his reply; and then he went on in a curious objurgation, in four or more languages, addressed to the half-breed who was currying Miss Inez's horse.

"They do not treat horses quite as we do," said Lonsdale, trying to be condescending.

"Donno what you do to 'em," said Ransom civilly enough: "there's a good many ways to spile a horse. These here Greasers knows most of 'em."

"Will you come into the stable, and look at my bay?" said Lonsdale artfully. "I do not like to trust him with these fellows."

The old man understood that this was a bribe, as distinctly as if Lonsdale had offered him half a crown. But no man is beyond the reach of flattery, — as the old saw says, we are at least pleased that we are worth flattering, — and he accompanied the Englishman into the other wing of the stable buildings. Having given there such advice as seemed good, he loitered, as Lonsdale did, in the open courtyard.

"Is there any news from above?" said the Englishman, pointing in the direction of the road up the river.

Ransom had not had time to determine on his answer. He would have been glad to know what the ladies had told Lonsdale. As he did not know, he fell back on his policy of general distrust.

"Them redskins was back yesterday. All got so drunk couldn't tell nothin'."

"I wish I could hear from Capt. Nolan," said Lonsdale, — not as if he were asking a question.

"Needn't be troubled about him," said Ransom gloomily: "he'll take care of himself."

"I think he will," said the Englishman, with an easy good-nature, which failed him as little in meeting Ransom's brevities, as when he met little Inez's impertinences, — "I think he will. But I would be glad to know there was no fighting."

Ransom said nothing.

The other waited a moment, and, finding that he should draw nothing unless he gave something, risked something, and said, —

"Capt. Nolan has no better friend than I am. I never saw him ; but I know he is an honorable gentleman. And I do not want to see him and his country at a disadvantage when they meet these idolaters and barbarians."

The words were such as he would not, perhaps, have used in other circles. But they were not badly chosen. Certainly they were not, considering that his first object was to detach the old man from the policy of reserve. Ransom himself had often called the priests "them idolaters" in his talk with Miss Perry, with Inez, and even with the White Hawk, — in faithful recollection of discourses early listened to from Puritan pulpits. But not in Orleans, least of all in his master's house, never even from his *confrères* in Capt. Nolan's troop or with Harrod, had he heard the frank expression of a dislike as hearty as his own.

His own grim smile stole over his face, not unobserved by the Englishman.

"The truth is, Mr. Ransom," said Lonsdale, following his advantage, "there are a plenty of reasons why your country should make war with Spain, and why my country should help you if you will let us. But, when that war comes, let it be a war of armies and generals and fleets and admirals. Do not let an honorable gentleman like Mr. Nolan be flung away in a wilderness where nobody can help him."

He had said enough to change the whole current of Ransom's thought and plan. Wisely or not, Ransom took into his favor a man who held such views as to the Spanish monarchy. He inwardly cemented a treaty of peace with Lonsdale, based on information which for years he had carried in the recesses of a heart which never betrayed confidence.

The well-informed American reader should not need to be told, that not only through the West, but wherever there were active young men in the American army, at that time, the hope of "conquering or rescuing" Mexico — as the phrase was — had found its way as among the probable or the desirable futures of the American soldier. When Taylor and Scott entered Mexico in triumph, in 1846, they were but making those visions of glory which had excited Alexander Hamilton and his friends nearly fifty years before. A curious thing it is, among the revenges and revelations of history, that Hamilton's great rival, Burr, blasted his own fame and ruined his own life, by taking up the very plan and the very hope which Hamilton had nursed with more reason, and, indeed, with more hope of success, a few years before. Silas Perry himself was not more interested in the plans of Miranda, the South American adventurer, than was Alexander Hamilton. And in Miranda's early schemes, as is well known, he relied on the co-operation, not of undisciplined freebooters from the American States, but of the American army under the direction of the American President. When, under President Adams, that army was greatly enlarged, — when Washington was placed at its head, with Hamilton for the first in command under him, — this army was not to act in ignoble seaboard defences. It was recruited to be stationed at the posts which have since become cities on the Ohio and the Mississippi ; and, when the moment came, Hamilton was to lead it to Orleans, and, if God so ordered, to Mexico. "Only twenty days march to San Antonio," says one of those early letters, anticipating by a generation the days of Houston and David Crockett.[1]

Of course all these plans were secrets of state. Not too much of them is now to be found in the archives of Washington, or in the published correspondence. The War Department was, very unfortunately, — or shall we say, very conveniently? — burned, with its contents, in 1800. But no such secrets could exist, no such plans could be formed, without correspondence — private indeed, for more than success hung on the privacy — with the handful of loyal Americans who lived in Orleans. They were, to the last drop of their blood, interested to see such plans succeed. Their co-operation, so far as it could be rendered fairly, must be relied on when the moment for action came. Oliver Pollock, already spoken of in these pages, who had supplied powder to Fort Pitt in those early days of Washington's battles, when powder was like gold-dust, had, before this time, left Orleans for Baltimore. There he was able to give to the Government such advice as it needed. When such an agent as Wilkinson, or Freeman, or Nolan, was despatched to Orleans, he confided what he dared to such reliable men as Silas Perry or Daniel Clark.

In Silas Perry's household there were many secrets of business or of state ; but none were secrets to Seth Ransom. True, there was a certain affectation maintained, as to what he knew, and what he did not know. When the time came for a revelation, Silas Perry would make that revelation, for form's sake. He would say, "Ransom, I am going to send two boxes to Master Roland, by the 'Nancy,' to Bordeaux." But then he knew that Ransom knew this already ; and Ransom knew that he knew that he knew it. There were occasions, indeed, when Silas Perry was humiliated in the family

---

[1] Wilkinson's letters to Hamilton, and Hamilton's in reply on this subject, are still extant in MS.

counsels, because he was obliged to ask for Ransom's unoffered assistance in secret matters. There was a celebrated occasion, when Mr. Perry had lost the will of Gen. Morgan, which that officer had intrusted to him for safe and secret deposit. Silas Perry had put it away, without whispering a word of it to any one, not even to his sister, far less to Inez ; and he had forgotten it through and through. And at last, years after, a messenger came in haste for it, Gen. Morgan being ill, and wishing to change it. Mr. Perry came from the counting-house, and spent hours of a hot day in mad search for it. And finally, when he was almost sick from disgrace and despair, Eunice called Ransom to her.

The old man entered, displeased and disgusted.

"Ransom, Mr. Perry has lost an important paper."

"Know he has."

"It is the will of Gen. Morgan, and the general has sent for it."

"Know he has."

"My brother cannot find it."

"Know he can't."

Eunice even — whom he loved — was obliged to humiliate herself.

"Do you remember his ever speaking to you of it?"

"Never said a word to me."

Eunice had to prostrate herself further.

"Do you think you could find it?"

"Could, if he told me to."

"Ransom, would you find it? he is very much troubled about it."

Ransom's triumph was now complete ; and he led his humbled master and mistress to the forgotten crypt where the will was laid away.

To such a man, the general plan of Hamilton, Miranda, the English Cabinet, and the American Government, was known as soon as it had been confidentially discussed between Gen. Wilkinson and Silas Perry. It was as safe with him as with the English foreign secretary ; far safer, as has proved since, than it was with Wilkinson.   Ransom knew now, therefore, that within four years past the co-operation of an English fleet, an American army, and Spanish insurgents had been among things hoped for by the most intelligent men in his own country.   And so the few words which Lonsdale spoke now led him instantly to the hasty conviction that Lonsdale was a confidential agent in a renewal of the same combination.

I am afraid this discussion of politics has been but rapidly read by the younger part of those friends who are kind enough to hurry over these lines.   Let me only say to them, that, if they will take the pains to read it, they will find the first step in the course which this country marched in for sixty years.   That course eventually gave to it Texas, and afterward California.   Among other things, meanwhile, it gave to it Oregon, and all east of Oregon.   And, when Kansas and Nebraska came to be settled, came the question, " How ? "   And out of that question came the great civil war, which even the youngest of these young readers does not think unimportant.

And, indeed, there needed powers not less than the statesmanship of Adams and Rufus King, the chivalry of Hamilton, and the fanaticism of Miranda, to bring about a marvel like that of peaceful talk between Seth Ransom and an Englishman.

" Do not let an honorable gentleman like Mr. Nolan be flung away in a wilderness where no one can help him." These were Lonsdale's words of frankness.

" Said so myself.   Said so to him, and said so to Mr. Harrod.   Told 'em both it was all dam nonsense.   Ef the Greasers was after 'em, told 'em to get out of the way, and wait for the folks up above to settle 'em."

"Well ! " said Lonsdale eagerly, " and what did they say ? "

"They said they was ready for 'em.   They said they was nobody at Noches that dared follow where they was goin':

they wasn't enough men there. An' they wasn't when we was there. Mr. Harrod an' I counted the horses, we did. They wasn't enough when we was there. But," after a pause, "they's been more men sent 'em since. Hundred an' sixty men went from this place over here, — went two months ago to Noches." Another pause. Ransom looked over his shoulder, made sure there were no listeners, and dropped his voice : "Sent word of this to the cap'n. Got his message back yesterday. He left for home a week ago yesterday."

"God be praised!" said Lonsdale so eagerly that even Inez would have had some trust in him. "If only he runs the lookout at Nacogdoches ! "

"He passed within ten miles on 'em while they was dancin' and figurin' with the ladies," said the old man, well pleased. "Guess he won't run into their mouths this time."

"If he gets safe home," said the other, "he will have chances enough to come over here, with an army behind him."

"Mebbe," was the sententious reply. But Ransom doubted already whether he had not gone too far in his relations to an officer of the English crown, as he chose to suppose Lonsdale to be ; and his confidences for this day were over.

Was he wise, indeed, in trusting "The Man I Hate," so far as he had done ?

We shall see — what we shall see.

CHAPTER XXII.

BATTLE.

"The cowards would have fled, but that they knew
Themselves so many, and their foes so few."
                                        Cymon and Iphigenia.

THE question whether Spain and America should meet in
battle in the forests of Texas was, at that moment, already
decided, although Ransom and Lonsdale did not know it.
The descendants of Raleigh and Sydney and Drake and
Hawkins, of Amyas Leigh and Bertram and Robinson
Crusoe and their countrymen, were to take up the gage
of battle which had lain forgotten so long, and were to meet
in fight the descendants of Alva and Cortez and Pizarro,
and De Soto and Philip the Second.

And for fifty years that battle was to go on ; not on the
seas as in Drake's days and Howard's, but on the land,
in sight of the very palaces Cortez had wondered at, and in
the very deserts in which De Soto had wandered.

And, when the glove was first picked up, poor Philip
Nolan, alas ! was the brave knight who stood for the faith
and for the star of Sidney and Howard.

Of the tragedy which followed, in the twenty-four hours
since we saw him, history has left us two accounts — one, the
journal of Muzquiz, the officer whom we saw kissing his hand
at Chihuahua ; and the other, the tale of Ellis Bean, the
youngest of Nolan's companions. They differ in detail, as
is of course ; but, as to the general history of that cruel
day, we know the story, and we know it only too well.

The custom of Nolan's camp was always that a third of the little party should keep the night-watch while two-thirds slept.   It had happened, naturally enough, that the five Spaniards — as the Mexicans of the party were always called, when they were not called "Greasers" — made one of the three watches.   And, as destiny ordered, these five were on duty on the night after Crooked Feather left with his message.   "As destiny ordered," one says : had they not been there, Philip Nolan perhaps would never have been a martyr, and these words had never been written.   Destiny, carelessness, or treachery, that night put these five men on guard. It was the 21st of March ; and in that climate, to such men as these young fellows, there was little hardship in such beds as they had provided.   They slept, and their leader slept, as hunters sleep after one day of work, and before another of enterprise.   He had not confided to any of them but Blackburn the plan for an immediate return.

Of a sudden the trampling of horses roused him.   It was dark ; still he judged it past midnight.   The fear of a stampede, or of Indian thieves, was always present, and Nolan was on his feet.   He hailed the guard.

No answer !

He left the little shed in which they were sleeping.   The guard were gone.

"Blackburn ! Bean ! Cæsar ! The Greasers are gone ! Call all the men ! "

In the darkness the men gathered.

From their wall of logs they peered out into the forest. It was not so dark but they could see here a figure passing and there.   Nolan and the others hailed in Spanish, and in various Indian tongues ; but they got no answers.

"Who will come to the corral with me ?" cried their fearless leader.

Half a dozen men volunteered.

They crossed to the corral to find that the horses were safe.   It was no stampeding party. Philip Nolan knew at that instant that he had not Indians to fight against, but the forces of the Most Catholic King of Spain ; one hundred and sixty of them too, if Miss Eunice had been right in her counting.

Of this he said nothing to his men. He bade each man charge his rifle ; but no man was to fire till he gave the word. He looked for his own double-barreled fowling-piece. It was gone. One of the "Greasers" had stolen it, as he deserted.[1]

This act made their bad faith the more certain, and revealed to the men, what Nolan never doubted, the character of their enemies. He bade them keep well covered by the logs, and so they waited for the gray of the morning.

Nor did they wait long. A party of the besiegers approached. Nolan showed himself fearlessly.

"Take care how you come nearer," he cried. "One or other of us will die if you do."

They halted like children, as they were bidden.

"Who will come with me this time ? " said he ; and again the volunteers were all that he could ask.

"No, not with rifles ! Lay down your rifles." And he stepped forth unarmed from the little enclosure ; and they, without gun or pistol, followed.

Again Nolan hailed the enemy in Spanish.

"Do not come near, for one or other of us will be killed if you do." On this there was a consultation among the enemy ; and, with a white flag, an Irishman whose name was Barr came near enough to talk with Nolan in English. He said his commander was a lieutenant named Muzquiz, and he justified Eunice's count of a hundred and sixty men. Unless Nolan had more men than he seemed to have, fight was hopeless, Barr said.

"We shall see that," said Nolan. "What terms do they offer us ? "

---

[1] The piece was afterward seen by Lieut. Pike ; and Muzquiz, the Spaniard, describes the theft.

Barr was not authorized to offer any terms. The orders of Muzquiz were to arrest them, and send them prisoners to Coahuila.

"Arrest us!" said Nolan, "when you know I have your governor's permit to collect these horses for your own army in Louisiana, and to bring in goods, if I choose, to pay the Indians for them; do you mean to arrest me?"

Barr said he could say nothing of that. Muzquiz had come to arrest them, and he expected them to surrender "in the name of the king."

Nolan turned to his men; but he needed not to consult them. They knew what Spanish courtesy to prisoners was too well. "Let them fight if they choose," was the sentiment of one and all. Barr went back to his master; and Nolan and his companions to the little log enclosure, which was yesterday only the poorest horse-pen, and was to-day a fort beleaguered and defended.

Who knows what, even with such odds, the end might have been! These gallant Spanish troopers, ten to one, did not dare risk themselves too near. But, not ten minutes after the sharp-shooting began, Nolan exposed himself too fearlessly, was struck by a ball in the head, and fell dead, without a word.

Muzquiz had brought with him a little swivel, on the back of a mule. He did not dare risk his men before the Kentucky and Mississippi sharp-shooters. But it was easy fighting, to load this little cannon with grape-shot, and fire it pell-mell upon the logs. If one of his men exposed himself, a warning rifle-shot showed that some one was alive within. But the Spaniards kept their distance bravely, and loaded and fired the swivel behind the shelter which the careful Muzquiz had prepared.

Within the pen there were various counsels. Ellis Bean, the youngest of the party, probably offered the best; which was, that at the moment the swivel was next discharged they should dash upon it and take it, trusting to the Spaniards' unwillingness to die first. "It is at most but death," said Bean ; "and we may as well die so as in their mines." And two or three of the boldest of them held with Bean. But the more cautious men said that this was madness. And so, after four hours of this aiming into the thicket from behind the logs, they loosened the logs on the side opposite the swivel, and then took the opportunity of the next discharge to escape from their fortress into the woods, bearing with them two wounded men, but leaving the body of their brave commander.

There were but nine well men left, after the desertion, and these two wounded fellows. Each man filled his powder-horn ; and to old Cæsar, who had no gun, was given the remaining stock of powder to carry. For a few minutes their retreat was not noticed. They got a little the start of the swivel-firers. But the silence of the pen-walls told a story ; and the Spaniards soon mustered courage to attack an empty fortress. Nothing there but Phil Nolan's body, and the little stores of the encampment !

Warily the host followed. Mounted men as they were, they of course soon overtook these footmen. But they kept a prudent distance still. No man wanted to be the first shot ; and the whir of an occasional bullet would remind the more adventurous that it was better to be cautious. At last, however, they made a prize. Poor Cæsar, with his heavy load, had lagged ; and, as he had no gun, a brave trooper pounced upon him. All the powder of the pursued troop was thus in the hands of the pursuers.

The next victory, announced by a cheer of Spanish rapture, was the surrender of one of the wounded men. He could not keep up with his friends, and he would not delay them. He was seen waving a white rag, and was surrounded by the advance with a shout of victory.

So passed six hours of pursuit and retreat. Muzquiz sent a body in advance, to command, with their carbines, both sides of the trail he knew his enemy would take. But so cautious was the Spanish fire, that the fortunate fellows passed through this defile without losing a man. Well for them that the Spaniards believed so religiously in the distance to which the Kentucky rifle would carry lead! Six hours of pursuit and retreat! At last Fero, who was more like a commander than any others in the little company, and Blackburn the Quaker, called a halt. They counted their forces. All here, but he who had insisted on surrendering himself, — save, alas! Cæsar.

Every man's horn was nearly empty. Unless Cæsar could be found — all was lost!

No. He cannot be found!

They are brave fellows; but there is nothing for it, but to hoist a white flag, which Muzquiz welcomed gladly.

He knew now what he could do, and what he could not do. He knew he could not make Spanish troopers with their carbines stand the sure fire of the Kentucky rifle. He knew Nolan was dead. The danger of the expedition was at an end. His own advancement was sure. In any event, it was victory.

Muzquiz therefore sent in Barr the Irishman again, and this time bade him offer terms. The little party was to return to Nachitoches, and never come into Texas any more. In particular they were to promise to make no establishment with the Indians.

To this they replied, that he might have saved himself trouble. This was just what he wanted to do. But they added that they should never give up their arms.

They were assured that this was not demanded: only they must agree to be escorted back to Natchitoches.

To this they agreed, if they might go back and bury Nolan. Muzquiz consented to this. The party marched back together, and buried him. But no man knows his resting-place. Nolan's River, a little branch of the Brassos, is the only monument of his fame.

The whole party then turned eastward, and marched good-naturedly enough together to Nacogdoches. Once and again the Spaniards had to accept of the superior skill of the Americans, in building rafts, or constructing other methods for crossing the swollen streams. So they arrived at the little garrison. Which were the conquerors?

It would have been hard to tell, until the morning after their arrival, when the Americans were disarmed, man by man, and handcuffed as criminals.

From that moment to this moment, the words " Spanish honor " have meant in Texas " a snare and a lie."

CHAPTER XXIII.

AT SAN ANTONIO.

"Of all their falsehood, more could I recount,
But now the bright sun 'ginneth to dismount;
And, for the dewy night now doth draw nigh,
I hold it best for us home to hie."

SHEPHERD'S CALENDAR.

APRIL crept by at San Antonio; but it only crept. The easy winter-life, which was not wintry, passed into the life of what ought to have been a lovely spring-time; for not at Nice or Genoa, better known, alas, to the average American reader than San Antonio, can spring be more lovely than it is there. But it was not lovely. Major Barelo assured Eunice on his honor that he had no news from Muzquiz's force above. He began to assure her, that, if they had met the hunters, he certainly should have heard of it before this. Miss Perry tried to believe this, and she tried to make Inez believe it. But still the days hung heavy. The little entertainments of the garrison seemed heartless and dull. What was a game at prison-bounds, or a costume-ball, or a play of Cervantes, or a picnic at the springs, when people did not know whether dear friends were alive or dead, or in lifelong captivity? How could one hunt for prairie-flowers, and analyze them and press them, when one remembered the ride across the prairies, and wondered where they were who shared it?

Poor Inez had her own cause of anxiety, which burned all the more hotly in her poor little heart because she was too proud to speak of it, even to Aunt Eunice. Where was Will Harrod? If he had joined Capt. Phil before Crooked Feather did, why had not Crooked Feather brought one word, or message, or token? If he had not joined Capt. Phil? — that question was even worse. Oh, the whole thing was so hollow! That one should eat and drink and sleep, should go to balls and *tertulias* and reading-parties; that Lieut. Gonzales should lift one into the saddle, and talk bad English with one for the hours of a ride; that Mr. Lonsdale should hang round all the evening, and talk of every thing but what he was thinking of, and she was thinking of, and Aunt Eunice was thinking of, — it was all a horrid lie, and it was terrible.

White Hawk was her only comfort. Dear child! she knew she was her only comfort; and, with exquisite instincts, she took upon her the duties of a comforter without once affecting that she took them. But she could make Inez forget herself, and she did. She would spin out the pretty lessons in writing, on which Inez had begun with her. She would lead her to talk about the spelling tasks and the reading lesson, which in Inez's new-fledged dignity as a tutor she was giving. Then she would play teacher in her turn. They found porcupine's quills; and a lovely mess they made of things in dyeing them with such decoctions as White Hawk invented. They embroidered slippers for Eunice, for themselves, for Major Barelo, and for dear Aunt Dolores; even for old Ransom, they embroidered slippers as the winter and spring went by. Inez was becoming a proficient in other forms of wood-craft. Ah me! if Will Harrod had come back, she could have talked to him before the spring went by, in pantomime quite as expressive as his own, and far more graceful.

But then, just when they came back from a tramp on the beautiful river-side, with old Ransom and one and another attendant, laden down with their roots and barks and berries, and other stuff, — as the old man called it, — the first sight of the garrison brought back the old terrible anxiety. Inez would rush to Aunt Dolores or to Aunt Eunice, and say, "Is there any news?" as if this happy valley was no happy valley at all, and as if she could not forget how far parted she was from the world.

Old Ransom took on himself to school her, in his fashion, more than her aunt thought wisest.

"Een," he said to her one day as they rode, "ye mus'n' take on so much as ye do for the cap'n. The cap'n's all right, he is. He told me heself he should be back at the river 'fore March was over. Them mustangs ain't good for nothin' ef you sells 'em after May, 'n' the cap'n knew that's well as I did. 'N he says, says he, 'Ransom,' says he, 'I shall be in Natchez first week in April. I shall send two hundred on 'em down the river to Orleans in flats,' says he ; ''n I shall go across to the Cumberland River, through the Creek country, with the others.' That's what he says to me. He knows Bowles, the Injen chief — always did know lots of the redskins. 'N he says to me, 'I shall go to the Cumberland River to be there 'fore April's over, time for the spring ploughing.'"

Every word of this was a lie ; but it was a lie invented with so kind an object, and, indeed, so well invented, that the recording angel undoubtedly dropped a tear of compassion and regret commingled, as he wrote it down.

Poor Inez tried to believe it true.

"You never saw Crooked Feather again, Ransom, did you ?"

Ransom paused. He doubted for a moment, whether he would not boldly create a second conversation with Crooked Feather, in which that chief should describe an interview with William Harrod. But no! this was too much. For the old man loved the truth in itself, and did not ever intend to swerve from it. What he had said about Nolan and the horses, he believed to be the absolute truth of things. He had put it in the form of a conversation with Nolan, because he could thus most distinctly make Inez apprehend it, baby as she was in his estimation still. But, as to Harrod, he believed as implicitly that he had been scalped within the week after he left them. Believing that, he had no romance to invent which should restore him to the world.

After a pause — not infrequent in his colloquies — he assumed a more didactic tone. It would, at another time, have delighted Inez ; but now the weight at her heart was too heavy. Still she beckoned the White Hawk to come up and ride by their side ; and the old man went on with his lecture.

" I never see him, Een, and I never want to. Niggers is bad ; French folks is bad ; English is wus ; and Spanish is wus then them, by a long sight ; but redskins is the wust on 'em all. They's lazy, that's one thing ; so is niggers. They's fools, that's one thing ; so is the mounseers. They's. proud as the Devil, that's one thing ; so is the Englishmen. They'll lie 's fast 's they can talk : so'll the Spaniards ; 'n' they'll cheat and steal, and pretend they can't understand nothin' you say all the time. They's a bad set. I gin your old chief (Crooked Feather he said his name was, but he lied ; it wasn't — didn't have no name) — I gin him his sugar, 'n I turned him out of the warehouse, 'n I told him ef I ever see him ag'in, I'd thrash him within an inch of his life. He pertended he didn't know nothin', 'n that he didn't know what I meant. But he knew enough to make tracks, 'n I haint ever seen him sence, 'n I haint wanted to, neyther. Redskins is fools 'n liars 'n thieves 'n lazy, 'n aint no good any way."

Ma-ry understood enough of this eulogy on her old masters to laugh at it thoroughly : indeed she sympathized, and said to Inez, —

" Ma-ry knows, yes. Ransom knows, yes. Crooked Feather bad, lazy, steal. O Inez, Inez ! darling dear, all bad, all lie, all steal ;" and she flung down her reins in a wild way, and just rested herself fearlessly on the other's shoulder, and kissed her once and again, as if to bless her that she had taken her from her old taskmasters; then she took the reins again, and made her pony fly like the wind along the road, and return to the party, as if she must do something vehement to express her sense of her escape from such captivity.

Thus Ransom tried — and tried not unsuccessfully — to turn Inez's thoughts for a moment from questions of Nolan and Harrod.

But not for a long respite. The moment they passed the gate of the little wall, which in those days, after a fashion, bounded the garrison, it was evident that something had transpired. The lazy sentinel himself stood at his post with more of a military air. On the military plaza were groups of men together, in the wild gesticulation of Spanish talk, where usually at this hour no one would be seen. Certain that some news had come, Inez pushed her horse, and Ransom in his respectful following, kept close behind her. She would not ask a question of the Spanish officers whom they dashed by; but she fancied that in their salute there was an air of gravity which she had certainly never seen before, — a gravity which the sight of two smiling, pretty girls, dashing by at a fast canter, certainly would not in itself have excited.

Arrived in the courtyard, the excited girl swung herself into Ransom's arms, gathered up her dress, and rushed into her aunt's room. The White Hawk needed no help, but left her pony as quickly, and followed Inez. Eunice was not there at the moment; but, just as Inez had determined to go in search of her, her aunt appeared at the door. Oh, how wretchedly sad in every line of her face, and in the eyes which looked so resolutely on poor Inez! The news had come, and it was bad news!

Eunice gave one hand to each, and led them both into the inner room. She shut the door. She made Inez lie down. Oh, how still she was! and how still they were!

She sat by the girl's side. She held her hand. She even

stroked her forehead with the other, before she could speak. At last, —

"O my darling, my dearest! it is all too true! It is all over."

Inez was on her elbow, looking straight into her eyes.

"Inez, my darling, they met; they found him only the day after he wrote to us. They fought him — the wretches — ten to his one. They killed him. They have taken all the others prisoners ; and they are all to go to the mines, to slave there till the king shall send word to have them killed. O my darling, my child!"

Inez looked her still in the face.

"Who else is killed? Tell me all, dear aunt, tell me all!"

"My darling, O my darling! I cannot hear that anybody but Nolan was killed. They killed him at their first fire, and he never spoke again. Dear, dear fellow! oh, what will his little wife say or do?"

It was the first time that in words Eunice had ever told Inez that Nolan had married the pretty Fanny Lintot, whose picture Inez had seen. In truth, he had married her just before he left Natchez.

"They say they took our people prisoners on terms of unconditional surrender. Inez, they say what is not true. Will Harrod, and all those men with Nolan, would have died before they would have been marched to the mines. But, my darling, I have told you all I know."

"There is no word from — from — from Capt. Harrod?" asked Inez, finding it hard to speak his name even now.

"Oh! no word for us from anybody. There is only a bragging despatch with 'God preserve Your Excellency many years,' from this coward of a Muzquiz, — this man who takes an army to hunt a soldier. Why, I should have thought he had met Bonaparte hand to hand!

"The Major sent for me. He is so kind! And dear Dolores — oh, she is lovely. He told me all he knew. He promised to tell me all. Perhaps the prisoners will come this way: then we shall know.

"But what a wretch I am! I have been praying and hoping so that I might break it to you gently; and I have only poured out my whole story without one thought. Dear, dear Inez, forgive me!"

She was beside herself with excitement. In truth, of the two, Inez seemed more calm. But she was, oh, so deadly pale! She tried to speak. No! she could not say a word. She opened her lips, but no sound would come. Nay, even the tears would not come. She looked up — she looked around. She saw dear Ma-ry, her eyes flooded with tears, her whole eager face alive with her sorrow and her sympathy. Inez flung herself into her arms; and the tears flowed as she sobbed and sobbed and sobbed upon her shoulder.

Eunice told Inez that Major Barelo had told her all. She thought he had. The loyal Spanish gentleman had kept his secret well.

He had not told her all. The bragging despatch from Muzquiz had been accompanied with a little parcel. This parcel contained the ears of Philip Nolan! The chivalrous Muzquiz, the representative of the Most Catholic King, had cut off the ears of the dead hero, to send them in token of victory to the governor!

So low had sunk the chivalry which in the days of Lobeira gave law to the courtesy of the world!

Of this accompaniment to the despatch, Barelo had said nothing to Eunice Perry; nor did she know it till she died.

We know it from the despatch in which the Castilian chief announces it.

CHAPTER XXIV.

"I MUST GO HOME."

"Now with a general peace the world was blest ;
    While ours, a world divided from the rest,
    A dreadful quiet felt, and, worser far
    Than arms, a sullen interval of war :
    Thus when black clouds draw down the laboring skies,
    Ere yet abroad the wingèd thunder flies,
    A horrid stillness first invades the ear,
    And in that silence we the tempest fear."

                                        Astræa Redux.

POOR Inez !   Poor Eunice !

They kept their grief to themselves as best they could.
But every one in the garrison circle knew there was a grief
to keep, though no one, not even Donna Maria, suspected
the whole of it, and no one could quite account for the depth
of the ladies' interest in the freebooters.   Eunice said boldly
that it would prove to be all a mistake, which De Nava and
Salcedo would surely regret.   That Mr. Nolan was an
accomplished gentleman, they all knew, for he had visited
Antonio again and again : he had danced in their parties,
and dined at their tables.   She said he was Gayoso's friend,
and Casa Calvo's friend, and that they were not the men
she took them for, if they did not resent such interference
from another province.   She said boldly, that there would
have to be some public statement now, whether the King of
Spain meant to protect his subjects in Louisiana against
other subjects in Mexico.   So far Eunice carried talk with a
high spirit, because she would gladly give the impression, in

the garrison circle, that she and Inez were wounded with a sense of what may be called provincial pride. The inhospitality exercised toward Nolan to-day might be exercised toward them to-morrow.

But, while Eunice Perry took this high tone in the long morning talks of the ladies, her own heart was sick with the secret her brother had confided to her. She knew that Orleans and Louisiana were Spanish only in name. Did not De Nava and Salcedo know this also? Was not this bold dash against Nolan the first declaration of the indifference of Spanish commanders to all directions from Louisiana, now Louisiana was French again? And, if it were so, ought not Eunice Perry be looking toward getting her white doves to their own shelter again as soon as might be?

She determined, not unwisely, to confide to Ransom the great secret of state which her brother had intrusted to her. In doing this, she knew she would not displease Silas Perry, who would have told Ransom within a minute after he had heard it, for the mere convenience of not having to perplex himself by hiding from his right hand what affected both hands every moment.

Eunice was not displeased that for once she could take the old man by surprise. She chose, as she was wont to do for private conferences, a chance when they were riding; for, while the old stone walls of the garrison might have ears, the river, the prairie, and the mesquits had none.

"Ransom, you know why all the people in Orleans speak French?"

"They's French folks, all on 'em, mum, they is. Them Spaniards is nothin' Ain't real Spanish, none on 'em. Gayoso, he'd lived in England all his life. This one has to talk French. Sham-Spanish all on 'em, they is."

"Yes, Ransom, the King of Spain sends over officers who speak French, because the people are French people."

"Yes'm, all French folks once; had French governors. Awful times, wen your brother fust come there, — when they

tried to send the Spanish governor packing, — good enough
for him, too.   He caught 'em and hanged 'em all — darned
old rascal, he did.   Awful times !   He was a Paddy, he was ;
darned old rascal ! "

"Yes, Ransom, and a very cruel thing it was.   Well, now,
Ransom, the King of Spain is frightened ; and he has given
Orleans back, and all the country, to the French."

"Guess not, Miss Eunice ! " said the old man quickly,
really surprised this time.

"Yes, Ransom, there is no doubt of it ; but it is a great
secret.   The French general told my brother, and he bade
me tell no one but you and Inez.   Do not let these people
dream of it here."

"No, marm, and they don't know it now.   Ef they knew
it, I should know.   They don't know nothin'."   Ransom
said all this slowly, with long pauses between the sentences.
But Eunice could see that he was pleased, — yes, well pleased
with the announcement.   His eyes looked, like a prophet's,
far into the distance before him ; and his face slowly beamed
with a well-satisfied smile, as if he had himself conducted
the great negotiation.

"Good thing, Miss Perry ! guess it's a good thing.   Mr.
Perry did not go for nothin'.   Them French don't know
nothin'.   King of Spain, darned fool, he don't know nothin'.
Ye brother had to go 'n tell 'em."

"No, Ransom, I do not think my brother told them.   But
he says he is glad to belong to the side that always wins."

"Guess Mr. Perry told 'em, ma'am," was Ransom's fixed
reply.   "They's all fools — don't know nothin'."

Eunice had made her protest, and did not renew it.   She
knew she should never persuade the old man that he and
Silas Perry together did not manage all those affairs in the
universe which were managed well.

"My brother is well pleased, Ransom, and so is Roland.
Roland is quite a friend of Gen. Bonaparte."

"Yes'm, this man always wins.   Say his soldiers cum over

here to learn fightin'. Say Gen. Washington had to show 'em how. Say Roshimbow's comin' over to the islands now. I knew that one, Roshimbow, myself; held his hoss for him one day, down to Pomfert meetin'-house, when he stopped to get suthin to drink at the tavern. Gen. Washington was showin' him about fightin' then, and so was old Gen. Knox, and Col. Greaton; and now he's been tellin' this other one. That's the way they knows how to do it. French is nothin'; don't know nothin.' This other one, he's an Eyetalian."

"This other one," who thus received the art of war at second-hand from Col. Greaton of the Massachusetts line, and from George Washington, was the person better known in history as Napoleon Bonaparte.

"Ransom, if there is one whisper of war between France and Spain, we must get back to Orleans. I am sure I do not know how. Or if there is war between England and France again, or between England and Spain. Indeed, I wonder sometimes that we ever came; but we acted for the best."

She hardly knew that he was by her, as she fell back on these anxieties. But it was just as well. The old man was as sympathetic as her mother would have been.

"I should not be troubled, mum. It's peace now, and the major here thinks it's like to be. So does the gov'nor and the general. Heerd 'em say so yesterday. It's peace now, and it's like to be." Here a long pause. "Ain't no cause to be troubled. Miss Inez liked the ride comin', and she'll like it goin'. There's two or three of the Greasers here will go where I tell 'em, and three of the niggers too, ef you don't like to ask him for soldiers. Shouldn't take no trouble about it. When you want to go, ma'am, we'll go. I'll tell 'em the king sent word we was to go." And his own smile showed that he was not displeased at the prospect of leaving behind him a community which he held in deeper scorn than the Orleans which he loved while he despised.

"I hope we may not have to go, Ransom; but you must

keep your eyes open and your ears, and we will be ready to go at an hour's warning."

" Yes'm, the sooner the better."

The truth was, that the signal came sooner than Eunice expected, and in a way as bad as the worst that she had feared. Late in the afternoon of a sultry day in June, — a day which had been pronounced too hot for riding, — the ladies had just returned from a bath in the river, and were not in full costume, when a clamor and excitement swept among the garrison, and, in spite of Major Barelo's precautions and the Donna Maria's, made way even into the rooms of the American ladies. The White Hawk ran out to reconnoitre and inquire.

A band of Spanish troopers, with great fanfarons of trumpets, and even with little Moorish drums, came riding into the plaza, and in the midst, with a troop behind as well as before, a little company of eleven bearded men, dirty and ragged, heavily ironed lest they might leap from their horses, and, without arms, overthrow a hundred Spanish cavalry. These were the American prisoners. They had been kept a month at Nacogdoches, listening to lies about their release, and at last were on their way to Chihuahua and the mines.

The White Hawk, with her usual indifference to regulations, walked right down to this wretched coffle, and in a minute recognized Blackburn, who had seen her at Nacogdoches. Without attempting a word of English, she asked him in pantomime where Harrod was, for the girl saw that he was not in the number. Blackburn did not conceal his surprise. He had taken it for granted, as they all had, that Harrod and the others had been held by the Spaniards. He told the girl, in gestures which she perfectly understood, that they had never seen Harrod, nor King, nor Adams, nor Richards, since, with old Cæsar, he parted from them in the autumn.

Then she ventured on the further question, to which, alas! she knew the answer, — Where was Capt. Nolan? Ah, me !

the poor fellow could only confirm the cruel news of two months before. His quick gesture showed where the fatal shot struck, and how sudden was his death. Then he told, in a minute more, that all this was but the morning after Crooked Feather left them. He called her to him, and bade her stroke his horse's neck, and lie close against his fore-leg as she did so. She was as quick and stealthy as a savage would have been in obeying him; and in an instant more she was rewarded. He slid into her hand, under the rough mane, the little prayer-book which Eunice had sent to Nolan. Blackburn himself had taken it from his leader's body when they buried him; and though, Heaven knows, he had been stripped and plundered once and again since, so that nothing else was left him that he could call his own, the plunderers were men who had a certain fear of prayer-books, — if it were fear which reverenced, — and, for good reasons and for bad, they had left him this and this alone.

"Come again! Come again!" said the White Hawk fearlessly; and she hurried away from the troop, with the news she had collected. In a minute more she had joined the ladies.

"Troopers come — Ma-ry — Ma-ry — troopers. Nolan's men come, — five, five, one!" and she held up her fingers. "Poor men! they are all — what you call — iron — iron — here, here — on hands — on feet. Blackburn come: me talk to Blackburn, Blackburn tell all. Darling, darling, Will Harrod never found them! Will Harrod never saw them! O darling, darling dear! Will Harrod all safe, — all gone home, — Orleans, — darling, darling dear!"

"Who says he's safe?" cried poor Inez, starting to her feet.

"Me say so, — me say he never saw Nolan, — never saw Blackburn. Blackburn said he was here. Blackburn wonder very, very much, Will Harrod not here. Blackburn tell me, — tell me now, — Will Harrod never come, King never come, Adams never come, Richards never come. Blackburn say all here. Nobody come but old Cæsar and Blackburn. Old Cæsar here now: me see old Cæsar."

Inez had fallen back when she saw that Harrod's safety was only the White Hawk's guess. But now she started.

"Dear, dear old Cæsar! let me go see him too;" and they ran. But the prisoners had already been led away; and there needed formal applications to Barelo — and who should say to whom else? — before they could talk with the poor old fellow.

To such applications, however, Barelo was in no sort deaf. If he had dared, and if there had not been twenty or thirty days' hard travel to the frontier, he would have given permits enough to Ransom and Miss Perry and Mlle. Inez and the White Hawk to have set every one of the "bearded men" free; he would have made a golden bridge for them to escape by; for Major Barelo could and did read the future. This was impossible. But old Ransom daily, and one or other of the ladies, saw the prisoners, and, while they could, ministered to their wants.

White Hawk's first story was entirely confirmed. Neither of the escort of the ladies had ever been seen on the Tockowakono or Upper Brassos. The men thought they had deserted, and gone back to Natchez; but Inez of course, and Eunice, knew that Harrod had never deserted his friend.

"No! the Apaches have him, or the Comanches."

"They *had* him! they *had* him, Eunice! But they keep no prisoners alive!" and, in a paroxysm of weeping, Inez fell on her aunt's lap; and the pretended secret of her heart was a secret no longer to either of them.

It was Inez's wretchedness, perhaps, which wore more and more on Eunice as the summer crept by. Perhaps it was the wretchedness of the miserable handful of men kept in close confinement at Antonio. Month after month this captivity continued. More and more doubtful were Cordero's and Herrara's words, when Eunice forced them, as she would force them, to speak of the chances of liberation. As September passed, there came one of the flying rumors from below, of which no man knew the authority, that the King of Spain had quarrelled with the French Republic. This rumor gave Eunice new ground for anxiety as to her position ; and she was well disposed to yield, when Inez one night broke all reserve, and, after one of the endless talks about the mysteries and miseries around them, cried out in her agony, —

"I must go home ! "

CHAPTER XXV.

COUNTERMARCH.

> "*Berenice.* — Tis done !
> Deep in your heart you wish me to be gone ;
> And I depart. Yes, I depart to-day.
> —' Linger a little longer ? ' Wherefore stay ?
> To be the laughing-stock of high and low ?
> To hear a people gossip for my woe ?
> While tidings such as these my peace destroy,
> To see my sorrows feed the common joy ?
> Why should I stay ? To-night shall see me gone."
>
> RACINE.

EUNICE slept upon the girl's ejaculation ; and the next morning she was determined. She went at once to her brother's brother-in-law, and said to him that their visit had lasted nearly a year, that the very circumstance impended by which her brother had limited it, and that frankly she must ask him for such escort as he could give her to Natchitoches. Once at Natchitoches, she would trust herself to her own servants' care, as they should float down the Red River.

The major was careworn, evidently disliked to approach the subject ; but, with the courtesy of a host and of a true gentleman, tried to dissuade her. He asked her why a breeze between Bonaparte and his sovereign should affect two ladies in the heart of America. Was this affectation ? Had he heard that Louisiana was to be French again ? Did he want to come at her secrets ?

Eunice looked him bravely in the eye before she answered. She satisfied herself that he was sincere ; that he did not know that great state secret which had been intrusted to her, and which would so easily explain her anxiety.

"I do not know when my brother will sail on his return. Suppose the First Consul of France chooses to say that he shall not return?"

"Then your niece will be here under the protection of her nearest American relations."

"Suppose Gen. Victor, with this fine French army of which you tell me, passes by St. Domingo, and lights upon Orleans. How long will my friend Casa Calvo defend that city, with a French people behind him, and a French army and fleet before him?"

"He will defend it quite as long without the aid of the Mlles. Perry as with," was Barelo's grave reply, made as if this contingency were not new to his imaginings.

"And if my brother and my nephew be with Gen. Victor, if they land in Orleans, surely they will expect to find us there," said poor Eunice quite too eagerly.

"My dear sister," said the Spanish gentleman gravely, "do not let us argue a matter of which we know so little. I am only anxious to do what you wish: only I must justify myself to Don Silas Perry, in event of any misfortune. I cannot think that he would approve of my sending you two ladies into a scene of war."

"Then you believe that war impends!" cried Eunice, more anxious than ever. "My dear, dear brother, what madness it was that we ever came!"

This was not a satisfactory beginning. It was the determination, however, as it happened, of the route which the little party took, and took soon,—by one of those chances wholly unhoped for when Eunice approached the major. On the very afternoon of that day, the monotony of the garrison life, which had become so hateful to both the ladies. was broken up by the arrival of an unexpected party. Mr. Lonsdale had returned, with a rather cumbrous group of hunters, guides, grooms, and attendants without a name, with whom he had made a long excursion to the mines of Potosi, The arrival of so large a party was a great event in the garrison.

Greatly to the surprise of Miss Perry and her niece, who had excused themselves from a little re-union which called together most of the garrison ladies, a visitor was announced, and Mr. Lonsdale presented himself. Inez was fairly caught, and, at the moment, could not escape from the room, as she would have done gladly. She satisfied herself by receiving him very formally, and then by sitting behind him and making menacing gestures, which could not be seen by him, but could be seen perfectly by her aunt and Ma-ry. With such assistance Eunice Perry carried on the conversation alone.

With some assistance, he was fired up to tell the story of what he and his party had done, and what they had not done ; to tell how silver was mined, and what was a "*conducta.*" He told of skirmishes with Indians, in which evidently he had borne himself with all the courage of his nation, and of which he spoke with all the modesty of a gentleman. But, as soon as Eunice paused at all, Mr. Lonsdale, as his wont was, shifted the subject, and compelled her to talk of herself and her own plans. Not one allusion to poor Nolan : that was too sad. But, of American politics, many questions ; of the politics of the world, more. Who was this man, and why was he here ?

"When I was in Philadelphia and New York they called Mr. Jefferson the pacific candidate. Will he prove to be the pacific president ? "

"You more than I know, Mr. Lonsdale. It was President Adams who made peace with the First Consul."

"I know that, and I know the Mlles. Perry are good Federalists." Here he attempted to turn to see Inez, and almost detected her doubling her fist behind his back. "I had a long talk with Mr. Jefferson, but I could not get at his views or convictions."

"He would hardly mention them to a — to any but an

intimate friend," said Eunice rather stiffly, while Inez represented herself as scalping the Englishman.

"No, no! of course not!   Yet I wish I knew.   I wish any man knew if the First Consul means war or peace with England, or war or peace with America."

Eunice saw no harm here in saying what she knew.

"Gen. Bonaparte means peace with America, my brother says and believes.   My nephew has been intimate at Malmaison, and my brother has seen the First Consul with great advantages.   He thinks him a man of the rarest genius for war or for peace.   He is sure that his policy is peace with us, — with America I mean."

"You amaze me," said Mr. Lonsdale.   "I supposed this general was one more popinjay like the others, — a brag and a bluster.   I supposed his history was to be strung on the same string with that of all these men."

And in saying this Lonsdale did but say what almost every Englishman of his time said and believed.   Nothing is more droll, now it is all over, than a study of the English caricatures of that day, as they contrast "the best of kings" and "the Corsican adventurer."   How pitiless history chooses to be!

In one of these caricatures, George III. figures as Gulliver, and "*Gen. Buonaparte*" is the King of Liliput!

Eunice could well afford to be frank at this time, whether Lonsdale were Conolly, Chisholm, Bowles, or any other English spy.

"My last letters from my brother are very late.   He was certain then of peace between England and France; and of this I have spoken freely here."

Lonsdale certainly was thrown off guard.   His whole face lighted up with pleasure.

"Are you sure? are you sure?   Let me shake hands with you, Miss Perry.   This is indeed almost too good to be true!"

Eunice gave him her hand, and said, —

"Let us hope the new century is to be the century of

peace, indeed. Shall we drink that toast in a glass of rain-water?" and, at a sign from her, the White Hawk brought him a glass of pure water from a Moorish-looking jar of unglazed clay.

"Ma-ry, my dear child," said the Englishman slowly, with the tears fairly standing in his eyes, "do you know what comes to those who give others a cup of cold water?"

Eunice had never seen such depth of feeling on his face or in his manner; and even Inez was hushed to something serious.

As he put down the glass, he passed Miss Perry, and in a low tone he said, —

"May I speak with you alone?"

Eunice, without hesitation, sent the girls to bed. Who was this man, and what did he come for?

"Pardon me, Miss Perry, you know of course how much you can trust of what is secret, in this cursed web of secrets, to our young friends. You may call them back, if you please. You may tell them every word I tell you. But I supposed it more prudent to speak to you alone. As I came across the Rio Grande I learned, and am sure, that Gov. Salcedo has gone to Orleans. That means something."

Of course it did. The transfer of Salcedo to the government of Louisiana must mean more stringent and suspicious government of Orleans. Did it mean war with America? Did it mean war with France?

"I thought," continued the taciturn Englishman, stumbling again now, "I thought — I was sure — you should know this; and I doubted if our friends here would tell you. In your place, such news would take me home ; and therefore I hurried here to tell you. We made short work from the river, I assure you."

"How good you are!" said Eunice frankly, and smiling even in her wonder why this impassive Englishman, this spy of Lord Dorchester or of Lord Hawksbury, should care for her journey.

"How good you are. You are very right. Yet to think that I should want to go nearer to that brute Salcedo! For really I believe it is he, Mr. Lonsdale, it is he who murdered our friend. But I do — I do want to go home. Oh! why did I come? I asked my brother that this morning."

"The past is the past, dear Miss Perry. Your question is not, Why did you come? but, How shall you go?"

"And how indeed?" said she sadly. "My brother virtually refuses me an escort. I do not know why. He wants to keep us here."

"Major Barelo hates, dreads, despises, this Salcedo, — this cruel, vindictive, 'moribund old man,' as I overheard him say one day, — as heartily as you do, or as I do. But, all the same, he is a soldier. De Nava or Salcedo may have ordered every man to be kept at this post, or within this intendancy."

"They have ordered something," said Eunice; and she mused. Then frankly, "Oh, Mr. Lonsdale! you are a diplomatist: I am a woman. You know how to manage men: for me, I do not know how to manage these two girls. They manage me," and she smiled faintly. "Forget you are an official, and for twenty-four hours think and see what an English gentleman can do for a friend."

She even rose from her chair in her excitement: she looked him straight in the face, as he remembered her doing once before; and she gave him her hand loyally.

Lonsdale was clearly surprised.

"Why you call me a diplomatist, I do not know. That I am a gentleman, this you shall see. Miss Perry, I came into this room, only to offer what you ask. Because the offer must be secret if you decline it, I asked you to send the young ladies away."

Then he told her that he had reason to believe, — he said no more than that, — he had "reason to believe" that a little tender to an English frigate would be hanging off and on at Corpus Christi Bay, on the coast below San Antonio. He

knew the commander of this little vessel, and he knew he
would comply with his wishes in an exigency. Wherever the
" Firefly " might be, her boats could push well up the river.

" Your brother will give you escort in this command, without the slightest hesitation ; and, once on a king's vessel,
you need no more," he said eagerly.

Eunice was surprised indeed.

" Could we wait for her, down yonder on the shore ? What
would these girls do in such a wilderness ? "

" There will be no waiting," he said quietly but firmly.
" The moment I suspected your danger, — I beg your pardon,
your anxiety, — I sent two of my best men down the coast
to signal Drapier. His boats will be at La Bahia if you
determine to go. They will be there, on the chance of your
determining."

" Mr. Lonsdale! how can I thank you ? I do thank you,
and you know I do. Let me call Ransom. Major Barelo
shall give us the escort ; nay, we really need no escort to
Bahia. The girls shall be ready, and we will start an hour
before sunset to-morrow."

She called the old man at once. She gave her orders in
the tone which he knew meant there was to be no discussion.
She said no word of a secret to be preserved : she had determined at once to trust the English spy's good faith. She
and her doves would be out of this Franciscan and Moorish
cage before the setting of another sun. Better trust an English spy than the tender mercies of Nemisio de Salcedo, or
the ingenious wiles of Father Jeronimo and his brothers !

Major Barelo was surprised, of course, but clearly enough
he also was relieved. Lonsdale was right when he guessed
that Elguezebal and he could easily give escort between the
fort and the bay, while they might not send any troops as far
away as the Red River. " With my consent not a bird
should leave Texas for Louisiana ; " this was always Salcedo's
motto. The wonder was that he himself crossed that sacred
barrier.

And by five o'clock of the next day the dresses were packed, and the good-bys were said. Old Ransom had drawn the last strap two holes farther up than earlier packers had left it. He had scolded the last stable-boy, and then made him rich for life by scattering among all the boys a handful of *rials*, — "bits" as he called them. He had lifted the girls to their saddles, while Miss Eunice more sedately mounted from the parapet of the stairs ; and then the two troops, one English in every saddle and stirrup, the other French as well in its least detail, filed out into the plaza. Both were extraordinary to a people of horsemen, whose Spanish equipments were the best in the world. Major Barelo and dear Aunt Dolores stood on the gallery ; and he flung out his handkerchief, and said, "Good-by."

"Just as dear papa said on the levee ! Oh, dearest auntie, if he could only be there to meet us ! Why, auntie, it was a year ago this living day !"

Sure enough, it was just a year since the little Inez's journeyings had begun. She was a thousand years older.

An hour's ride out of town, and then the sun was down ; but here were the tents pitched and waiting for them. So like last year ! but so unlike ! No old Cæsar, alas ! Inez's last care had been to visit him in the lock-up, and to promise him all papa's influence for his release. No Phil Nolan, alas ! and no Will Harrod ! Eunice confessed to Lonsdale that, if she had had imagination enough to foresee the wretched recollections of the camp, she could not have braved them. But Inez, dear child, was truly brave. She said no word. She was pale and thoughtful ; but she applied herself to the little cares of the encampment, which a year ago she would have lazily left to her cavaliers, and she made the White Hawk join her.

Lonsdale also was eager and careful. But oh the difference between the elaborated services of this man, trained in cities, and the easy attentions of those others, born to the wilderness, and all at home in it !

Ransom, with all his feminine sympathy, felt the lack of what they had last year, and managed, in his way, to supply it better than any one else could. His vassals had served the supper better than could have been hoped ; the beds were ready for the ladies, and as soon as the short and quiet meal was over they retired.

Lonsdale lighted a cigar, called the old man to him, and invited him to join him. No, he would not smoke, never did ; but when Lonsdale repeated his invitation he sat down.

"You are quite right, Mr. Ransom. The ladies like this camp-life better than any quarters they would have given us yonder."

He pointed over his shoulder at some little buildings of an outpost of the "Mission."

Ransom did not conceal his disgust as he looked round.

"See the critters furder," said he : "treat us jest as they treated them redskins last spring when they got um. They would ef they wanted to. See um furder. Et's them cussed black goats 'n rope-yarn men that's at the bottom o' this war agin the cap'n — Cap'n Nolan. The cap'n couldn't stand um, he couldn't ; he told um so, he did. He gin um a bit of his mind. Cussed critters never forgot it, they didn't — never forgot it. Cap'n gin um a bit of his mind, he did. Cussed critters is at the bottom of this war. See um furder."

"But you have to see them a good deal at Orleans, Mr. Ransom, do you not ? There is no Protestant church there, is there ? "

"Guess not. Ain't no meetin'-house there, and no meetin'. Ain't nothing but eyedolaters, 'n' immigis, 'n' smoke-pans, 'n' boys in shirts. See um ! guess we do, the critters. Bishop comes round to dine. Likes good Madeira and Cognac 'zwell 'zanybody, he does. Poor set, all on um. Ignorant critters. Don't know nothin'. No ! ain't no meetin'-house in Orleans."

"Do they give Mr. Perry or Miss Perry any trouble about their religion? Do they wish them to come to church, or to the confessional ? Did they baptize Miss Inez ? "

"Do they? I see um git Mr. Perry to church ef he didn't want to go!" and the old man chuckled enigmatically. "They's ignorant critters, they is; but they knows enough not to break they own heads, they do."

"You have heard of the inquisition?" persisted Lonsdale.

"Guess I have. Seen the cussed critters when I was at Cadiz in the 'Jehu:' that's nineteen years ago last summer. Never had none here to Orleans, never but once!" And this time he chuckled triumphantly. "They didn't stay long then, they didn't. Went off quicker than they come, they did. I know um. Cussed critters."

Lonsdale was curious, and asked for an explanation.

The old man's face beamed delight. He looked up to the stars, and told this story: —

"Best guv'nor they ever had, over there to Orleans, was a man named Miro. Spoke English heself most as well as I do. Married Miss Maccarty, he did — pretty Irish girl. Wasn't no real Spanisher at all. Well, one day, they comes one of these dirty rascals with a rope's end round him — brown blanket coat on — comes up from Cuba, he does — comes to Gov. Miro. Gov. Miro asked him to dinner, he did, and gin him his quarters. Then the cussed fool sends a note to the guv'nor, 'n he says, sez he, that these underground critters, these Inky Sijoan they calls um over there; they'd sent him, they had, says he; and mebbe he should want a file o' soldiers some night. Says so in a letter to the guv'nor. So the guv'nor, he thought, ef Old Nightgown wanted the soldiers he'd better have um. 'N' he sent round a sergeant 'n' a file of men that night, he did, at midnight, 'n' waked up Old Nightgown in his bed. 'N' Old Nightgown says, says he, he was much obliged, but that night he didn't need um. But the sergeant says, says he, that he needed Old Nightgown, 'n' as soon as the old fool got his rawhide shoes tied on, the corporal marched him down to the levee, 'n' sent him off to Cadiz, he did; 'n' that's the last time the Inky Sijoan men come here — 'n' the fust time too. Gov. Miro the best guv'nor they ever had over there. Half Englishman."

Lonsdale appreciated the compliment. His cigar was finished. He bade the old man good-night, and turned in.

CHAPTER XXVI.

HOMEWARD BOUND.

> " So they resolved, the morrow next ensuing,
>   So soon as day appeared to people's viewing,
>   On their intended journey to proceed ;
>   And overnight whatso thereto did need
>   Each did prepare, in readiness to be.
>   The morrow next, so soon as one might see
>   Light out of heaven's windows forth to look,
>   They their habiliments unto them took,
>   And put themselves, in God's name, on their way."
>
> *Mother Hubberd's Tale.*

So short a journey as that from San Antonio to the Gulf seemed nothing to travellers so experienced as Miss Perry and her niece. As for the White Hawk, she was never so happy as in the open air, and especially as on horseback. She counted all time lost that was spent elsewhere, and was frank enough to confess that she thought that they had all escaped from a feverish wild dream, or what was as bad as such, in coming away from those close prison walls. The glorious weather of October, in a ride over the prairies in one of the loveliest regions of the world, could not but raise the spirits of all the ladies ; and Mr. Lonsdale might well congratulate himself on the successful result of his bold application to Miss Perry.

As they approached the Gulf, he kept some lookouts well in advance, in hope of sighting the boat or boats from the " Firefly " which he expected. But Friday night came with no report from these men ; and, although they had not returned, he was fain to order a halt, after conference with Ransom, on a little flat above a half-bluff which looked down upon the stream.   The short twilight closed in on them as they made their supper.   But after the supper was finished, as they strolled up and down before going to bed, a meteor, far more brilliant than any shooting star could be so near the horizon, rose above the river in the eastern distance ; and as they all wondered another arose, and yet another. "Rockets!" cried Mr. Lonsdale well pleased.   "Roberts has found them ; and this is their short-hand way of telling us that they are at hand. — William," he said, turning to the thoroughly respectable servant who in top-boots and buck-skins followed his wanderings in these deserts, — "William, find something which you can show to them."   The man of all arts disappeared ; and, while the girls were yet looking for another green star in the distance, they were startled by the "shirr-r" of a noisy rocket which rose close above their own heads, and burst beautiful above the still waters.   Another and another followed in quick succession, and the reply was thus secure.   The White Hawk was beside herself with delight.   She watched the firing of No. 2 as Eunice might have watched the skilful manipulations of Mme. Le Brun. William was well pleased by her approbation.   He did not bend much from the serenity of a London valet's bearing, but he did permit the White Hawk herself to apply the burning brand to the match of the third rocket.   The girl screamed with delight as she saw it burst, and as the falling stick plunged into the river.

"To-morrow morning, Miss Inez, your foot is on the deck, and these pleasant wanderings of ours are over forever." Even Inez's severity toward the man she tried to hate gave way at his display — so difficult for a man of his make — of emotion which was certainly real and deep.

"But, Mr. Lonsdale, no Englishman will convince me that he is sorry to be on the sea."

"*Cela dépend.*   I shall be sorry if the sea parts me from near and dear friends."

"As if I meant to be sentimental with old Chisholm or Conolly, because he had been good to us!" This was Inez's comment as she repeated the conversation to her aunt afterward. "I was not going to be affectionate to him."

"What did you say?" asked Eunice, laughing.

"I said I was afraid Ma-ry would be seasick," said the reckless girl. "I thought that would take off the romance for him." None the less could Eunice see that the rancor of her rage and hatred were much abated, as is the fortune often of the wild passions of that age of discretion which comes at eighteen years.

Mr. Lonsdale had not promised more than he performed. Before the ladies were astir the next morning, two boats were at an improvised landing below the tents. Ransom had transferred to them already all the packs from the mules; and there needed only that breakfast should be over, and the ladies' last "traps" were embarked also, and they were themselves on board. A boatswain in charge received Mr. Lonsdale with tokens of respect which did not escape Inez's eye. As for the White Hawk, she was beside herself with wonder at the movements of craft so much more powerful than any thing to which the little river of San Antonio had trained her. As the sun rose higher the seamen improvised an awning. The current of the river, such as it was, aided them ; and before two o'clock the little party was on the deck of the " Firefly " in the offing.

Nothing is prettier than the eagerness of self-surrender with which naval officers always receive women on their ships. The chivalry of a gentleman, the homesickness of an exile, the enthusiasm of a host, — all unite to welcome those whose presence is so rare that they are made all the more comfortable because there is no provision for them in a state of nature. In this case, the gentlemen had had some days' notice that the ladies might be expected.

It was clear that Lonsdale was quite at home among them, and was a favorite. Even the old salts who stood at the

gangway smiled approval of him as he stepped on board.
He presented young Drapier and Clerk, the two lieutenants
who held the first and second rank ; and then, with careful
impartiality, the group of midshipmen who stood behind.
Then he spoke to every one of them separately.   "Good
news from home, Bob ?   Mr. Anson, I hope the admiral is
well ; and how is your excellent father, Mr. Pigot ? "   A
moment more, and a bronzed, black-browed man, in a military undress, came out from the companion.   He smiled as
he gave his hand to Lonsdale, who owned his surprise at
meeting him.

"Miss Perry," said he at once, "here is one friend more,
whom you have heard of but never seen.   One never knows
where to look for the general," he said, laughing, "or I also
should be surprised.   Let me present to you Gen. Bowles,
Miss Perry.   Miss Inez, this is Gen. Bowles, — I think I
might say a friend of your father's."

This extraordinary man smiled good-naturedly, and said, —

"Yes, a countryman of yours and of your brother's, Miss
Perry ; and all countrymen are friends.   The people in
Orleans do not love me as well as I love the Americans who
live among them."

Eunice was not disposed to be critical.   "Mr. Lonsdale is
very kind ; and I am sure we poor wandering damsels are
indebted to all these gentlemen for their welcome," said she.
She had learned long since, that in times like hers, and in
such surroundings, she must not discriminate too closely as
to the antecedents of those with whom she had to do.   Inez
could afford to have "hates" and "instincts," like most
young ladies of her age.   But Eunice had passed thirty, and
was willing to accept service from Galaor, if by ill luck she
could not command the help of Amadis.   The truth was, that
Gen. Bowles had been known to her only as a chief of
marauding Highlanders might have been known to a lady of
Edinburgh.   For many years he had been, in the Spanish
wars against England, the daring commander of the savage

allies of the English. He was her countryman, because he was born in Maryland. But, as soon as Gen. Howe came to Philadelphia, Bowles had enlisted as a boy in the British army. It was after the most wild life that ever an adventurer led, — now in dungeons and now in palaces, — that she met him on the deck of an English cutter.

His eye fell upon Inez with the undisguised admiration with which men were apt to look on Inez. When he was presented to Ma-ry in turn, he was quick enough to recognize — he hardly could have told how — something of the savage training of this girl. She looked as steadily into his eye as he into hers. Compliment came into conversation with less disguise in those days than in these ; and so the general did not hesitate to say, —

"But for that rich bloom, Miss Ma-ry, upon your cheek, I should have been glad to claim you as the daughter of a chief, — a chief among men who have not known how to write treaties, nor to break them."

Ma-ry probably did not follow his stately and affected sentence.

"My name on the prairies is the White Hawk," said she simply.

"Well named," cried Bowles ; and he looked to Eunice for an explanation, which of course she quickly gave. The passage was instantaneous, as, among the group of courteous gentlemen, the ladies were led to the cabin of the captain, which he had relinquished for them ; but it was the beginning of long conferences between Gen. Bowles and the White Hawk, in which, with more skill than Eunice had done, or even Harrod, he traced out her scanty recollection of what her mother had told her of the life to which she was born.

The stiffness of the reception and welcome of the ladies was broken, and all conversation for the moment was made impossible, by the escape of two pets of the girls, from the arms of a sailor, who had attempted to bring them up the

ladder.   They were little Chihuahua dogs, — pretty little
creatures of the very smallest of the dog race, — which
Lonsdale had presented when he had returned to San Antonio, as one of the steps, perhaps, by which he might work
into Inez's variable favor.   The little things found their feet
on deck, and dashed about among swivels, cat-heads, casks,
and other furniture, in a way which delighted the midshipmen, confounded the old seamen, and set both the girls
screaming with laughter.   After such an adventure, and the
recapture of Trip and Skip, formality was impossible ; and,
when the ladies disappeared into Lieut. Drapier's hospitable
quarters, all parties had the ease of manner of old friends.

Ransom, with his own sure tact, and under the law of
"natural selection," — which was true before Dr. Darwin
was born, — found his way at once into the company of the
warrant-officers.   Indeed, he might be well described by calling him a sort of warrant-officer, which means a man who
takes much of the work and much of the responsibility of
this world, and yet has very little of the honor.   As the men
hauled up the little anchor, and got the boats on board, after
Ransom had seen his share of luggage of the party fairly
secured, an old sailor's habits came over him ; and he could
hardly help, although a visitor, lending a hand.

It was not the first time he had been on the deck of an
English man-of-war ; but never before had he been there as
a distinguished visitor.   He also, like his mistress, if Eunice
were his mistress, knew how to conquer his prejudices.   And,
indeed, the order and precision of man-of-war's-man's style,
after the slackness, indolence, and disobedience of the Greasers, was joy to his heart.   He could almost have found it in
him to exempt these neat English tars from the general doom
which would fall on all "furriners."   At the least, they could
not speak French, Spanish, or Choctaw ; and with this old
quartermaster who offered him a lighted pipe, and with the
boatswain who gave him a tough tarred hand, he could
indulge in the vernacular.

Hardly were these three mates established in a comfortable nook forward under the shade of the foresail, when an older man than the other Englishman presented himself, and tipped his hat to Ransom respectfully in a somewhat shame-faced fashion.

The old man looked his surprise, and relieved the other's doubts by giving him a hard hand-grip cordially.

"Why, Ben, boy, be ye here? Where did ye turn up from?"

The man said he enlisted in Jamaica two years before.

"Jes so, the old story. Can't teach an old dog new tricks. Have some tobaccy, Ben? Perhaps all on ye will like to try the Greasers' tobaccy. Et's the only thing they's got that's good for any thing, et is." And he administered enormous plugs of the Mexican tobacco to each of his comrades, neither of whom was averse to a new experiment in that line. "Woll, Ben, et's a good many years since I see ye. See ye last the day Count Dystang sailed out o' Bostin Harbor. Guess ye didn't go aloft much that v'y'ge, Ben?"

The other laughed, and intimated that people did not go aloft easily when they had handcuffs on. The truth was, he had been a prisoner of war, and, under some arrangements made by the Committee of Safety, had been transferred to the French admiral's care.

"'N when did ye see Mr. Conolly, Ben?" asked Ransom, with a patronizing air.

The man said Mr. Conolly had never forgotten him, that "he was good to him," as his phrase was, and got him exchanged from the French fleet. But Mr. Conolly afterward went to Canada ; and Ben had never heard from him again.

"I've heerd on him often," said Ransom, with his eyes twinkling: "Guv'nor o' Kannydy sent him down here to spy out the country. Thort they wa'n't no rope to hang him with, he did : didn't know where hemp grew. Down comes Conolly, and he sees the gineral, that's Wilkinson, up river ; 'n he tells the gineral, and all the ginerals, they'd better fight

for King George, he does, 'n that the king's pay was better
nor Gineral Washington's. Darned fool, he was. Gineral
Wilkinson fooled him. Major Dunn fooled him, all on um
fooled him. Thought he'd bought um all out, he did!"
and Ransom chuckled, in his happiest mood; "thought he'd
bought um; 'n jest then in come a wild fellow, — hunter, — 'n
he asked where the English kurnel was, he did, 'n he says the
redskins 'n the English 'd killed his father 'n mother; 'n he
says he'll have the kurnel's scalp to pay for it; 'n after he
hollered round some time, old Wilkinson he put him in irons,
'n sent him away; 'n then the kurnel — Conolly — he took
on so, 'n was so afeerd he'd be scalped, that he asked the
gineral for an escort, he did, 'n so he went home. Gineral
gin the hunter a gallon o' whiskey, 'n five pounds of powder,
to come in there 'n holler round so."

And old Ransom contemplated the sky, in silent approval
of the deceit. After a pause he said, —

"They wus some on um over there among the Greasers,
thought this man was Col. Conolly" (pause again). "They
didn't ask me, 'n I didn't tell um. I knew better. I see
Conolly when I see you fust, Ben" (grim smile), "when we
put the irons on you, aboard the 'Cerberus' 'fore she went
down. I knew Conolly." Another pause; then, somewhat
tentatively, —

"This man I never see before; but he knows how to
saddle his own horse, he does;" this in approval, Lonsdale
being "this man" referred to.

The others said that they took "this man" into Vera Cruz
the winter before, with his servants. The talk of the "Firefly" was, that while they had been sounding in Corpus
Christi Bay they had been waiting for him. Who he was,
they did not know, but believed he was First Lord of the
Admiralty, or may be a son of Lord Anson, or perhaps of
some other grandee.

"Ye don't think he's that one that was at New York, do
you?" said Ransom. "I mean the Juke, they called him —

old king's son. I come mighty near carrying him off myself one night, in a whale-boat."

The men showed little indignation at this allusion to Royal William, the Duke of Clarence, — "by England's navy all adored," though that gentleman was said to be. But they expressed doubts, though no one knew, whether Mr. Lonsdale were he. If he were, the midshipmen were either ignorant or bold ; for, when Inez compelled them to sing that evening, they sang rapturously, —

> " When Royal William comes on board,
>   By England's navy all adored,
>   To him I sometimes pass the word,
>   For I'm a smart young midshipman."

The White Hawk proved a better sailor than Eunice had dared to hope. Her wonder at what seemed to her the immense size of the little vessel, and at all its equipment and movement, was a delight to Inez and even to the less demonstrative Ransom. The young gentlemen were divided in their enthusiastic attentions to these charming girls, and the three or four days of their little voyage were all too short for the youngsters ; when, with a fresh north-west breeze, they entered the south-western mouths of the great Mississippi River, and so long as this breeze served them held on to the main current of the stream. For that current itself, the breeze was dead ahead, and so the " Firefly " came again to an anchor, to the grief of the ladies more than of their young admirers.

Eunice Perry and her " doves " had retired to dress for dinner, when, from a French brig which was at anchor hard by, a boat was dropped, which pulled hastily across to the Englishman. In these neutral waters there was no danger in any event, but a white handkerchief fluttered at her bow. A handsome young man in a French uniform ran up on the " Firefly's " deck. He spoke a word to Capt. Drapier, but hardly more ; for, as they exchanged the first civilities, Eunice and Inez rushed forward from the companion, and Inez's arms were around his neck.

"My dear, dear brother !"

CHAPTER XXVII.

HOME AS FOUND.

"And I will see before I die
The palms and temples of the South."

TENNYSON.

"Is it not perfectly lovely?" said Inez to her brother, as she ran ashore over the little plank laid for a gangway. "Is it not perfectly lovely?"　And she flung her arms about him, and kissed him, as her best way of showing her delight that she and he were both at home.

"You are, pussy," said Roland, receiving the caress with as much enthusiasm as she gave it with; "and so is the White Hawk, whom I will never call Ma-ry; and to tell you the whole truth, and not to quarrel with you the first morning of home, dear old Orleans is not an unfit setting for such jewels. Oh, dear! how good it is to be at home!"

The young officer seemed as young as Inez in his content; and Inez forgot her trials for the minute, in the joy of having him, of hearing him, and seeing him.

So soon as Mr. Perry had understood the happy meeting at the river's mouth, he also had boarded the "Firefly." Matters had indeed fallen out better than even he had planned; and the embarkation planned in grief by Eunice, and in what seemed loyalty by Mr. Lonsdale, proved just what all would have most desired.　Mr. Perry had the pleasure of announcing to Lieut. Drapier and the other English officers peace between England and France.　They had heard of the hopes of this, but till now the announcement had lingered.   At the little dinner improvised on the deck of the "Firefly," many toasts were drunk to the eternal peace of England and France ; but, alas ! the winds seem to have dispersed them before they arrived at any mint which stamped them for permanent circulation.

With all due courtesies, Mr. Perry had then taken his own family on board the "Antoinette," a little brig which he had chartered at Bordeaux, that he might himself bring out this news. Of course he begged Mr. Lonsdale to join them as soon as he knew that that gentleman's plan of travel was to take him to Orleans. Drapier and Clerk manifested some surprise when they learned of this plan of travel, as they had supposed the "Firefly" was to take him to Jamaica. They learned now, for the first time, that Lonsdale had errands at Fort Massac and the falls of the Ohio and Fort Washington. The young officers looked quizzically at each other behind his back, as if to ask how long he might be detained at Orleans. But whoever Lonsdale was, and however good a friend he was, they did not dare to talk banter to him,—as Miss Inez and as Ransom did not fail to observe.

So with long farewells, and promises to meet again, the two vessels parted. Gen. Bowles said to Eunice, as he bade them good-by, that he was the only person on board the "Firefly" who was not raging with indignation at the change of plans. "The middies are beside themselves," he said. "So, indeed, am I ; but my grief is a little assuaged by the recollection that Gov. Salcedo would hang me in irons in fifteen minutes after the 'Firefly' arrived. True, this is a trifling price to pay for the pleasure of sailing along the coast with three charming ladies ; but if I do not pay it, I have the better chance to see them again."

" And also," he added more gravely, "I have the better chance to learn something of this Apache raid in which your interesting charge was carried from home, of which, Miss Perry, I will certainly inform you."

The "Antoinette" had slowly worked her way up the stream. At nightfall, on the second night, she was still thirty miles from the city. But, as the sun rose on the morning of the third day, Roland had tapped at the door of the ladies' cabin, and had told them that they were at the levee in front of the town. Of course Inez and Ma-ry were ready for action in a very few moments ; and, as Roland waited eager for them, they joined him for a little ramble, in which Inez should see his delight as he came home, and both of them should see Ma-ry's wonder.

It is hard even for the resident in New Orleans of to-day to carry himself back to the little fortified town which Inez so rejoiced to see. As it happens, we have the ill-tempered narrative which a M. Duvallar, a cockney Parisian, gave, at just the same time, of his first impressions. But he saw as a seasick Frenchman eager to see the streets of Paris sees : Inez saw as a happy girl sees, who from her first wanderings returns home with so much that she loves best. The first wonder to be seen was a wonder to Inez as to the others : it was the first vessel ever built in Ohio to go to sea. She lay in the stream, proudly carrying the American colors at each peak, and was the marvel of the hour. But Inez cared little for schooners, brigs, or ships.

She hurried her brother to the Place d'Armes, which separated the river from two buildings, almost Moorish in their look, which were the public offices, and which were separated by the quaint cathedral, — another bit of Old Spain. Over wooden walks, laid upon the clay of the *banquette* or sidewalk, she hurried him through one and another narrow street, made up of square wooden houses, never more than a story high, and always offering a veranda or "*galerie*" to the street front. Between the *banquette* and the roadway, a deep gutter, neatly built, gave room for a little brook, if one of the pitiless rains of the country happened to flood the town. Little bridges across these gutters, made by the elongation of the wooden walks, required, at each street-crossing,

a moment's care on the part of the passenger. All this, to
the happy Inez, was of course ; to the watchful White Hawk,
was amazement ; and to Roland all was surprise, that in so
many thousand details he had forgotten how the home of his
childhood differed from the Paris of his manly life. The
fine fellow chattered as Inez chattered, explained to the
White Hawk as he thought she needed, and was every whit
as happy as Inez wanted him to be. "There is dear M. Le
Bourgeois. He does not see us. Monsieur ! Monsieur !
You have not forgotten us, have you ? Here is little Inez
back again. And how are they at Belmont ? Give ever so
much love to them ! " And then, as she ran on, " And there
is Jean Audubon ! Jean, Jean ! " and when the handsome
young fellow crossed the street, and gave her both hands,
"Oh, I have such beautiful heron's wings for you from Antonio ; and Ransom has put up two nice chapparal birds for
you, and a crane. I made Major Barelo shoot him for me.
And, Jean ! did you ever see a Chihuahua dog ? Ma-ry and
I have two, — the prettiest creatures you ever did see. This
is Ma-ry, Mr. Audubon. — How do you do, Mme. Fourchet ?
We are all very well, I thank you."

So they walked back from the river, — not many squares :
the houses were farther and farther apart ; and at last a
long fence, made of cypress boards roughly split, and higher
than their heads, parted them from a garden of trees and
shrubs blazing with color and with fruit. The fence ran
along the whole square ; and now the little Inez fairly flew
along the *banquette* till she came to a gateway which gave
passage into the garden. Here she instantly struck a bell
which hung just within the fence ; and there, protected by a
rough shelter, — a sort of wooden awning, arranged for the
chance of rain, — she jumped with impatience as she waited
for the others to arrive, and for some one within to open.
She had not to wait long. In a minute Ransom flung
the gate open, and the girl stood within the garden of her
father's house. The old man had landed long before them,

and had come up to the house to satisfy himself that all was fit for the family and its guests.

"Come, Ma-ry, come !" cried Inez, as she dashed along a winding brick alley, between palm-trees and roses, and myrtles and bananas, oranges in fruit, great masses of magnolia cones beginning to grow red, and the thousand other wonders of a well-kept garden in this most beautiful of cities, in a climate which is both temperate and tropical at a time. "Oh, come, Ma-ry ! do come, Roland ! Welcome home ! welcome home !"

She dashed up the broad high steps of the pretty house, to a broad veranda, or "gallery," near twelve feet deep, which surrounded it on every side. Doors flung wide open gave entrance to a wide hall which ran quite through the house, a double door of Venetian blind closing the hall at the other end.

On either side, large doors opened into very high rooms, the floors of which, of a shining cypress wood, were covered in the middle by mats and carpets. The shade of the "gallery" was sufficient in every instance to keep even the morning sunlight of that early hour from the rooms. Ransom's forethought, and that of a dozen negro servants who were waiting to welcome her, had already made the rooms gorgeous with flowers.

The happy girl had a word for every Chloe and Miranda and Zenon and Antoine of all the waiting group ; and then she was beside herself as she tried at once to enjoy Roland's satisfaction, and to introduce Ma-ry to her new home. It was impossible to be disappointed. Roland was as well pleased and as happy as she could wish ; and, because she was so happy, the White Hawk was happy too.

"See, Roland, here is the picture of Mme. Josephine you sent us. And here is your great First Consul ; and very handsome he is too, though he is so stern. I should think Mme. Bonaparte would be afraid of him. See, I hung them here. Papa had hung them just the other way, and you see they looked away from each other. But I told him that would never do: it seemed as if they had been quarrelling."

"Madame's picture is not good enough, as I told you when I sent it. The general's is better. But nothing gives his charming smile. You must make papa tell you of that. I wish we had Eugene's. If he becomes the great general he means to be, we shall have his picture engraved and framed by the general's side."

"Oh! there are to be no more wars, you know. Eugene will be a planter, and raise sugar, as his father did. We shall never hear of Gen. Beauharnais again."

And then she had to take Ma-ry into her own room, and show her all the arrangements in which a young girl delights. And Ransom was made happy by seeing Mr. Roland again at home. And these joys of a beginning were not well over before the carriage arrived from the " Antoinette " with the more mature elders of the party, who had not been above taking things easily, and riding from the levee to the house.

But it was impossible not to see at breakfast that Mr. Perry was silent and sad, in the midst of all his effort to be hospitable to Mr. Lonsdale, and to make his son's return cheerful. And at last, when breakfast was over, he said frankly, "We are all so far friends, that I may as well tell you what has grieved me. Panton came on board as we left the vessel.

"He tells me that this horrid business yonder has been too much for the poor girl."

Inez's face was as pale as a sheet. She had never spoken to her father of the beautiful lady whose picture Philip Nolan had showed her. She had always supposed that there was a certain confidence or privacy about his marriage to Fanny Lintot ; and, as the reader knows, not even to Eunice had she whispered it before they heard of his death. But now it was clear that her father knew ; and he knew more than she knew.

"Yes," continued Mr. Perry. "There is a child who will never remember his father and mother. But this pretty Fanny Lintot, not even the child could keep her alive. 'What should I wish to live for?' the poor child said. 'I shall never know what happiness is in this world. I did not think I should be so fortunate as to join my dear Phil so soon.' And so she joined him."

Poor Inez! She could not bear this. She ran out of the room, and the White Hawk followed her.

CHAPTER XXVIII.

"Who saw the Duke of Clarence?"

Henry IV.

"AUNT EUNICE," said Roland, with all his own impetuosity, when they had all met for dinner, "there is no such soup as a gumbo filé, — no, not at Malmaison. *Crede experto,* which means, my dear aunt, 'I know what I am talking about.' And, as Madame Casa Calvo is not here, you may help me again."

"Dear Roland, I will help you twenty times," said his aunt, who was as fond of him as his mother would have been, and, indeed, quite as proud. "I am glad we can hold our own with Malmaison in any thing."

"We beat Malmaison in many things. We beat Malmaison in roses, though Mlle. Hortense has given me a ' Souvenir ' from there, before which old Narcisse will bow down in worship. But we have more than roses. We beat Malmaison in pretty girls," this with a mock bow to the White Hawk and to Inez; "and we beat her in gumbo."

"How is it in soldiers, Mr. Perry?" said Mr. Lonsdale, with some real curiosity. "And is it true that we are to see the renowned Gen. Victor here with an army?"

"That you must ask my father," said the young fellow boldly. "He is the diplomatist of the family. I dare say he has settled it all with Mme. Josephine, while I was obtaining from Mlle. Hortense some necessary directions about the dressing of my sister's hair. — My dear Inez, it is to be cut short in front, above the eyebrows, and to flow loosely behind, *à la Naiade affranchie.*"

"Nonsense!" said Inez. "Did not Mlle. Hortense tell you that ears were to be worn boxed on the right side and cuffed on the left? She was too kind to your impudence."

"She made many inquiries regarding yours. And, dear Aunt Eunice, she asked me many questions which I could not answer. Now that I arrive upon the Father of Waters, I am prudent and docile. I whisper no word which may awake the proud Spaniard against the hasty Gaul or the neutral American. I reveal no secret, Mr. Lonsdale, in the presence of the taciturn Briton: all the same I look on and wonder. The only place for my inquiries — where I can at once show my modesty and my ignorance — is at the hospitable board of Miss Eunice Perry. She soothes me with gumbo filé, she bribes me with red-fish and pompano ; in the distance I see cotelettes and vol-au-vents, and I know not what else, which she has prepared to purchase my silence. All the same, I throw myself at the feet of this company, own my gross ignorance, and ask for light.

"Let me, dear Mr. Lonsdale, answer your question as I can. Many generals have I met, in battle, in camp, or in the ballroom. Gen. Bonaparte is my protector ; Gen. Moreau examined me in tactics ; Gen. Casa Bianca is my friend ; Gen. Hamilton is my distinguished countryman. But who, my dear Aunt Eunice, is Gen. Bowles? and of what nation was the somewhat remarkable uniform which he wore the day I had the honor to meet you, and to assure you that you had grown young under your anxieties for your nephew?"

Now, if there were a subject which Eunice would have wished to have avoided at that moment, it was the subject which the audacious young fellow had introduced.

In spite of her, her face flushed.

"He served against the Spaniards at Pensacola," said she, with as much calmness as she could command. Everybody was looking at her, so that she could not signal him to silence ; and Mr. Lonsdale was close at her side, so that he heard every word.

"A countryman of yours, Mr. Lonsdale? Where, then, was the red coat? where the Star and Garter?"

Lonsdale was not quick enough to follow this badinage; or he was perhaps as much annoyed as Eunice, that the subject was opened.

"Gen. Bowles is not in the king's service," he said; "yet he is well thought of at the Foreign Office. I dined with him at Lord Hawksbury's."

"At Lord Hawksbury's?" said Mr. Perry, surprised out of the silence he had maintained all along.

Lonsdale certainly was annoyed this time, and annoyed at his own carelessness; for he would not have dropped the words, had he had a moment for thought. His face flushed, but he said, —

"Yes. It was rather a curious party. Gen. Miranda was there, who means to free Mexico and Cuba and the Spanish main, — the South American Washington of the future, Miss Inez. This Gen. Bowles was there, in the same fanciful uniform he wears to-day. There was an *attaché* of your legation there, I forget his name; and no end of people who spoke no English. But I understood that Gen. Bowles was an American. I did not suppose I should be the person to introduce him to you."

"Why does Lord Hawksbury ask Gen. Bowles to meet Gen. Miranda, sir?" said Roland, turning to his father.

"Why do I ask an *élève* of the École Polytechnique to meet Mr. Lonsdale? — Mr. Lonsdale, that Bordeaux wine is good; but, if you hold to your island prejudices, Ransom shall bring us some port which my own agent bought in Portugal."

"I hold by the claret," said Lonsdale, relieved, as Roland thought, that the subject was at an end. Now, Roland had no thought of relieving him. If Englishmen came to America, he meant to make them show their colors.

"No man tells me," he said, "what nation that is whose major-generals wear green frock-coats cut like Robin Hood's, with wampum embroidered on the cuffs. I am only told that this unknown nation is in alliance with King George and Gen. Miranda."

"Gen. Bowles is the chief of an Indian tribe in this region, I think," said Lonsdale, rather stiffly.

"Oho!" cried the impetuous young fellow, "and the Creeks and the Greasers, with some assistance from Lord Hawksbury and King George, are to drive the King of Spain out of Mexico. Is that on the cards, Mr. Lonsdale?"

Lonsdale looked more confused than ever.

"You must ask your father, Mr. Perry. He is the diplomatist, you say."

"But is this what the Governor of Canada is bothering about? Is this what he sent Chisholm and Conolly for, sir?" said Roland, turning to his father. "Not so bad a plot, if it is."

The truth is, that Roland's head was turned with the military atmosphere in which he had lived ; and, like half the youngsters of his time, he hoped that some good cause might open up, in which he, too, could win spurs and glory.

At the allusion to Chisholm and Conolly, two secret agents of the Canadian Government in the Valley of the Mississippi, Inez turned to look gravely upon her aunt. As, by good luck, Mr. Lonsdale's face was also turned toward Eunice, Inez seized the happy opportunity to twirl her knife as a chief might his scalping-knife. Ma-ry understood no little of the talk, but managed, savage-like, to keep her reserve. Mr. Perry felt his son's boldness, and was troubled by it. He knew that all this talk must be annoying to the Englishman.

"The plot was a very foolish plot, Roland, if it were such a plot as you propose. If John Adams had been chosen president again, instead of this man who is called so pacific, —if some things had not been done on the other side which have been done, — I think Gen. Hamilton might have brought a few thousand of our countrymen down the river, with Gen. Wilkinson to show him the way. Mr. Lonsdale can tell you whether Admiral Nelson would have been waiting here with a fleet ; they do say there have been a few frigates in the Gulf : as it is, all I know is, that fortunately for us we found the ' Firefly ' there. Mr. Lonsdale knows, perhaps, whether a few regiments from Canada might not have joined our men in the excursion. But we have changed all that, my boy ; and you must take your tactics and your strategies to some other field of glory."

The truth was, that all the scheme of which Mr. Perry spoke had been wrought out in the well-kept secrecy of John Adams's cabinet. As he said himself once, such talent as he had was for making war, more than for making peace.

As it proved, the majestic, and to us friendly policy of the great Napoleon, gave us Louisiana without a blow ; but in the long line of onslaughts upon Spain, which the United States have had to do with, this was the first.

The first Adams is the historical leader of the filibusters.

Miss Inez did not care a great deal about the politics of the conversation. What she did care for was, that Lonsdale appeared to be uncomfortable. This delighted her. Was he Chisholm ? was he Conolly ? Her father had hushed up Roland, with a purpose. She could see that. But she did not see that this involved any cessation in that guerilla war with which he persecuted the Englishman.

" That must have been a very interesting party which you describe, Mr. Lonsdale. Is Lord Hawksbury a good talker ? "

" Yes — hardly — no, Miss Perry. He talks as most of those men in office do : he is all things to all men."

"Was the Duke of Clarence there ? " said Inez, with one bold, wild shot. Since Ransom had expressed the opinion that their guest was this gentleman, Inez was determined to know.

Lonsdale's face flushed fire this time ; or she thought it did.

" The duke was there," he said : "it was just before he sailed for Halifax."

But here Eunice came to his relief. She looked daggers at the impertinent girl, asked Mr. Lonsdale some question as to Lieut. Drapier, and Inez and Roland were both so far hushed that no further secrets of state were discussed on that occasion.

CHAPTER XXIX.

"WHERE SHALL SHE GO?"

> " From her infant days,
> With Wisdom, mother of retired thoughts,
> Her soul had dwelt; and she was quick to mark
> The good and evil thing, in human lore
> Undisciplined."
>
> COLERIDGE.

THE White Hawk dropped into her new life with a simplicity and naturalness which delighted everybody. From the beginning Silas Perry was charmed with her. It was not that he tolerated her as he would have tolerated any person whom Eunice had thought best to introduce to his house: it was that by rapid stages he began by liking her, then was fond of her, and then loved her. She was quite mistress of the spoken English, so much so that Inez began to fear that she would lose her pretty savage idioms and fascinating blunders. Indeed, there were a few Apache phrases which Inez insisted on retaining, with some slight modifications, in their daily conversation. How much French and Spanish the girl understood, nobody but herself knew. She never spoke in either language.

It would be almost fair to say that Roland taught her more than Inez did. In the first place, he taught Inez a good deal which it was well for a provincial girl — a girl of two cities as petty as Orleans and San Antonio — to learn, if she could learn it from her brother, seeing her life had been so much restricted, and her outlook so much circumscribed. Roland was quick and impulsive; so, indeed, was the White Hawk; but he was always patient in explaining himself to her, and he would not permit Inez, for mere love's sake, or fancy's sake, to overlook little savageries as he called them, in the girl's habit or life, merely because they seemed pretty to her. "She is an American girl," said he: "by the grace of God you have rescued her from these devils, and she shall never be annoyed by having people call her a redskin." And never had teacher a quicker pupil, never had Mentor a Telemachus more willing, than the White Hawk proved to be under the grave tutelage of Inez and her brother.

These pages, which are transparent as truth herself, may here reveal one thing more. The present reader, also, has proved herself sharp-sighted as Lynceus since she engaged in reading these humble annals of the past. This reader has observed, therefore, from the moment the "Firefly" met the "Antoinette" in the South Pass, that the handsome young American gentleman, and the beautiful girl rescued from captivity, were placed in very near propinquity to each other, and that they remained so. The author has not for a moment veiled this fact from the reader, who is, indeed, too sharp-sighted to be trifled with.

It is now to be stated that the White Hawk observed it quite as soon as the reader has done. The White Hawk maintained a very simple as it was a very intimate and sweet relation with Roland Perry whenever she and he were with Inez and Eunice, or the rest of the group which daily gathered at his father's. But the White Hawk very seldom found herself alone with Roland Perry; and, when she did, the interview was a very short one. Roland found himself sometimes retiring early from the counting-room, wishing that she might be in the way. But she never was in the way. He would prepare one and another expedition to the lake, to the plantation-house, and the like. On such expeditions the White Hawk went freely if the whole party went; but not for a walk or ride out to the English Turn, did she go with him alone.

Roland Perry did not know whether this was accident or no ; did not even ask, perhaps. But it is as well that this reader should understand the girl, and should know it was no accident at all.

One day they had all gone together to a pretty meadow by the lake, under the pretence of seeing some races which the officers of the garrison had arranged. Roland took the occasion to try his chances in sounding Ma-ry about a matter where he had not had full success in his consultations with his aunt.

"Ma-ry," said he, "tell me about the night when Inez was lost in Texas, — by the river, you know."

"Oh, poor Inez! She was so tired! she was so cold !"

"How in the world did you find her ? "

"Oh, ho ! Easy to find her ! I went where she went. Footstep here, footstep there, footstep all along. Leaf here and leaf there — broken leaf, torn leaf — all along. Then I heard her cry. She cried war-whoop, — hoo, hoo, hoo! — just as I taught her one day. Easy to find her."

" And you brought her in on your back ? "

"No: nonsense, Mr. Perry. You know she came on foot, the same as she walks now with Mr. Lonsdale."

" And the others — were they all at home while you looked for her ? "

" At home ? Dear auntie was by the fire, waiting, and praying to the good God. Ransom, he built up the fire, made it burn, so I saw the smoke, red smoke, high, high, above the black-jacks and the hack-berries. Black men, — some at home, some away. All the rest were gone."

" This Capt. Harrod, — where was he, Ma-ry ? "

"Oh ! Capt. Harrod ? Capt. Will Harrod ? Capt. Harrod rode, — had rode, — no, Capt. Harrod had ridden back. All wrong ; all wrong. Had ridden back on the trail — on the old trail ; ridden fast, ridden well, ridden brave, but all wrong. Had ridden back to camp where we had lunch that same day. All wrong. Poor Capt. Harrod ! "

"Why did he ride back, Ma-ry, if it was all wrong?"

"Capt. Harrod not know.   Capt. Harrod saw Inez's foot-mark.   Capt. Harrod saw it was moccason mark; all the same moccason Inez wore at breakfast this morning.   Capt. Harrod see moccason mark; no, saw moccason mark.   Capt. Harrod thought it Apache boy; thought Apaches caught Inez, — carry her away, same like they carry Ma-ry away — carry me away."

"And he went after them?"

"All men went, — all but Ransom and the black men and Richards.   All went — rode fast, fast — very fast; and found no Inez."

And the girl laughed.   "Inez all happy by the fire.   Inez all asleep in the tent."

"Ma-ry, was Capt. Harrod very good to Inez?"

And so you think, Master Roland Perry, that, because this girl is a savage, you are going to draw your sister's secrets out of her, do you?   Much do you know of the loyalty of women to women, when they choose to be loyal.

"Capt. Harrod very good to Inez, very good to auntie, very good to Ma-ry:" this with the first look analogous to coquetry that Roland had ever seen in his pupil.

"Good to everybody, eh?   And who rode with Capt. Harrod, or with whom did he ride as you travelled?   Who rode with Inez?   Who rode with you?"

"I rode with him, auntie rode with him;" and then, correcting herself, "he rode with me: he rode with auntie. Auntie very pleasant with him.   Talk, talk, talk, all morning.   I not understand them.   Talk, talk, talk.   Inez and Ma-ry ride together."

This was a combination of pieces which Roland had not thought of.   He followed out the hint.

"How old was Capt. Harrod, Ma-ry?"

"Old?   I do not know.   He never said; I never asked."

"No, no! you never asked; but was he as old as Ransom? Was he as old as my father?"

Ma-ry laughed heartily.

"No, no!   No, no, no!"

"Was he as old as — Mr. Lonsdale there?"

"Me no know — I mean I do not know.   Mr. Lonsdale never tell me;" and she laughed again.

"Which was older, — Harrod, or Nolan?"

"Oh! I never see, I never seed — I never saw Capt. Phil. Capt. Nolan all gone before I saw Inez.   I saw Inez at Nacogdoches."

"And did Inez like Capt. Harrod very much, Ma-ry?"

"Oh, ho!   I think so.   I like him very much.   Auntie, oh! auntie like him very much.   Oh! I think Inez like him very much.   Ask her, Mr. Roland; ask her."   And the girl called, "Inez, my darling, Inez, come here!"

But Inez did not hear: perhaps it was not meant that she should hear.

"No, no!" said Master Roland interrupting, but so much of a man still that he did not know that this little savage girl was playing with him.   "Do not call her.   She can tell me what she chooses.   But, Ma-ry dear, what makes Inez unhappy?   When she is alone, she cries: I know she does. I see her eyes are red.   When she is with us all, she laughs and talks more than she wants to.   She makes believe, Ma-ry.   Ma-ry, what is the trouble, the sorrow of Inez?"

No, Roland: Ma-ry is very fond of Inez, and she is very fond of you; but if you want Inez's secrets you must go to Inez for them.   This girl of the woods will not betray them.

"Inez very, very fond of Capt. Phil Nolan.   Inez very, very sorry for poor lady who is dead, and little baby boy. When Capt. Phil Nolan was here, here in Orleans, Capt. Phil Nolan told her, told Inez, all story, — all the story of beautiful girl who is dead.   Fanny, — Fanny Lintot.   Capt. Phil Nolan showed Inez picture — pretty picture, — oh, so pretty! — of Fanny Lintot.   Told her secret.   Inez told no one.   No, Inez not tell auntie, not tell me.   Now gone, all gone.   Fanny Lintot dead.   Capt. Nolan dead.   Only little, little baby boy.   Poor Fanny Lintot!   Poor Inez very sorry.

But, Mr. Roland, you not ask her. No, no, no! do not ask her."

"Not I," said Roland, led away by the girl's eagerness, and not aware, indeed, at the moment, that he had been foiled.

Mr. Silas Perry had soon made the same remark which the eagle-eyed reader of these pages has made, that his son and his ward were thrown into very close "propinquity," and into very near communion. He had, or thought he had, reasons, not for putting an actual stop to it, but, on the other hand, for not encouraging it ; and he speculated not a little as to the best way to separate these young people a little more than in the easy circumstances of their daily life. He had consulted his sister once and again in his questionings. She had proposed a removal to the plantation. But he dreaded to take this step. The exigencies of his business required his presence in the city almost every day. He was happy in his family ; and, after so long a parting, he hated to be parted long again.

Matters brought themselves to a crisis, however. He came into Eunice's room one evening in serio-comic despair.

"Eunice, you must do something with your Indian girl. She is on your hands, not on mine. What do you think? I saw something light outside the paling just now. I went out to see what it might be, in the gloaming ; and there was Ma-ry, bobbing at a crawfish hole for crawfish, as quietly as you are mending that stocking. She might have been little Dinah, for all anxiety about her position. She never dreamed, dear child, that it was out of the way."

"What did you say?" said Eunice, laughing.

"It was not in my heart to scold her. I asked her what her luck was "—

"And then looked for another crawfish hole, and sat down and fished by her side?"

"No," said he ; "not quite so bad as that. I told her it was late, that she must not stay out late ; and she gathered up her prizes prettily, and brought them in. She never resists you a moment; that is the reason why she twirls us all round her fingers. I don't know what to do. It would break Inez's heart to send her away, not to say mine. She gave Chloe the crawfish for breakfast."

"There is Squam Bay?" said Eunice interrogatively.

"I had thoughts of Squam Bay. Heavens, how she would upset the proprieties there! I wonder what Parson Forbes would make of her. I would almost send her to Squam Bay for the fun of seeing the explosion.

"You see," after a pause, "Squam Bay is better than the nuns here, and it is worse. The nuns will teach her to embroider, and to talk French, and to keep secrets, and to hide things. The people there will teach her to tell the truth, where she needs no teaching; to work, where she needs no teaching; to wash and to iron; to make succotash; and to reconcile the five points of Calvinism with one another, and with infinite love. But this is to be considered: with the nuns she is close to us, and Squam Bay is very far off, particularly if there should be war."

"Always war?" asked Eunice anxiously.

What troubled Eunice was that this conversation, having come to this point, never went any farther. Forty times had her brother come about as far as this; but forty times he had put off till next week any determination, and next week never came. The girl was too dear to him; her pretty ways were becoming too necessary for him; Inez was too fond of her; and home-life, just thus and so, was too charming. At any given moment he hated to break the spell, and to destroy all.

This was, however, the last of these conferences. The next morning, immediately after family prayers, Silas Perry beckoned his sister into his own den.

"It is all settled," he said half gayly, half dolefully.

"What is settled?"

"Ma-ry yonder, the savage, is to go to the Ursulines."

"Who settled that?" asked Eunice, supposing this was only the forty-first phase of the talk of which last night showed the fortieth.

"Who settled it? Why, Ma-ry settled it. Who settles every thing in this house? What is the old story? It is repeated here. Ma-ry manages Ransom; Ma-ry manages Inez; Ma-ry manages you. And you and Inez and Ransom manage me."

"We and Roland," said Eunice.

"As you will. If Ma-ry does not manage him too, I am much mistaken. Any way, the dear child has given her directions this time, with as quiet determination as if she had been yourself, and with as distinct eye down the future as if she had been Parson Forbes. She wants to go to the Ursulines, and to the Ursulines she is to go."

The Ursulines' convent was at this moment the only school for girls, of any account, in Orleans, not to say in Louisiana.

"What did she say?"

"She said that all the things she knew were things of the woods and the prairies and the rivers. She said Inez was kind, too kind; that you were kind, too kind; that everybody was kind. But she said that she was never to go back to the woods, never to live in them. She must learn to do what women did here. If she staid in this house, I should spoil her. She did not put it in these words, but that was what she meant. If she went to the nuns, she should study all the time, and should never play. Here, she said, it was hard, very hard, not to play."

"What will Inez say?"

"I dare not guess. Ma-ry has gone to tell her."

"And what will Roland say?"

"I do not know, nor do I know who will tell him."

CHAPTER XXX.

MOTHER AND CHILD.

> " Smile not, my child,
> But sleep deeply and sweetly, and so beguiled
> Of the pang that awaits us, whatever that be
> So dreadful, since thou must divide it with me."
>
> SHELLEY.

So it was settled, and settled by herself, that poor Ma-ry should go into a convent-school. The freest creature on earth was to be shut up in the most complicated system of surveillance.

Ransom was well-nigh beside himself when he found that this step had been determined on, in face of his known views, and, indeed, without even the pretence of consultation with him. For the next day gloom was in all his movements. He would not bring Mr. Perry the claret that he liked, and pretended there was none left. He carried off the only pair of pumps which Roland could wear to the governor's ball, and pretended they needed mending. Inez sent him for. her hat; and he would not find it, and pretended he could not. For a day the family was made to understand that Ransom was deeply displeased.

He made a moment for a conference with Ma-ry, as he strapped her trunk. The only consolation he had had was the selection of this trunk, at a little shop where they brought such things from France.

" Ma-ry," said he, " they'll want you to go on your knees before them painted eye-dolls. Don't ye do it. They can't make ye noway, and ye mustn't do it. Say ye prayers as Miss Eunice taught ye, and don't say 'em to eye-dolls. They'll tell ye to lie and steal. Don't ye do it. Let um lie as much as they want to; but don't ye believe the fust word they‑tell ye. They won't give ye nothin' to eat but frogs, and not enough of them. Don't ye mind. I'll send round myself a basket twice a week. They won't let me come myself, 'cause they won't have no men near um but them black-coated priests, all beggars, all on um, and them others with brown nightgowns. Let them come; but I shall make old Chloe go round, or Salome, that's the other one, twice a week with a basket, and sunthin' good in it, and anough for three days. An' you keep the basket, Ma‑ry, and sponge it out, and give it back to her next time she comes. Don't let them nuns get the baskets, 'cause they ain't any more like um. They's white-oak baskets, made in a place up behind Atkinson; they ain't but one man knows how to make um, an' I make old Turner bring um down here to me. Don't ye let the nuns get the baskets."

Ma‑ry promised compliance with all his directions; and the certainty of outwitting the "eye-dollaters" on the matter of her diet threw a little gleam of comfort over the old man's sadness.

She went to the Ursulines. The Ursulines received her with the greatest tenderness, and thought they never had a more obedient pupil.

And this was the chief event in the family history of that winter. With the spring other changes came, necessitated by a removal to the plantation. Although this was by no means Silas Perry's chief interest, he had great pride in it; and he did not choose to have it in the least behind the plantations of his Creole neighbors. Roland had brought from the polytechnic school some pet theories of science which he was eager to apply in the sugar-mills; and he did not find it difficult to persuade Lonsdale to join him, even for weeks at a time, when he went up the coast. A longer expedition, however, called them away, both from the counting-house and from the plantation.

Gen. Bowles had not forgotten his promise. Inez and Roland both twitted Aunt Eunice with her conquest over this handsome adventurer. It was in vain that Eunice said that he was well known to have one wife, and was even said to have many. All the more they insisted that no one knew but all these savage ladies might have been scalped in some internecine or Kilkennyish brawl, and that the general might be seeking a more pacific helpmeet. The truth about Gen. Bowles was, that he was one of the wildest adventurers of any time. Born in Maryland, he had enlisted in King George's army just after Germantown and Brandywine. He had been a prosperous chief of the Creeks. He had conferred, equal with equal, with the generals who had commanded him in the English army only a few years before. He had been an artist and an actor, in his checkered life ; he had been in Spanish prisons, and had been presented at the English court.

One day, when a very distinguished Indian embassy had brought in a letter from him to Eunice, Roland undertook to explain all this to Mr. Lonsdale.

"And now, Mr. Lonsdale," said the impudent youngster Roland, who had chosen to give this account to him, as coolly as, on another occasion, he had cross-questioned him about the same man, " and now, Mr. Lonsdale, weary of diplomacy, he proposes to leave the throne of Creekdom. He lays his crown at Miss Perry's feet ; and she has only to say one little word, and he will become a sugar-planter of distinction on the Côté des Acadiens, with Miss Perry as his helpmeet, to cure the diseases of his people, and with Mr. Roland Perry, *ancien élève de l' École Polytechnique,* to direct the crystallization of his sugar."

The truth was, as it must be confessed, that the general's letters had usually been made out of very slender capital. He would write to say that he was afraid his last letter had miscarried, or that he should like to know if Miss Ma-ry remembered a house with a chimney at each end ; whether she had ever seen a saw-mill, or the like. For a man who had nothing to say, Gen. Bowles certainly wrote to Miss Perry a great many letters that winter. But on this occasion Eunice was so much absorbed, as she read, that she did not give the least attention to Roland's raillery.

"Hear this ! hear this ! Roland, go call your father. This really means something."

Mr. Perry came, on the summons.

Eunice began : —

GENERAL BOWLES TO MISS PERRY.

TALLADEGA, CREEK NATION, April 19, 1802.

MY DEAR MISS PERRY, — I can at last send you some tidings which mean something. If you knew the regret which I have felt in sending you so little news before, you would understand my pleasure now that I really believe I may be of some use to your charming *protégée.*

"Well begun," said the irreverent Roland. "We shall come to the sugar-plantation on the next page."

"Hold your tongue, sir," said his father ; and Eunice read on : —

I have just returned from a "talk," so called, with some of the older chiefs of the Choctaw and Cherokee nations. So soon as I renewed the old confidence which these men always felt in me, I made my first inquiries as to raids from the west into the territories north of us, in the year 1785, or thereabouts. The Cherokee warriors knew nothing of our matter.

But the Choctaw chiefs, fortunately, were better informed. As to the time there can be no question. It was the year 1784, well known to all these people from some eclipse or other which specially excited them.

A party of Choctaw chiefs, embodying all that there are left of the once famous Natchez, who, as your brother tells us, have just now appeared in literature, — a party of Choctaw chiefs crossed the Mississippi, and even the Red River, in quest of some lost horses. This means, I am sorry to say, that they went to take other horses to replace the lost ones. They met a large roving body of Apaches. They saw them, and they were whipped by them. They recrossed the Mississippi much faster than they went over.

These savages of the West had never, to my knowledge, crossed the Father of Waters.   But on this occasion, elated by their success, they did so ; and then, fortunately for the Choctaw people, they forgot them.   They were far north ; and hearing of a little settlement from Carolina, low down on the Cumberland River, they pounced on it, and killed every fighting man.   They burned every house, and stole every horse.   Then the whites above them came down on them so fast that they retired as best they might.

It is they, I am assured, who are the only Apaches who have crossed the Mississippi in this generation.   It is they, as I believe, who seized your little friend and her mother.

If you have any correspondents in the new State of Tennessee, they ought to be able to inform you further regarding the outpost thus destroyed.   I cannot learn that it had any name ; but it was very low on the Cumberland, and the time was certainly November, 1784.

"There is more ! there is more !" screamed Roland, seeing that his aunt stopped.

"There is nothing more about Ma-ry," said Eunice, who felt that she blushed, and was provoked beyond words that she did so.

"More ! more !" cried the bold boy, putting out his hand for the letter ; but his aunt folded it, and put it in her pocket.

And a warning word from his father, "Roland, behave yourself," told the young gentleman that for once he was going too far.

CHAPTER XXXI.

ON THE PLANTATION.

" Those sacred mysteries, for the vulgar ear
Unmeet; and known, most impious to declare,
Oh! let due reverence for the gods restrain
Discourses rash, and check inquiries vain."

Homeric Hymns.

LITTLE enough chance of finding any thing by raking over the wretched ashes of that village burned eighteen years before.　Still every one would be glad to know that the last was known; and, if one aching heart could be spared one throb of agony, every one would be glad to spare it.

The wonder and the satisfaction excited by Gen. Bowles's letter held the little party in eager talk for five minutes; and then Mr. Lonsdale, who happened to be of the plantation party that day, filled up the gap in the practical and definite way by which, more than once, that man of mystery had distinguished himself.

"I do not know what friends Mr. Perry may have, or what you may have, in Tennessee State," said he almost eagerly; "but I hope, I trust, Miss Perry, that you will put your commission of inquiry into my hands.　I have loitered here in your *dolce far niente* of Louisiana much longer than I meant, as you know.　What with this and that invitation, I have staid and staid in Capua, as if, indeed, here were the object of my life.　But my measures were all taken last week.　I asked Mr. Hutchings to select a padrone and boatmen for me; and he has hired a boat which, I am told, is just what it should be. Pardon me for saying a 'a boat:' I am told I must call it a *voiture.* Your arrangements are fairly Venetian, Miss Perry. Men seem to know but one carriage."

"Oh, call it a galliot!" she said, "and we shall know what you mean."

"If you would only be Cleopatra," said Mr. Lonsdale, with high gallantry, and he bowed.

"I shall be late in delivering my commissions at Fort Massac ; but I shall be there before any one else leaving Orleans this spring. Pray let me make your inquiries regarding this dear child's family."

Loyally said, and loyally planned, Mr. Lonsdale. If this man is a diplomatist, or whatever he be, he has twice come to the relief of Eunice by a most signal service, offered in the most simple and manly way. Even the suspicious Inez looked her gratitude, through eyes that were filled with tears.

The plan was too good not to be acceded to. Roland begged to go as a volunteer on the expedition ; and Mr. Perry insisted on it, that he must see to the stores.

"Pardon me, Mr. Lonsdale, but your countryman Mr. Hutchings does not know as we do what the Mississippi demands. I shall provision your galliot, or rather Ransom will ; for, if I undertook to do it without his aid, he would countermand all my directions. I may as well from the first confess to him that I am at his mercy."

"Take care, Mr. Perry, for I am almost as much a favorite with him as you are. That is, his pity for my ignorance, not to say his contempt for it, takes with me the place of his affection for your house. If you tell him to store the galliot for both of us, he will strip the plantation. ' Aint nothin' fit to eat, all the way up river,' he will say. ' All on 'em eats alligators and persimmons. Don' know what good codfish and salt pork is, none on um.' "

Everybody laughed.

"Capital, capital, Mr. Lonsdale ! You have studied the language of the country at its fountain."

"We will not let Ransom starve us, Mr. Lonsdale; but certainly we will not let him starve you."

The reader of to-day, who embarks at New Orleans for the mouth of the Ohio in a steamboat which is "a palace above and a warehouse below," has to take thought, in order to make real to himself a voyage, when Lonsdale and Roland could not expect, even with extra good luck, to reach their destination in two months' time. Slow as travelling was from Philadelphia or Baltimore across the mountains, many a traveller would have taken a voyage from New Orleans to an Atlantic seaport, that he might descend the Ohio, rather than ascend the Mississippi.

In this case, every preparation was made for comfort and for speed, on a plan not very unlike that on which Inez and her aunt started on their journey for Texas.

By a special dispensation, in which perhaps, the vicar-general and bishop assisted, not to say the pope himself, Ma-ry was liberated from the convent school to be present at the last farewells. The evening was spent at the plantation with affected cheerfulness, as is men's custom on the evenings of departure; and with early morning the two travellers were on their way. Mr. Perry took his own boat as they went up the river, and went down to the city to his counting-house, taking Ma-ry to a new sojourn with the Ursulines, in which her docility must show the pope that she had not abused his gracious permission for a "retreat."

Eunice made her preparations for a quiet week with Inez. Dear little Inez! she was more lovely than ever, now that there was always a shade of care about her. How true it is that human life never can be tempered into the true violet steel without passing through the fire! And Inez had passed through. It was the one bitter experience of life in which nobody could help her. Eunice knew that. She would have died for this child to save her sorrow; and yet without sorrow, nay, without bitter anguish, this lively, happy girl could never be made into a true woman. That Eunice knew also.

And, while Inez suffered, all Eunice could do was to sit by, or stand by and look on, — to watch and to pray as she did that night by the camp-fire.

"Now we are rid of them all, auntie, we can go to work and get things into order. There is no end of things to be done, and you are to show me how to do them all. What in the world will come to the plantation when you go off to be Duchess of Clarence, or maybe queen of England, if I do not learn something this summer?"

"Could you not push the Duke of Clarence into a butt of malmsey, and be well rid of him? Then you would be free from your terrors. For me, I have not yet seen him, and I don't know how I shall like him. Go, get your apron, and come with me."

And so the two girls, as Mr. Perry still called them fondly, had what women term a "lovely time" that day. No such true joy to the well-trained housekeeping chief, as to get rid of the men occasionally an hour or two early. Eunice and Inez resolved that they would have no regular dinner, just a cup of tea and a bit of cold meat; and that the day should.be devoted to the inner mysteries of that mysterious Eleusinian profession, which is the profession of the priestess of Ceres, or the domestic hearth.

And a field-day they had of it. The infirmary was inspected, and the nursery, the clothing-rooms, the kitchen, and the storehouses. Inez filled her little head full, and her little note-book fuller. They were both in high conclave over some pieces of coarse home-woven cotonnades, — a famous manufacture of their Acadian neighbors, — when a scream was heard from the shore, and Mr. Perry was seen approaching.

The ladies welcomed him with eager wonder. He was tired and evidently annoyed, but relieved them in a minute from personal anxiety about Ma-ry or any near friend.

"Still my news is as bad as it can be. I have come back to send it up to Roland there and Mr. Lonsdale. This Morales, this idiot of an intendant, means to cut off from the people above the right of sending their goods to Orleans."

"Cut off the right of depot!" cried both the girls in a word. They both knew that the prosperity of Orleans and the prosperity of the West alike depended on it ; nay, they knew that peace or war depended upon it. They heard with the amazement with which they would have heard that the intendant had fired the cathedral.

"Yes, the fool has cut off the permission for deposit. Of course I supposed it was a blunder. I went round to my lord's office, and saw the idiot myself. He is as mad as a March hare. I reminded him of the treaty. The right is sure for three years more against all the intendants in the world. The crazy coot rolled his eyes, and said that in the high politics treaties even sometimes must give way. High fiddlestick! I wish his Prince of Peace was higher than he has been yet, and with nothing to stand upon!"

"Did you speak of the — the secret?" said Eunice, meaning that Louisiana was really Napoleon's province, or the French Republic's, at this moment, and no province of Spain.

"I just hinted at it. So absurd, that there should be this pretence of secrecy, when the 'secret' has been whispered in every paper in the land! But, indeed, the men who are most angry below say that this is Bonaparte's plan, that he wants to try the temper of the Kentuckians. He is no such fool. It is another piece of Salcedo's madness, or of the madness which ruled Salcedo's. Perhaps they want at Madrid to steal all the value from their gift. Clearly enough there is a quarrel between old Salcedo the governor, and this ass of a Morales. The Intendant Morales will do it, or says he will do it all the same ; and the governor does not interfere. But it is all one business : it is that madness that sent Muzquiz after our poor friend ; it is that madness which appointed Salcedo, the old fool, here. Madrid, indeed!"

"What will the river people say?" asked Inez.

"I do not know what they'll say," said her exasperated father, who had by this time talked himself back into the same rage with which he had left the intendant's apartments ;

"but I know what they will do. They will take their rifles on their shoulders, and their powder-horns. They will put a few barrels of pork and hard-tack on John Adams's boats, which are waiting handy for them up there. They will take the first rise on the river after they hear this news ; and they will come down and smoke this whole tribe of drones out of this hive, and the intendant and the whole crew will be in Cuba in no time. Inez, mark what I say. This river and this town go together. The power that holds this town for an hour or a day against the wish of the people above holds it to its ruin. Remember that, if you live a hundred years."

"The whole army of Cuba could be brought here in a very few weeks," said Eunice thoughtfully.

"Never you fear the army of Cuba. The general who ever brings an army from the Gulf against New Orleans, when the sharp-shooters of this valley want to hold New Orleans, comes here to his ruin. Inez, when New Orleans and the Western country shall learn to hold together, New Orleans will be one of the first cities of the world ; and you, girl, are young enough to live to see it so."

All this he said, as Eunice fairly insisted on his drinking a cup of coffee and eating something after his voyage. All the time, however, the preparations were going forward, to order which he had himself come up the river. The lightest and swiftest boat in the little navy of the plantation was hastily got ready to be sent with the bad news to Roland and Lonsdale. Nobody knew whether the intendant had forwarded it. Nobody knew whether he meant to. But, since Oliver Pollock and Silas Perry forwarded gunpowder to Washington six and twenty years before, they knew the way to send news up the river when they chose, and he did not choose that any intendant of them all should be ahead of him.

The boat was ready before half an hour was over. The occasion was so pressing that Ransom himself was put in charge of the expedition and the despatches. The other party had a day the start of them. But Ransom took a double crew that he might row all night, and hoped to overhaul them at their camp of the second evening.

CHAPTER XXXII.

THE DESOLATE HOME.

"Still, as they travel, far and wide,
Catch they and keep they a trace here, a trace there,
That puts you in mind of a place here, a place there."

BROWNING.

RANSOM returned a good deal earlier than anybody expected. He came in the middle of the night with as cross a crew of boatmen as ever rowed any Jason or Odysseus. He had compelled them to such labors as they did not in the least believe in.

He reported to Eunice before breakfast.

" So you caught them, Ransom ? "

" Yes'm.   Come up with um little this side Pointe Coupée. They was in camp. Good camp too. All right and comfortable.   Mr. Roland understands things, mum."

" And you didn't see the Spaniards ? "

" Yes'm — see um.   Didn't see me though — darned fools. See them fust night out. They was all asleep in the Green Reach.   See they fires, lazy dogs ! didn't go nigh um, 'n they didn't know nothin' about us ; passed right by um, t'other side of the river. That's all they's fit for. Calls um coast-guards.   Much as ever they can do is to keep they own hats on."

" And what message did the gentlemen send ? "

" Said they was all well, and had had very good luck ; 'n they wrote two letters — three letters here, for you and Miss

Inez, 'n Mr. Perry. I'd better take his'n down to him myself. I'm goin' down to-day."

"And did you come back in one day, Ransom?"

"Yes'm. Come down on the current. Come in no time, ef these lazy niggers knew how to row. Don't know nothin'. Ought to 'a' been here at three o'clock. Didn't git here till midnight. Told um I'd get out 'n walk, but ye can't shame um nor nothin'. They can't row. They don't know nothin'."

This was Ransom's modest account of a feat unsurpassed on the river for ten years — indeed, till the achievements of steam left such feats for the future unrecorded.

" And you saw no one coming down ? "

"Yes'm. See them Spanish beggars agin, and this time they stopped me. Couldn't 'a' stopped me ef I didn't choose; but there's no use quarrelling. They was gittin' ready for they siesta, 's they calls it, lazy dogs! right this side o' Mr. Le Bourgeois's place, — pootiest place on the river. We was on t'other side, and they seed us, and fired a shot in the air ; and I told the niggers to stop rowin'. Made the Spanishers — them's the coast-guard, they calls um — come out and meet us. They asked where we'd been. I told um we'd been cat-fishing. They asked where the fish was. I said we hadn't had no luck. They asked if any boats had passed me, and I said they hadn't, 'cause they hadn't. They asked me to take a note down to the intendant, 'n I said I would; 'n I got it here. Guess I shall give it to him about Thanksgivin' time."

This, with a grim smile of contempt for the snares and wiles of the Spanishers.

"O Ransom ! you had better take it to the intendant's to-day."

" I'll see, mum. Sartin it's for no good, 'cause they's no good in um. They's all thieves 'n liars. Mebbe it's for harm, 'n ef it is, they'd better not have it."

" Well, show it to Mr. Perry, Ransom, any way."

To which the old man made no reply, but withdrew ; and

then the ladies undertook the business of letter-reading and breakfasting together. The letters would not tell many facts. They might show to the skilful reader something of what was in the heart of each writer, as he left for such long and solitary journey. But this story hurries to its end, and these intimations of feeling must be left to the reader's conjectures.

Whatever they said, the ladies had to satisfy themselves with these letters for months. The news which Lonsdale and Roland carried was enough to turn back most of the downward-bound boats which would else have taken their letters. Such boats as did attempt the gauntlet were seized or threatened at the different Spanish posts ; were searched, perhaps, by *guarda costas*, so called ; and nothing so suspicious as letters, even were these the most tender-looking of billets to the sweetest of ladies, was permitted to slip through.

It is true that some cause, either the bitter protests of the American factors, or some doubts engendered by despatches from home, postponed until October the final proclamation of the famous interdict by which New Orleans was self-starved and self-besieged. Its effect on the upper country was none the less for the delay.

The ladies settled back into that simple and not unprofitable life so well known to our grandmothers, so impossible to describe to their descendants, or even for these descendants to conceive,— a life unpersecuted by telegrams, by letters, by express-parcels ; a life which knew nothing of that " stand and deliver," which bids us reply by return of post ; or, while the telegraph-messenger waits in the hall, to give a decision on which may rest the happiness of a life. For Eunice and Inez, the great events were, perhaps, to see that a crew of Caddoes drifting down the river with their baskets were properly welcomed ; perhaps to spend the day with Mme. Porcher, at her plantation just below ; perhaps to prepare for the return visit when the time came ; perhaps to go out of a Saturday evening to see the Acadians dance themselves almost dead to the violin-music of Michael, the old white-haired fiddler ; perhaps for Inez to keep her little school daily, in which she taught the little black folk the mysteries of letters ; and all the time, certainly, for both of them, the purely domestic cares of that independent principality which was called a plantation.

Mr. Perry came up to the plantation about once a week, but only for a day or two at a time. His stay would be shorter than Eunice had ever known it, and there was anxiety in his manner which it had never known before. Every thing combined to make that an anxious year for Orleans. Though this ridiculous intendant had pretended not to know the secret of its transfer to France, many men did know that secret early in the spring, and before summer all men knew it. That Gen. Victor with an army of twenty-five thousand Frenchmen was on his way to take possession, was a rumor which came with almost every vessel from Philadelphia or from England. Gen. Victor and his army did not appear. What did appear was another army, a starving army of poor French men and women from San Domingo, driven out by a new wave of the insurrection there. It was not the first of such arrivals. They always made care and anxiety for the little colony. Not only were the poor people to be provided for, but the cause of their coming had to be talked over in every family in Louisiana. A successful rising of slaves in San Domingo had to be discussed in the hearing and presence of slaves now well enough satisfied in Louisiana. This year, this anxiety had reached its height. The Spanish intendant, who had precipitated war on his own head from up the river, so soon as the Western sharp-shooters could arrive, frightened himself and his people to death with terrors about insurrection within. The French began to whisper that their own countrymen were coming. The handful of Americans chafed under the unrighteous restriction on the trade for which they lived there.

"BY THE KING.
A proclamation !
In the name of the King !

Know all men :

That His Most Christian Majesty commands that the sale of all clocks bearing upon them the figure of a woman, whether sitting or standing, wearing the cap of Liberty, or bearing a banner in her hand, is henceforth, forever, absolutely prohibited in the colony of Louisiana.

Let all faithful subjects of his Majesty govern themselves accordingly.

Long live the King."

To see such a proclamation printed in the miserable "Gazette," or posted at the corner of the street, was something to laugh at; and at the old jealousies of other days, between the French circle and the Spanish circle, Mr. Perry could afford to laugh again. But here, in matters much more important, was jealousy amounting to hatred, for causes many of which were real; and every man's hand, indeed, seemed to be against his brother.

It was therefore, at best, but a sad summer and autumn ; and Miss Perry succeeded in persuading her brother to remove the little family to the city earlier than was their custom, that he might at least have in town what she called home comforts, and that, if any thing did happen, they might at least be all together.

"We cannot be of much use," she said ; "but at least we shall be of no harm. Besides, if we go, we shall take Ransom : I know he will be a convenience to you, and you may need him of a sudden."

Whether Ransom would be of any real service, Mr. Perry doubted. But it was very true that he was glad to have his cheerful little family together ; and in the comfort of a quiet evening to forget the intrigues, the plots, the alarms, and the absurd speculations, which were discussed every day in his counting-room, now that there was little other business done there. In the old palmy days of Gov. Miro, even under the later dynasties of Casa Calvo and Gayoso, if any such complications threatened as now impended, Mr. Perry would have been among the favored counsellors of the viceroy ; for vice-roys these governors were. He would not have hesitated himself to call, and to offer advice which he knew would be well received. But times were changed, indeed. Instead of one king, there were three. Here was Morales, the intend-ant, pretending that he did not care whether Gov. Salcedo approved or did not approve of his doings. Here was Sal-cedo himself : was he old enough to be foolish and in his dotage, as some people thought? or, was he pretending to be a fool, and really pulling all the strings behind the curtain? And here was young Salcedo, his son, puffing about, and pretending to manage everybody and every thing.

One night, at a public ball, this young Salcedo set every-body by the ears. The men drew swords, and the women fainted. Just as the dance was to begin, and the band began playing a French contra-dance, the young braggart cried out, "English dances, English dances!" He was a governor's son : should he not rule the ballroom? Any way, the band-master feared and obeyed, and began on English contra-dances. The young French gallants would not stand this, and cried out, "French, French, French!" There were not Spaniards enough to out-cry them ; but Salcedo, and those there were, drew their swords. The Frenchmen drew theirs. The women screamed. The American and English gentle-men let the others do the fighting, while they carried the fainting women out. The captain of the guard marched in with a file of soldiers, presented bayonets, and proceeded to clear the hall. It was only this absurd extreme which brought people to terms. The women were revived, and the dancing went on. What with young Salcedo's folly, old Sal-cedo's jealousy, and Morales's wrong-headedness, some such bad-blooded quarrel filled people's ears every day.

Under such circumstances, the simple life of the city had all gone. Mr. Perry's counsels, once always respected at headquarters, were worthless now.

This intendant knew his estimate among the Americans,

and with their nation, only too well ; but he pretended to make that a reason for distrusting him. The absurd dread of the Americans, which first showed itself in the treachery to poor Philip Nolan, showed itself now in unwillingness to hear what even the most cautious Americans had to say.

In the midst of such anxieties, as they expected Roland from hour to hour, there came in his place, by the way of Natchez, only this not very satisfactory letter : —

ROLAND PERRY TO EUNICE PERRY.

FORT MASSAC, Aug. 31, 1802.

MY DEAR AUNT, — We have been up the Cumberland River ; and I am convinced that I have seen the ruins of dear Ma-ry's home. There is not stick nor stem standing of the village, — save some wretched charred beams of the saw-mill, all covered with burrs, and briars, and bushes. But, that this is the place, you may be sure. We have been up to the next settlement, which was planted only three years later ; and they know the whole sad story, just as Gen. Bowles has told you. The bloody brutes came in on the sleeping village, just in the dead of night. The people had hardly a chance to fire a shot, none to rally in their defence. They slaughtered all the men, and, as these people said, they slaughtered all the women ; but it seems dear Ma-ry and her mother were saved.

Which baby she is, from which mother of these eight or ten families, of course I cannot tell, nor can these people. But they say that, at Natchez, there is an old lady who can. An old Mrs. Willson, — all these people were Scotch-Irish from Carolina, — an old Mrs. Willson came on to join her daughter, and arrived the spring after the massacre. Poor old soul, she had no money to go back. She has loitered and loitered here, till only two years ago. Then she said there would be more chance of her hearing news of her child if she went farther south and west ; and so when somebody moved to Natchez he took with him this Mother Ann ; and, if she is alive, she is there still.

She is possibly our Ma-ry's grandmother. If anybody knows any thing of the dear child's birth, it is she.

And this is all I can tell. I am sorry it is so little ; so is poor Lonsdale, — the heartiest, most loyal companion, as he is the most accomplished gentleman, it was ever a young fellow's luck to travel with. You will think this is very little ; but it has cost us weeks of false starts and lost clews to get at what I send you.

You will not wonder that you do not see me. You will believe me that I am well employed. Make much love for me to dear Ma-ry and to my darling Een.

Always your own boy,
ROLAND PERRY.

This letter had been a strangely long time coming. Had it perhaps been held by the Spanish authorities somewhere? Eunice had another letter, a letter in Lonsdale's handwriting; but she read Roland's first, and then, grieved and surprised that her boy was not coming, she gave it to his father.

Mr. Perry read with equal surprise and with equal grief.

"What does it mean?" said she.

"It means," said he, after a pause, — "it means that he thought the chances were that the coast-guard would get that letter, and so it must tell very little." Then, after another pause, "Eunice, I am afraid it means that the boy has mixed himself up with recruiting the Kentuckians to come down here on the next rise of the river. Why they did not come on the last rise, is a wonder to me; but I suppose they were waiting for these fools to strike the last blow. They have struck it now. As I told you, Morales has published his 'interdict.' The old fool Salcedo pretends to shake his head; but it is published all the same, and, now they have done it, they shake at every wind. They believe, at the Government House, that twenty thousand armed men, mounted on horses or alligators or both, are now on their way. The intendant shakes in his shoes, as he walks from mass to his office. Roland has been bred a soldier. He is an eager American. He certainly has not staid for nothing, when his heart and every thing else calls him here. What does your Mr. Lonsdale say?"

Mr. Lonsdale said very little that could be read aloud, as it proved. In briefer language than Roland's he told substantially the same story. Mother Ann, at Natchez, — if Mother Ann still lived, — was the person to be consulted regarding Ma-ry's lineage.

There seemed to be more in Mr. Lonsdale's letter than

was read aloud to Mr. Perry, or even to Inez. But poor Inez was growing used to secrets and to mysteries. Poor girl! she knew that of one thing she never spoke to Aunt Eunice. Who was she, to make Aunt Eunice tell every thing to her? It seemed to her that the world was growing mysterious. Her lover left her, if he were her lover, and never said a word to tell her he loved her; and no man knew where his body lay. Her dear Ma-ry, her other self, was caged up on the other side of those hateful bars. Her own darling brother, lost so long, and only just back again, — he had disappeared too. Nothing but these letters, months old, to tell what had become of him. And now, when Aunt Eunice had a letter from where he was, that letter was not read to Inez, as once every letter was: it was simply put away after one miserable scrap had been read aloud, and people began discussing the situation as if this letter had never come.

But the letters were to work Inez more woe than this; for Eunice determined to follow up, as soon as might be, the clew they gave.

So was it, that some weeks after, when a change was to be made in the Spanish garrison at Concordia, opposite Natchez, she availed herself of the escort of a friendly officer going up the river, who was taking his wife with him, and determined for herself to make an inquiry at that village for "Mother Ann." She had never ceased to feel that on her, first of all, rested the responsibility in determining Ma-ry's future, and in unravelling the history of her past.

CHAPTER XXXIII.

ALONE.

> " Much was in little writ, and all conveyed
> With cautious care, for fear to be betrayed
> By some false confidant, or favorite maid."
>
> DRYDEN.

" Ah, well!" wrote Inez, in the queer little journal which she tried to keep in those days, "so I am to learn what life is. They take their turns; but one after another of these I love most leaves me, till I am now almost alone. I will try not to be ungrateful, but I am very lonely."

And here the poor girl stopped; and such was the eventfulness of her life for weeks after, that she does not come to the diary again. As it is apt to happen in our somewhat limited human life, the people who have most to do have little chance, or little spirit, to sit down night by night, to tell on paper how they did it.

Her aunt's absence must of necessity be three or four weeks in length. They parted with tears, you may be sure. It was the first time they had been parted, for so long a separation, since Inez could remember. She was now indeed put to the test to show how well she could carry on the duties of the head of the household.

And Chloe and Antoine, and even old Ransom, would come to her for orders, in the most respectful way, from day to day. " As if I did not know," Inez said to Ma-ry, in one of their convent interviews, " that they were all going to do just what they thought best, and as if they did not know that I knew it."

Once a fortnight, under the rules for girls' schools, which St. Ursula had arranged before the barbarians had cut off her head at Cologne, Inez was permitted to visit Ma-ry for an hour in the convent parlor. Once a month, under some such dispensation from the holy father at Rome as has been spoken of, Ma-ry was able to return the visit for the better part of a day. For the rest, their intercourse went on in correspondence, with the restriction, not pleasing to two such young ladies, that the letters on both sides were to be examined before they reached their destination by Sister Barbara. Inez took such comfort as she could, by going to mass on Sunday at the chapel of St. Ursula, where she could see Ma-ry, and Ma-ry could see her. But, excepting these comforts, the two girls had to live on in hope that Whit-Sunday would come at last, and then Ma-ry was to be liberated from the study and the imprisonment to which she had so bravely submitted.

Poor Inez's anxieties were not to be the questions of good or bad coffee, or tender steaks or tough. Every thing seemed to conspire against the peace of that little community ; and in that little community the bolts seemed to fall hottest and fastest on the household of Silas Perry.

The community itself was in the most feverish condition. M. Laussat had arrived, with a commission from the First Consul to govern the colony, as soon as it was transferred by Spain ; for all mystery about the transfer from Spain to France was now over. Besides old Salcedo, "moribund," and young Salcedo, impudent and interfering, and the Intendant Morales, idiotic and pig-headed, here was this pretentious popinjay, Laussat.

You would have said that the French people would have been pleased : now they could dance French contra-dances when they chose.

Not so much pleased. The Spanish rule had been very

mild. Hardly a tax, hardly any interference, before this fool came in. Oh for the old .days of Miro, and then we would not ask for any French ruler!

And M. Laussat, or Citizen Laussat, without a soldier to walk behind him or before him, with nothing but a uniform and a few clerks, is swelling and puffing, and talking of what our army is going to do.

But where is "our army"?

It does not come.

Gov. Salcedo invites him to dinner, and is civil. Young Salcedo makes faces behind his back, and is rude. Meanwhile the bishop is cross with the Free-Masons, and says the Jacobins are coming; and all the timid people are watching the negroes, and say Christophe or Dessalines is coming. Men who never sat up all night, except at a revel, are watching their own kitchens for fear of secret meetings.

"Ah me!" poor Inez says, "were there ever such hateful times? When will Roland come? When will Aunt Eunice come? When can I go back to the plantation?"

One afternoon Mr. Perry came home later than usual, and looked even more troubled than usual. He changed his coat, and made ready for dinner, apologized to Inez for making her dinner late, and then bade the servant call Ransom.

"I do not think he is in, papa. He has not come home since I sent him down to you."

"Why, that," said her father, "was but little after noon. He came, and I gave him his papers for the 'Hannah.' The 'Hannah' cast loose, and was gone in twenty minutes. Tarbottle stood on the quarter, and waved his hat to me, as they drifted by the office. Where can the old fellow have gone?"

These were the first words, remembered for days afterward, about a mysterious disappearance of the good old man. One more of Inez's stand-bys out of the way.

For that afternoon Mr. Perry gave himself no care. So

often was Ransom out of the way that there was an open
jest in the family, which pretended that he was major-domo
in another household, and spent half of his time in it. Mr.
Perry needed him this evening; but he often needed him
when he had to do without him. He merely directed that
word should be brought to him of Ransom's return, and
made no inquiry.

But when it appeared, the next morning, that Ransom had
not slept at home, matters looked more serious. A theory
was started that he had gone down the river with the "Hannah," to return with the river-pilot; but an express to the
vessel, which was making but slow progress, settled that idea.
A message up to the plantation showed that he was not
there. A note from Capt. Tarbottle made sure that the old
fellow had landed safely from the brig; but from that moment not a word could be heard of poor Ransom.

Mr. Perry's anxiety was much greater than he could
describe to Inez. The girl was so much attached to her
old protector that his death would be to her a terrible
calamity. To Inez, therefore, Mr. Perry affected much more
confidence than he felt. The truth was, that if the old man
had not carried much such a charmed life as crazy men
carry in Islam, he would have been put out of the way long
before. In this mixed chaotic population of French, Spanish, Portuguese, Italians, Sicilians, English, Irish, negroes,
and Indians, Ransom was going and coming, announcing
from moment to moment, to men's faces, that they were all
thieves and liars and worse. How he had escaped without
a thousand hand-to-hand battles, was and had been a mystery to Silas Perry. Now that Ransom was gone, his own
conviction was simply that the hour had come, which had
been postponed as by a miracle. After three days of inquiry,
he was certain that he should never see Ransom again. The
blow of a dirk, and a plash into the river, would make little
echo; and the Mississippi tells no tales.

No one said this to poor Inez; but poor Inez was not

such a fool but she suspected it. She did not like to tell her father how much she suspected, and how much she feared. She did write to her aunt; and she poured out her fears, without hesitation, to Ma-ry. If Sister Barbara or Sister Horrida wanted to read this, they were welcome.

Weary with such anxieties, the poor girl sat waiting for her father one evening, even later than on the day when Ransom disappeared. At last she called Antoine to know if his master had spoken of a late dinner. "No, monsieur had said nothing." Then Antoine might make ready to walk with her to the counting-room; and Antoine might take a bottle of claret with him: perhaps her father was not well.

The sun had fairly set. The twilight is very short; and even at that hour the street, never much frequented, was still. The girl almost flew over the ground in her eagerness. But the counting-room was wholly locked up; no one was there. Indeed, no one was in the neighborhood.

Papa must have stopped at Mr. Huling's. They would walk round that way; and they did so. With as clear a voice as she could command, and with well-acted indifference, she called across the yard to Mr. Huling, who was smoking in his gallery, and who ran to her as soon as he recognized her voice.

No. As it happened, he had not seen Mr. Perry all day. He expected him, but Mr. Perry had not come round. He had thought he might have gone up the river. Had Miss Perry any news of old Ransom?

Mr. Huling was the American vice-consul, and Inez was half tempted to open her whole budget of terrors to him. But she knew this would displease her father. Indeed, he was probably at home by this time, waiting for her. She said as much to her friend, left a message for the ladies, and withdrew. So soon as she had passed the garden she fairly ran home.

No father there!

A message to the book-keeper brought him round to wonder, but to suggest nothing. Mr. Perry had left the counting-room rather earlier than usual, had walked down the river bank : that was all any one had observed. The old man was not a person of resource, and could only express sympathy.

And so poor Inez was left indeed alone. What a night that was to her ! How it recalled the horrible night on the Little Brassos ! Only then it was she who had drifted away from the rest of them : now she was the fixture, and every-body — everybody she loved — had drifted away from her. One by one, they had all gone. Nobody to talk to, nobody to consult, nobody even to cry with. Ma-ry gone, Roland gone, her aunt gone, poor old Ransom gone, and now papa gone ! Vainly she tried to persuade herself that she was a fool ; that papa was at Daniel Clark's card-party, or had stopped for a cup of tea with the Joneses. But really she knew that papa did not do such things without dressing, and without sending word home. Papa would never frighten her so. She tried to imagine sudden exigencies on shipboard which might have called him down the river for the night. This was a little more hopeful. But she did not in her heart believe this, and she knew she did not. The girl was too much her father's confidante, he talked with her quite too freely and wisely about his affairs, for her to pretend to take this comfort solidly.

She went through the form of ordering in the dinner, and ordering it out again. She wrapped her shawl around her, and sat on the gallery, to catch the first footstep. Footstep ! No footsteps in that street after nine at night ! She watched the stars, and saw them pass down behind the magnolias. When Fomalhaut was fairly out of sight, she would give it up and go to bed. As if she could sleep to-night !

And yet, poor tired child, she did sleep ; she slept then and there. And she dreamed. What did she dream of ? Ah me ! What did poor Inez dream of most often ? She was sitting in the gallery. Her shawl was round her head, as she dreamed ; and there was a quick footstep in the street.

Then some one stopped, and knocked hard at the street-gate. And then, as she sat, she could see a head above the gate, — a head without a hat on. And the head spoke in the darkness; it cried loud: " Ransom, Ransom ! Cæsar, Cæsar ! Miss Eunice, Miss Eunice ! Miss Inez, Miss Inez ! "

It was the head of William Harrod, and it was William Harrod's voice which called.

Inez was well waked now. With one hand she seized the hall-bell, and rang it loud to call Antoine. She dashed down the steps, not waiting an instant, nor seeing the winding garden-path. She rushed across the circular grass-plat, and through the shrubbery to the gate. She unbolted the gate, flung it back, and threw it open. But there was no one there ! Inez thought she heard receding steps in the darkness ; but, if so, it was but an instant. By the time Antoine was by her side, all was midnight silence.

The girl compelled the frightened Antoine to run with her to the corner of the street. But all was still as death in the cross-street to which she led him. And she was obliged to return to the house, wondering, had she been asleep, and had she dreamed ? Could dreams be as life-like as this was ? Inez confessed to herself that she had dreamed of William Harrod before ; but never had she seen his face or heard his voice in a dream which had such reality as this.

It will not do to say that she passed a sleepless night. There are few sleepless nights to girls of her age and health. But the sleep was broken by dreams, and they were always dreams of horror. All alone she was indeed ; and such was their life in Orleans, that there were strangely few people to whom the girl could turn for counsel.

So soon as she thought it would answer in the morning, she went out herself to see Mr. Huling, resolved to intrust all her agonies to him, as she should have done at the first, she now thought. Alas ! at sunrise, Mr. Huling had gone down the river, on an errand at the Balize, which would detain him many days. There was only a consul's clerk, a stranger, clearly inefficient, though willing enough, with whom Inez could confide. She did intrust him with her story, but she did not make him feel its importance. He promised her, however, to call on Mr. Daniel Clark or Mr. Jones, and on young Mr. Bingaman, and to be governed by their advice. He undertook to persuade her that she was unduly alarmed. Her father was visiting some friend. He would be back before the day was over. For such is the way in which ignorant and inefficient men usually treat women.

Inez had more success in rousing the interest and sympathy of Mr. Pollock, one of her father's companions and frends. But even he, interested as he was, did not want to alarm the city vainly. Nor did Inez want to. He sent an express to the plantation, and lost half a day so, in justifying Inez in her certainty that her father was not there. And in such useless fritter, which she knew was useless, the day was wasted, before he brought the consul's clerk to an understanding of who Silas Perry was, and that some inquiry as to his welfare was incumbent on the Americans in Orleans, and on those who represented them.

A horrible day to Inez. She was becoming a woman very fast now.

Just before dark, when her loneliness seemed the most bitter ; when she had done every thing she could think of doing, had turned every stone, and felt that she had utterly failed, that she had as little resource as poor old M. Desbigny the book-keeper had, — she heard an unexpected sound ; and one of the little Chihuahua dogs which the girls had brought with them from Antonio — the token of Mr. Lonsdale's attention — jumped upon her lap.

"One being that has not left me, that tries to find me." This was Inez's first thought, as she fondled the little creature ; and there was a sort of guilty thought mingled with it, that she had never been specially attentive to her pet. He was a pretty creature, but he was Mr. Lonsdale's present. Ma-ry had been much more attentive to hers ; but Inez had willingly enough left her dog to a little black boy at the plantation. And now this little forsaken wretch, grateful for such scant favors as Inez had bestowed, had followed her down the river. How did he get here to be her companion when she had no other?

Are you sure of that, Inez?

As she bent over the little wretch to fondle him, she felt a real sinking of heart at finding that it was not Skip, after all, but Trip. Now, Trip was Ma-ry's dog, and not hers. Trip had escaped from convent fare to the more luxurious home he was first used to. Inez was so angry that she took him in both hands to push him from her lap, — when her hand closed on a little bit of paper wound tightly round his back leg, so colored with charcoal as to match the hairless skin precisely.

In an instant Inez had clipped the thread which bound it, and took the scrap to the light.

As it unrolled, it was a strip of paper several inches long, very narrow. Not one word of writing on it! Ma-ry had not meant to risk any secrets. But in dingy red characters, — Inez knew only too well where that red came from, — in the Indian hieroglyphic with which she and Ma-ry had whiled away so many rainy days, was a legend which answered, oh, so many questions!

There was the sign of Ransom, an eye strangely cocked up to heaven; the sign or token of Mr. Perry, two feathers, cut in the shape to which the old-fashioned penmen always trimmed their goose-quills.   Around these signs was a twisted rope, doubly wreathed.   And Inez knew that this meant that both Mr. Perry and Ransom were in prison. But this was not all, but only the beginning.   In long series, there was the rising sun ; there was the roof of a house ; there was a hawk, a tree ; strange devices defying all perspective and all rules of design.   But Inez knew their meaning, and wrought out the sequence from the beginning.   The legend directed her to take, with her brother's field-glass, a little before the sun rose the next morning, some station from which she could see the top of the Ursuline convent.   Ma-ry could tell her by the pantomime of the Indian race, what she dared not commit to paper, for fear some adept in the Indian hieroglyphic might catch poor Trip as he worked his way from the convent garden.

Of all the wonders which Roland had brought home from Paris, nothing had delighted Ma-ry so much as this field-glass, which he had selected from the workshop of the Lerebours of the day.   Often had she expatiated to him and to Inez together, on the advantages of this instrument to people who were surrounded with enemies.   More than once had Inez, and once in particular, as she now remembered, had her aunt, tried to explain to Ma-ry that as most people lived they were not surrounded with enemies, and that the uses of the field-glass were, in fact, pacific.   But this girl had grown up with the habit of questioning every rustling leaf.   She had not been persuaded out of her theory.   All this talk Inez remembered to-night, as she wiped the lenses of the field-glass, and as she reconnoitred the garden to make sure which magnolia-tree best commanded the roof of the Ursulines' convent.

CHAPTER XXXIV.

"Short exhortations need." — *Neptune in* OVID.

BEFORE it was light, — long before the time Ma-ry had indicated in her blood-red letter, — Inez was working her way up the tall magnolia which stood south of the house. She had taken a garden-ladder to the lower branches, and now scrambled up without much more difficulty than the lizards which she startled as she did so. How often in little-girl days had she climbed this very tree, Ransom approving and directing! And how well she remembered the last victorious ascent for a white bud that seemed to defy all assault; and then, alas! the prohibition which had crowned victory, and robbed it of all its laurels, as her aunt and even her father had joined against her, and bidden her never climb the tree again!

Ah me! if only either of them were here, she would not disobey them now! How wretched to be her own mistress!

The field-glass was swung around her neck by its strap; and the girl brought in her hand the end of a long narrow pennon of white cotton cloth. When she had attained a station which wholly commanded the roof of St. Ursula's shrine, Inez pulled up by the pennon a fishing-rod which she had attached to it, — one of the long canes from the brake which are the joy of the Louisiana anglers, — and thrust the rod high above her head into the air, so that the pennon waved bravely in the morning breeze. With this signal Inez knew she could say, "I understand," or by rapid negatives could order any thing repeated.

And then she had to wait and wait again, her eye almost glued to the eye-piece. She could at last count the tiles on the roof-tree of the convent. She could see a lazy lizard walk over them, and jump when he caught flies. The Ursulines' is not far away from Silas Perry's garden; and, but for the more minute signals of the pantomime, she would not have needed the field-glass at all.

Ready as she was, she did not lose one moment of poor Ma-ry's stolen time. Inez at last saw the girl appear upon the corridor of the schoolroom, — what in older countries would have been called a cloister, and perhaps was in St. Ursula's fore-ordination. She passed rapidly along to the corner where a China-tree shaded the end of the gallery. Without looking behind her, she sprung upon the railing; she was in the tree in a moment, and in a moment more had left it, to stand unencumbered on the roof of this wing of the spacious buildings.

When people in a house are looking for a person out of a house, there is no point so difficult for them to observe as the top of that house; and there is no point which they so little think of searching.

Ma-ry had had less to do with houses than any person in Orleans, if one excepts a few old Caddo hags who crouched around the market; but she had made the observation just now put on paper, before she had been in Nacogdoches an hour.

If eleven thousand virgins of St. Ursula searched for her in eleven thousand niches, or under eleven thousand beds, they would not find her; and, while they were searching, she would be telling the truth, — a business at which she was good, and which St. Ursula herself probably would not disapprove.

The girl turned to Silas Perry's garden, saw the pennon, and clapped her hands gladly.

The pennon waved gracefully in sympathy.

Then the pantomime began. Grief, — bitter grief; certainty, — utter certainty; and then the sign for yesterday. She was very sorry for the news, she was certain it was true, and she had only known it yesterday.

The pennon waved gently its sympathy, and its steady " I understand."

The girl walked freely from place to place, and made her gestures as boldly as a mistress of ballet would do in presence of three thousand people.

Ransom was taken nine days ago. He is now in the soldiers' room under the court-house, next the cathedral. Ever since, they have been trying to find Mr. Perry alone. Day before yesterday they found him and took him. He is in the governor's own house. After early mass yesterday, one of the fathers came to the convent, as was his custom. After he had confessed three novices, he had a talk with Sister Barbara. He told her what Ma-ry told Inez. Sister Barbara told Sister Helena, in presence of a Mexican girl whom Ma-ry had been kind to. The Mexican girl told Ma-ry.

Ma-ry thought that Ransom and Mr. Perry were both to be sent to Cuba.

Cuba was intimated by an island which would be reached by a voyage of ten days, — an island in which there were a thousand Spanish soldiers.

Lest any news should be sent after this vessel, an embargo on all vessels would be ordered for a fortnight. The embargo was denoted by rowers, who were suddenly stopped in their paddling. Ma-ry had to repeat this signal, because the pennon waved uncertainty. When she was sure all was understood, she kissed her hand, and then, pointing to the rising sun, bade Inez keep tryst the next day but one.

The glad pennon nodded its assent cheerfully, and Ma-ry disappeared.

News indeed !

Inez wrote this note to Mr. Bingaman : —

INEZ PERRY TO MICAH BINGAMAN.

THURSDAY MORNING.

MY DEAR MR. BINGAMAN, — I have just learned, and am certain, that my father is in confinement in the government house.

Old Ransom, our servant, who disappeared ten days ago, is shut up closely in the guard-house.

Both of them are to be sent to Cuba ; and, for fear the news shall be sent down the river, an embargo will be proclaimed to-day.

I beg you to press up the consul's clerk to some prompt action. Cannot Mr. Clark be sent for ?

Respectfully yours,
INEZ PERRY.

Well written, Inez ! You are becoming a woman, indeed ! Sister Barbara does not teach one to write such letters ; and I am not sure that even St. Ursula fore-ordained them, or looked down to them through the prophetic vista of many years.

Antoine was sent with this note to Mr. Bingaman ; and really glad, for the first time, that there was any thing she could do, Inez ordered her breakfast, and sat down, determining very fast what she would do next.

And this time the girl ate her breakfast with a will.

As she finished it, she heard a question at the back steps of the corridor, on the brick walk which led to the kitchen, and then a sort of altercation with the smart Antoine.

"Ask Miss Perry," said a stranger in very bad French, which Antoine knew was no Creole's, "if she does not want to buy some *filé.*"

Antoine did not reflect that his young mistress overheard every word ; and with accent more precise than the stranger's, but with expression far less civil, told him to go to hell with his sassafras, that the sassafras of Little Vernon was worth all other sassafras, and that he was to leave the garden as soon as might be.

Inez needed no nerving for her first contest with Antoine. She rang sharply.

"Antoine, you are never to speak to any person so in my house. Go beg the man's pardon, and bid him come in."

Antoine went out, mumbled some apology, and returned much crestfallen with the huckster.

Inez had never said " my house " before.

Inez rose. She scarcely looked at the man, who was, indeed, the wildest creature that even the Sunday market could have shown her. Bare feet, red with mud which must have clung to them for days ; trousers of skin patched with cottonade, or cottonade patched with skin ; hair bushy and curling, covering and concealing the face ; and the face itself browned so that it would be hard to say whether it were Indian, mulatto, or Spanish, by the color. A miserable Indian blanket torn in twenty holes, of which the largest let through the wearer's head, gave the only intimation as to his nationality.

Inez lifted the dried leaves in her hand, tasted some of the fibres, and said, —

" Your *filé* is very good ; I wish you had brought us more. Take the basket into the herb-room." Then to the obsequious Antoine, who led the way, " No, Antoine, wait at the gate for Mr. Bingaman's message : or no, Antoine ; go, ask him if he has no answer for me. I will show the man upstairs."

The savage shouldered his basket, and followed Inez. She threw open the door of a corner room in the attic story. He brought the basket in, and kicked the door to behind him ; and then, and not till then, did Inez rush to him, seized both his hands in hers, looked upon him with such joy as an hour before she would have said was impossible, and then said, —

" Am I awake? Can it be true? Where did you come from ? "

"Dear Miss Inez," said Will Harrod, "it is true ; you are wide awake ; and your welcome," he added boldly, " pays for the sufferings of years."

"Welcome ! You knew you were welcome, Will ! "

She had never called him " Will " before ; and they both knew it. Her cheeks flushed fire, and they were both, oh ! so glad and so happy !

"There never was a time when I needed you so much," said she eagerly, as she made him sit down.

"There never is a time when I do not need you," said he bravely.

"But why are you in all this rig? I thought I must not let Antoine know."

"I am afraid you are right. You are certainly prudent and wise. Heavens! How careful I have been for the last forty-eight hours! Are they all crazy here?"

"I believe the governor is crazy. The intendant is surely. But do you know what they have done? My father is in prison, and Ransom, dear old Ransom, too."

"In prison?"

"In prison, and are to go to Cuba. You know what that means. But I feel now as if something could be done, now you are here. How are you here? Oh, Mr. Harrod, they all told me you were dead!"

And here the poor girl fairly cried; and, for a moment, lost her self-command.

"Did you think I was dead?" said he eagerly.

"Think so? I knew so till Tuesday night: then I dreamed I saw your head over the garden gate, and it called me, — twice it called me."

"Yes," said Harrod laughing; "and it called very loud, and it called Cæsar and Ransom too. But, before anybody could come, the men with sticks were after the head, and the poor head had to run, and to hide again till this morning. I gave them the slip this time."

"It was you? It was you? Then, I am not a fool! But, Mr. Harrod, you called Cæsar: do you not know?"

"Know, my dearest Miss Inez? I know nothing. I only know, that after escaping from those rascally Comanches, after starving to sleep, and waking so crazy with hunger that I thought I was in purgatory, after such a story of struggle and misery as would touch a Turk's heart, I came out at Natchitoches for help, to be clapped into their guard-house.

Then I knocked two idiots' heads together, blew out what brains one had with his own gun, trusted to my friendly river again, and worked my way down on a log to Point Coupée, to be arrested again by a *guarda costa.* I bided my time till they were all blind drunk one night, stole their boat, and floated down here, to be arrested, this time, for stealing the boat. But I am used to breaking bounds. Tuesday I took refuge with some friendly Caddoes, and, by Jove! the savage protects what the white man hunts to death. My own costume was not so select as this. I owe this to their munificence."

"I thought you were dressed like a prince," said Inez frankly. "Now you have come, all will be well."

Then came a little consultation. Inez explained to him the reign of terror in which they lived, so far as it could be explained. But she found, first of all, that she must break his heart by telling of Phil Nolan's fate, and Fanny Lintot's. All through his perils, he had heard no word of that massacre. His calling for Cæsar had given her the first suspicion of his ignorance.

How much there was to tell him, and how much for him to tell her!

Inez bravely told the horrid story of Phil Nolan's death. She told him, as frankly as she could, why she did not at first believe that he was in the party; and then, how Cæsar had confirmed her. But all hope for his life was over, she said, when Mr. Perry had found the news of Richards's treason, and the others, as Mr. Perry had found it, and as the reader has heard it. Two years had gone by since the gay young man had bidden them good-by in sight of the San Antonio crosses.

"But now you have come," she said again bravely, "all will be well; and now we must look forward, and not back. Do you remember that?"

"It has saved my life a hundred times," said he. "God only knows where I should be," he added reverently, "if I had not remembered to look up, and not down."

"These people have lost the track of you, as the knocker of heads together. You have now only to dress, pardon me," said she, really merry now — to think that she should ever be merry again! — "and to shave, and then you may walk unrecognized through our valiant army. Go into my brother's room," she said. She led him in, and unlocked the wardrobes. "See what you can find: there must be some razors somewhere."

"If my right hand has not lost its cunning," said Harrod, entering into her mood.

"Take what you find," said she. "I wish only dear Roland were here to help you. He is not as stout as you are, but perhaps you can manage."

And so she hurried down-stairs, happy enough, to forget for a minute or two her weight of anxiety.

CHAPTER XXXV.

SAVAGE LIFE.

" And as his bones were big, and sinews strong,
Refused no toil that could to slaves belong,
But used his noble hands the wood to hew."

Palamon and Arcite.

WILLIAM HARROD had indeed lived through a lifetime of horrors in the period since he had parted from these ladies above San Antonio Bexar.

It is of such adventures that the personal history of the pioneers who gave to us the Valley of the Mississippi is full ; but it is very seldom that personal history crowds together so much of danger, and so much of trial, in so short a time.

So soon as he knew that he was a prisoner, Harrod frankly accepted the situation of a prisoner, with that readiness to adapt himself to his surroundings which gave at once the charm and the strength to his character. He was to be a slave. The business of a slave was to obey. That business he would learn and fulfil ; not, indeed, with the slightest purpose of remaining in that position, but because a man ought to make the best of any position, however odious. With the same cheerful good-temper, therefore, with which he would have complied with a whim of Inez, whom he loved, or a wish of Eunice, whom he respected, he now complied with a whim of the Long Horn, whom at the bottom of his heart he hated, and whom he would abandon at the first instant. Nor was here any treachery to the Long Horn. If Harrod or the Long Horn could have analyzed the sentiment, it was based on pride, — the pride of a man who knew so thoroughly that he was the Long Horn's superior that he need not make any parade about it. He submitted to his exactions as a sensible person may submit to the exactions of a child whom for an hour he has in charge, but for whose education he has no other opportunities, and is not responsible.

Day after day, therefore, the Long Horn had more and more reason to congratulate himself on the slave he had in hand. He did not congratulate himself. A process so intricate, and so much approaching to reflection, did not belong to the man or to his race. But he did leave to Harrod, more and more, those cares for which the women of his lodges were too weak, and for which he was too lazy; and of such cares, in the life of a clan of shirks and cowards, there are not a few.

Harrod himself was able to learn some things, and to teach many, without his pupils knowing that they were taught. This does not mean, as a missionary board may suppose, that he built a log-cabin, sent to Chihuahua for primers and writing-books, and set the Long Horn and the False Heart to learning their letters and their pot-hooks. He taught them how to take care of their horses; and many a poor brute, galled and wincing, had to thank him for relief. He simplified their systems of corralling and of tethering. And on his own part, thorough-bred woodman as he was, his eyes were open every moment to learn something in that art which is so peculiarly the accomplishment of a gentleman, that no man without some skill in it can be called a chevalier.

It was to such arts that he soon owed a dignity in the tribe which materially tended to his own comfort, and ultimately effected his escape.

The great wealth of the Indians of the plains of the Colorado of the West, and even of the mountains, was in their horses. They treated them horribly, partly from ignorance, partly from carelessness, but not because they did not value them. It is a mistake of the political economists to suppose that selfishness will compel us to be tender when our passions are aroused. Of course the easiest way to obtain a good horse was to steal him, as these fellows had stolen Harrod's. In periods either of unusual need or of unusual courage, they pounced on a Spanish outpost, and so provided themselves. Perhaps they won horses in fight, as the result of a contest in which large numbers overpowered small, —the only occasion in which they ever fought willingly. Failing such opportunities, they were fain to catch the wild horses, and, after their fashion, to break them to their uses. They were passionately fond of horse-racing, which is not to be counted as only an accomplishment of civilized men.

So great is the power of the man over the brute, that one man alone, and he on foot, can, in the end, walk down and take captive even the mustang [1] of the prairies. It would be only in an extreme case, of course, that that experiment would be tried. But two men alone can catch their horses from a herd even of wild ones, almost as well as if they had more companions. If they be mounted, so much the easier for them.

In the sublime indolence of the Comanche chiefs, therefore, horses beginning to fail, the Long Horn and the Sheep's Tail each of them detached a slave to the hard job of taking three or four horses each for them, which they would next have to break to the saddle.

The method of capture is based on the habit of the wild horse to keep at or near his home. He knows that home as well as the queen-bee knows hers ; and his range is probably not much wider than that through which her subjects wander. Each herd has its captain, or director ; and this director does not lead it more than fifteen, or at the utmost twenty miles, in one direction. When he has passed that limit, he returns, and leads his herd with him to the region which is familiar to them.

---

[1] The derivation is said to be from the Spanish "*mestaña,*" — that which is common property, or belongs to the state, "*mesta.*"

The hunter observes this limit for any particular herd of horses, and then knows what his duty is. He builds a corral ready for his captives. Then one of the two pursuers, if the party be as small as in Harrod's case, follows the herd even leisurely. They only follow close enough to have their presence observed. The stallion who leads, leads at such pace as he chooses, avoiding the pursuer by such route as he chooses. If the herd turned against the pursuer, they could trample him into the ground. But they do not turn : they avoid him. The pursuer keeps steadily behind. At a time agreed upon, one of the two men stops with his horse for rest and sleep ; the other "takes up the wondrous tale," and for twelve hours keeps close enough to the wandering herd to keep them moving ; in turn he stops and sleeps ; but his companion is awake by this time, has found the trail, and keeps the poor hunted creatures in motion. There is no stop to sleep for them ; and so jaded and worn down are they by a few days and nights of this motion — almost constant and without sleep — that at last no thong nor lasso is needed for their capture. You may at last walk up to the tired beast who has lost his night's rest so long, twist your hand into his mane, and lead him unresisting into the corral you have provided for him. Poor brute ! Only let him rest, and you may do what else you will.

On such an enterprise Will Harrod was sent with the Crooked Finger, a young brave who was young enough to have some enterprise, and proud enough to be pleased at being trusted with so good a woodman as Harrod. Each of them was respectably mounted, — not very well mounted, for the Long Horn and the Sheep's Tail had but few horses, or they would not be hunting more, and they wanted the best horses for themselves. Nor, for this line of horse-taking, was speed so essential. The young fellows found the herd, and made a good guess as to its more frequent haunts ; then they built their little corral; then they took a long night's sleep; then they started for the trail, soon found it, and soon overtook the animals they sought. Harrod was magnanimous as always; he bade the Crooked Finger take the first rest; he would follow the herd through the twelve hours of that moonlight night, and at dawn of the sun the Crooked Finger must strike in. When Harrod had reason to suppose that he was well on the trail, he also would stop, and he and his horse would sleep.

For two days and two nights this amusement continued. An occasional pull at some dried meat kept soul and body together; and the horses and the men followed their uneventful round, which was, in fact, a very irregular oval.

As Crooked Finger finished his second tour of service, he saw Harrod just mounting for his third. They simply nodded to each other; but Harrod dismounted, and busied himself with his horse's mouth and rein. Crooked Finger approached, and gave some brief report of the day's pursuit, to which Harrod replied by the proper *ughs;* and then, as Crooked Finger dismounted, he seized the savage in his iron arms, much as he remembered to have been seized himself by the Long Horn, fastened his elbows tight behind him with a leather thong, and kicked his horse so resolutely that the horse disappeared. Harrod's horse was tethered too tightly to follow him.

"Good-by, Crooked Finger," said Harrod good-naturedly. "Here is meat enough, if you are careful, to take you to the lodges. I am going home."

The vanquished savage made not a struggle, and uttered not a sound. In Harrod's place he would have scalped the other, and he knew it. He supposed that Harrod did not scalp him, only because he had no scalping-knife.

Harrod was free; and, so far did he have the advantage of the tribe, that they made no attempt to follow him. And he never feared their pursuit for one moment. But he did fear other captors, and he feared want of food. This meat provided for the hunt would not last forever. This somewhat sorry beast he rode must have time to feed. The hunting of a man who has neither knife, gun, nor arrows, is but poor hunting, — for food, not very nutritious; and poor Harrod knew that the time might come when he should be glad of the sorriest meal he had ever eaten in a Comanche lodge. But Harrod was free, and freedom means — ah! a great deal!

This chapter cannot tell, and must not try to tell, the adventures of days and weeks, even of months, at last lengthening out into the second year of his exile, as, by one device and another, the poor fellow worked eastward and still eastward. He came out upon the lodges of the Upper Red River, where Phil Nolan had smoked the pipe of peace only the year before. He found the memory of his great commander held in high esteem there; and he had wit to represent himself as a scout from his party, only accidentally separated from them for a few days. Nicoroco remembered the calumet of peace, and tidings had come to him of Nolan's discipline of One Eye, a memory which served Will Harrod well; and, after a sojourn of a few days with Nicoroco, Harrod proceeded, refreshed, upon his way.

It was after this oasis in the desert of that year's life, that the most serious of his adventures came. He had been hunted by a troop of savages, of which nation he knew not, but whom he dared not trust. He was satisfied that the time had come when he must do what he had all along intended to do, — abandon his poor brute, who was more and more worthless every day, and trust himself to the swollen current of the magnificent Red River. Such raft as he could make for himself must bear him down till he could communicate with the pioneer French settlements, and be safe.

He knew very well, in this crisis, that it was the last step which would cost. But Harrod was beyond counting risks now: he risked every thing every day.

It is not so easy to make a raft, when one has not even a jack-knife. Trees do not accidentally rot into the shapes one wants, or the lengths one can handle. But Harrod's ambition for his raft was not aspiring. Two logs, so braced and tied that they should not roll under him, — only this, and nothing more, was the raft which he needed. In a long, anxious day, the logs were found. With grape-vines mostly, and with the invaluable leather thongs which had been his reins so long, the obdurate twisted sticks were compelled to cling together. Their power of floating was not much; but they were well apart from each other in one place, and there Harrod wedged in a shorter log, which was to be his wet throne. And so, with a full supply of poles and misshapen paddles, he pushed off upon his voyage. The boiling and whirling stream bore him swiftly down; and there was at least the comfort of knowing that the last act of this tedious drama had come. How the play would turn out, he would know before long.

Day after day of this wild riding of the waters! And, for food, the poorest picking, — grapes, well-nigh raisins for dryness, astringent enough at the best; sassafras bark was a flavor, but not nourishing; snails sometimes; and once or twice a foolish fish, caught by the rudest of machinery: but very little at the very best. "How many hired servants of my father have bread enough and to spare!" said poor Will Harrod; for he was very hungry.

Where he was, he did not know: only he was on the Red River above "the Raft." His hope was to come to "the Raft:" then he should only be two or three days from the highest French farms. Only two or three days, Will Harrod, with nothing to eat! Armies have perished, because for twenty-four hours the regular ration did not come.

Even the Red River could not last forever. At last he came to a raft, so thick and impassable that he hoped it was the Great Raft. Any reader who has seen the tangled mass of timber above a saw-mill can imagine what the Great Raft was, if he will remember that it was made up, not of felled logs, but of trees with their branches, as for centuries they had been whirled down the stream. First formed at a narrow gorge of the Red River, it extended upward, at this time, one hundred and thirty miles. The river flowed beneath. Soil gathered above. Trees took root, and grew upon it to be large and strong. In high water the river found other courses round it. On parts of the Raft a man could travel. Through parts of it, a canoe could sail. It was this wreck of matter, — this "*tohu va bohu*," — the utter confusion of water which was not land, and land which was not water, which marked for Will Harrod the end of his navigation.

With the precious thongs, a bit of sharp flint, and the tail of an imprudent cat-fish, as his only baggage, he landed on the bank not far above the water-line, and boldly pushed down on the southern shore. He thought Nachitoches could not be a hundred miles away ; and that night he slept well. The next day he made good time. Little to eat, for no cat-fish rose to his bait ; still that night he slept well. The next day came the worst repulse of all.

A bayou back from the stream — all gorged with bark and trees and wreck like the main river — cut off his eastward course. Nothing for it but to return !

Never ! That way was sure death. Will ventured on the Raft itself. To cross the bayou proved impossible. One could not swim there : one could not walk there, more than one could fly. But the river itself was here more practicable, — not for swimming, but for walking. So old was the Raft that the logs had rotted on the surface, and weeds and bushes had grown there. It was more like a bit of prairie, than of river. One must watch every step. Still one could walk here ; and, though the channel was very broad here, Will Harrod held his course, slowly and not confidently.

No food that day ! not a snail, not a grape, not a lizard, far less red-fish or cat-fish. And that night's sleep was not so sound. Water is but little refreshment, when one breakfasts on a few handfuls of it, after such a day ; but with such breakfast Will Harrod must keep on. Keep on he did ; but he knew his legs dragged, that he missed his foothold when he ought not, and that his head spun weirdly, that he did not see things well.

"This is one way to die," said poor Will aloud. And then, sitting on a moss-grown cypress stick, he looked wistfully round him ; and then, when a belated grasshopper lighted by his side, with a clutch of frenzy he snatched the creature, and held him helpless in his hand.

Victory !

The grasshopper, yet living, was tied tight to the end of the little thong which had served for a line all along. A stout acacia-thorn, one of a dozen at Harrod's girdle, was tied in a knot just above. And, with cheerfulness he had thought impossible, he went to the nearest open hole, to bob and bob again for his life.

But how soon the dizziness returned ! How many hours did he sit there in the sun ? Will Harrod never knew. Only at last, a gulp, a pull at the cord, and a noble fish — food for three or four days, as Will Harrod had been using food — was in the air, — was flapping on the so-called ground at his side.

Victory !

With the bit of sharpened stone which had served him all along, he killed the fish, opened him, and cleaned him. Little thought or care for fire ! He returned carefully to his lair, to put by the sacred implements of the chase, which had served him so well. Weak as he was, he tripped, — his foot was tangled in a grape-vine, — and he fell. As he disentangled himself, he could see an alligator rise — not very rapidly, either — from the stream, make directly to the prize ; and, before poor Will was free, the brute had plunged with the fish into the river.

"Miss Inez," said he, as in the evening they sat in the gallery, and he told this story, "I never despaired till then. But my head was swimming. The beast looked like the very Devil himself. I lay back on the ground, and I said, 'Then I will die.' And, will you believe me ? I fell asleep.

"I woke up, — I do not know how soon. But, as I woke, my one thought was of sitting and bobbing there. What had I seen when I was bobbing? Had not I seen a log cut with an axe? Why did I not think of that before? Because I could only think of my bait and my line. Was it cut by an axe? I went back to the stream. It was cut by an axe. It was an old dug-out, — a Frenchman's *pirogue*, bottom up. How quick I turned it over! Where it came into that bayou, it could go out. I laid into it my precious line and cutting-stone. I broke me off sticks for fending-poles. I was strong as a lion now. I bushwhacked here, I poled there, I paddled there. In an hour I was free; and then the sun was so hot above me, that I fainted away in the bottom of the canoe."

"You poor, poor child!" sobbed the sympathizing Inez.

"And, the next I knew, it was evening, and an old Frenchman held me in his arms, at the shore, and was pouring milk down my throat in spoonfuls. Weak as I was, I clutched his pail, and he thought I should have drunk myself to death. He did not clap me in irons, though I did come from above."

CHAPTER XXXVI.

IN PRISON, AND YE VISITED ME.

> "Curse on the unpardoning prince, whom tears can draw
> To no remorse, who rules by lions' law,
> And deaf to prayers, by no submission bowed,
> Rends all alike, the penitent and proud."
>
> *Palamon and Arcite.*

BUT Miss Inez and Master William did not spend that morning in telling or in hearing this tale. It is from long narratives, told in more quiet times, that we have condensed it for the reader.

No. They had other affairs in hand.

Inez had been diligently at work preparing her costume for the day, before Antoine had summoned her to breakfast. Chloe had been as diligently at work in the laundry, while breakfast went on.

While Harrod made his toilet, — a matter of no little difficulty, — Inez made hers.

At last he came down-stairs, shaven and shorn, washed and brushed, elegantly dressed, with a ruffled shirt, an embroidered waistcoat, and a blue coat; dressed, in short, in the costume of civilized Europe or America, as he had not been dressed for two years.

He went through the hall, and from room to room of the large parlors down-stairs, but saw Inez nowhere. In the front parlor was a little sister of charity, who seemed absorbed in a book of devotions. Harrod touched his hat, and asked if he could see Miss Perry; to which the sister, without so much as raising her modest eyes to the handsome Kentuck-ian, only replied, "*Pas encore.*"

Harrod struck the bell which stood in the hall, and sum-moned Antoine. The respectful servant wondered if he had left the garden gate open, but did not distress himself. Har-rod bade him call his mistress. Antoine thought she was in the parlor, but, as he looked in, saw no one but the sister of charity. She asked him also if he would summon his mis-tress. Antoine said he did not know where she was, but he would try.

The minute he was well out of the hall, the sister of charity hopped up, and executed a pirouette, to Harrod's amazement, clapped her hands, and ran across the room to him. "So, sir, I knew you after two years' parting, and you did not know me after an hour's! That shows who understands masquer-ading best."

"Who would know you, with that ridiculous handkerchief tied round your mouth and nose, and those devout eyes cast down on your prayer-book? At the least, you cannot say my disguise covered me."

"Indeed," said Inez, laughing, "that was its weakest side."

And she proceeded to explain her plans for the day. She was going to the prison to see old Ransom. Her father was out of the question. But an interview with Ransom could be gained, she thought; for she believed, as it proved rightly, that no such calendar of sisters was kept at the prison gate, that the warders would know of a certain new-comer, wheth-er she were or were not *en règle.* Of her own costume Inez had no doubt whatever.

And so they parted, — Inez for this duty, Harrod to see the American consul, Mr. Pollock, Mr. Bingaman, and the other Americans, and to determine what should be done in this rudest violation yet of the rights of the American resi-dents in Orleans.

At the Palace of Justice — if it may be so called — Inez

had even less difficulty than she had apprehended. The place was not strictly a prison. That is, the upper stories were used for the various purposes of business of the fussy administration of the little colony ; and, below, a dozen large cells and a certain central hall had been by long usage set apart as places of confinement, barred and bolted, for prisoners awaiting trial, and for anybody else, indeed, who, for whatever reason, was not to be sent to the prison proper.

To the sentinel on duty at the door, Inez simply said, —

" You have a sick man here."

" Two, my lady. Will my lady tell me the name of the sinner she seeks ? "

" If there be two," said Inez, speaking in Spanish, with which the French sentinel was not so familiar, " I will see them both ; " and, acknowledging his courtesy as he passed, she entered into the general prison, where nine or ten poor dogs sat, lay, or paced uneasily. Among them she instantly saw Ransom, sitting handcuffed on a chest.

He did not recognize her, and she affected not to see him ; but she passed close to him, and said quite aloud in English, " Ransom, take care that you are very sick when I come to-morrow." Then she passed on into the side cell, which had been opened at her direction. The particular Juan or Manuel who was lying there had not expected her ; but he was none the worse for the guava-jelly she left him, nor that she sponged his hands and face from the contents of the generous canteen she bore. She read to him a few simple prayers, visited the other invalid in the same fashion, and was gone.

The next day, however, Inez had three patients. She had soon disposed of those whom she saw the day before, and then found herself, as she had intended, alone with Ransom, who lay on the shelf in his cell with a few leaves and stems of the sugar-cane under him.

Ransom explained, that on the day he was missed, having been lured away, just as he left the brig, into a narrow street

where none "but them Greasers" lived, — as he was talking
with the man who had summoned him, he was caught from
behind, his arms pinioned behind him, he tripped up, steel
cuffs locked upon his feet, and in this guise was carried by
four men into a neighboring *baraca.* As soon as night fell,
his captors brought him to the Government House. They
had since had him under examination there three times.
They had questioned him about Nolan and Harrod, about
Mr. Perry and Roland, about Lonsdale and the "Firefly,"
and about Gen. Bowles. They had asked about the message
sent up the river by Mr. Perry the previous spring. But
specially they had questioned him about the Lodge of Free-
Masons, to find whether Mr. Perry, Mr. Roland, or Mr.
Lonsdale belonged to it; and about what Ransom knew,
and what he did not know, of the movements of one Sopper,
an American, whom the authorities suspected of raising a
plot among the slaves.

Now, the truth was that Ransom knew Sopper very well.
He probably knew Ransom better than he did any other
person in Orleans, where the man was, indeed, a stranger.

"They'd seen me with him, Miss Inez. He's a poor
critter; hain't got no friends, any way, 'n I wanted to keep
him out o' mischief. He's one of them Ipswich Soppers, —
no, he ain't: he came from Sacarap, — they was a poor set;
but they did zwel as they knew how. They'd seen me with
him, so I knew they was no use of lyin' about it, 'n I told
'em I knew him, cos I did."

"Ransom, there is never any use of lying," said poor Inez,
doing something to keep up her character.

But it was clear that Ransom's examination had been of
that sort which did nobody any good, and him least good of
all. Inez could see, as he detailed it, that he had made the
authorities suspect him more than ever; and, from the tenor
of the last examination, she saw that the authorities thought
that he was an accomplice in the negro plot, regarding which
they were most sensitive.

"Tain't no account, mum, any way, now Mr. Perry knows I'm here : he'll go to the guvner, and the guvner 'll have to let me out.   Didn't have no way to send ye word, or I'd 'a' sent before."

Then Inez told him that her father had been seized also.

The poor old man started from his bed, and could hardly be kept from rushing to the rescue.

In one instant he saw the position ; and in the same instant his whole countenance changed, and his easy courage fell.

Often as he had thwarted Silas Perry, and often as he had disobeyed him, in his heart he was a faithful vassal, and nothing else.   He would have "died with rapture if he saved his king ;" but when that king was checkmated his truncheon fell at once.

Inez went farther, and said her fear was that they would both be sent to Cuba for trial.

"No, Miss Inez : ef your father's in prison, they ain't no more trial for me.   Tried me three times a'ready, and I give em a bit o' my mind each time.   No.   They's done with me."   And he sank into silence.

Inez broke it with a consolation she did not feel.

"Keep up good spirits, dear Ransom," she said.   "We are all at work for you.   Mr. Harrod has come home, and he is at work, and Mr. Bingaman and the consul.   Aunt Eunice got home last night, and she will work for you.   Mr. Lonsdale will work.   We shall never let you come to harm."

The old man sat silent for a moment more.   Then he said calmly, "No, mum, they's done with me.   Bingaman's no account, never was, unless he had Mr. Perry to tell him what to do.   Ain't none on 'em knows what to do, ef Mr. Perry don't tell 'em.   Capt. Harrod, he's a gentleman ; but they don't none on 'em know him here.   No, mum, they's done with me."   And he made another long pause.   "They'll send ye father to Cuby, and they'll hang me.   They'll hang me down by the arsenal, — jest where they hanged them Frenchmen. It's just like 'em ; 'n I told 'em so, I did. Says I, 'you hanged them Frenchmen, and you know you've been all wrong' ever since ye did it,' says I. But they didn't hang 'em theyselves : they didn't dare to. Darned ef they could get a white man in all Orleans to hang 'em. Cum to the 'Hingham Gal,' — she was lyin' here then, — 'n there was a poor foolish critter in her, named Prime, 'n they offered him twenty doubloons to hang 'em ; 'n he says, says he, 'I'm a fool,' says he, and he was a fool, 'but I ain't so big a fool,' says he, ' as you think I be,' says he ; 'n they had to get a nigger to hang 'em, cos no white man would stand by 'em. That's what they'll do with me,'' said poor old Ransom.

In speaking thus, Ransom was alluding to O'Reilly's horrible vengeance upon the Creole gentlemen who had engaged in a plot to throw off the Spanish rule more than twenty years before.

" Ransom," said the girl, sobbing her heart out, "if they hang you they will hang me too." Then she promised him that she would return on Sunday, bade him be sure he was sick in bed at noon, and with a faint heart found her way home.

She would have attempted more definite words of consolation if she had had them to offer. But Harrod's report of yesterday had not been encouraging. The consular clerk had been roused to some interest, but to no resource. The embargo had been proclaimed. That had confirmed Inez's news, and had awakened all the merchants. Harrod had made him, the clerk, promise to call on the governor with him at one o'clock. By way of preparing for that interview, he made one or two visits among English and American merchants, when suddenly, to his disgust, he found himself evidently watched by a tall man of military aspect, though not in uniform. Harrod was close by the Government House. He determined, at least, to strike high and to die game. He would not be jugged without one interview with the governor in person.

He entered the house, — went by as many sentinels as he could, by what is always a good rule, pretending to be quite at home, giving a simple hasty salute to the sentries, — and so came to the governor's door, as he had been directed. Here he had to send in his card; but he was immediately admitted.

He explained that he had expected to be joined by the American consul. His message, however, was important, and he would not wait.

"And what is your honor's business?" said the courtly governor.

"It is to ask on what ground Mr. Silas Perry is held in confinement, and to claim his release as an American citizen."

"Don Silas Perry in confinement!" said the governor with a start of surprise, which was not at all acted. He was surprised that this Mr. Harrod should have come at his secret. "Where is he in confinement?"

"No one knows better than your excellency," said Harrod, who noted his advantage: "he is imprisoned under this roof. Your excellency can show me to his apartments, unless your excellency wishes me to take your excellency there."

This was a word too much, and probably did not help Master William. It gave his excellency time to rally, and to ask himself who this brown, well-dressed man of action and of affairs might be.

"You have sent me your card," said he: "you have not explained to me who has honored me by introducing you, nor do I understand that you represent the American consul. I think, indeed, that the American consul is not in the city, that he is at the Balize."

"Your excellency does not wish to stand upon punctilio," said Harrod. "The consul's clerk will be here in five minutes. The American consul will be here to-night. It is in the name of the Americans of the city that I speak."

The governor looked his contempt. "His Majesty the

King of Spain has given these gentlemen permission to reside here to attend to an unfortunate commerce, all but contraband, which will end in a few months at latest ; but his Majesty has never been informed, till this moment, that these gentlemen expected him to consult them in the administration of justice." Then, as if he were weary of the interview, he turned to a servant who gave him a card, and, as if to dismiss Harrod, said, " Show this gentleman in."

To Harrod's dismay, the military man entered, who had tracked him in the street.

He thought that his game was up, and that he was to be put into the room next to Mr. Perry's. But he had no disposition to surrender a moment before his time came. Without noticing hint or stranger, he said, —

" If your excellency despises the Americans here, you may have more regard for the Americans at home. Your excellency has the name of a friend of peace. Your minister at home is called the Prince of Peace. Your excellency has simply to consider, that, if Mr. Silas Perry and Mr. Seth Ransom are not free to-morrow night, a courier will carry that news to the Tennessee River in ten days, to Kentucky in five more. Let it once be known that two American citizens have been sent to Cuba, and ten thousand riflemen from Kentucky and Tennessee will muster at their ports to avenge them. The boats are there, as your excellency knows ; the river is rising, as your excellency knows. Whether the ' Prince of Peace ' will thank you for what your excellency brings down hither upon the river, your excellency knows also." And William Harrod rose. " I see your excellency is engaged. I will find the vice-consul, and will return with him."

" Stay a moment," said the military gentleman, " stay a moment, sir. Do I understand that Mr. Perry is in confinement ? "

" He is under lock and bar in this house, sir," said Harrod fiercely.

"And for what crime?" said the stranger.

"For no crime under the heavens of God," said Harrod, now very angry, "for no crime, as you would say if you knew him. You must ask his excellency on what accusation."

"I will take the liberty to ask his excellency that question," said the other. "Mr. Perry is my near friend," he added, turning to the governor; "he is the near friend of the King of England, to whom he has rendered distinguished services. I know your excellency too well to think, that, at this critical juncture, your excellency would willingly thwart the government I represent, by the arrest of a person whose services, I had almost said, we require."

The picture was a striking one, as these two fine young men stood, the one on each side of the governor, who was himself to the last degree annoyed, that by his own blunder he had lost the one great advantage in Spanish statecraft, the advantage of dealing with each alone.

"My dear Mr. Lonsdale," he said, giving to the English diplomatist his hand, "if you will do me the favor to dine with me, I can explain perhaps what you do not understand. If our young friend here, the ambassador from Kentucky, will meanwhile study the Constitution of the United States, he will understand perhaps that I cannot treat with envoys from separate States. — Good-morning, sir:" this sharply to Harrod. "If you will take an early lunch with us, it is waiting now:" this courteously to Lonsdale.

"I am greatly obliged," said Lonsdale coolly. "I have business with this gentleman. I will do myself the honor of calling again." And, with hauteur quite equal to what might be expected from the Duke of Clarence, he withdrew.

CHAPTER XXXVII.

FACE TO FACE.

" A brave heart bids the midnight shine like day,
Friendship dares all things, when love shows the way."
Andromaque.

As they left the Government House, Harrod hastily explained to Lonsdale who he was, and told what he himself knew of the passages of these dark days, and why he knew so little. Lonsdale explained who he was,—that he had but just landed from his own galliot, in which he had brought Miss Perry, and the old lady whom Miss Perry had gone to Natchez to find. But they had left Natchez before any bad news, even of Ransom's disappearance, had arrived there; and the first intelligence Mr. Lonsdale had had of either calamity was in the words he had heard William Harrod use at the governor's.

He had parted from Miss Perry only at the landing, having promised to join her again at her own house within an hour. He was therefore sure that up till her arrival at home she had had no intimation of the wretched news.

Harrod was quick enough to observe that in his language there was a certain air of authority, as if he had a right to protect Miss Perry, and to be consulted intimately in her affairs. For this, Harrod had not been prepared by Inez's hurried narrative. Inez had spoken of Mr. Lonsdale as the English gentleman whose escort they had received in coming from Texas ; but she had scarcely alluded to him again.

The two went hastily to Mr. Perry's house, filling up, as each best could, the immense gaps in the information which each had, as to these matters in which each had personal reasons for intense interest. Let them do their best, however, there were large chasms unfilled. For what reason was Mr. Perry arrested? For what, poor Ransom? What new motive could they now bring to bear? And should William Harrod not make good his threat of sending a courier through Gen. Bowles's country into Tennessee and Kentucky?

Inez was away on her first visit to the prison when the young men arrived. They found Eunice in all the agony of surprise, anger, and doubt, having received, from the very incompetent lips of Antoine and Chloe, such broken account as they could give of the little which Miss Inez had chosen to intrust to them. Eunice was writing to the consul as they entered. By her side was the lovely white-haired Mother Ann, who had come so gladly with Eunice, certain that she should find her lost grandchild, and who now found herself in the midst of another tragedy so strange. The beautiful old lady had not learned the lessons of sixty years in vain. Her face had the lovely saint-like expression of the true saint, who had never shirked life in a convent, but who had taken it in its rough-and-tumble, and had come off conqueror and more than conqueror.

"Never mind me, dear Eunice," she said, in her half-Quaker way: "let us do what we may for thy brother first, and for this brave old fellow who loves my dear girl so. What is a few hours to me, now I am so safe, so sure, and so happy?"

Upon their rapid consultations Inez came in, still in the sister's costume. She flung herself into Eunice's arms, and sobbed out her grief. A common cause gave frankness and cordiality to her welcome of Lonsdale such as she had never honored him with before. Then came rapid conferences, and eager mutual information. Inez could tell, and Harrod could tell, to this group, what had not been revealed to

Antoine and to Chloe of Ma-ry's information.   Harrod and Lonsdale had to tell of the governor's coldness, and the dead-lock they were at there.   But both of them agreed that they must go at once to the American consulate to report ; and Lonsdale said, very simply, that he could and would bring in all the intercession of Mr. Hutchings, the English consul.   Such an outrage made a common cause.

"And we and this dear, dear, dear lady, will go, — we can go on foot, dear aunt, — and liberate my darling from the convent."   This was Inez's exclamation, and then she stopped. "But what a blessing that she was not liberated before! Where should we be now, but for the White Hawk?"

Then they all turned to Harrod and to Lonsdale, to make sure that they should not want her at the convent still.   But it was agreed, that they now had, in all probability, all the information that Ma-ry could give.   The chances were vastly against their gaining more.

"I must have the dear child here," said Eunice promptly.

"Thank God you say that !" said Inez.

And, so soon as she could transform herself into Miss Inez Perry, they were all three on their way.

It was not the regulation day for seeing visitors ; there had been no chance to consult the pope or the vicar-general ; and St. Ursula had not provided in her last will for any such exigency.   But Eunice was so forceful in her quietness, and dear "Mother Ann" was so eager in her quietness, for she did not say one word, that even Sister Barbara gave way ; and Inez was obliged to own to herself, that even she could not have improved on the method of the negotiation.   Sister Barbara disappeared.   She was not gone long.   She came back with the White Hawk, to whom she had said nothing of her visitors.

The moment the pretty creature entered the room, the quiet, lovely grandmother sprang across like a girl, and flung her arms around her, and kissed her again and again.   "My dear, dear, dear child !"   This was all she could say.   The girl's likeness to her murdered mother was enough for the other mother who had brooded over her loss so long.

And Ma-ry, dear child, kissed her, and soothed her, and stroked her beautiful white hair, and said little loving words to her, now as a child might do, just learning to speak, now as a woman of long experience might do. How much these two would have to tell each other, and to learn from each other! And the first meeting was all that the eager heart of either could demand.

"Dear, dear, dear grandmamma," for the child had been teaching herself this word in anticipation. "Was she not very lovely?"

"My darling, she was very lovely. You are her image, my child. I knew you were named Mary. My sister was named Mary, and you are named for her. I have here," and she pointed to her heart, "your dear, dear mother's last letter. She says she had named you 'Mary,' and she says you were the only baby in the settlement, and the pet of them all. And I was to come and help take care of you when you were a baby; and now at last I have come."

Sister Barbara was as much affected as the others. She agreed with Miss Eunice, that it was not probable that Ma-ry's studies would flourish much under the stimulus of this new element in her life. And it was also so improbable that any similar case had transpired in the eleven thousand experiences of the eleven thousand virgins, that their memoirs were not even consulted for a precedent; and failing the vicar-general and the pope, as above, Sister Barbara consented that the White Hawk should go home with the visitors, and stay till next week. Alas, for Sister Barbara! "to-morrow never comes," and "next week" never came for this return to study.

Ma-ry, meanwhile, signalled to Inez, to ask whether she might not be needed on the house-top the next morning. Things might be mentioned in the house which needed to be published there. But Inez re-assured the loyal girl; and in five minutes more her little packet was ready, and she kissed Sister Barbara " good-by," forever, — as it proved.

"But the little dog, ma'm'selle, — the little dog. He will be wretched without you, and you will be wretched without him."

With the gravity of a bishop, and with a penitent's conscience smiting her, Ma-ry explained that she had not seen the little dog since yesterday. And Inez hastened to add that he was safe at home. And so, with some jest on the dog's preferring the fare at one house to that of the other, they parted. And thus, to use the common phrase which Miss Edgeworth so properly condemns, Miss Ma-ry's " education was finished."

They met the gentlemen at dinner. Antoine and Felix were tolerated as long as might be; and, for so long time, the talk was of Harrod's experience, of Lonsdale's trials, of Mrs. Willson's wanderings, and of Ma-ry's recollections. But, as soon as these two worthies could be dismissed, serious consultations began again.

The two consuls had had as little success as the unofficial gentlemen had had. Indeed, they had anticipated no success. Arbitrary as the Spanish rule always was, it had till lately been sensible and mild until Salcedo, to whom, rightly or not, Harrod ascribed the change of policy which had swept even De Nava away, and whom Harrod made responsible for Nolan's murder. Under Salcedo, the rule had been abrupt, tyrannical, and inexplicable.

"You would think," said Lonsdale, " that the approaching cession to the French prefect would make the Spaniards more tolerant and gentle. But, on the other hand, they seem to want to cling to power to the last, and to show that Laussat is nobody. Laussat is a fool, so our consul thinks, — a fussy, pretentious fool. He came here as prefect, with great notions, with great talk of the army behind him; and he has not yet so much as a corporal's guard for his ceremonies. The Spaniards make fun of him; and even the Frenchmen cannot make much else of him.

"Yes: if he were not here, we should fare better. From this double-headed government, it is hard to know what we may look for. One thing is fortunate," he added dryly: "we have three or four frigates and their tenders, within a day of the Balize. I have bidden Hutchings send down word that they are to be off the Pass till they have other orders."

Eunice only looked her gratitude; but she certainly blushed crimson. Inez was forced to say, "How good you are!" But this time she was frightened. Even she did not dare to say, "Who are you?"

But who was he? Who was this man who said to the English fleet, "Sail here," or "Sail there," and it obeyed him? And why did Aunt Eunice blush? What had they been doing and saying at Natchez, and in this six-days' voyage down the river? Was Aunt Eunice to be Duchess of Clarence, after all?

The truth was, that Mr. Lonsdale and Aunt Eunice had come at each other very thoroughly. First, their correspondence had helped to this; for nothing teaches two people who have been much together, how much they rest on each other, as an occasional separation, with its eager yearning for messages or letters. Horace Lonsdale needed no teaching on this matter. Eunice was perhaps surprised when she found how lonely a summer was, in which she did not see him as often as once a week. After this parting, had come the renewed intimacy at Natchez; and, from the first, they found themselves on a personal footing different from that of the spring. She had found him the loyal and chivalrous English gentleman which, indeed, he had shown himself from the first moment that she had known him. He had found her always the same unselfish woman she was then and there. It had been hard for him to come at her, to give to her the whole certainty of his enthusiastic admiration; because Eunice Perry was quite out of the fashion of asking herself what people thought of her, or, indeed, of believing that they thought of her at all. If the truth were told, Horace Lonsdale had not been used, in other circles, to meet women as entirely indifferent to his social position as was Eunice Perry. He might, indeed, have travelled far, before he found a woman so indifferent to her own accomplishments, so unconscious of remarkable beauty, and so willing to use each and every gift in the service of other people, as she.

To pay court to this unconscious vestal, was no easy matter. So Horace Lonsdale thought. Words or attentions which many a pretty countrywoman of his would have welcomed with delight, in the false and unbalanced social habits of London in those days, passed by Eunice Perry as if he did not exist, had never spoken the word, or offered the attention. He found very soon, that, if he meant to render her service, it must be by serving those she loved ; and he counted himself fortunate, and fortunate he was, that the chaotic condition of the times in which they moved gave him, once and again, the opportunity to do so.

The absurd stories as to who and what he was had, of course, their share of foundation. He was a younger son of the distinguished family whose name he bore, and had been placed in the English Foreign Office, when yet young, for education and for promotion. Choosing to use the opportunities of his position, in a time when every day furnished the material for a romance, instead of flirting at Almack's or riding in Hyde Park, he had been intrusted with one and another confidential duty, in which he had distinguished himself. As the new century opened, the plots of Miranda in Cuba and on the Spanish Main, the insurrection in St. Domingo, and the certainty of a change in Louisiana, made it necessary for his chiefs to seek more accurate information than they had, as to the condition of the Spanish colonies. Such a man as Lonsdale would not shrink from an appointment which gave him almost *carte blanche* in travelling in those regions, then almost unknown to Europe. His social standing, his rank in the diplomatic service, and the commission he was intrusted with, gave him the best introductions everywhere. And, when the ladies of our party met him at Antonio, he was in good faith pursuing the inquiries regarding the power of Spain which had been confided to him.

The absurd story that he was the Duke of Clarence had grown up in some joke in a London club; but it had found its way to one and another English ship on the West India station, and from these vessels had diffused itself, as poor jokes will, in the society of almost every place where Lonsdale made any stay. In truth, it was very absurd. He was five years younger than the duke, was taller and handsomer. But he had light hair worn without powder, a fresh healthy complexion, so that, as Inez afterward told him when she condescended to take him into favor, he looked so handsome and so much as one wanted a king's son to look, that everybody took it for granted that he was one. However that might be, the rumor was sometimes a very great convenience to Horace Lonsdale, and sometimes such a bore and nuisance as to arouse all his rage. He said himself, that, whatever else it did, it always doubled the charges on his tavern bills.

Lonsdale had not let the favorable opportunity pass, which his visit to Natchez, and the escort he gave Eunice Perry to New Orleans, afforded him. He told her, like a gentleman, that her love and life were inestimably precious to him; that the parting for a summer had taught him that they never could be parted again. And Eunice, who for fifteen years had let the admiration of a hundred men drift by her unobserved and unrequited; who had quietly put fifty men on their guard that they should come no closer, and had sent fifty away sadly who would not take her hint, and pressed too near, — Eunice told him the truth. She told him that once and again, in the anxieties of that summer, she had caught herself wishing for his sympathy and counsel, — nay, if the truth must be told, for a cheery tone of his, or a cheery look of his, before she had wished even for her brother's help, or for Inez's love; and, when she said this to Horace Lonsdale, Horace Lonsdale was made perfectly happy.

But all this narrative, so uninteresting to the young reader of seventeen, who seeks in these pages only the history of her country, does but interrupt the story of the fate of Silas Perry and Seth Ransom.

The formal interview with the Spanish governor, and with Laussat the French prefect, took place the next morning after Lonsdale and Miss Perry came down the river. Only these two officers with their secretaries, and the fussy young Salcedo in a very brilliant uniform, were present to represent the French and Spanish Governments: to represent the insulted merchants, only the English and American consuls, with Mr. Lonsdale and William Harrod, were admitted.

And, oh the horrors of the red-tape of a Spanish inquiry! Ransom had not exaggerated when he said they copied what he said four times for the king to read. And what with soothing Laussat's ruffled dignity by interpreting into French, and meeting Castilian punctilio by talking Spanish, while every person present spoke English and understood it, the ordinary fuss was made more fussy, and the ordinary misery more miserable.

But no promise, either of a trial or of a release, could be extorted. Laussat, the Frenchman, talked endlessly; but he had, and knew he had, no power, — strictly speaking, he had no business there. The same might be said of young Salcedo, who talked, however, more than any one but his father, and to no purpose. He had come, as was his wont, without being asked. The governor had summoned Laussat, only as a later man in power used to invoke Mr. Jorkins when he wanted to avoid responsibility. The governor himself said little, and explained nothing. The consuls made their protests, made their threats, which were written down "for the king to read;" but the governor declared he was under orders. Count Cornel, Minister of the Colonies at Madrid, had written thus and so ; and who was a poor local governor to stand one instant before Count Cornel?

After this had been said six times, and the protest had

been five times renewed, Lonsdale rose, and said gravely, —

"Then we must leave your excellency. The transaction appears to me much more serious than your excellency thinks it. Your excellency claims the right to send British subjects secretly to Cuba for trial. We resist that right : I say *resist*, where my colleague said *protest*. I ought to inform your excellency, that I sent directions this morning to his Britannic Majesty's naval officer in command below the Pass. That officer will search every vessel coming down the river, and will rescue any British subject he finds on board, though that subject be on a ship-of-war of the King of Spain."

There was a moment's silence. Gov. Salcedo himself did not maintain the haughty look of indifference which he had pretended. He looked Lonsdale steadily and anxiously in the eye. Laussat pretended not to hear what was said. The secretaries prepared four copies for the king.

"And will the American squadron look for American citizens ? " said the governor at last, with a sneer.

"I think there are no American vessels of war there," replied Lonsdale quietly. "If they were, Mr. Clark would communicate with them, I suppose."

"And how does your order, Mr. Lonsdale, affect the persons whom you say are our prisoners ; for whom, observe, I disclaim all responsibility ? "

"Your excellency cannot mistake me. Silas Perry and Seth Ransom are both subjects of George the Third."

"The American consul has claimed them as American citizens," said the governor in excitement. "And you must pardon me, Mr. Lonsdale : your ignorance is that of a stranger ; their nationality is perfectly known here. No person so important in the American interest, always excepting the honorable consul, as Mr. Silas Perry ; unless, indeed, Señor Ransom's claim is superior to his, as he certainly supposes it to be."

"I speak of facts," replied Lonsdale, — "facts everywhere

known. These men were born British subjects. It is true that the State of Massachusetts, in which they were born, is no longer a part of the British empire; but these men, born under the flag of England, were not residents of Massachusetts when that change took place. They have never forfeited their allegiance to the King of England, nor his protection. They are under the English flag to-day."

Everybody was amazed at this bold position so suddenly assumed by this calm man. For a moment there was silence. Then the governor said, —

" It is too late to-day ; but, if the men can be found in this jurisdiction, we will learn from them to what nation they belong."

" And when shall we have this privilege," asked Mr. Lonsdale boldly, " of seeing the prisoners, who, as I had understood, were not known by your excellency to be imprisoned ? "

" To-morrow is Sunday," said the governor with equal coolness. " I understand that it will be disagreeable to Englishmen and Americans to attend to business then. Shall we say Tuesday ? "

" No day better than Sunday for an act of the simplest justice," said Lonsdale.

The governor had committed himself; and it was agreed that after mass the same party should meet again.

And then the English and American gentlemen were bowed out of the room ; and the four clerks completed their four memoirs for the king.

CHAPTER XXXVIII.

WHAT NEXT?

*" To-morrow is behind." — *DRYDEN.

THAT night was an eventful night in the little American "colony." Daniel Clark's magnificent mansion, the consulate and its dependent offices, Davis's rope-walk on Canal Street, and, indeed, every vessel in the stream, had its great or little consultation of outraged and indignant men. It was not the first time in which the handful of Americans in Orleans had had to consult together as to their mutual protection. We have still extant the little notes which Daniel Clark from time to time sent up to Gen. Wilkinson, who commanded the American army, and whose quarters were as near as Fort Adams in Mississippi, arranging for the co-operation of the Americans within and the Americans without when the time should come. And the army was not unwilling to make the dash down the river. It was·held in the leash not too easily. Constant Freeman and other tried officers knew to a pound the weight of those honeycombed guns on the Spanish works ; they longed to try a sharp, prompt escalade against those rotten palisades ; and there was not a man of them but was sure that the handful of Franco-Spanish troops would give way in half an hour before that resolute rush, when it should be made. Whether, indeed, the gates were not first opened by the two hundred insulted and determined Americans within, would be a question.

It was all a question of time, for the two or three years of which this story has been telling.   The Americans within the city were always believing that the time had come.   Gen. Wilkinson was always patting them on the back, and bidding them keep all ready, but to wait a little longer.   Recent revelations in the archives of Spain have made that certain which was then only suspected, that this man was at the same time in the regular pay of the King of Spain and of the Government of the United States.   There is therefore reason to doubt how far his advice in this matter was sincere.   But, as the end has proved fortunate, a good-natured people forgets the treason.

They would abide the decision of the governor and the prefect, to be rendered the next day.   If then the prisoners were not surrendered, why, that meant war.   After the counsels of this night, the Americans were determined.   A messenger should be sent up the river in a canoe ; and, lest the water-guard arrested him, Will Harrod should go up by land through the Creek country.   Harrod did not decline the commission, though he preferred to remain within, where, as he believed, would be the post of danger.   So soon as the consultation was ended, he hurried to Mr. Perry's house to tell the ladies such chances as the meeting gave.   But he was too late for them that evening.

It was in the loveliness of early morning the next day, with every rose at its sweetest, every mocking-bird vieing with its fellow, every·magnolia loading the air with its rich perfume, that the brave fellow came running down into the garden, and found Inez there.   He told her hastily what was determined, and that the wishes of these gentlemen, which he must regard as commands, compelled him to leave her and her aunt, just at the time, of all times, when he wanted to be nearest to them.

" Dear Inez," he said boldly, " you know that I would not move from your side but in the wish to serve you.   You know that I have no thought, no wish, no prayer in life, but that I may serve you.   You do not know, that, for two years and more, I have thought of you first, of you last, of you always; that there is no wish of my heart, nay, no thought of my life, but is yours, — wholly yours. I should die if I were to part from you without saying this; and I wish, my dear Inez, that you would let me say a thousand times more."

He had never called her Inez, of course, without that fatal "Miss;" far less, of course, had he ever called her "dear."

But the gallant fellow had resolved, that come what might, and let Inez say what she may, he would call her "dear Inez" once, if he died for it. Now he had made a chance to do so twice before he let her answer. And so he waited bravely for her reply.

Poor Inez!

She looked up at him, and she tried to smile, and the smile would not come. Only her great eyes brimmed full of tears, which would not run over. She looked down, she turned pale; she knew she did, and he saw she did. Still he waited, and still she tried to speak. She stopped in their walk, she turned resolutely toward him; and now she was so pale, that he grew pale as she looked up at him. And she gave him her hand slowly.

"I will speak," she said, almost gasping, that she might do so, — "I will speak. Will Harrod, dear Will Harrod," a smile at last, or an effort at a smile in all her seriousness, "I love you better than my life."

And then she could hardly stand; but there was little need. Will Harrod's arms were round her, and there was little danger that she should fall. And then they walked up one avenue, and down another, and they talked back through one year, and forward through another, and tried to recall — yes, and did recall — every single ride upon the prairie in those happy days, — what he said above the Blanco River, and what she said that day by the San Marcos Spring; and if he ought to have thought that that cluster of grapes meant any thing, and if she remembered the wreath of the creeper;

and all the thousand nothings of old happy times, when they dreamed so little of what was before them. For one happy quarter-hour now, they even forgot the dangers and miseries of to-day.

Yes; and when they came back to them, as back they must come, oh, how much more endurable they were, and how much more certain was she and was he, that all would come out well! If he must go to Natchez, why, he must; but no parting now could be so terrible as that other parting, when they did not know.

They went in to join the party at breakfast. Harrod was ready to kiss Inez twenty times in presence of them all. But Inez was far more proper and diplomatic. Still, as she passed her aunt, she stooped and kissed her, and said in a whisper, —

"Darling auntie, you have not told me your secret, but you are welcome to mine."

And, happier than any queen, she went through the pretty ministries of the table; and Ma-ry knew, by intuition, that every thing was well.

Was every thing well? That, alas! must be decided at the formal hearing of the forenoon, when the prisoners were to be brought forward, "if they could be found within this jurisdiction."

It proved, as might be expected, that they "could be found," although, to the last, the governor and his son and the intendant had said, and the prefect had intimated, that they would not acknowledge that they knew any thing about either of them.

"It is all like Pontius Pilate, and Herod, and Annas the high priest," said Asaph Huling. "Shifting and shirking, and only agreeing in lying!"

So soon as the consuls and Mr. Lonsdale and Harrod had appeared, and made their compliments, the governor's son nodded, and a sort of orderly disappeared. In a moment

Ransom entered, and, in a moment more, Silas Perry on the other side. Ransom's beard had grown, and his clothes were soiled; evidently none of the elegances of hospitality had been wasted upon him; but he was fully master of the position; he came in as if he were directing the policemen who brought him; he bowed civilly to Mr. Huling, to Mr. Hutchings, to Mr. Harrod, and to Mr. Lonsdale; but, as for the prefect and the governor, they might as well have been statues in the decoration. He took a seat, and the seat which was intended, by a sort of divine instinct, and sat, as if he were the lord high chancellor, before whom all these people had been summoned.

Silas Perry was neatly dressed, and had not, in fact, been left to suffer personal indignity or inconvenience: but he was pale and nervous; he seemed to Lonsdale ten years older than when he saw him last. Harrod had never seen him before; but Mr. Perry's delight at seeing Ransom re-assured him. "Are you here, my dear Ransom," said he, "and what for? I thought they had thrown you into the river."

The secretaries hastily wrote down for the king's information the fourfold statement that Don Silas had supposed that the major-domo Ransom had been thrown into the river.

"Donno, sir," replied Ransom in a lower tone. "Had me up three times, cos they wanted to hear the truth told 'em, for a kind of surprise, you know. Donno what they want now."

"Then you are a prisoner too, Ransom?"

"Guess I be. Darbies knocked off, jest afore I come upstairs."

And Ransom looked curiously at both windows, as one who should inquire how easy it might be to break these two governors' heads together by one sudden blow, and, with one leap, emancipate himself from custody; but he had no serious thought of abandoning the company he was in.

The governor tapped impatiently; and a kind of major-domo with a black gown on, who had not been present the day before, came and told Ransom to be silent. Mr. Perry told him the same thing, and he obeyed.

"We have no necessity for any formal investigations," said the governor, in a courtly conversational manner, which he was proud of. "I had almost said we are all friends. Many of us are. I hope Don Silas recognizes me as one. But all purposes will be best answered if Don Silas will mention to these gentlemen his name, his age, and his nationality."

Lonsdale shuddered. If the Yankee should say, "Silas Perry, age sixty-two, an American citizen," he would be out of court. But Mr. Perry answered firmly, —

"I should like to know where I am. If this is a court, I demand to know what I am tried for."

"Indeed this is no court, my dear friend," said the courtly governor: "we have met, at the request of these gentlemen, for a little friendly conversation."

"Then I hope these gentlemen and your excellency will converse," said Mr. Perry bitterly. "I have always found I profited more by listening than by talking."

"You do yourself injustice, Don Silas. We had a question here yesterday which only you, it seems, can answer. These gentlemen, in fact, asked for your presence, that we might obtain satisfaction."

"If I am to obtain any," said Perry undaunted, "I must know whether I am a prisoner here to be badgered, or a freeman permitted to go at large. As a freeman, I will render any help to these gentlemen or to your excellency, as I always have done loyally, as your excellency has more than once acknowledged to me. As a prisoner, I say nothing, — no, not even under a Spanish examination."

This with a sneer, which the governor perfectly comprehended.

"You ask," said he, "precisely the question which you are here to answer; or, rather, the answer may be said to depend upon your answer to my friend here. The American consul here is claiming your person as an American citizen. The British consul intervenes, and, as I understand the matter, claims you as a subject of George the Third. It is impossible for us here even to consider their claims, till we know in what light you hold yourself."

"I a subject of George the Third!" cried Perry incredulously. "I did not think George the Third himself was crazy enough to say that; and I believe his Majesty has heard my name."

But, at the moment, he caught Lonsdale's eager and imploring eye. Lonsdale waved in his hand a card ; and Silas Perry was conscious, for the first moment, that he also held one. Ransom had slipped it into his hand, as he rose to address the governor ; but till now he had not looked at it. He paused now, and read what was written on it.

"I have claimed you as a British subject. The English fleet is off the Pass, and will take you off if you admit the claim. Ransom too. The governor is afraid. Take our protection. — LONSDALE."

Silas Perry read the card, nodded good-humoredly to Lonsdale ; and while the governor, amazed at the manifest deceit which had been practised, hesitated what to say, Mr. Perry himself took the word.

"I can relieve your excellency of any question. I am a citizen of the United States. I was born in Squam, in Massachusetts, in the year 1741. When I was twenty-one years of age I removed to the Havana. With every penny of my purse and every throb of my heart, I assisted in that happy revolution which separated those colonies from the British crown. And lest, by any misfortune, my children should be regarded subjects, either of George the Third or of Charles the Third, on my first visit to England after the peace, at the American embassy, I renounced all allegiance to the King of England, and obtained the certificate of my

American nationality from that man who has since been the honored President of my country. So much for me.

"With regard to this good fellow, I presume the consul is technically right. Seth Ransom was born a subject of George the Third. He did not reside in the United States when the treaty of peace was made ; nor has he resided there since. He is undoubtedly, at law, a subject of the King of England."

So saying, Silas Perry sat down. The four secretaries provided four transcripts for the gratification of their king.

"How is this?" said the governor himself, turning to Ransom. "Have you understood what the gentleman has said?"

Seth Ransom had been contemplating the ceiling, still in the character of the Lord Chancellor.

"Understood all I wanted to," said he. "Perhaps you didn't understand, cos he spoke English. Ef you like, I'll put it in Spanish for you."

For, as it happened, the etiquettes of yesterday had not been observed. The parties had begun with English : with English they went on. But Ransom, for his own purposes, now changed the language.

"You can ask me what you please," said he. "But, if you have not sent the king the other things I told you, you might read them over ; for I shall tell you the same thing now."

The governor turned up the record of Ransom's first examination. He then said, with a sneer, —

"This reads : 'Seth Ransom, being questioned, states that he is a citizen of Massachusetts, one of the United States of America.' But I understand Don Silas, that this is a mistake, and that we are to say that you are a subject of King George the Third."

"You can say what you like," said Ransom fiercely, in a line of Castilian wholly his own, which was, however, quite intelligible to the governor, and the four secretaries who toiled after. "You know as well as I know that whatever you say will be a lie, and, if you say that, it will be the biggest lie of all."

Ransom spoke hastily, and in his most lordly air of defiance, but not so hastily but they could all follow him ; and the secretaries noted his language in such short-hand as they could command.

Mr. Hutchings, the English consul, availed himself here of the pretence that they were conversing as friends in the governor's office, and that none of the forms of court were observed.

"Ransom," said he, "all that we want to prove is, that you never appeared before a magistrate, and made oath of your citizenship. Of course we all know where you were born."

Ransom listened superciliously, with one eye still turned to the heavens.

"You don't want me to be lying too, Mr. Hutchings. 'Them eyedolaters do, cos it's their way. But you don't."

And he paused, as if for reflection and for recollection.

Lonsdale took courage from the pause to say, —

"Of course, the king's officers have no claim on you ; but we are all friends now, and all the king's officers want is a right to befriend you."

A bland smile crept over Ransom's face.

"Much obliged," said he : "they's befriended me afore now."

Then, as if this "solemn mockery" had gone far enough, he turned to the governor, and said, again in Spanish, —

"I will tell you all about it. When the war began, Gen. Washington wanted powder, — he wanted it badly ; and he said to old Mugford that he'd better go down the bay, and catch some English store-ships for him. And I volunteered under Mugford, and went down with him. And we took the powder, and drove those fellows out of Boston."

The Castilian language furnished Ransom with some very

happy epithets — as terms of reproach, not to say contumely
— with which to speak of the English navy and army.

The secretaries, amazed, wrote down this ridicule of a
king.

"After Mugford was killed, I went out again, — first with
Hopkins, and then with Manly. And, the first time, I went
to Hopkins's shipping-office, down at Newport; and I swore
on the Bible that I'd never have any thing more to do with
George the Third, nor any of that crew, — poor miserable
sons of dogs as they were; and, when I went with Manly,
I shipped at old Bill Coram's office, and he had a Bible
too, and I swore the same thing again."

Of all which the secretares made quadruplicate narrative.

"That time his fellows caught us," continued Ransom,
pointing over his shoulder at Lonsdale. "We were under
the Bermudas, waiting for the Jamaica fleet; and there came
a fog, and the wind fell; and, when the fog rose, I'll be
damned if we were not under the guns of a seventy-four, —
the 'Charlotte;' and they boarded us, and carried every
man to England. And that's the only time I ever ate his
bread," — pointing again to Lonsdale, — "black stuff, and
nasty it was too. That was at Plymouth.

"I lived there a year. And once every month a miserable
creature in a red coat — one of his fellows — came and asked
us to take service in the king's navy. And there was some
dirty Spanish and Portuguese, and niggers [this in English],
— lying dogs, all of them, — that did. But all the Americans
told him to go to hell, and I suppose he went there, because
I have never seen him since.

"And at last there was an exchange, — exchanged a thousand of us against a thousand of his fellows we had. Poor
bargain he made too! And that time they took me over to
France; and they made me captain of the squad, because I
could speak their lingo, — the same as I speak yours, because
you do not know any better. And there we saw the man
that told the King of France what he'd better do, — same

man that fixed the lightning-rod on Boston Light. King
George did not know how. King fixed it wrong, — did every
thing wrong."

The secretaries, amazed, entered these statements on
King George's knowledge of electricity.

"White-haired old man he was, — long-haired man, — sort
of a Quaker; and he came and asked all that were Americans to come to his place, and take the oath. So I took it
there, — that's three times. And he gave me my certificate,
— 'purtection' they call it," — turning to the secretaries to
give them the word in English, — "and when any of his men
— the king's, I mean — see that, why, they can't take a fellow
out of any ship at all. And there it is: if you think your
king would like to know what it says, I'll read it to you. I
always keep it by me; and these fellows of yours, when they
stole every thing else I had the day you sent them after me,
they didn't find it, because I did not choose to have them.
You'd better tell that to the king. Tell him they are all fools,
and good for nothing."

By this time Ransom was worked into a terrible passion.
He still commanded himself enough, however, to hold the
precious paper out, and to read in English, —

"KNOW ALL MEN,

By these presents, that Seth Ransom, of Tatnuck, Worcester County, in
the Commonwealth of Massachusetts, one of the United States of
America, hath this day appeared before me, and renounced all allegiance
to all kings and powers, save to the Commonwealth of Massachusetts,
and, in especial, all allegiance to King George the Third, his heirs and
successors.

"And the said Seth Ransom hath hereby given to him THE PRO-
TECTION of the United States of America in all and every of his
legal enterprises by sea or by land, of which these presents are the certificate.

"Signed,
"BENJAMIN FRANKLIN,
"Minister of the United States.

"Witness,

"WILLIAM TEMPLE FRANKLIN,
"Passy, near Paris, June 16, 1781."

Ransom knew the paper by heart. He read it as an orator, — with some break-down on the long words.

This short address produced no little sensation. Two secretaries crossed to take the paper to copy it. Ransom stepped forward to give it to them, stumbled and fell as he did so. When he rose, he apologized, — affected to have given it to one of the men; they were in turn almost persuaded each that the other had it. Between the three, the paper could be nowhere found; and Ransom cursed them with volumes of rage because they had stolen it so soon.

" Have you any further inquiries to make, Mr. Hutchings? or have you, Mr. Lonsdale? " asked the governor, addressing the English gentlemen with his courtly sneer.

Before they could reply, Ransom rose again, and waved his hand. Like Lockhart before the Red Comyn, he seemed resolved to "make sicker."

" Beg your pardon," said he in English : " I forgot to say that I know you want to hang me ; I knew that the first day you shut me up there. Ef you think anybody's forgotten how t'other one — the Paddy governor — hung them French gentlemen, it's because you think we's all fools. None on 'em's forgot it. O'Reilly, the other one, died screamin' and howlin' in his bed, because he see the Frenchmen all round his room pointin' at him. You know that as well as I do. Now you'd better hang me. After you've hanged me, you can think up a pack of lies, and send 'em to the king to tell him what you hanged me for."

And then the old man sat down with a benignant smile. His happy allusion was to that most horrible judicial murder committed in the last century, of which he had spoken to Inez. For generations the memory of that horror did not die out in the colony. It was the very last subject which Salcedo would willingly hear alluded to ; and this old Ransom knew perfectly well : for that reason he chose it for his last words.

After a ghastly pause, Salcedo said again, with some difficulty, —

"Have you any further inquiries to make, gentlemen?"

"I have only to protest, in all form," said the plucky English consul, "against a transaction which strikes at the root of all commerce among nations. I shall report the whole business to the Foreign Office, and I know that it will meet the severe censure of the king."

The governor bowed. He turned to Mr. Huling: —

"Have you any remarks to offer?"

"I make the same protest which my clerk made yesterday."

And he read it, as it had been put on paper. He added, —

"I assure your excellency, in that friendship to which your excellency referred just now, that no act could be so fatal to friendly relations for the future. Let me read to your excellency from the debate in the Senate of the United States of the 23d of February last. I received the report only last evening. The Secretary of State instructs me to lay it before your excellency; and I am to say that the Administration has the utmost difficulty in restraining the anger and ardor of the country. If your excellency will note the words used in debate, they mean simply war. It is to fan the flames of such anger that your excellency orders our friends sent to Cuba for trial;" and he read from the warlike speeches of White and Breckenridge.

The governor listened with courtly indifference. When Mr. Huling had done, and handed the papers to a secretary, the governor said contemptuously to that officer: —

"You need not trouble yourself. His Majesty has read that debate three weeks ago: at least I have; I have no doubt he has."

Laussat, the French prefect, bowed, and took the papers. He read them with an interest which belied the contempt affected by the other.

All parties sat silent, however. The evident determination of the governor to yield no point made it difficult to re-open the discussion.

William Harrod was the first to speak. With no training

for diplomacy, and no love for it, he rose abruptly, and took his hat.

"I understand your excellency to declare war against the United States : in that case, I have no place here."

"You will understand what you choose, young man," said the governor severely. "I have never understood why you appeared here at all ; and I do not even now know why I do not arrest you for contempt of His Most Catholic Majesty."

"Let me ask," said Lonsdale, "if your excellency will not consent to some delay in the measures you propose toward our friends, — a communication home, or with the city of Washington? "

"I have already said, Señor Lonsdale, that the officers of the King of Spain do not call councils of foreign powers to assist them in their administration of justice."

Lonsdale bowed, did not speak again, but took his hat also, very angry. At this moment, however, to the undisguised surprise even of the oldest diplomatists in the group, their number was enlarged, as a footman ushered into the room Roland Perry. He was well known to all there, excepting the French prefect Laussat and Harrod. He was dressed from head to foot in leather, and the leather was very muddy. His face was rough with a beard which had seen no razor for a fortnight, and was burned brown by a fortnight's sun and air. He held in his hand the sombrero which he had just removed, and a heavy riding-whip. He crossed the room unaffectedly to the governor, and gave him his hand.

"Your excellency must excuse my costume, but I am told that my despatches require haste."

He turned to his father : —

"My dear father, I am so glad to see you! you must have been anxious about my disappearance," and he kissed him.

He shook hands cordially with the consuls and with Lonsdale. He offered his hand to Harrod : —

"It is Mr. Harrod, I am sure."

He bowed to all the secretaries, and to Salcedo's son.

He shook hands cordially with Ransom. Then, turning to the governor with the same air of confident command, as if really everybody had been waiting for him, and nothing could be done until he came : —

"Will you do me the honor to present me to the prefect — M. Laussat, I believe ?"

The governor, chafing a little at this freedom, did as he was asked, reserving for some other moment the rebuke he was about to give to this impudent young gentleman.

Laussat hardly understood the situation. But he had learned already that the etiquettes of America were past finding out.

"I had the honor of meeting your excellency at the house of Citizen La Place," said Roland ; "but I cannot expect that your excellency would remember such a youngster. I hope your excellency left the Baroness of Valcour in good health, and your excellency's distinguished father."

Laussat also postponed the snubbing he was about to administer, not certain but he was snubbed himself already.

Roland, with the same infinite coolness, turned to the governor, who was trying to collect himself. Roland opened a large haversack, very muddy, which had hung till now from his shoulder.

"This despatch, your excellency, is from Señor Yrujo, the Spanish minister at Washington. I left him only a fortnight Thursday. His excellency bids me assure your excellency of his most distinguished consideration. And this despatch, Citizen Laussat, is from the French minister. I am charged with his compliments to you."

This use of the word "citizen," which was already out of vogue, was necessary to Roland's consummate air of superiority over the braggart Frenchman.

"And now, gentlemen, as I see these despatches are long, will you excuse my father, and my old friend Ransom here, to both of whom I have much to say ? Your excellency does not know that it is nearly a year since we have met."

This outrage was more than the "moribund old man" could stand.

"You are quite too fast, Mr. Perry. I know very well when you went up the river to foment war in Kentucky. I know very well that you failed, and went to Washington on the same errand. I know that these despatches will tell me of your further failure. If you wish to converse with your father, it will be in this palace, where I will provide accommodations for both of you."

"Your excellency is very kind," said the young man with infinite good-humor. "When your excellency and Citizen Laussat have read these papers, you will perhaps think it better to accept my father's hospitality than to offer him yours."

Then, as if such badinage had gone far enough, he turned with quite another air to Laussat : —

"M. Laussat," he said, with an air of an equal, "this diplomacy has gone far enough. New Orleans and Louisiana are in fact, at this very moment, a part of the United States. The First Consul has sold them to the President for a large and sufficient compensation. Nothing remains but the formal act of cession."

"Impossible !" cried Laussat, starting from his seat. "My despatches say nothing of it."

"I know not what they say," said the young man, "and I do not care. Perhaps you will do me the favor to look at mine."

He took from his pocket a billet, which, as he showed to the prefect, was written at Malmaison, with the stamp of the First Consul's cabinet on the corner. It was in the handwriting of Mme. Bonaparte, — a playful note thanking Roland for the roses he had sent her. The young man turned the first page back, and pointed to a postscript on the last page, in the cramped writing, not so well known then as now, of Napoleon Bonaparte.

The words were these : —

MY DEAR SON, — We speak of you often, and we wish you were in France. Say to your honored father, who knows how to keep a secret, that I have sold Louisiana to Mr. Monroe. He well knows my friendship to America : let this prove it to him again. He will use this note with discretion.   Health,

    25 Germinal.   Year XI.   BUONAPARTE.

The prefect read them, and read them again. "*Lâche, imbecîle, traître !*" he said, between his teeth, as he gave back the note to Roland.

"Your excellency may be curious to see the First Consul's autograph," said Roland ; and he handed the little billet to the governor in turn. The governor read it, as Roland stood by; but, as he was about to give it to the secretaries, Roland put it in his pocket.

"Your excellency will pardon me. It is my note — and a note from a lady.

"And now," he said, in that quiet tone of command which became him so well, which he had inherited from his father, "as among friends, we must confess that this kind announcement from the First Consul puts a new arrangement on all our little affairs in this room. Your excellency will perhaps permit my father to dine at home ; and I think Ransom will find us some good sherry in which to drink prosperity to France and to Spain."

But the "moribund old man" sat with his head upon his breast, pondering. This was the end, then, of Phil Nolan's murder ; this was the end of Elguezebal's watchfulness; this the end of interdicts and protests, and all the endless restrictions of these weary years. God be with Mexico and Spain !

He said nothing.

Roland turned to Laussat : "Will your excellency not use your influence with the governor ? " he said.

Laussat looked the fool he was, but said nothing.

The English and American gentlemen rose. "I am to report, then, to Lord Hawksbury," said Lonsdale, "that the

Spanish Government is indifferent to the friendship of England." He took his hat again, as to withdraw.

" I am to write to Mme. Bonaparte," said Roland Perry, " that M. Laussat says the First Consul is a coward, an imbecile, and a traitor. Gentlemen, we seem to have our answers."

The poor old governor raised his head. " I shall be glad of a little conference with his excellency the prefect, our friend M. Laussat. Will you gentlemen await us in the next salon ? "

They waited fifteen minutes. At the end of fifteen minutes Mr. Perry and Ransom joined them. There was a civil message of excuse from the governor, but he did not appear ; nor was Laussat visible through the day.

And so they left the governor's house in triumph. Roland Perry could hardly come close enough to his father. He assured himself that he was well, and then his first questions were for news from Texas. Had Cæsar been set free ? Had any of Phil Nolan's party returned ?

No ; but Barelo had good hopes. The trials[1] were proceed-

---

1 A regular trial was given them, of which the proceedings are extant. Don Pedro Ramos de Verea conducted the defence (will not some Texan ·name a county for him?), and the men were acquitted. The judge, De Vavaro, ordered their release, Jan. 23, 1804 ; but Salcedo, alas! was then in command of these provinces : he countermanded the degree of acquittal, and sent the papers to the king. The king, by a decree of Feb. 23, 1807, ordered that one out of five of Nolan's men should be hung, and the others kept at hard labor for ten years. Let it be observed that this is the royal decree for ten men who had been acquitted by the court which tried them.

When the decree arrived in Chihuahua, one of the ten prisoners, Pierce, was dead. The new judge pronounced that only one of the remaining nine should suffer death, and Salcedo approved this decision.

On the 9th of November, therefore, 1807, the adjutant-inspector, with De Verea, the prisoner's counsel, proceeded to the barracks, where they were confined, and read the king's decision. A drum, a glass tumbler, and two dice were brought; the prisoners knelt before the drum, and were blindfolded.

Ephraim Blackburn, the oldest prisoner, took the fatal glass and dice, and threw 3 and 1 . . . . = 4
Lucian Garcia threw 3 and 4 . . . . = 7
Joseph Reed threw 6 and 5 . . . . = 11

ing with infinite slowness ; but Barelo and all men of sense hoped still that Spanish honor would be vindicated, and these men, who had certainly enlisted in faith in De Nava's pass, would be set free, — a hope, alas ! not to be verified.

David Fero threw 5 and 3	= 8
Solomon Cooley threw 6 and 5	= 11
Jonah [Tony] Walters threw 6 and 1	= 7
Charles King threw 4 and 3	= 7
Ellis Bean threw 4 and 1	= 5
William Dowlin threw 4 and 2	= 6

Poor Blackburn, having thrown the lowest number, was hanged on the 11th of November.

Ellis Bean afterward distinguished himself in the revolt against Spain, which freed Mexico.

Cæsar had got detached from the party, and was seen by Pike, high up on the Rio Grande.

Of the end of the life of the other prisoners, no account has been found.

We owe these particulars to the very careful researches in Monterey, of Mr. J. A. Quintero, who has taken the most careful interest in the fame of Philip Nolan.

People who are fond of poetical justice will be glad to know that Salcedo was killed in the first effort for Texan liberty in 1813.   But so, alas ! was Herrara.

CHAPTER XXXIX.

A FAMILY DINNER.

*" Thus for the boy their eager prayers they joined,
Which fate refused, and mingled with the wind."*

Iliad.

As the little procession passed along the streets, there was
almost an ovation offered to Mr. Perry and to Ransom.
From every warehouse and counting-room some one ran out
to felicitate them. Indeed, the merchants of every nation
had felt that here was a common cause ; and Silas Perry was
so universally respected that his release was a common
victory. Roland walked on one side of his father, and Lonsdale on the other, while Harrod renewed his old acquaintance with Ransom. Ransom confessed to him, that of all
the strange events of the day his appearance had surprised
him most. For, if there were any thing regarding which
Ransom had expressed himself with confidence for two years
past, it was the certainty that William Harrod had been
scalped, burned at the stake, and indeed eaten.

It was necessary to respect the open secret of the First
Consul's postscript so far that to no person could the result
of Mr. Monroe's negotiation be distinctly told. It had, of
course, been hoped for and suspected already. In fact, what
with delays in the draft of the treaty, and delays in transmis-
sion, the definitive intelligence did not arrive till some time
later. It was convenient for the governor, for his staff, and
for Laussat and his, to speak slightly of the intelligence.
But this was of no account to those who knew the truth ; and,

as it happened, to all others the "law's delay" involved no consequences of evil.

Roland hastily told his story to his father. His inquiries regarding Ma-ry, and the communications he had to make to the governors of Kentucky, of Tennessee, and of the Northwest, had taken him far up the River Ohio, and late into the spring. He had determined — wisely as it proved — not to return with Lonsdale, who had in the meanwhile crossed to Fort Niagara and to Montreal, and then had descended the Mississippi. Roland had preferred to go to Washington, to make full statement there to Mr. Jefferson and his father's old correspondents of the excited condition of Orleans, knowing that he could return by sea with more certainty than by land and the river.

At Washington he had heard the celebrated war debate of February. Mr. Jefferson had not received him into any close confidence : that was not Mr. Jefferson's way. But he had told him of his hopes that Orleans might be bought for the United States ; and Mr. Madison had bidden him encourage the merchants to hold out a little longer. At the French legation he was treated more cordially. They gave him a welcome which the State Department of that day did not know how to give, and late one night the French minister sent to him, and asked him if he would take his despatches to Laussat when he returned.

"As it happened," said Roland, "I had within the hour received this note from Mme. Bonaparte. Old Turner had brought it to me, riding express from Baltimore almost as I have ridden from Tybee. A fortunate curiosity had led Turner to carry the rose-bushes to Malmaison himself. He was still looking at the garden when he was summoned by a lackey to the house, was asked who he was, and had confided to him Mme. Bonaparte's billet. She came into the hall, and gave it to him with her own hand, with a sweet smile. Something in what she said made Turner think the note was more than a compliment. Any way, he had seen enough of

Paris, he said. The 'Lady Martha' was ready for sea at Bordeaux; and, having his letter, he took post-horses, and rode night and day till he came there.

"And then, sir, they made the 'Lady Martha' spin. Wood and iron never crossed that ocean so quickly before. He ran into Baltimore in twenty days, heard from Pollock that I was at Washington, and came across with this scrap of paper."

Roland felt the importance of the message thus intrusted to him, so soon as he had read it. To no human being in Washington did he dare intrust it; and he could not make out, in the few minutes he had for trying, whether the French minister had received any corresponding intelligence. He sent at once to the Spanish legation, to offer to carry their despatches to the governor of Louisiana. Then he crossed to Baltimore, where the " Lady Martha " had been unloading some oil and wine; and, without a minute's loss of time, she loosed from the pier, and went down the bay.

"With a spanking breeze we ran," said the young fellow. " By the time we were off Hatteras it was a gale. But old Turner never flinched. Give him his due. The next night it was a north-easter,— blew like all the furies! How she walked off! Turner said she might run so till I said the word. I never said it. Dark it was, — dark as Egypt; wet, cold, even snow in that gale. But Turner did not stop her, and I did not stop her."

"I suppose the light-house at San Augustine stopped her," said his father, laughing.

"No, sir; but the breakers off Tybee Sound stopped her; and there, I am sorry to say, is the 'Lady Martha,' or what is left of her, this day."

"She could not have run her last in a better cause," said his father warmly.

"That's what I said to Turner. We got ashore, sir, all safe. I landed with this bag, and with no dry rag on me. I told an officer we found there, that I had government despatches. He mounted me on the best horse in Georgia. That beast took me, to whom do you think? — to Aunt Eunice's old admirer, Gen. Bowles ; and Gen. Bowles has sent me through since, as if I had been a post-rider of the First Consul's. If Aunt Eunice is not kind to the general now, she is graceless indeed."

Lonsdale could, this time, take the joking for what it was worth. They were now at the house. The news was in the air, and all the ladies flew to the gate to welcome them.

What a Sunday it was, to be sure ! How much to be told publicly, how much to be told privately, how much to be explained ! and how many questions to be asked, how many mysteries to be solved ! Fortunately there was very little to be done. Roland had come dashing up to the house with the best stride of one of Gen. Bowles's chargers, at a very un-Sunday like pace.

" Lucky for you, you were not in Squam," said his father. " All the tithing-men in Essex County would have been after you."

" Better after me than before me, my dear father. I am not sure whether all Essex County would have overhauled that bright bay whom Zeno is stuffing with corn in the stable now."

He had flung the rein to Antoine, and rushed into the house to hear the amazing tale of the women, as to his father's arrest and Ransom's.

"I was hardly dressed for diplomacy," said he ; "but I thought the sooner I contributed my stock of news, the better."

" Certainly," said Lonsdale : " you were none too soon. We had all played up our last pawns, and the governor was implacable."

" Casa Calvo will be angry enough," said Mr. Perry, " when he knows how like an ass Salcedo has behaved. But his visit here just now seems to be simply one of ceremony."

Before dinner was announced, Will Harrod succeeded in

luring Mr. Perry away into the room which was called his office, and laying before him, with a young man's eagerness, such claim as he had for Inez's hand. A blundering business he made of it, but her father helped him.

"My dear boy," said he, "this is hardly matter for argument. I do not think my girl would have taken a fancy to you, had you not been a Christian gentleman. More than that, my boy: I fancy you have found favor in her eyes because you are one of Philip Nolan's friends. For me, I have always supposed that some man would want to take a girl so lovely to his heart — well, as I took her mother; and, if you will only love this child as I loved her, why, I can ask nothing more."

Harrod's eyes were running over. He could only repeat the certainty, which he said two years of constancy had given him a right to proclaim, that Inez would be dearer to him than his life.

Eunice was never known before to apologize for a dinner; and never in after-life did she so apologize.

"But, Roland, we were so wretched this morning! If we had only known you were coming, why, we would have killed for you any beast fat enough on the place."

"And why did you not know, dear auntie? Why had you not signal-officers in the Creek country to telegraph my coming? Is the general so tardy in his attentions? Why, I had but to ask, and the finest horses his lieges ever stole were at my command."

Much fun there was, because people were supposing, all through the dinner, that those had met who had never met, and that everybody understood every thing.

"One question, Mr. Lonsdale, you will permit me to ask," said Harrod: "I have puzzled myself over it not a little. To what good fortune do I owe it that you followed me into the governor's den on Thursday? To tell you the truth, I had seen you in the street, and had thought you were some intendant or other who meant to arrest me. I had been dodging all sort of catchpolls for three days of disguise."

"You were not far from right," said Lonsdale quizzically.

Everybody laughed, and looked inquiry.

"What do you mean?" said the blunt Kentuckian, taking the laugh good-naturedly. "For really that was a great stroke of luck; but for you, I believe we should all three be in the Gulf, or near it, at this hour."

Lonsdale laughed again; and then, in a mock whisper across the table, he said, —

"I met a man in the street with my best frock-coat and waistcoat on, and I followed him to see where he was going. He went to the governor's house, and I went too."

One scream of laughter welcomed the announcement, and Harrod and Inez laughed loudest of any.

"Woe is me!" she cried. "Woe is me! I am the sinner, as I always am." And she laughed herself into a paroxysm again. "Oh, Mr. Lonsdale, if you could have seen him that morning! I turned him into Roland's room, and bade him fix himself up; and he has opened the large wardrobe, and helped himself to the clothes Roland bade you leave there."

And the girl screamed with delight at the transformation.

"And very nice clothes they are," said Harrod, joining in the fun. "And, when Mr. Lonsdale visits me in Kentucky, I will replace them with the handsomest hunting-suit in the valley.

"How was I to know? There were some thread-paper things there, which I see now would fit our diplomatic friend here; but, for a broad-shouldered hunter like me, give me Mr. Lonsdale's coat and waistcoat. Indeed, Mr. Roland," he said, "I shall patronize the English tailors. Your French snips do not give cloth enough."

"We can make common cause,' said Lonsdale. "The coat and waistcoat fit you so well that I will double my orders when I send to London; and, as you say, you can bid the Frankfort snips duplicate yours when you send there. We will play the two Dromios."

The little speech was wholly unconscious. So far had

Lonsdale looked into the future in these two or three days, so happy to him, though so anxious to all, that he quite forgot that the others had not accompanied him in those fore-looks, not Eunice herself, from whom he thought he had no secret.

Quick as light, and pitiless as herself, Inez caught the inference, and proclaimed it. She clapped her hands, while Eunice first, and Lonsdale in sympathy, turned crimson.

"Bravo, bravissimo!" cried the light-hearted girl. "The first American citizen adopted in the new State of Louisiana is his Royal Highness the Duke of Clarence. On the Acadian coast he will establish his vineyard for the growth of grapes and the manufacture of malmsey. From a throne on the levee, he will rule Great Britain, Ireland, and France, when his royal father at length throws off the uneasy crown. Mistress Inez Perry will be appointed first lady of the robes. But where, oh! where, my dear Aunt Eunice, where shall we find him a duchess? How would Mlle. Selina de Valois do?"

"She will not do at all," cried Lonsdale; his light heart, and the sense of so many victories, conquering all reticence. "The duchess is found; the throne is in building; the coronet is ready in the wardrobe upstairs, if the Prince of Kentucky, Cavalier of the Red River, and Marshal of the Big Raft, have not needed it for purposes of his diplomacy; all that the Duchess needs is her brother's good-will, and " —

"And what?" cried Inez, laughing still.

"The presence of her niece as bridesmaid, when she gives her hand to 'The Man I Hate.'"

And the taciturn and undemonstrative Mr. Lonsdale, to Ma-ry's unspeakable delight, waved his fruit-knife as if he would scalp Inez, and bear off her luxuriant tresses as a trophy.

The frankness of this bit of by-play was more like the style of Sir Charles Grandison's days than Eunice really liked; and Mr. Perry, to relieve her, said, —

"Nobody has told me how you all knew where I was, or where Ransom was."

Inez nodded to Ma-ry, and made a sign with her hand.

"May I ?" asked Ma-ry of her grandmother, who did not at all understand, and gave assent from the mere joyous habit of the day, by accident.

So Ma-ry sprung from her seat, ran across the room, skipped upon a side-table, and there repeated the signals which had told where Mr. Perry was shut up, and where they should find Ransom.

Ransom, meanwhile, had honored the occasion as he honored few ceremonies in life. He appeared in a handsome black coat and breeches, with a white necktie. Some footman whom he had seen in Paris, in some livery of mourning, may have suggested the costume. Eunice might have given a state ball to a travelling emperor, and Ransom would not have assumed this dress except to please himself. When he did assume it, all parties knew that he was entirely satisfied with the position. He filled Roland's glass with some of the favorite claret.

" Here's ye father's own claret, Mr. Roland ; found the bin this morning."

Then Roland knew that all was sunny.

" As the governor did not honor us, we need not order up the sherry. Indeed, I am not sure that Ransom could have found it," said Mr. Perry, looking good-naturedly at the dear old fellow.

Perhaps Ma-ry's welcome to Roland had been the prettiest of all. Although Mrs. Willson had felt at ease with Lonsdale and Eunice, Roland seemed to her the oldest friend of all. It was he who had wrought out the whole inquiry ; it was he who had traced her from village to village, from State to Territory, and through him that Eunice had found her, and that she had found her darling. And now that she saw the sun-browned young fellow the hero of the day ; now that he was constantly coming back to dear Ma-ry's side, to ask her this and to tell her that, and to praise her for the central service which she had rendered to them all, — the old lady felt

more at ease with him than with Mr. Perry, of whom she
was afraid ; with Mr. Lonsdale, whom she never half understood ; nay, even more than with Mr. Harrod, the Kentuckian.

And Ma-ry ! She had gained every thing in this year, the
young man thought, and she had lost nothing. She was a
woman now. Yes ! but she was a lovely girl as well. She
could give him both her hands ; she could look up as frankly
as ever in his face ; she could talk to him of the thousand new
experiences of the year ; and yet, in all the simplicity of her
bearing, there was never one word or gesture but the finest
lady at a ball at Malmaison might have been glad to use.
And Ma-ry was not afraid to tell him how well he looked,
and how glad she was that he had come. A long, jolly,
home-like dinner : they loitered at the table, almost till twilight came. Then Eunice said, —

"Will it not be pleasanter on the gallery ? I will order
coffee there."

But Roland retained them.

"Let me tell you all," he said, "what I was telling Mr.
Harrod. At Fort Washington whom should I meet but a
fine little fellow, Inez, a good mate for you some day, who
fascinated me at the very first. He had just come over from
Frankfort, and had on his nice new uniform, his bright shoul-
der-knots, and his new sword. He was a little bit homesick
withal. Well, I remembered how homesick such a boy feels.
I asked them to introduce me ; and they introduced to me
Ensign Philip Nolan."

Everybody started. "Philip Nolan ! "

"Yes, he is the cousin of our dear Phil. Did not I want
to hug him ? I did tell him more of our Philip than he knew.
I told him of poor Fanny Lintot, and the little baby cousin
there."

"One day we will tell him," said Silas Perry solemnly,
" how much the country owes to his cousin's cruel martyr-
dom. If our brave friend Phil Nolan had not gone to

Texas, these rascals would never have got their terror of the Valley men. It was he who taught them how near was Kentucky to Potosi. The moment they learned that, they lost their heads.

"From Phil Nolan came Salcedo's madness.

"From their frightened despatches home, came the easy gift of all this country to France.

"From Salcedo's madness comes the uprising of the Western hunters, and the first real recognition of the West by the Congress of America.

"Good fellow! in all his wildness, Philip Nolan never was afraid.

"He has done more for his country than he meant.

"In all his rashness, he has served her so that she can never pay her debt to him.

"Listen to me, Inez: I shall not live to see this, but you and your children will.

"What Casa Calvo calls Nolan's mad act has given Louisiana to your country: it will give her Texas.

"When the tug comes, you will find that every Spaniard dreads the prowess of Philip Nolan's race, and that every Kentuckian remembers the treachery of Philip Nolan's murder.

"Poor fellow! how often I have heard him say that he did not know what country he served, or what army gave him his commission.

"This cousin, his namesake, is more fortunate. Ransom, fill the glasses. We will drink this young ensign's health.

"To Ensign PHILIP NOLAN, ladies and gentlemen. May the young man never know what it is to be

"A MAN WITHOUT A COUNTRY!"